FOOD
MY PEO

FOOD OF MY PEOPLE

THE EXILE BOOK OF ANTHOLOGY SERIES
NUMBER NINETEEN

CO-EDITED
AND WITH AN INTRODUCTION AND AN AFTERWORD BY

CANDAS JANE DORSEY

URSULA PFLUG

EXILE
editions

singular fiction, poetry, nonfiction, translation, drama, and graphic books

Library and Archives Canada Cataloguing in Publication

Title: Food of my people / co-edited and with an introduction and afterword by
    Candas Jane Dorsey, Ursula Pflug.
Names: Dorsey, Candas Jane, editor. | Pflug, Ursula, 1958- editor.
Series: Exile book of anthology series (Exile editions Ltd.) ; no. 19.
Description: Series statement: The Exile book of anthology series ; number nineteen |
    Short stories.
Identifiers: Canadiana (print) 20200334417 | Canadiana (ebook) 20200334670 |
    ISBN 9781550969092 (softcover) | ISBN 9781550969108 (EPUB) |
    ISBN 9781550969115 (Kindle) | ISBN 9781550969122 (PDF)
Subjects: LCSH: Food—Fiction. | LCSH: Short stories, Canadian—21st century. |
    CSH: Short stories, Canadian (English)—21st century.
Classification: LCC PS8323 .F66 2020 | DDC C813/.60803564—dc23

Cover art by R Type/iStock Photo
Text and cover design by Michael Callaghan
Typeset in Fairfield, Hellas Fun, Perpetua Tilting, Optima and Zapf Dingbat fonts at
Moons of Jupiter Studios
Published by Exile Editions Ltd ~ www.ExileEditions.com
144483 Southgate Road 14 – GD, Holstein, Ontario, N0G 2A0
Printed and Bound in Canada by Gauvin

We gratefully acknowledge the Canada Council for the Arts, the Government of Canada,
the Ontario Arts Council, and the Ontario Creates for their support toward our
publishing activities.

Canadian sales representation: The Canadian Manda Group,
664 Annette Street, Toronto ON M6S 2C8 www.mandagroup.com 416 516 0911

North American and international distribution, and U.S. sales:
Independent Publishers Group, 814 North Franklin Street,
Chicago IL 60610 www.ipgbook.com toll free: 1 800 888 4741

for all those who have nourished us

Dessert

Digestif

May we suggest, for your future dining pleasure...

FOOD AND MAGIC

INTRODUCTION

Once a long time ago as writers measure time, I was asked to contribute a story to an anthology of "mojo conjure stories:" fantastical stories of everyday magic. Uncomfortable with poaching from the everyday magics of other cultures, I begin to wonder, What is the everyday magic of my own people? I'm a fourth-generation settler on Treaty 6 land, from dirt-poor Scots and English stock, and by the time I was born, our potluck family reunions were marvels of potato salads and baked ham, Tupperware full of lemon squares, corn on the cob – seemingly practical feasts with only a hint of magic around the edges, such as that time Danny Berry stepdanced. I realized our mojo was inextricably linked with our food: that flapper pie recipe from the graham cracker box (a pie only known on the Canadian prairies and a little crescent to their south), those terrifyingly green jellied salads, that other pie made of saskatoon berries we had picked ourselves on the Kootenay Plains, the fresh-baked white bread, and the fast and slapdash custardy pudding one makes from the last of the loaf when it gets dry...and, of course, our comfort fast food of Kraft Dinner and Prem with frozen or fresh green peas on the side... So, I wrote "The Food of My People."

After it was published by Ursula Pflug and Colleen Anderson in *Playground of Lost Toys* (Exile Editions, 2015 but, alas, without the recipe), I found that every time I did a reading from it, people would come up afterward and swap family recipes, including one year when Ursula and I were both at the International Conference for the Fantastic in the Arts. I said to her, "Look at the interest here! We should do an anthology of speculative fiction on the theme of food – with recipes!" Ursula pitched it to Michael Callaghan at Exile, and the long road to this moment began.

I love working with my co-editor, who is brilliant, canny, talented – and very patient. I also love all the stories in this book and admire their authors extravagantly for what they have cooked up. Together, we have created a rich and various buffet for you to enjoy, just as excessive and various as at those extended-family gatherings of half a century ago. (Let the would-be chef beware: some of these recipes can be made in our world – with great results! – and some are only appropriate to the parallel worlds from which they came. As my great-grandmother, after whom I am named, used to say, "Use your own judgement!"). So let's start our feast with the story that began it all, and you will see as you read the anthology how wonderfully it ended up.

Candas Jane Dorsey

THE FOOD OF MY PEOPLE

Reenie's dad worked on the rigs. Before the accident he was only home one week in six or eight. He was working so they could have a good future, Reenie's mom said. Reenie loved him dearly but sort of the same way she loved certain library books she took out from the Bookmobile when it came around, but knew she couldn't keep forever, that she had to share with the others whose dates were stamped in the back by Jan the librarian.

Right after the accident, Reenie was only allowed to see him through a glass window, where he lifted two fingers in a tiny wave, and Reenie would spread her fingers on the glass and watch the bandaged stranger with a nervous smile. Reenie's mom could go in the room, with special clothes on. But they didn't go very often, because Reenie's mom, Lori, had to work at the dollar store.

Lori took her hand one day and they went over to the next door of the row house where they lived, and Lori rang the doorbell.

"Hang on, I'm coming!" The door opened, and Reenie looked up with awe at the woman in the calf-length cotton pants and the floral top. She'd never seen anyone as big around as she was tall like that. Lori was tiny – Reenie was already almost up to her shoulder and, Lori said, gaining on her every day – and thin as a rail, and wore thin jeans, cowboy boots, and shirts with little pearl snaps that Reenie loved to touch and, since she went to school, to count. Lori said that when Reenie was a big girl she could have one of them shirts. This big woman wore what seemed like enough flowered chintz to make a sail and float her away.

"Well, hi there!" the woman said, looking down at Reenie, then up at her mom.

"I'm Lori Gervais from next door," her mom said.

"Everybody calls me Cubbie, at least everybody polite." The woman laughed out loud, at which certain parts of her shook in an alarming way, as if there was something alive under her skin. Reenie shrank behind her mom and held on tight.

"I was wondering if you knew someone who could take care of my girl at noon and after school while I go to work?"

The woman – Cubbie – looked down at her and smiled. "Hello, Renée, honey," she said, and Reenie went cold with a mixture of fear and delight. Not even Lori called her by her real name. She thought nobody but her and her mama and daddy knew it. And how did *the lady* know it?

"Reenie's daddy is French," said Lori. "Say hello to Mrs. Cubbie."

"Just Cubbie," said Cubbie. "My husband was Jake Cubb, godrestisoul, but since I been looking like a beach ball, I been called Cubbie by everybody, adult, child, or dog."

"Hello, Cubbie," Reenie – Renée – said bravely. "I'm six."

"Well, that's a wonder," said Cubbie, smiling at her, and then to Lori, "She can come to me."

"I can't pay you much," said Lori, looking aside.

"I don't want your money," said Cubbie. "Noon hour don't work for me, so you send Renée to school with her lunch in a bag. When she gets home, she can come right here. Make me a sugar pie now and again, we'll call it even."

There was some back-and-forth about that, but by the time it was over they found themselves sitting at Cubbie's kitchen table, eating home-made doughnuts rolled in cinnamon and table sugar. Lori was telling Cubbie about the dollar store.

Renée had no idea that people made doughnuts. She thought they came from Tim Hortons.

That was the start of it.

>·<

The next day, Reenie's mom walked her to school like always. "Now you eat your lunch in the lunchroom and remember to go next door to Auntie Cubbie when you go home."

Reenie remembered.

That day Cubbie said they were going to put together a jigsaw puzzle. Cubbie showed Renée a box with little bits of picture jumbled up inside, with some of the pieces upside down, and some of them with their little stubby fingers tangled up with each other. Then she showed the lid and said how the jumbly bits all fit together and made that picture that was on the lid.

The whole idea was amazing to Renée. How did she get almost halfway to the age of seven without hearing about this thing?

"Don't you have them in that school you go to?" Cubbie asked.

Renée tried to explain about the school kind of puzzle, with only 10 or 26 pieces, made of wood, no box-with-a-picture-on, and educational.

"Don't look so sad. Not your fault that school is kinda backward!" Cubbie laughed and jiggled. "These ones are what regular people do, not educational so much."

Not only did Cubbie have a whole cupboardful, some of them in old, worn boxes with old-fashioned pictures on them, but she had a special felt cloth she put on the table beforehand. "Got it from Sara Martin." Renée knew she meant the Sara Martin catalogue from which Lori got the set of three nesting stainless steel bowls, and the special support bra for well-endowed women to prevent backache and that would last for five years guaranteed.

"You choose the picture you like," said Cubbie. Renée put her finger on a big red dot with no detail.

"That one's a little tough for a starter," said Cubbie, "and I usually save it for a special time. You never know when you might have a tricky problem, and if nothing else, making one of these clears your thoughts. But for a first-timer with nothing much on her mind, you best pick something a mite easier."

Renée picked a puppy dog in a basket and fell into a trance of shape and colour until Cubbie said, "That's enough for today." She rolled the whole puzzle up in the tablecloth, presto, and tucked it up on the shelf above the puzzles, pushing back a crocheted afghan in pink, yellow, and lime green. "I bet you're hungry."

They went behind the kitchen island and Cubbie showed Renée how to make Jell-O. She wouldn't let Renée near the hot water but, after the ice cubes were in, Cubbie let her stir it. The Jell-O was orange. Cubbie mixed in a can of fruit cocktail and put it all in a fancy copper dish she called a mould. Renée loved how the ice made a flat little tinkle against the Jell-O mould, but even more she loved how when the Jell-O hardened and when it was turned out on the plate, the fruit cocktail pieces floated in an orange sky, a sky that jiggled like Cubbie's laughing folds and tasted like Kool-Aid.

The next day when Lori dropped Reenie off at school, they both went to the office. "I hear you got French immersion here," said Lori. "Reenie's daddy is French and I want to put her in that." The principal called another teacher from outside the door, a fancy-looking lady with dyed hair. This was the French immersion teacher, call-me-Madame, who looked at Reenie's admission card and said, in a voice with the same music in it as her dad's voice, "So, Renée, you wan' to come wit' us an' learn *français*, eh?"

"Yes, ma'am," said Renée. So, from that day on she went to Madame's classroom, and things got strange. She had to do everything *en français*. Count, ask to go to the bathroom, everything. Some of the kids knew how *parler français* real good, but Renée was, like most, slow and stumbly.

"I don't want to go," she said to Cubbie. "Two kids make fun of me. I was smart in my other class. I got all correct on my worksheet. I got to work on the computer. In French immersion they only have three computers at the back, and we have to sit around in a circle and talk *français*. I hate it."

"Why do you think your mom put you in there?" Cubbie said, not mean, not agreeing with Renée or disagreeing, just asking. Renée shook her head, trying not to cry.

"Well, tell you what, honey," Cubbie went on. "You sit down there with some of this delicious Jell-O and finish off that puzzle and think on the answer."

Cubbie unrolled the puzzle, with its finished edges and mysterious middle, and Renée was so instantly absorbed that she hardly noticed how she finished her Jell-O.

There was one piece with two fingers of pink and the rest of it white. It reminded her of her father, in his peculiar suit of bandages. She laid the piece down in the centre space and started looking for another white and pink piece. She thought about how her father would come home from the rigs and call for her by her real name. He'd say what he always said, "*Viens-tu, ma petite chou!*" and when she came running, he'd call out, "*Bonjour, bonjour, ma petite Renée.*" He'd lift her up so she could see over his shoulder to the top of the fridge, that magic secret place only her dad could reach. His tattooed arms were strong and he'd bounce her up and down until she shrieked.

Wait a minute. Here was another pink bit. It was the puppy's nose! And Renée remembered that the teacher said, "*Bonjour*" too. "*Bonjour*" was *français* and *français* was French…"M*a petite chou*" was "*My little darling…*"

A little white puppy sat in a nasty pink basket. Renée liked the puppy, but if she had a puppy like that she'd let it sleep on her pillow, not put it in a basket like an Easter egg. The puzzle was done and Renée's dish was empty.

"Cubbie, can I have more Jell-O? *S'il vous plaît?*"

Cubbie laughed. "See there, *ma petite*, I told you puzzles would help." It turned out that Cubbie knew how to speak French too. Maybe it was just what people did, but nobody knew in her old school, like nobody knew about proper jigsaw puzzles. She had to come to the city for that. So Renée would figure it out, and teach her mother too, and when Daddy got better…but there her thoughts hit a rock and turned aside. She put her nose back into the Jell-O.

Well, it wasn't that easy. Like her mom said: "Reenie, nothing in life comes easy." There was so much to learn all over again. A whole new set of numbers before she could count. A whole new set of words. A bunch of sounds she'd never made before. "Put your mouth like an O and say E," said Madame, which made Renée's mouth sore at first.

Celeste and Marie-Claire ragged on her, but Madame and Lori and Cubbie all said, "Don't rag back, be a better person." That was easier said than done, as Cubbie would say, but Renée worked at it. The weeks went on, some of them slow, and some fast. Every day Reenie worked at school, then came to Cubbie and played, did a little puzzle, ate some cookies or a piece of pineapple upside-down cake, then went home with Lori.

Sometimes they went on the bus to see Renée's daddy. They had to go a long way in the big hospital, up two elevators. Now they let Reenie in too if she put on the gowns and gloves, but she couldn't hug him. She said, *"Je t'aime, Papa!"* from across the room, and from inside the bandages her daddy said, *"Très bien, ma petite chou! Je t'aime aussi!"* and waved his two pink fingers at her. Lori would say something like, "You stay and tell your dad what you're doing in school. I'm just going to talk to the staff," and Reenie would try to think of a story from school that didn't involve being teased or forgetting *un mot en français*. Sometimes she told him about Cubbie. He would murmur a word or two.

One day he said, "Not much happens here. It's pretty much same old, same old."

After they left, Lori was usually pretty quiet. Reenie could relate to that. She was learning it was better to be quiet when she was worried about something – especially what she was starting to think of as *same-old, same-old* worry. Because even worrying got boring sometimes, though she didn't think she could explain that to her mom, so she didn't try.

>ı<

One Saturday, the doctor met Lori in her dad's room. Lori said, "Reenie, you go sit on that chair outside a minute," and she and the doctor talked in low voices, standing beside her dad's bed. When they were done, Lori came out and said, "Just say hello to your father and then we'll go, kiddo. He's real tired today." So, Renée said, "*Je t'aime, Papa!*" in a tiny voice, and her dad waved his fingers at her, and then Lori and Reenie went home.

On Monday, Renée wasn't concentrating and got three wrong on her math sheet. After school she ran to Cubbie's with a sick stomach and held out the sheet with its red red ink.

"You put that by for now, and let's try to make *crêpes* tonight," Cubbie said. "Maybe if it works out, we can make dinner for your mom. Me, I never made these yet, so it's gonna be a special adventure. Meanwhile, you go see what kind of puzzle you want to start up."

Soon she was deep in a picture of a mom in a long blue dress holding a little baby. The lady and the baby had gold plates behind their heads. Reenie was trying to do the border first, like Cubbie taught her, but she had found the face of the mom, so she carefully cleared a place on the felt right around where she thought the face should go. It went on well from there. It was a pretty easy puzzle, actually.

She heard Cubbie say, "You look like you been rode hard and put away wet. You sit down there by Renée and put a few pieces in that there puzzle." Reenie looked up in surprise to see Lori, her face tired and flat under her make-up. The metal legs of the bridge chair scraped on the linoleum as Lori pulled it out. She sat down at the side of the table with a sigh.

"It's a mom, like you," said Reenie. "Pretty."

Lori laughed. "More famous than me, that's for sure. You know, we had that picture in church when I was little."

Lori and Ren, Reenie's dad, had had one of their special discussions about church. Ren said he didn't know what Reenie's grandparents would have thought if they saw Reenie was growing up without going to church. Lori said that if he wanted her to go so bad, he could stay home and take her. Then Ren said that he was working to give them a better life, and Lori said Reenie was turning out just fine, and Ren said he couldn't argue with that, that's for sure, and they went back to cooking hot dogs on the grill. That was back home in Fahler; well, back in their *old* home. This was home now.

"Fahler's the honey capital of Canada," said Renée to Cubbie.

"Well, that's a wonder," said Cubbie. "You both were born up there, then?"

"Yep, just a little honey from Fahler," said Lori. "The kids used to tease me about that until I cried. I was so glad to shake the dust of that place off my feet and then, damned if I didn't end up back there with Ren. Pardon my French."

"How come 'Pardon my French' means 'Sorry I swore'?" asked Reenie. "Because in Frenchimmersion nobody swears.

Except the teacher said Celeste said a bad thing when she called me stupid. But Mommy, I *am*..." Reenie's lip trembled despite herself. She got down and ran to get her backpack. "Here's my test. I got three wrong. I'm sorry." She began to sob. Lori reached out and put an arm around her shoulder, gathered her in.

"Those damn kids. Are you crying just because of three wrong in subtraction?"

"I promised...to be good while Daddy was in the hospital."

Lori looked up at Cubbie. It seemed to Reenie that Lori didn't know what to say. What Cubbie said didn't really make sense either. "You're not much more than a kid yourself. Give yourself a break."

Lori took Reenie's chin and turned her face so they could see each other's eyes. "Reenie, honey, I just didn't want any temper tantrums, I didn't mean you couldn't make a mistake or two. Everybody makes a mistake or two. You shoulda seen me today trying to add up all the stuff this one old lady had in her cart. I had to do it three times. She was mad as he...heck at me, but I got it right in the end. That's all that matters, kiddo."

"Well," said Reenie, "that's a wonder." She wiped her eyes and nose on her sleeve. "Okay. You gonna help me with my jigsaw?"

Lori laughed her little laugh, more like a snort. "You don't like the weather, wait five minutes," she said.

"Cubbie's making *crêpes*."

"I haven't had *crêpes*" – her mom said it more like *craypse* – "since I was knee-high to a grasshopper. My granny used to make them."

"Well, it's my first time, so don't expect granny quality," said Cubbie. "But it's worth a try. All else fails, we'll have a Kraft Dinner."

"I never tried to make them myself, me," Lori said, rummaging in the box for blue dress pieces. "They hard?"

The upshot was that Renée finished her puzzle alone while Cubbie and Lori learned how to make *crêpes*.

When it was time, Cubbie let Reenie set the yellow Arborite kitchen table. Reenie put out the pink plastic place mats and carried three sets of knives and forks – Cubbie called them "silverware" and they were brighter and paler than the knives and forks Lori had got from the dollar store. Then they all sat down and ate the *crêpes*. They were basically to pancakes what Lori was to Cubbie, and then with stuff all wrapped up in them. They were good.

"Reenie's named after her daddy," Lori said between bites. "His name is René too, without the extra 'e' at the end. But everybody calls him Ren." Reenie didn't know that. She sat very quietly. "Ren's in the burn unit over at the University Hospital. He got caught in a blowout. He was lucky. The other three didn't make it."

Reenie didn't understand that. "Like I didn't make three questions on my arithmetic?"

"That's not what I meant, hon," said Lori.

"What did you mean?"

Lori looked at Cubbie. Finally, she said, "It means they were too badly hurt, sweetie. They died."

Renée didn't ask out loud. Was Ren going to die?

>‹

The next day after school it was time to choose a new puzzle. Reenie was looking at the pictures, and she was trying to choose between some dogs dressed up in people clothes, and a Where's Waldo, when Cubbie came up behind her.

"I think you should start on this one today," she said, reaching up to a higher shelf of the puzzle closet. She handed Renée a puzzle box that had "1000 PIECES" printed on the side.

"That's a lot of pieces," said Reenie.

"One thousand," said Cubbie. "But if you put your mind to it, you can do it all right."

The picture on the box was of some people working. There were a lot of pipes and rails around them. A lot of the puzzle was different colours of grey. "It looks hard," said Reenie.

"It is hard," said Cubbie. "If things were different, maybe you could work up to it slower, but from what your mom said last night, we don't have that kind of time."

"Can you help me?"

Cubbie shook her head. "No, honey. If I helped you, it wouldn't work, and you don't want that."

"I guess not."

"Trust me, honey, that's the right answer. Just start the way I showed you, with the edges first. It's just one piece at a time, just like the other ones."

The edges of this jigsaw were just as hard as the middles of other puzzles. By the end of the first day she hadn't even found all the edge pieces, and the parts that she had found and put together didn't join up. When Lori came, Reenie went home dispiritedly, and after their dinner, bologna and cheese sandwiches because Lori was tired, Reenie did homework. They had started multiplication, which had a special chant with it called the times tables. She had to write out her one- and two- and three-times tables. She suddenly realized when she got to the threes that there was a pattern that made them easier and easier. She took a new piece of paper and wrote them out in good.

"Look, Mom!" she said. "They're pretty!"

"That's good, kiddo," said Lori. Reenie put her homework in her backpack.

Lori hugged her. "See, you'll be acing that arithmetic stuff in no time."

"Mom, it's called *mathematiques*!"

"Kid, it's called bedtime."

The next afternoon as she sat down to the puzzle table, she saw the piece with the eyes right away. They were just a bit like how her daddy's eyes looked when he smiled down at her. She reached out for the piece. It felt warm. She knew it should go right in the middle. She knew she should finish the border first, but instead she placed the eyes piece in the middle of the felt and looked back into the box. She remembered the pink pieces of the other puzzle. Would pink pieces in this one be easier to find?

Reenie thought for a minute. She hardly noticed Cubbie bringing her a glass of lemonade. She sipped it while she stirred her finger around in the box. The pieces were all every which way. That wasn't right. There was only a picture on one side. She looked at the table.

"Cubbie, how big is this puzzle? I mean, is it as big as the table?"

"Oh, no, there's plenty of room around a puzzle that size." Cubbie went back to her baking. It was chocolate chip day, but Renée hadn't even remembered to ask for batter. She got up on her knees on the chair and leaned over the table.

"You be careful you don't tip over!" Cubbie called from the sink without even looking.

"Well, that's a wonder!" Renée said to herself, but she didn't get down. She tilted the box and carefully poured out all the pieces onto the table. Then she began to turn all of them over onto their cardboard backs so the colours faced up. As she did, she looked for the face-coloured pieces – lots of different face colours from pink like her dad to brown. She put all those pieces over on the left side of where she had put her daddy's eyes, where the middle of the puzzle was going to be.

After a bit, she noticed that she could also sort the other colours into colour families at the same time – grey, and black, and blue, and even some green she hadn't noticed before – so she went back and did that. She also started to put all the edge pieces over on the right edge of the table.

This took a long time. She sat down and sipped her lemonade. Two chocolate chip cookies on a plate had appeared on the other bridge chair when she wasn't looking, so she ate one while she looked at the face pieces.

After the cookie was done, she reached out and finished the middle face. The more she looked at it, the more she thought he looked like her daddy. Then she realized that the green pieces were the colour of his shirt. She remembered from before the accident. He had more than one of those shirts, and he wore them every workday. She realized for the first time that there was a patch with his name embroidered into it, René, sewn on just above the left pocket.

The other people had green shirts too, with name patches: "Sam" and "Nadine" and "Jeff." Their faces looked sad to Renée, even though they were smiling. Were they the ones who "didn't make it?" Were they sad because they were dead? Maybe it was Reenie who was sad because they were dead. She would be sad if her dad were dead, that's for sure.

"She's right patient, that one," said Cubbie.

"Reenie is?" said her mom, sounding surprised. Reenie hadn't noticed her come in, but she couldn't stop now. The pieces of the puzzle were starting to make sense. Lori picked up the cookie plate and absently ate the cookie while she started looking for edge pieces. But Reenie kept doing the middle.

"Were Jeff and Nadine and Sam friends of Daddy?" Renée asked as she worked.

"How'd you know that, baby?"

"Says on their shirts," said Renée. "See?"

"Those *are* a bit like the rig company shirts," said Lori. "But these are blue."

"Green," said Renée.

"So they are," said Lori.

After their tuna melt and soup Reenie went to bed early, she was so tired! "Well, that's a wonder!" Lori said, and came and kissed her goodnight. But when she was in bed, in the grey darkness that was never quite black because of all the city lights, Reenie couldn't sleep for a while, worrying about stuff.

By Friday Reenie was so tired when she went to school that Lori had to tell her three times to hurry up. Finally, Lori grabbed her hand and hurried her along. Why on earth was she such a slowpoke? When it was her turn to answer,

Madame had to ask her twice. When Reenie came into Cubbie's, Cubbie said, "What's your daddy's favourite kind of pie?"

"Saskatoon," said Renée. "Why?"

"While you're finishing that jigsaw, I think I'll bake me a saskatoon pie. You and your mom and I can have a piece when she comes to get you tonight. Can't hurt."

"Can you come talk to me?"

"You just work away there, and I'll work away in here. Pie's kinda labour-intensive."

When her mom came to Cubbie's door, Reenie didn't hear the knock. She was deep into the pieces of her daddy. By supper, Renée had finished all the face and his left arm, but his right arm was only half there, and the legs still weren't done.

Cubbie had added extra macaroni and grated cheese to a Kraft Dinner to make it stretch, and she had cut one of the saskatoon pies for their dessert. Reenie could hardly concentrate on finishing her Kraft Dinner for the enticing smell of the pie sitting there above her dinner plate, but she was good and ate every bite of macaroni first.

"We can't keep coming over here to eat," said Lori. "We'll eat you out of house and home."

"If I can't make Kraft Dinner for my friends now and again, it's a pretty poor home," said Cubbie comfortably, clearing the plates at the counter. "Keep your fork."

Renée licked every bit of cheese off the fork before she took the first bite of pie. Usually, she liked to start at the crust end and work her way down to the tip, saving the best part for last. But today she very slowly and carefully lined up her fork across the tip so it was perfectly even, then gently pressed. The triangle that tilted onto her fork was as perfect as she could make it. She put it into her mouth and it melted on her tongue as if it were something else besides pie: air or water or blood or *mathematiques*.

"We should go home right after the dishes," said Lori. She was eating her pie the same way, slowly and gently. "I'm sure Reenie has homework."

Before Reenie could protest, Cubbie said, "Let her bide for tonight and work on her puzzle. She's that worried about her dad."

"I am too," said Lori.

After the last bite of the saskatoon pie, Reenie remembered to ask to be excused before she got down and went back to the puzzle on the bridge table. She put three or four pieces in fast, and Lori came and helped her a bit with background, then went off to the kitchen to dry dishes for Cubbie.

There was a really hard part on her dad's right leg that wasn't coming clear. Renée looked through all the pieces that were left. What she needed wasn't there.

"Cubbie, there are some bits missing!"

"Maybe they got stuck in the box," Cubbie said. "Look in the lid too. And check if they fell on the floor."

Renée found two pieces stuck in the corner of the box lid where it had split a little, and one sticking up from the pile of the shag carpet right by the fern stand beside the puzzle table. That almost did it. Then she found the one with the right thumb on it, on the floor way over underneath the coffee table. Now how did it get there? She imagined it scuttling over on its little puzzle feet while they were having dinner. She giggled as she turned it all four ways. There! It fit! That was it for the hand and legs! There were only a few more pieces...

Renée sighed with relief. The puzzle was done. Then she blinked at Lori and Cubbie. They were sitting on the couch watching TV. The clock above the couch had both hands pointing to the nine. That was wrong! That was fifteen minutes past her bedtime! Reenie walked over and sat by her mom, drooping against her shoulder.

"My goodness, kiddo, we better get you home!" Lori said. Reenie was so sleepy she wanted her mom to hoist her up, but Lori said, "Oof, you're too big! You have to use your own feet."

"Take the rest of the pie," urged Cubbie. "Have it for breakfast."

Reenie giggled at the idea.

"Nothing like saskatoon pie to round out a healthy breakfast," said Lori. "Why not? Ren loves this pie more than almost anything."

"Except you two," said Cubbie.

They did have pie for breakfast. The phone rang while they were eating it. Lori came back from the call grinning. "Put your coat on, kiddo," she said jubilantly. "We're going to see your daddy! He took a turn for the better last night!" She hugged Reenie.

As they went out, Cubbie was on her porch, hanging her delicates wash on a wooden rack that unfolded like an accordion, and they went over to her.

"Cubbie, we're going to see my daddy!" said Reenie. Cubbie hugged them, then left her hand on Renée's shoulder to hold her back as Lori started away. "You did well this week," she said quietly.

"You made the pie," said Renée.

"You did well," Cubbie repeated. "Your daddy is going to be fine now. You can stop worrying."

"Hurry up, Reenie, we'll miss the bus!" Lori called. She ran.

>·<

It was all winter before her daddy could come home, and when he did, he leaned on crutches and was thin as a rake, Cubbie said – but he was home.

Renée and Cubbie didn't talk much about what happened. All Cubbie said was, "When my Mr. Cubb was first sick, I did the red dot. I put on my grandmother's girdle, and I'll tell you, *that* was a stretch, more ways than one. I had my mother's floral polyester dress, and I bought support pantyhose in an egg from Vic's Super Drugs. But we had 10 more good years together."

"What was *his* favourite pie?"

"Flapper," Cubbie said, and let out that big laugh that set all her rolls to quivering again. "Me, I like a good bread pudding. That's easy to make. Flapper pie, now, takes a meringue topping and cream filling, easy to mess those up. The only easy thing is the graham wafer crumb crust."

>·<

Time settled down and quit stretching out, so it went on in a relaxed and happy way for a few years without seeming to take as long as those few months had taken. Renée's dad went to vocational retraining and became a health-and-safety officer, which Renée thought was a pretty strange kind of a thing – didn't everybody want health and safety? She and Cubbie talked that over one day.

"Accidents happen," said Cubbie. "But they don't have to always happen. Things can be done." Reenie thought of the puzzles and pie, and smiled a little. She learned to make bread pudding with Cubbie and Lori, and later attended to the making of flapper pie, and all four of them ate it.

One June day when Lori came to tell Reenie it was time to come home, Cubbie said, "You have some time tomorrow? I'd like us to make an angel food cake, and maybe you all could pop over for supper Friday."

"What's the occasion?" Lori joked.

"It's my eightieth birthday," said Cubbie, "and I thought the four of us might want to celebrate a tad."

"No way you're 80!" said Lori.

"I sure am!" Cubbie laughed and set her rolls to quivering, but Renée noticed then, and the next day as they all worked in Cubbie's kitchen, that there weren't as many rolls as there used to be, and more wrinkles. Under Cubbie's arm when she reached up to get down the multi-coloured sprinkles for the angel food, a fold of skin now swung, and her neck was wattled. The world swung a little too and settled down in a new path. Cubbie was 80 years old!

As she stirred seven-minute icing on the stove (Cubbie said store icing in a tub was the devil's work, and if the day came that she couldn't scratch-build icing for a cake, she might as well be in her grave), Lori said, "You know, Reenie's old enough now to stay late after school, or come home and let herself in. You don't have to be bothered with her if you don't want."

Reenie held her breath. But Cubbie said, "Let her come. She's no trouble. She earns her keep."

>‹

One day in January, Renée came in all bundled up and unwound the scarf she was wearing. She and Lori had made it themselves, after Cubbie taught them to knit, and Renée's dad even took a turn. It was made of three balls of wool of three different colours, and was a little wonky here and there, but it wrapped around four times with room to tie, so Reenie liked it.

Cubbie was working in the kitchen, and Reenie went to help her turn the chocolate chip cookies out onto the cooling rack. She knew how to make them herself now.

Suddenly Cubbie sat down, hard, on the easy chair she kept in the kitchen, and said, "Renée, please take those cookies out and then turn off the oven."

"But there's more…" Renée looked at the shade of Cubbie's face, and turned off the oven.

"You need to get my phone and call 911 for me, honey," Cubbie said. Renée called, and when the operator told her to, she brought the cordless phone to Cubbie so Cubbie could have a word with the lady at the other end. Before you could say Jack Robinson, Cubbie's house was cluttered up with paramedics – Pete and Kate, by their name tags – fussing with a stretcher and making the place seem very small. When they helped Cubbie up from the chair, Renée sat down in her warm spot, mostly to stay out of the way, but also because it seemed like the last warm spot in the kitchen.

Cubbie on the stretcher under a beige blanket made a mound like bread dough until paramedic Pete raised the head end so Reenie could see her face again.

"Hold on a sec," Cubbie said as they began to wheel her out. "Kate, dear, you're tall. Reach up there on top of the fridge and get down that cookie jar? Just put it on the table there." Paramedic Kate carefully lifted down the cookie jar. It was shaped like a mother cat in a storybook with a hat and a shawl, and matched the salt and pepper set that always sat on Cubbie's table.

"Renée, you look in there and find my spare key. You come in and out like usual, and keep my plants watered too, if you don't mind."

"Okay, Cubbie."

"Go home now and stay there, tell your folks what happened. She'll be fine," Cubbie said to the paramedics. "Go get me my purse, Renée, honey, I'll need it."

Renée ran to Cubbie's lacy bedroom to get the worn red leather purse, and brought it to the stretcher. Cubbie put her arm around her and kissed her cheek.

"You did real good," she said. "Don't worry, now. I'll call when I know what's what."

After they left, Renée carefully lifted off the cookie jar lid – it was the whole of the cat's head, which was a bit uncanny. Inside were a lot of bits of paper – mostly crochet patterns and recipes, plus Cubbie's pair of embroidery scissors shaped like a crane, and a key ring with two keys hanging from it, labelled *FRONT* and *BACK* on bits of white tape. She put it on the table.

Then she turned the oven back on and used two teaspoons to put out the last batch of cookies onto a baking sheet. While they baked, she licked out and washed up the batter bowl, and while they were on the cookie rack, she washed and put away the cookie sheets. She stacked the cooled cookies, separating the layers with waxed paper, into one of Cubbie's cookie tins, the one with the peacock on the lid. She washed the cooling rack and put it away. She watered the plants and looked around the house. Everything was the way it should be.

She turned out the lights and, taking the cookie tin, her coat and scarf and mitts, and her school backpack, she locked up after herself and went home to wait for Ren and Lori.

They ate two chocolate chip cookies each while they waited for news. Lori put the rest in the freezer against a special occasion.

>·<

As had happened with Renée's father years earlier, Cubbie's stay in hospital seemed to get longer the more optimistically the doctors talked. Lori and Ren and Renée visited her quite a bit. Cubbie seemed to get thinner in the bed, smaller, older, a stranger walking away down a long road: Renée looked around at some of the other old folks on the same ward and realized that this is how it happens.

It was like looking backwards through binoculars into her parents' future, and her own. She didn't like it.

The day Cubbie had been in hospital exactly three months, when Reenie went over to water Cubbie's plants, she went to the puzzle cupboard. She and Cubbie hadn't done many puzzles the last little while. The one she wanted wasn't on the shelves she could reach. She went and got the kitchen stool and climbed up to reach the top shelf. It was right at the back, at the bottom.

With trepidation, she took down the red dot puzzle. She carefully put all the other boxes back, climbed down, and put the kitchen stool in its place. She went back home and got the chocolate chip cookies out of the freezer. She put two on Cubbie's Bunnykins plate to defrost. She rolled out the felt cloth onto the bridge table, put the puzzle box in the cloth, and opened the lid.

This was a puzzle that had to be worked from the outside in. It had 2500 pieces, and every one of them red. In the end, it would be just a big round red dot. Even finding the edges took days, let alone placing them.

It was the hardest thing. With her dad, it had been putting back something that wanted to get better anyway, just giving a little shove. With the red puzzle, it was just the opposite. She was fighting something back, something immature and growing that just wanted to be alive, to be everywhere, to eat and eat no matter who else went hungry. She had to fight the energy these uncontrolled cells had.

Renée had to fight herself, too. She had to fight the shame she felt that her younger self had been like that, so hungry in her heart. She had to fight her guilt that she hadn't noticed Cubbie getting thinner and sicker in time to work on it earlier, when it would have been easier. But she fought. Every day she added more pieces.

One day, Ren was home early so Renée asked him to help her make a bread pudding for dinner. She was so tired.

"We can have it for dinner, and take some of the leftovers up to Cubbie," she said. "She told me she hates that hospital food."

"Renée, *ma chou*, I don't think she'll be able to eat any. She's pretty sick, you know."

"Why does she have to be sick, anyway?"

"It's entropy. We French have a saying about it, you know. *Tout passé, tout lasse, tout casse.* It means that—"

"I know what it means, Papa, I'm in French immersion, OK?"

"No need to be rude, *p'tite*."

"*Je m'excuse, Papa.* But let's just try, OK?"

So they did try, and ate the pudding for supper with Kraft Dinner. "Comfort food," said Lori.

"Cubbie food," said Reenie.

The next day at the hospital, Cubbie was sitting up in a chair. She took the lid off the Tupperware, took her Rogers silver-plate spoon that Renée had brought, and ate almost all of the bread pudding. "That was just fine, girl."

"Daddy helped me cut the bread," said Renée. "We buttered it with real butter."

"You learned what I taught you pretty good. You know, I'm leaving you my things. You might need them later, when you grow up."

"You need them *now*, Cubbie!" Reenie protested. She was afraid of entropy, but she needed to know. "Cubbie, did we use it all up? You know, on Daddy?"

Cubbie looked at her sharply. "It don't work that way, child. It's like water. It just flows down."

"So it's always there?"

"If you can get at it, it sure is."

Renée went home to her puzzle. Every day that week Cubbie sat up in a chair. Renée began to think that she might be able to manage. At night she couldn't sleep, dogged by shadows in her room made by the lights as cars whooshed by on the service road outside. Seemed like there were more cars than Renée had ever noticed, but then again, she usually slept better.

All week she worked on the spiralling, closing eye of the puzzle, until by Friday suppertime she was at the centre.

The hole for the last piece was heart-shaped: not heart like a greeting card but shaped like the actual heart in the Heart Association brochure on Cubbie's TV table. But there were no more pieces on the table. She reached into the box and felt around. The box was empty.

The heart of the puzzle was missing.

It wasn't in the box. It wasn't on the floor. She looked all through the living room and down beside all the couch cushions. She took every puzzle out of the puzzle cupboard and opened the boxes one at a time, rummaged through the pieces of each one before she put it back. The centrepiece wasn't there either.

All weekend she searched Cubbie's house. She went through Cubbie's bedroom, feeling like a trespasser, but driven to it. She searched the lavender-smelling drawers, even under their shelf-paper lining. She took all the sensible shoes out of the bottom of the closet and searched behind them. She glimpsed red at the back of the closet but it wasn't the puzzle piece. It was a beautiful pair of red, open-toed, high-heeled pumps that she couldn't imagine Cubbie ever wearing. Among the clothes, the swatch of red she saw in a garment bag at the side wasn't the puzzle piece but a red velvet evening gown with a strapless sweetheart bodice and a full skirt. She had always known there was more to Cubbie than met the eye. Cubbie couldn't die now; she just couldn't die. Cubbie was a bundle of life; this was the proof she always had been. How could death come for her so soon? The lady in the next bed at the hospital was 99 and still telling stories. It wasn't fair.

Reenie searched the spare room, the bathroom with its shelf of scented bath oils, the mud room, and the porch. She searched the basement, its toolbox and good wood. Nothing.

Finally, she searched her own room at home, in case somehow she'd tracked the piece back when she came home one time.

Rien. Nothing.

By Sunday afternoon, when it was time to go to the hospital, Renée was ready to cry at the drop of a hat. At least she didn't need her winter coat. It was the first nice spring day.

"Maybe she's too tired to go," Lori said to Ren. "She spent all weekend doing housework over there, and she has school tomorrow."

"Let her go, *cherie*," said Ren. "Her heart fairly beats on our Cubbie."

Renée thought about this all the way over on the LRT. Hearts and heartbeats – difficult and complicated, and a terrible challenge. When she got to Cubbie's room Cubbie was back in bed. She had an oxygen tank on one side and a drip-controlling machine on the other, and on its IV stand was clamped a box full of monitors that were hooked up to a plastic pincher on Cubbie's finger.

"Hello, my loves." Cubbie hugged Lori, and Ren awkwardly bent over for his own hug. They talked a few minutes about the kind of things they always did. If it hadn't been for the beeps and humming of the machines, it would have been calming.

Then Cubbie beckoned Renée closer. "Come over here so I can hug you! Lori and Ren, why don't you go get a coffee so I can talk to my girl?"

Renée wended her way between the equipment and approached the hospital bed with its metal edges. Cubbie took her hand. Her warm comforting grip was the same, even though she looked flat as an empty plastic bag, lying there covered only by a single white sheet. Her crocheted afghan was folded on the chair.

"Are you cold, Cubbie?" Renée asked.. "Do you need your afghan?"

"My lovely Renée," said Cubbie. "Don't worry, I'm fine."

"I'm doing the red puzzle for you," whispered Renée, finally telling her secret. "I've done it all, but one piece is missing."

Cubbie winked at her. "That's why I've been feeling so good. Thank you, child."

Then she did a strange thing. She opened her mouth and stuck out her tongue at Renée.

On her tongue was the last piece from the heart of the puzzle.

"Oh, give it back," begged Renée. "Please! It's the last one…"

But even as she watched, the red puzzle piece, the triangular three-legged one from the very heart of the round red puzzle, began to dissolve and lose its edges. It soaked into Cubbie's tongue until nothing was left but a bright red stain, as if Cubbie had been sucking on those red Valentine cinnamon hearts. Cubbie closed her mouth and swallowed, smiling as if around a sweet taste.

Reenie began to cry.

Cubbie squeezed her hand gently. "I'm an old woman," she said. "A person can't live forever."

"But Papa...he...we..."

"It wasn't the right time for him. We just helped the Universe see that. But for me, it's the right time. It happens to everyone."

"I don't like it!"

"The Universe never asked us if we do or we don't. It is what it is."

"It is what it is...?"

"That's my girl. Give me a kiss goodbye, now, Reenie. You won't see me again."

It was the first time Cubbie had used Renée's nickname.

Renée squeezed Cubbie's hand hard and leaned in to kiss her pale, frail, wrinkled cheek. Cubbie kissed Renée on both cheeks and smiled at her. "Now, my girl. Don't forget all I taught you."

"Oh, Cubbie," said Renée. She put Cubbie's hand up to her cheek, where both their hands got wet with Renée's tears.

She was just pulling herself back together when Lori and Ren came back from the coffee machine with their covered paper cups. "Come on, Reenie," said her mom. "Cubbie has to rest now. We can see her again next Saturday." Lori couldn't help it. She didn't know.

"Bye-bye, dear," said Cubbie. "You know I love you. Remember."

"Goodbye, Cubbie," said Renée. "I love you too. I won't forget. I promise."

She didn't cry all the way home, but she felt like it. The only reason that she didn't was Lori and Ren didn't know what was going to happen, and Renée didn't know how to explain it to them.

They were very practical people. It had been a trial to her and Cubbie sometimes.

>‹

When Renée and her parents got home, Renée went next door. She had to water the plants, she said.

Through the wall she could hear her parents talking, but not what they were saying. Cubbie always said these places had walls like paper.

She walked slowly to the table with the red puzzle on it, the proof of her failure to save Cubbie's life, the puzzle with the heart missing.

But that's not what she saw. The puzzle lay there complete, the heart-shaped centrepiece in place as if she had never searched all of Cubbie's row house and theirs too, trying to find it, as if she'd never seen it dissolve on Cubbie's tongue and be swallowed.

She walked forward slowly and reached out her hand to touch the piece. It was smoothly fitted in, as if by Cubbie's gentle, precise hand. It felt warm.

"Cubbie," she whispered. "I'll remember everything. Everything. I promise."

Through the wall, she heard the phone ringing, the call from the hospital.

Cubbie's (really, my mother, Marie Dezall Dorsey's) Bread Pudding

Preheat oven to 350°F

In a deep (4+ inches) round, 8" or 9" casserole dish, mix either:

2 eggs and ¾ cup sugar   or   3 eggs and 1 cup sugar.

Note: This isn't about measuring-cup cooking. Use a coffee cup if you want, but not one of the big ones.

Add:

1 cup milk

Cube and, if desired, butter all the leftover crusts and heels of bread you've saved in a bag in the fridge. If necessary, top up with enough sliced bread, cubed, to fill the dish to within 1" of top. (Cubbie and her tribe use white bread and white sugar and make a pale pudding, but darker breads and brown sugar will make a darker pudding.)

Add:

Some raisins if desired (a handful or two, or a cup. You know, some).

Stir perfunctorily.

Cover with:

More milk

Stir again if you feel like it. Or not.

Top with:

Liberal amount of cinnamon and a touch of nutmeg.

Bake in 350°F oven for about one hour or microwave oven for approximately 10-12 minutes (time depends on the microwave). It is done when it rises, the top is slightly brown (in conventional oven), and if when pudding is pricked with a toothpick, toothpick emerges clean.

Putting a custard, caramel or chocolate sauce on top is revisionist, but not a mortal sin.

Equally delicious served hot or cold.

Gluten-free note: If making with gluten-free bread, you probably will have to use the larger number of eggs for binding, even in the smaller sized dish. Gluten-free breads differ widely in composition, so consider your first attempt a test.

WIDOW

Richard Van Camp

That summer of the pandemic
the wheetago returned to live with us

We bathed him out at Pine Lake
while the people prayed

We blanketed him
smudged him
fed him
fed him more
fed him again

He was death white and cold
his aunties cut his hair
trimmed his nails with the tool
they use to sharpen axes, chainsaws

They dressed him in a black ribbon shirt
laced with red and white
green in the back
tendrils of hope

They made seven of these shirts
so we could see him coming from anywhere
on any day

With blue jeans
white socks
a belt and black runners from Kaeser's
he almost looked human

He would smile every once in a while
when kids ran by
or played around him

He would smile

I was always so shocked when I saw
how yellow his teeth were
when he yawned
or curled wide his upper lip while listening to
something none of us could hear

His skin, over time, discoloured to that
of the webbing you see on old-time rawhide snowshoes

The handlers put upon him
were men with big sticks
walkie-talkies
the uncles
the Special Constables
the JP
watching his every move

After some time they let him free
reminded him if he was ever hungry
to go to the Red House in Indian Village

The family there would cook for him day and night
they were very traditional and could
cook the old-time bone grease

They would pound and pound caribou bones into a pulp
adding a little boiled water at a time

Even better
they'd go out and grab handfuls of crystal snow
in Spring and add it or they'd use
snow from the spruce boughs
and pound and pound
boiling it to make bone grease

They had lots of caribou
ever lots
and they wanted to meet him
they said their great-grandparents were good
friends with him
when he was alive

He walked the community
strode it
paced it
after a while
there were no break-ins anymore
and your insomnia grew

People would cruise the streets at night to watch him
some would walk with him
ask him questions
he would never answer

One night you parked and walked to him
he stopped and watched you
taking his time
first one eye and then the other
just like that porcupine in the branch
I once told you about

Do not be amazed
your auntie told you once if you ever see one
do not be amazed

But you were amazed
you got out of your truck
came to him
held his hand

It was burning
you were surprised
you got in your truck and drove away

That night you felt his breath under your body
and you slept for the first time
since your husband's funeral

Your hand ached for days
but you were happy
you caught yourself singing
looking out the window

Sometime later you woke
got dressed
found him by the Slave
the boat launch
Panty Point they call it

He'd walked down the landslide by himself
he was dusty
thirsty
listening to something past the water

He washed himself like a beaver
his hands over and over
his wrists and his face
the way he slurped the water
gently
you weakened

He stood
looked at you

You held your hand out and spoke to him
Nah

You took his hand again
he came to stay with you and he would watch you
your legs
how they were covered with psoriasis
dots of shame
scabs that flaked

You feasted him
and he ate
everything raw
while yours was cooked

He loved berries
you were surprised
he looked through your photo albums
pointed at pictures of your great-grandparents
made noises in his throat

He turned on your late husband's bush radio
and turned it to a station that was noise
he was listening for something
or waiting to hear from someone

He needed that hiss to sleep

One night you woke and he was in
your backyard dancing on fire
you put your glasses on and looked again
he'd dug a hole beside the fire that roared between you
put rocks in it

buried a caribou head in the hallowed earth
covered the head with rocks
then pushed the fire over the rocks

The head baked all morning
just like a barbeque

For lunch
he motioned with his jaw for you to taste it
he brought you a plate and utensils

Every piece of meat tasted different

He boiled a caribou head on the first
fire in a big pot and ate the tongue
eyes
brains
Indian Ice Cream
your first husband called it

You were too chicken to try
you realized this was the first time
since your husband died
that anyone cooked for you

When you were young
one of the rich white boys who wanted you
but couldn't have you
told everyone you had a smell
and that became a nickname for you
from everyone jealous of your beauty

The Unburied One frowned when you told him this
and held you

He smelled of something raw and sweet
fresh rain
a garden

The next night he held caribou hooves
offered them up to the moon
and placed them in the same hole
used the same stones
made a new fire by rubbing his fingernails together and
throwing sparks at old-man's-beard and twigs

He baked you marrow from the legs
he used his teeth to peel back the caribou hoof tops
like tree bark
and you discovered the sweetest delicacies underneath

The next night he boiled muskrat for you
pounded meat
with marrow and bone grease served on bannock

You started boiling soup bones
would sip broth from the same bowl
back and forth
each time you tasted the same shared soup
from his mouth to yours
it tasted sweeter and deeper

He boiled you rabbit soup with oats, and spooned
brains into your mouth
giggling
your chin slick with holy juice

One night you woke and he was scraping his bottom teeth
through the dead skin off the soles of your feet
he gripped your ankle with both hands and
dug in
each rake getting closer and closer to the meat inside you

His eyelids quivered and he never looked at you
you wanted him to look at you as you came
again and again
bucking
gushing

He smiled after and you smiled back
(you knew this would happen)
and he swallowed and smacked his lips before
holding you and drifting to sleep

One night he motioned to ask why you were alone

He motioned to your home and yard and to you
your beauty

You told him about your husband
how good he was to you
how he shielded you as best he could from the rumours
the shame name the town kept ready for you

when you got out of line
went to a dance or tried to sing at the talent show
The Unburied One shook his head and knelt before you
hugging your legs like you were a saint

After some time he would leave
to return bones and hooves to the cracks in stone
longer and longer away
the soles of your feet had never been softer
your days had never seemed longer

Your palm ached with searing fire and you loved it
held it between your thighs to feel him

He can smell me anywhere in the world
you said to yourself one day
as you put pictures of your first husband away

Your legs cleared up where he kissed you
your psoriasis slowly vanished
he sucked it all from you
every time you came

One day you arrived home and there was a note
on birch bark:
a calligraphy from the land:
a touch of spruce bough
three berries:
low bush cranberry
blueberry
and a berry that told you his alive name

A child's writing in scratches with animal blood:
they lied to you
you are delicious

You never saw him again but God
did your feet and hands burn when the snow fell
as you dug into the same hole he did
placing stones in hopes of seeing him
when the snow fell
when it rained
under stars

That's how you cooked now

You were amazed
you smelled of smoke
your house smelled of smoke
you slept with your eyes and doors wide open

Our town never looked your way or spoke your name again.

Old-time Cariboo Grease-bone
Best served for lunch on a plate with utensils

Ingredients:
- Caribou bones and handfuls of crystal snow

Preparation:
• Pound and pound caribou bones into a pulp, adding a little water (crystal snow) at a time, boiling it to make bone grease.
• Bury the caribou head and bone pulp in hallowed earth. Cover the head with rocks, then push the fire/coals over the rocks.
• The head bakes for a full morning, just like a barbeque. Eat and enjoy.

EATING OUR YOUNG

Casey June Wolf

Kenda watched the carnage through the break in the laundry room wall, sucking on her big toe anxiously. The family was savaging the thin remains of their youngest boy, her twin brother, Ken. Dale, Ken and Kenda's mom, nibbled, with her incisors and lips, the tight skin of an ankle, pulling it from its grip on the bone; James sank his teeth into the softer region of Kenny's midriff. A frayed electrical cord hung from the ceiling. The dim, twitching light of a naked bulb gave the meal an eerie look, as if it wasn't normal, didn't happen every day.

The presence of Kenda's toe against her tongue reassured her. She sucked vigorously, closing her eyes. To the sounds of sucking, chewing, snarling over the reluctant cadaver, she sank gradually into sleep.

>·<

Morning arrived with the shout of her biggest sister, Enid. "Up! School! Come make your lunch!"

Kenda tripped on tangling sheets as she leapt to the door. All seven kids would stampede to the washroom but she was closest and with luck might not have to wait.

Too late. Enid was mean again and wakened James before the rest. He was the biggest boy and Enid's favourite and slower in the bathroom than anyone. Kenda faltered at the closing door. "Can I come in, Jamie?"

"Wait your turn, Turd-Drop."

She sighed and looked at the bristling line of bigger kids squeezing toward her, and remembered Kenny last night. It was *not* going to happen to her today. She ran back to her room and began to change clothes, then climbed out the window, down the rose trellis, to the dirt. No one guessed her use of the garden. Here behind the rose she yanked her shorts down, piddled, and covered the pee before climbing the trellis again. At the window she listened, peeking cautiously over the sill.

The door had drifted open. Children cried and shouted, doors slammed, water ran. Enid yelled orders. Kenda wanted to climb back in and burrow in the blank oasis of the laundry room where she and Kenny slept. (Her idea. They'd been sneaking in to sleep together on piles of laundry for so long nobody thought about it anymore.)

No one was in the room.

Kenda slipped inside and went to the kitchen. Dale was making coffee. "Morning," she grunted. Kenda ran over to her. Dale bent down, eyes still on the measuring spoon, to receive her daughter's kiss.

Going to the table, Kenda climbed a padded chair and grabbed a blue-green Melmac bowl from the pile. Using both arms to lift the box, she shook a mound of flakes into her bowl, then sprinkled on sparkling white sugar. She nearly upset the milk tipping the jug over her bowl. Very carefully, she replaced it on the table.

An assortment of siblings was already shovelling cereal into their mouths, barking at each other, wrestling over the last of the toast or the toy in the empty box. Kenda put her spoon in the bowl and lifted out the first bite.

"SHIT-SMEAR!" James called. Her turn in the bathroom. Get up now and lose her cereal. Don't get up and lose her place in line. She couldn't get dressed till she was clean, and if she wasn't dressed when they were ready to leave... "*Too late!*" rang out her sister Heather's voice, and the bathroom door banged closed.

Crunching softly, Kenda slipped the spoon back into the bowl and lifted out the next bite. At least she'd already peed.

>‹

She was the smallest of the kindergarteners and people talked to her like her big owl eyes really belonged to a bird. They cooed and patted her and discussed her with each other as if she couldn't understand. Some girls got mad when people did things like that, calling them cutie and asking how many babies they would have when they grew up. But Kenda didn't mind. Any friendly attention seemed good. Her answering smile must have been goofy because they'd laugh and say nice things or hug her, and she liked that. So she was happy to go to school.

She looked around and there was Ken, whole and bruised and not meeting her eyes, sitting on his short stool in the kindergarten circle, where they always started their day. She was sad to see him and wanted to look away so she wouldn't have to remember last night. But he was her bestest brother, so she walked over and put her arms around him and said, "Hi, Kenny."

He looked down. There was a raw, lumpy scar behind his ear and his neck was one yellow bruise. She knew from before that the teachers wouldn't see it. She touched him sadly.

"Kenny," she said again.

Ken shrugged her hands off and whispered, "Go away." So she went away and sat on her own stool, hands on her lap.

>·<

Miss Streudel (Enid's nickname; she was really Miss Steedle) was as kind and fun as usual, although she was a bit impatient with Ken. He couldn't follow what she was saying and wasn't playing happily or "participating" – Miss Streudel liked kids to participate. Kenda tried to distract her from Ken by being bright and useful, helping her with games and retrieving things from the storage cubes. But this just made Miss Streudel squint at Ken even more. Kenda knew she wanted to say, "Why aren't you like your sister?" but they weren't allowed to say things like that here. Instead she said, "What's *wrong*, Ken?"

The more she bugged him the blanker he got. Eventually he was sent home with a note, and Miss Streudel had a short, intense talk with Enid, who had to come to pick him up. Enid looked mad at Ken, and when he looked up at her and his big yellow bruise stretched out, she looked even madder at him, but she didn't say a word to him, and not a lot to Miss Streudel.

Kenda wondered, watching them, why Miss Streudel couldn't see. She wondered if other kids ever came in torn and bruised. She'd never noticed. She wondered, for a second, why.

>·<

That night, dinner was a quiet affair. Kenda tried to hide in the laundry room again but they weren't having any of it. They sat like zombies around the table while Enid pointed at the serving platter and Ken obediently crawled up, tears beading in his eyes and dribbling down his cheeks. Even Enid looked stressed.

Dale came in with the carving knife and everyone stopped breathing. Kenda stared hard at her plate, hands clenched. She couldn't see what was going on, but she *heard*.

She heard the tip of the knife pop the threads that held Ken's buttons, and the shuffle of clothing as it was removed. She heard him settle back on the cold platter (she knew it was a cold platter – she had set it out, and the room was a cold room), and heard his tiny whimper. She imagined him squeezing his eyes shut. She wanted to grab him and run and hide. She stopped her breathing and tried to faint.

That night, for an extra bit of cruelty, the others threw the uneaten bits of Ken on the laundry room floor as a warning to Kenda. She would have to sleep all night with his bloody, pissy-smelling parts only a few feet away. She was lucky they hadn't thrown them on her sleeping pile.

>·<

"Come on, Kenny," Kenda said the next morning. He had crawled back together in the night and was congealing slowly, regrowing, knitting piece by piece like they always did, the scars and bruises slowly fading as the joins were made complete.

Kenny looked over weakly. She could see he was very tired. It's hard to rest when you have to go through this, and it was his second night in a row. She pitied him.

"Want to run away?" she whispered, knowing what he would say, what he always said.

But this time he didn't say anything. He just looked.

James was in the bathroom. Enid came down the stairs to the laundry room door and looked in, a pink hairbrush in her hand. Kenda saw the white, threadlike scars along her neck and face, down her arms and even over the bones of her bare toes.

"Is he okay?" Enid asked.

Kenda shook her head and nodded at the same time. Enid sighed hard and pushed up the sleeves of her housecoat.

"Okay," she said. "Turn around, Kenda. Let me brush your hair."

The bathroom door opened and James called out. "Hey, Shit-Stripe! What the hell did you do with my toothbrush?"

He came in holding a toothbrush covered in grimy flesh. His hands shook with fury and his face was red enough to burst.

Kenda was speechless. Ken shrank into the darkness behind the washing machine. Something dark dripped from him. He shouldn't be bleeding; he was all knitted up now.

"Oh, for Christ's sake, James," Enid said. "How the hell do you know it was her? Piss off."

James and Enid faced off for a brittle moment, then he stomped out of the room.

Enid took up the hairbrush again.

"Got to get a new carving knife," she said. "The old one's getting dull. I think it hurt Kenny too much." She pulled a bunch of bobby pins from her pocket and stuck a few between her teeth.

Kenda held her breath. Too many feelings hit together inside her all at once. She was battered, scared, desperate, tentatively mad. She wanted to bawl.

But.

Enid was right. She would make it better. She would make sure the knife was really sharp.

Kenda turned to her big sister, stared up at her. Enid grabbed her hair and started to pull the brush through it, sending little stars of pain through Kenda's scalp.

It would be better. It would help a lot. Relief washed slowly up. "I love you, Enid," she whispered. Enid's hand jerked, then resumed brushing, maybe a little less roughly.

A small movement by the washing machine caught Kenda's eye. A sick, sad, bloody boy, subsiding hopelessly to the floor.

Ken and Kenda's Breakfast

Ingredients:
- One bowl corn flakes, any brand
- White sugar
- Milk

Preparation:
• Combine ingredients in a breakfast bowl. May be served with white or brown toast.

RED LIKE CHERRIES OR BLOOD

Desirae May

The man sat on his porch and looked out over what you might call a yard, if you had decided to be generous. They were too far from town for fences but that also meant there were no children daring each other to ring the doorbell and run away. Or not often; it *did* happen on Halloween some years, drunk teenagers who got a good scare when he pulled the door open just as their feet hit the top step. Which was what they were after.

The house sat on a low hill at the end of a dirt road. Dry grass and nettles grew all around it, tangled as a head of unkempt greying hair. No one mowed the lawn or tended the garden. There were flowerbeds stretching the whole length of the verandah but they had been lost to weeds long ago. The field was dotted with junk; broken bottles, a spare tire, and an old Model T that could have been worth something if it weren't a rusted-out, mouse-infested mess.

The man and the woman did not live in the house, the way others might have lived in it; they merely inhabited the space. Waited.

She approached the door from inside. He turned an eye to her silhouette, trying to gauge her mood. On good days she would come outside and let him position her chair so she could enjoy some fresh air. But she was wearing her veil and that meant it was going to be a bad one.

There was one mirror in the house, above the sink in the bathroom. He insisted on keeping it so he could shave. She covered the glass with a towel whenever she was in there.

"It's a nice day," he said, in a language he kept expecting to forget but hadn't yet. "You should come out and keep me company."

Wrong tactic; she wheeled sharply away without saying a word and disappeared into the interior of the room. He might have known better than to say "should" to her but some lessons never did get learned.

The man sighed. Going after her would be no use. He stretched out his bony legs and folded his hands. Two crows dropped from the sky, wings outstretched. They found something dead in the grass and started to rip it apart.

>·<

He went by Mr. Greene. The townspeople, on the very rare occasions that they saw his companion, referred to her as Mrs. Hammersmith. These were not their real names.

But naming is a funny thing. Inhabit a moniker long enough and you start to look like it, or it starts to look like you. There were whole weeks where he thought of himself as Mr. Greene. He couldn't say the same for Mrs. Hammersmith. She never forgot anything.

Might have been kinder if she could; yes, it would have been. If they had both ended up brain-scrambled along with the rest of it. But kindness wasn't the point.

Everyone in the county called the nearest town the Hollow. That wasn't what appeared on maps or on the official census; it had been christened Oakdale by some dismal founder in the mists of history. There wasn't an oak in the place. But there was a dip in the land that the town nestled in, not impressive enough to be a ravine nor a valley. Just a hollow, and so the name.

There wasn't much to the town. Whitewashed buildings that had gone up during the Depression and hadn't changed since. Modest farmhouses, painted bright or dull colours at the owner's discretion. He drove in once every two weeks to pick up groceries.

Mr. Greene woke the morning of his errand to heavy rain. He turned over in bed and groaned. The raindrops drumming against the roof echoed inside of his head.

Mrs. Hammersmith was still asleep by the time he managed to pry himself out of the sheets. He thought about knocking on her door to ask if she wanted to come with him, but he knew the answer. Best to get going. The rain wasn't going to let up all day, he could smell longevity in the air.

He dressed in heavy rubber boots and a baseball cap with the brim tilted down. The rain got to him anyway, sneaking in behind the collar of his jacket. And the truck, of course, took forever to start. The radio wouldn't work, no matter what he did to it. He hated technology.

Which is to say that Mr. Greene was already in a glorious mood when his truck got stuck in the mud.

It was in as firm as a pig in shit. He yanked uselessly at the wheel, hit the gas and then released it. His exertions acted only upon himself. The truck, it seemed, was uninterested in moving.

Mr. Greene climbed out with a curse. By the side of the road a few leaves fell from a tree, as though the branches had shivered suddenly. When he spat on the ground it sizzled.

His hat fell off. The rain plastered his hair to his skull within minutes. He was sodden, a drowned rat in Wellingtons. He tried to dig the wheels out, splattering himself with mud up to the elbow. He pushed at the side of the vehicle. Hands up against the metal, straining. A squeal of rage escaped his clenched teeth.

And he felt it give. He smelled heat, a particular heat, and one that brought him back to the blacksmith's shop he'd swept out as a boy. Gleaming fire – coloured iron striking against the anvil.

The metal warped. It blistered under his fingers and re-solidified in their shape – not a handprint, not quite, but close. Too close, and he had promised himself that he wouldn't *do* that anymore. Mr. Greene fell backwards, panting.

He had cut his palm clear across. On what? There was no jagged edge.

"Mister Greene?" someone asked. "You okay?" It was a distinct *Mis—ter*, and a young voice.

Mr. Greene wiped water and hair out of his eyes. He squinted through the rain. The Beckett boy. One of them, anyway – they tended to blend together in a blur of gappy smiles and sunburn. "Zachariah," he asked, "is that you?"

"It's just Zach, sir," said the boy. "You need help up?"

Mr. Greene gritted his teeth. "I do not," he said. "I'm not *that* old, kid."

(He was, and then some.)

"Okay," said Zach. "Truck's still stuck, though."

He had a chain in the flatbed of his own vehicle. For hauling wood, he said. They attached it to the front of Mr. Greene's truck and hit the gas, mud flying. There was a long moment of strain during which he seemed to sink further in – and then he was near airborne, being dragged down the wet road, skidding sideways in a screech of rubber and dirt.

He got out to shake Zach's hand. The bloody one he kept tucked in his pocket, curled into a fist. The boy looked him in the eye. That was impressive. Mr. Greene had never been easy to look at, even before the scars. There was a sweet smell in the air. It lingered in the memory and the nostrils.

Zach had clammy, cold hands. At the time, Mr. Greene thought it was because of the rain.

>·<

"What do you suppose we are?" he asked, from the couch where he was sprawled on his back. The better to watch spiders spin their way across the ceiling.

Mrs. Hammersmith was sitting in a recliner and eating a TV dinner. It tasted like salt and ash, it always did, for both of them.

"What can you possibly mean?" she asked, pushing her limp potatoes around with a fork.

"We aren't vampires," he mused. "We don't drink blood. We can still go outside. And we aged."

She dropped her fork onto the card table in front of her with a sigh. "I hate when you get philosophical. A curse is a curse."

"We thought we were so lucky at first," he said. "That after everything, we had lived."

Mrs. Hammersmith turned on the television. It came to life in a crackle of static. *Wheel of Fortune*. He hated *Wheel of Fortune*. He hated he had opinions on *Wheel of Fortune*.

"Do you remember the feasts?" he asked. "Roast pig. Strawberries and clotted cream. Rabbit stew and venison seasoned with garlic and pepper. Beef so tender it fell off the bone. Slices of fresh fish. Pumpkin tarts. Potatoes with onion and bacon. Roast goose hot from the fire…"

"Apples," she said.

He got up and went out to the porch. Now he had gone and made himself hungry and there was nothing he could do about it. There was always a gnawing pain beneath his ribs, a streak of unfulfilled need. He could only wait for it to lessen. Food was so unsatisfying. Everything was – even the world, he thought, looking out at the sad grey sky, leached of all its colour.

(He couldn't starve to death, either. He'd tried. Yet the hunger still hurt. He had not passed far enough from life to escape it.)

Mr. Green paced the step. He threw a can at one of the crows. He watched a squirrel gnaw on the skull of one of its fellows. And then a long line of cars began to cross the horizon, heading toward the old graveyard outside of town. Everyone inside them wore black. A funeral.

In the car at the head of the procession, Mrs. Beckett dabbed a handkerchief to her face. Her son was dead.

>‹

He lay awake at night thinking about it. The cold handshake. The sweet smell. Finally, at the break of a lavender dawn, he crept into Mrs. Hammersmith's room and woke her up. It was decorated only in shades of white, blank as a sheet of paper.

"He was poisoned," he said.

She stared at him. Her face was lined and sagging, her hair silvered and thinning. But her eyes were still the blue of the deep ocean.

"You've cracked," she said with interest. "Finally. I knew it would happen."

"Young Beckett," he said. "That's who I mean."

"Did a little birdie tell you?" she asked. "Did it braid your hair, as well?"

"Woman," he said, "listen to me for a minute. I could smell it on him. And I'd know, wouldn't I? You and I, we would *both* know."

"I can't confirm your theory," she said. "I never met him."

He sat down on the edge of the bed. She tried to shove him off but he wouldn't go; eventually she dropped her head back down to the pillow. "I know," he said. "But I think we can prove it."

"Christ in heaven," she said. "*How?*"

"A test," he said. "There's always a test in cases like these." She pulled the blankets up over her head in disgust.

>ı<

She still went with him to the Beckett homestead the next day. It was always the family. That was the other thing they both knew.

They brought a pie. They had put it together, paging through a cookbook so ancient the pictures were etchings. It couldn't have been read by anyone but an expert. Or themselves. And it wasn't just a cookbook. "Do we have strawberries?" he asked. "Do we have cherries?"

They didn't, so he went outside and picked some. There were no fruit trees where they were. He had to go – afield. When he got back, he smelled of lightning. The fruit in the basket was too shiny, too plump. It sparked the appetite more than it should have. It almost glittered.

"I thought you weren't going to do that anymore," she said, sniffing him delicately. "Didn't you have some theory the magic would eventually run out, thus releasing you?"

People gave food to grieving families. It had always been so, even back in his day. One of his earliest memories was the procession of people bringing by preserves, and bread, and dried meats after his mother had passed. Sacks of beets or fruit from their orchards. Anything that would last.

It was scarlet fever, he thought. Or the sweating sickness. One of those diseases no one got any longer. Antibiotics, and so on.

It had been many, many years since he had thought of that day. Or her; her soft hands, her round face. How odd, that it should come back now. He had stopped rolling out dough. Mrs. Hammersmith tapped him on the elbow. He started moving again.

She was mixing things together in a bowl, ingredients that were too strange to mention. Small bones. Crushed flowers. Blood from the reopened wound on his hand (magic, always, requires sacrifice). A noxious liquid, thick and dark as an oil slick. It bubbled as it went in.

But she didn't pour it into the pie shell. Instead, it went into a tall glass, which she handed to him.

"Ready?" she asked.

He took a deep breath. "Yes," he said, and drank it down.

>ı<

They dressed in black to bring the food over. Mrs. Hammersmith kept fussing with her veil during the drive.

"Will you take that stupid thing off?" he asked. "You look like an Italian widow."

"Given the circumstances, I think it's appropriate," she snapped.

The Beckett home was one of the larger farmhouses in the area. It had Gothic windows, gingerbread edges, and dying plants hanging on the front porch. There was a rolling blond field out back. A reasonable site for a murder. A confluence with an expected narrative. He, of all people, knew how powerful stories could be.

The pie dish was covered in tinfoil and was still warm in his hands. He knocked on the door and shoved it at the first person who opened it. One of the children. A girl, with the same washed-out colouring as her brother. Big dark circles under her eyes. He cleared his throat. "For your parents," he said. She stared at him. The hand that took the pie spasmed with weakness.

But she was a polite girl, one correctly raised. "Would you like to come in?" she asked, tucking her hair behind her ears.

"We would," said Mrs. Hammersmith. She had her cane across her lap; she'd used it to steady herself while he got her chair up the stairs. Then she had hobbled up after it. It looked like a weapon in her hands. So did everything else.

The girl gave her an even more uncertain look. That fucking veil. She stepped aside to let them in.

It looked like he would have predicted. Inherited furniture and grandma's china figurines. Knitted afghans on the sofa and draped over a recliner. Pictures on the walls of family dating back a hundred years, showing men with full beards and women in high-necked dresses. A doll or a toy truck on the floor, here and there.

The parents were in the kitchen. The father, drunk. The mother, curiously sharp-eyed. She smiled at them and accepted their offering.

She was out of place. He understood that as soon as he saw her. Too shiny for this shabby world. Too beautiful for her husband, too cultured for this town. She had sold herself cheap at some point to get here. She knew it and resented it.

He'd known a woman like that, once.

"I don't believe we've met," she said.

"We don't live far," said Mr. Greene. "Just outside of town. I thought well of your boy. So," he nodded at the pie. He knew how good it looked. They'd made sure of that. Everyone would want a slice.

The children were all small, pale things. Knobby knees and elbows, mouths drawn in a tight line. He kept losing track of them as they moved in and out of his line of vision. There was the girl who had let them in. A toddler of indeterminate gender meandering, tugging at the edges of its diaper. A sulky teenager hanging on to the edges of the room. None of them looked very well. Not exactly underfed. Just – not healthy. Like each and every child was fighting off a cold.

They resembled their mother. Blonde with sleepy, deep-set eyes.

The pie was on the table, crisp and inviting and smelling like spice and hot fruit. But not only that. Every person in the room was turned toward it.

Mrs. Hammersmith tilted her strange, veiled head. "Why don't we all have a slice?"

There was power in her voice still. Mr. Greene knew she wouldn't have any – that would mean showing her face, which she rarely did around strangers now – but the same suggestion from him would have lacked impact. She spoke like someone who expected to be obeyed.

"Yes," said Mrs. Beckett. "We should. How nice." There was an odd, fixed smile on her face. She couldn't stop looking at Mrs. Hammersmith. But she went to get a knife and cut several thick slices from the pie.

She passed it out on plates that had roses around the border. He took one and broke the crust with his fork.

"May I ask," he said, "if it was an accident?"

"An illness," she said, and wiped at her eyes with the edge of her spotless white cardigan. "Zach was ill for a long time."

He looked toward the father but got no response. The man was so faded he might have been part of the wallpaper.

"I'm sorry to hear that," Mr. Greene said. "I saw him only last week. I wouldn't have guessed."

"Would you like to hear a story?" Mrs. Hammersmith asked. "It's about families."

She had their ears. They were worn out, grief-stricken. Yet they were eating that pie. And they were listening.

"I love stories," he said.

"I'm not sure that would be appropriate," Mrs. Beckett said. There was a little hiccup in her voice, a strain in her smile. She didn't look happy. She didn't like Mrs. Hammersmith, he realized. Two suns could not occupy the same sky.

"Oh," Mrs. Hammersmith said. "But it's such a good one. It starts with a beautiful girl. All the best stories do."

"I'd like to hear it," said Mr. Beckett, suddenly.

"Like I said, it starts with a girl. She lived in a cold and lonely village in the middle of a cold and lonely forest. The pines were so tall that the sun could only reach the ground in thin, watery shafts. She used to walk amongst those pines, wishing she could be anywhere else. Could be anyone else. And one day, she got her wish. Because the girl came upon a Prince, in those long-forgotten woods. He had been hunting wild boar, and lost track of his party.

"Oh, but he was a fine and handsome man. Broad of shoulder, strong of leg. Those calves! He wore a red riding habit with the King's crest on it. So she knew he was important.

"She was barely past the blush of girlhood, so beautiful the stars shone for her alone. Her face glowed like a brand. He fell in love instantly. He wanted her; he decided that he would have her. And so, he picked her up and put her on his horse and took her home.

"What could she say? He was a Prince.

"The Prince was already married. They always are. His wife was a fairly stodgy Princess from a few borders over. She knew how to make lace and sing opera and paint watercolours, but she never had anything interesting to say. And she wasn't pretty. Wasn't that the most important thing, the girl thought? Wasn't being pretty the most important thing in the world?

"The Prince made the girl his mistress. He installed her in her own apartment within the castle, and she had the kind of fineries she had always dreamed of. Gowns of silk and velvet hung in her wardrobe and ropes of diamonds from her neck. She wore perfumes that came across the ocean on great ships. Her skin was smooth as the snow outside, her eyes blue as the sky. No other men were allowed to touch her. They weren't even to look at her. Only him.

"There was one exception. The Prince, you see, had a scientific curiosity. It was not a potent one; like everything else about him it was lazy. But it was there. He had gathered around him a collection of human marvels: dog-faced boys, hunchbacks, girls with two heads. And a funny little dwarf, his legs twisted and bowed, his face wizened and ugly. It was he whom the girl got to know and to value. He wasn't considered a real man, not really, so the Prince never protested. The little man became the girl's favourite, more than all the fine lords and ladies. He never laughed at her. He never thought he was better than her, because he was so ugly and she was so beautiful. But on the inside, they were just the same.

"And he knew secrets. Dark and dangerous secrets, the kind that could kill or cure, and the kind that had to be done in the dark of night or under the full moon. He whispered them into her ear. She liked them better than all the music she had ever heard; all the books she had ever read."

"You say the sweetest things," Mr. Greene murmured. She shot him a glare, or he thought she did. It was hard to tell.

"The Prince became the King, as he eventually had to," she continued. "His court grew and grew. They ate whole deer and pigs roasted in the great fireplaces. Grain to be ground for flour came to the castle by the cartload. And every night a new cask of wine was opened. She had a place of honour at the table. Not by his side, not quite, but close.

"But that wasn't enough. Our girl, oh – she was *hungry*.

"She was tired of being alone in those fine rooms. She was tired of dancing only for the King's pleasure. Of waiting for him on long dull nights; of having to keep her hands so soft she couldn't even do needlework; of being a pretty little doll for him to play with, to dictate, to pose how he liked.

"She wanted that court – and that country – to turn round her like the sun through the sky. She wanted to be the Queen. Why couldn't they jump to her tune for a change?

"So wasn't it convenient, then, when the Queen herself sickened and died? Wasn't it just the thing?

"And so, the girl became a Queen. His advisors didn't like it, but he had long since stopped listening to them.

"Now there was only one step left in her ascent: she needed a child.

"The former Queen left behind a little daughter. There was no son, no heir. And what was a woman for, but producing a child, the desired and needed child? The girl needed a baby. She had never liked them, never wanted any, but she *needed* one. Too bad that her body – that body that men had lusted for, that the King had snatched from her home for his own use – was entirely barren.

"She tried for years. She drank potions, made sacrifices, and did everything she could. He was blaming her and she knew it. He was also getting old, grey hairs springing up, a belly forming. His eyes wandered to the young and fertile women in the court, and the peasant girls he rode past in the village.

"She started examining her face every night in the mirror, waiting for cracks to appear. She knew how all this was going to end.

"So, she asked her friend from the menagerie to procure for her a healthy newborn child. She went into seclusion as if she had been actually pregnant. And she waited for him to come back."

Mr. Greene touched the scars on his face, the ones that went all the way down, dividing him in two. "He failed," he said. "In case you're wondering."

Mrs. Hammersmith nodded. "He failed," she said. "And that was when she started to lose control.

"The little princess was growing up. As slender as a sapling and as gentle as the breeze. She was well-loved. Though not by the Queen. News of the girl's beauty and her sweetness travelled across the land. She was unspoiled, in a way the Queen had never been, not since the King took her to his castle and to his bed. She started to hate the girl. To see her as a competitor. What else did the Queen have, except her fading looks? She couldn't have anyone more beautiful in her court. Not even her own step-daughter.

"So, she tried to have her killed."

Mrs. Beckett had stopped eating. Her plate hit the table with a clatter. It was empty. "I don't understand what the point of this story is," she said. "What's wrong with you people?"

Mrs. Hammersmith squared her shoulders and tilted her head back. She raised a wrinkled hand, fine-boned still, and drew back her veil. Her eyes blazed. A flash of the old magnificence remained.

"My point," she said, "is that sometimes after you get too much of what you want, all that you have left is the wreckage you created chasing after it."

Mrs. Beckett abruptly stood up. She hit the table with a closed fist, making her children jump. "You need..." she started, and Mr. Greene knew what she was trying to say. You need to get out of my house, or, you need to leave. But she couldn't. There appeared to be something stuck in her throat.

Her face turned red. She gagged. She put both hands around her neck. She doubled over with her mouth wide open.

Something dropped out, landing on the table. It was a squat toad, black as pitch. It opened its own mouth, but not to croak.

"I killed him," it said in Mrs. Beckett's voice, and with that she fainted dead away.

>·<

(Back at the house, Mr. Greene had coughed up the toad himself after drinking Mrs. Hammersmith's potion. It felt like a hot coal working its way out. "Why am I the one who has to do this part?" he'd complained.

("Well, it isn't going to be *me*," Mrs. Hammersmith had said, and into the pie it went.)

>·<

Their drive home was quiet until Mrs. Hammersmith broke the silence. "Why did he matter?" she asked. "This boy. He wasn't special to you."

He glanced over at her as they bounced along the road. "Don't you ever feel guilty?" he asked. "For what we did?"

"No," she said. But she pulled the veil over her face once more.

>·<

It was a fine, starry night. They sat out on the porch together and enjoyed it.

She changed into a simple white gown, her face bare for now, turned toward the sky. He brought out a bowl of strawberries left over from the pie and balanced them on his knee.

He put one in his mouth. Ashes and salt. "Shit," he said, and spit it out.

"What?" she asked. She didn't take her eyes off the sky.

"I don't know," he said. "I thought something might have changed."

"What a strange punishment this is, Rumpelstiltskin," she said. "Once upon a time I would have given anything to live forever. Of course, I would have wanted to remain young as well."

"Don't we all," he said, though youth had never mattered so much to him. He'd always been ugly. But then, he'd always been a man. It hadn't needed to matter to him – the ugliness or the youth. "Would you do anything differently?" he asked. "If you could?"

She closed her eyes, thinking, and then she nodded.

Yes," she said. "I would have had that damned huntsman killed. Lie to me, will you."

He sighed. Only so much a person could change, really.

There were no red hot shoes in the world anymore. No talking mirrors. No glass coffins. An apple was only an apple. But the stars – those were the same as they had always been.

"We aren't doing so badly," he said, and tried to cover her hand with his for old time's sake. She slapped him away, which was about what he expected.

Pink 'n' Red Pie

Preheat oven to 180°C. (350°F)
Ingredients:
- 2 ½ cups strawberries, cut in half.
- 1 cup cherries (sour or sweet are both fine - sour will give a sweet/tart flavour to the pie)
- 1 cup sugar
- ¼ cup flour
- 2 tablespoons lemon juice
- Pie crust (store-bought is fine)
- 1 egg, beaten

Preparation:
• Combine the strawberries, cherries, flour, sugar, and lemon juice in a bowl. Mix and set aside.
• Flour cutting board. Roll pie crust into a circle. Fit it into a small to medium-sized pie plate. Don't trim crust yet.
• Roll out another pie crust into a circle the same size as your pie plate.
• Spoon filling into the pie plate. Cover with the remaining pie crust. Close edges of crust with a fork or your fingers so it has a scalloped appearance. Brush with egg wash and slice some vents into the top of the crust.
• Bake at 180°C. (350°F) for 40 to 45 minutes, until the crust is golden. Let cool on a wire rack for at least four hours before serving.

RUBY ICE

Lisa Carreiro

Xan never even takes off her coat. She comes inside just long enough to stoke the fire. Puddles from her boots evaporate in the rising heat from the wood stove. The cabin's cold, but tiny, so it warms up fast. It's better than what real Floe Riders get, which is maybe a bed on the forest floor. In winter.

What the hell am I doing here? I can't do this without my sister. Without Rejeanne.

But I smile at Xan like everything's fine.

I don't really know her, but I want Xan to stay 'til morning. She's just the guide who led me here though, so she goes back on the trail tonight – in the dark through a blizzard. Without me to slow her down, she'll hike for days without stopping, without sleeping, without eating. Without fear.

She's who I'm here to try to become. For at least 100 days, 'til the river ice breaks up, I'm here to learn.

One taste of Ruby Ice, though, and I'll be like Xan, walking for days with little food and no fear. I'll patrol forests and protect borders. I'll save anyone who's frozen or drowned or broken. I'll ride ice floes, watching for Bug Eaters who steal our ice. Maybe I'll even steal a few of their lambs next spring in retaliation. But first, I gotta get through this. I gotta eat that ice.

>‹

Rejeanne and I used to scrape ice with our fingernails and lick it, each declaring herself the winner in our make-believe tournaments. We ate shaved ice drizzled with precious syrup made from preserved strawberries, and I imagined Ruby Ice would taste as sweet. We practised every winter day. We leaped across chasms in the ice; we slipped into the freezing water; we returned home shivering. We'd try again the following day until spring weather ended our sport and we were left to jump from rock to rock instead.

Ruby Ice is all that stands between me and my dreams. Ruby Ice, and 100 days of hell.

>·<

At the Floe Riders' compound after Xan leaves, I sit at a scratched wooden table with 12 other Baby Riders. We steal peeks at each other. Some are taller than me, their legs as high as my waist, but I'm swift.

One glares at me like I'm a Bug Eater with the gall to sit with them. I wonder what Rejeanne would do, then look her in the eye. She sneers at me.

When the Doyenne enters, we all straighten up. On her cue, women from the kitchen set hand-sized bowls filled with crushed ice in front of us.

No hot food for us now. We're of the winter and of the floes.

The ice is red, maybe with real blood. Sheep's blood, I suppose, though maybe wolf's.

We grab spoons to eat that ice like it's hearty stew. It doesn't taste like berry juice ice, but nothing in it seems like blood either. It tastes like hardship.

I'm surprised when the ice is followed by thick-sliced bread and tangy cheese. So, we're not to live on river ice like the rumours say. A few Baby Riders chuckle quiet relief.

After the table's cleared, Doyenne raises an eyebrow. "Little girls," she says.

Like we're all children and not young women in our seventeenth and eighteenth years? I twitch.

"As of tonight, you're Floe Riders," Doyenne continues. "You're no longer at play. You probably know we got strict rules while you're in training. As of now, you say nothing to anyone unless you're spoken to. Don't talk to each other even if you met before – especially if you met before. Follow your trainers, do what you're told. Don't stray and don't argue. And no fighting, never."

Doyenne's wrinkly face looks kind of creepy when she steps underneath a flickering fluorescent light. "If one of you falls into the water, you don't see her. If one of you collapses in a snowbank, you don't know it."

I swallow like bread's lodged in my throat.

"You see a dead body, you pass it," Doyenne says. "Maybe mention it later if you remember."

Everyone bites their lips. We knew these brutal rules before we got here, but hearing those words from Doyenne's mouth pierces my heart like a shard of ice.

"Go to bed," is all she says after the briefest pause.

When I reach my cabin, the fire's extinguished. Steam rises from black ash inside the stove. Sooty water pools on the bricks beneath it. The heat from the earlier blaze still warms the cabin, but the draft through the window – through the walls – quickly chills it. I pull on my coat and climb into bed.

Wolves howl not far from the compound.

Their howls comfort me.

Wolfsong lulled me to sleep in my cradle, and tonight when I'm cold, hungry, and homesick; when I let the niggling doubt grow into a monster that sleeps with me, their howls are my sole comfort.

>‹

Rejeanne knew everything once.

"Bug Eaters steal our water, Lyla. So we steal their lambs." Rejeanne arranged twigs on our make-believe fire, ready with a layer of soggy bark and wet leaves. "It's been this way since the Old Ones moved into the mountains. Bug Eaters eat bugs and piss in drinking water. So we gotta guard the river!"

"Guard the river!" I leapt to my feet. Fist in the air, I was ready to fight any Bug Eaters who snuck in as far as our village, 10 days' walk from the border.

"They all got rotten teeth," Rejeanne continued. "You can smell them coming 'cuz they chew rancid sheep bones and never take baths."

"I had a bath three days ago," I said, then hid my dirty bare feet under leaves.

But Rejeanne looked up at the greying clouds. "Gonna rain tonight," she said. "Bug Eaters hide from rain."

"Scare-dy cats! They faint at the sight of blood, too."

"Yup," Rejeanne said, "they faint dead away. That's when we toss 'em in the river."

"But they can't swim so they all drown."

"Naw, Lyla, the Old Ones pull 'em out."

I frowned at this new, unexpected fact. "What inna hell would they do that for? Old Ones don't care. They don't drink water."

My wise elder sister looked at me like I was stupider than a Bug Eater.

"Old Ones don't drink wolf blood," she said. "Old Ones remember corner stores and candy bars. When water came from sinks. So Old Ones still save Bug Eaters, not just Us."

I was quiet with an open-mouthed, stupid-kid face for a whole minute, absorbing Rejeanne's newest lesson.

"Well," I finally said, "I ain't saving any Bug Eaters!"

Rejeanne raised an eyebrow and shook her head at me. "You can't save anyone. Ever."

><

The next day's blizzard doesn't stop the training. After a breakfast of porridge dotted with dried saskatoon berries, we 13 follow Doyenne into the woods. Snow sharp as blades cuts our cheeks. Since we could toddle, Rejeanne and I tromped through winter storms, but none like this. It's like it's been made especially to train weak little girls to survive.

When snowshoeing, Rejeanne and I opened our coats to freezing winds, but nothing prepared me for this: walking 'til my feet are so cold I can't feel them. Floe Riders sometimes lose fingers and toes, but I don't need that badge of honour. Not yet. Not 'til after I eat Ruby Ice.

We tromp single file across a sloping field of blue-white snow forever. From my place in line, fifth back from Doyenne, I can barely see her coat. The fourth marches one arm's length ahead of me, the sixth should be one arm's length behind me. The sixth is Gemini, the one who glared at me, and she stomps too close to my feet the whole uphill trek.

Two hours after noon we stop in a snow-covered meadow, where, to our shock, food awaits us. Plates loaded with hot mutton stew, thick with potatoes, carrots, garlic, and onions, and seasoned with dried rosemary, sit on blankets spread out like a picnic in the snow. The sparse chunks of mutton are leathery: some long-ago stolen lamb grown old and tough, and good only for wool and food for Baby Riders.

Gemini eats slowly like she's not even hungry. I suck the last bits from my fingers.

"Little girls," Doyenne says as the last of us hand back our emptied plates, "there's no shame if you choose to leave at any time. Simply follow one of the trainers back to the compound. No one will think less of you."

Three trainers appear from the woods, ready to lead away any Baby Riders who rise. All 13 stay. Perhaps if Doyenne had offered us the choice before we ate, someone might've given up. Not me. I imagine myself holding up a chunk of Ruby Ice like a trophy.

Doyenne whistles, waking me from my daydream, and we tromp back into the forest. We, little girls indeed, follow her like ducklings. Down a slippery trail. Beside the wide river. Across a swaying bridge so rickety I can't believe it'll hold one of us, let alone the entire troupe. Through a copse which is blessedly out of the wind and then – another shock – to a waiting truck. Its engine's running so someone, somewhere, procured fuel: petrol, battery, firewood for all I know.

We climb inside the empty box. Trainers hand us blankets. I fight sleep huddled under a grey blanket with green borders and a yellow sun stitched in one corner – my sister's old blanket. I grit my teeth and fight tears instead of sleep.

>ı<

On the fifth day, the sun a grey disc barely visible through clouds, my trainer Eedjia jogs ahead of me along a narrowing trail. I ate no breakfast. Dinner was a bowl of ruddy ice and a crust of bread.

Eedjia points ahead. "Follow that trail. It'll take you about two days to finish. You'll know where you are when it loops back. See you later." She turns away.

Trail? I look where she pointed at a forest filled with snow sculpted into miniature mountains by howling wind. I say nothing. Eedjia's gone already anyway.

I swallow my fear. I follow the upward slope between trees. Twice I stumble through snow-covered thickets. Late afternoon, I watch a deer drink and remember I haven't eaten anything except snow. The sun travels west, and I hike north until the path curves east back toward the river.

By the time the sun sets – late afternoon in midwinter – I'm hungry. The path veers north again and even west for a while. I listen for animals and search for shelter. Survival huts dot the region, built by the Old Ones when they first came to the mountains. They're never locked and some travellers even leave food for the next person. But nothing except snow and trees and more snow lies ahead.

I scrounge under the snow. Rejeanne and I knew where to hunt for frozen berries that still clung to bushes, but here, I have no idea where food's buried. I'm too far from water to fish and even if I snared a rabbit, I don't have my precious knife.

I can do this. Even without my knife; without knowing exactly where survival huts are, I'll finish the circuit. I've been hungry and cold before. *I'll build my own damn shelter using snow and leaves. I'll chew off boughs with my teeth if I have to.*

I follow the trail after dark, able to see fairly well with a nearly full moon. I know by the stars when it's close to midnight.

In shadows to my left I swear I finally see something. *I'm sleepwalking*, I think. *I'm dreaming.*

It's a lean-to, far superior to anything Rejeanne ever made, with the grey blanket and dried venison strips inside it. I stare at it, listening for another person. I hear no one.

>·<

Wolves run through a clearing in the valley. Every cell in me aches to join them. I howl just for fun and the hunger subsides a little.

Must be wolf's blood. We eat it. We become them. We run through dark forests, save travellers, protect our river. I'll eat Ruby Ice when I win the tournament and get to be the top. Champion, like Rejeanne.

Today, I'm just a Baby Rider with dreams. I drape the blanket over my shoulders and gnaw venison. In a copse, I dig up two frozen berries. Coming out into a clearing, I lurch backwards.

A spiderweb larger than me glimmers between two trees. I cry out before I realize it's human-made: twine covered with frost and blown snow. An old woman sits on the steps of her trailer home, lacing snowshoes. An Old One who might remember corner stores that sold candy.

Before everything went to hell, Rejeanne would say.

The woman's dog stands up, ears pricked. She chuckles and the dog relaxes. Flustered, I step backwards into the copse until I hear the river.

I reach the compound late that night just as Eedjia appears from the forest.

"I gotta learn to build a shelter that well," I say.

She almost grins, then silently takes my hand like I'm small, and leads me into the main building. No ice tonight, only hearty stew and chunks of bread. And nine Baby Riders left.

The next morning we devour porridge with nuts, but when we clean our bowls we're told to stay seated.

"Little girls," Doyenne says. "Young Floe Riders."

I sit straighter.

"Most of you can forage and find shelter…for one night. Most of you are accustomed to a little hunger, thirst, pain, or fear." She drags a chair across the floor with a wretched squeak, then sits on it backwards. "Eat when you can because you never know when you'll eat again." I swear she eyes Gemini when she says this. "When you trek the back-country you'll be cold or hot or tired. You'll be thirsty, your blood will come, the flies will bite. Yesterday, you ran into the forest without food or supplies, but learned you weren't alone.

"After training, though, you *will* be alone." Doyenne nods at the trainers who, on cue, dole out bulging leather pouches.

"Everything you need, you carry. A different pack for summer, rain, or snow. That's your winter pack."

I pull out smoked meat, antiseptic, waterproofed matches. My precious knife. A bar made from nuts, seeds, and honey. *Like candy the Old Ones ate when they had corner stores and factories and...*

"Don't be complacent." Doyenne stands up, hands spread out on the table. Small hands, like mine. "Riders with everything they need still die in storms or from animal attacks. You're responsible for packing every time you go Out There. Your trainers will help you decide what you need at any given time. Now get up and get out. Go!"

><

The trail's the one I hike every few days. The late winter sun's warm on my face. The ice creaks, like a monster that'll wake up soon. I creep from habit, hoping to spot a deer.

She's kneeling on the snowy riverbank opposite me.

A Bug Eater.

Silently, she hefts a chunk of ice the size of my torso and, without effort, stands up. Her hood falls back to reveal her face.

She doesn't look like someone who eats bugs. She could be my sister. *She could be me.*

She sees me, then snarls, baring very good teeth indeed, and dashes away still carrying the ice; even leaping over snow-covered logs like a deer.

Weak, rotten-toothed Bug Eaters.

I scramble across the frozen river. The Bug Eater's disappeared into the forest by the time I reach the opposite riverbank, but I follow her boot prints until someone pulls me to the ground.

"Never chase Them alone," Eedjia says. Her voice is as quiet as always.

She looked like me.

"Never," Eedjia repeats, standing and brushing snow from her pants. "Chances are, more are nearby."

"But…"

"No." Eedjia holds up a bare hand.

Where the hell are her mittens?

"You know the way things are." Eedjia shakes my arm. "Without our water, they got no lambs for us to steal."

"But…"

Eedjia shakes her head and hauls me away.

But she looked like me.

><

Five days later, Gemini hulks like a shadow in the forest. I bare my teeth at her and she slips away. She looks more like what I imagined a Bug Eater would look like. Maybe a Bug Eater crossed over here and stole one of ours – one who could be another sister to me – and left behind one of theirs. I'm as convinced of it as I am that we drink wolf's blood by the time I reach the copse.

Where Gemini waits, hands on hips. She's got fight in her and I'm her target. Neither of us talks, but her upper lip curls.

I sneer back and pass her, leaping over logs to the river. I pretty much skate across the ice, snarling Gemini already forgotten when the opposite bank is only a few slides away.

She surprises me. Me, who's aware of everything; best at listening to the forest; best at watching for Bug Eaters.

That's twice in five days I got caught off guard.

Gemini pins me face down on the ice. I turn my head so that one ear's pressed against it. Even while I'm thinking about what I'm gonna do to get her off me, I'm also listening for cracking ice.

Gemini doesn't speak, doesn't hit me, doesn't move. She's in some childish power struggle with me. She wants to win. She wants to eat Ruby Ice as much as I do.

I buck to wrench myself free. As soon as I reach the riverbank, but before I can run far, Eedjia catches me and drags me into the compound. She glares at me and places finger over lips before I protest. I follow complacently to Doyenne's den.

Doyenne's scratching notes on paper, real paper. The pencil doesn't stop moving when Eedjia presses me into a chair. Gemini and her trainer are right behind us, but Gemini's not silent. She's actually growling. That Baby Rider will rip open my throat if she can. Maybe she'll fight the trainers and Doyenne, too, tearing flesh like a wolf on its prey.

Only when Gemini's in a chair, her trainer's hands on her shoulders, does Doyenne stop writing and look at us. Her brown eyes move to the trainers next.

"Fighting," they say in unison.

Doyenne studies us like she's never seen either of us. I start to shiver. Gemini stops growling.

Doyenne rises and our trainers leave. She pulls a fat brown book with red stripes on its spine from her shelf and flips through it.

"Once upon a time," she says, "there was two little girls what couldn't stop fighting. They fought over breakfast and fought over blankets. They punched each other's cheeks and stole each other's boots. They dunked each other in the river and shot each other's dogs. They yelled in front of the judge and fought inside the jail. Judge says, 'You live on the east side of the river and you live on the west. In winter the west can take some of the river and in spring the east can take a few lambs.' Cargyle versus Pettit." Doyenne shuts the book with a thud and places it back on the shelf. "No training tomorrow, and special training the day after that."

>·<

Fire blazes in my wood stove. Eedjia brings me hot water with honey, porridge with dried berries and cream, fat sandwiches with cheese, meaty stew with potatoes and carrots, and squash soup with butter. *Eat when you can.*

The day indoors out of the cold with plenty of food is supposed to soften tough girls. Late in the night, Eedjia finally speaks. She sits at the foot of my bed and crosses her arms.

"This pisses me off, too," she says. "I'd rather be outside."

"It's 'cause Gemini..."

"This ain't about who started it. It's gotta end, Lyla. Spring's coming and we got a lot more to do before any of you can go into the forest alone. We got a helluva spring storm coming in a couple of days and it looks like the thaw's gonna crash into us a like a rockslide. We got no time for petty quarrels. Once you're all out there, you gotta look after each other as well as everyone in general." Her hands curl into fists. "Lyla, you can't take a Floe Rider pledge until you prove you can live up to it. That pledge is more than just words."

She opens the wood stove and tosses in another log. "Get some sleep. Tomorrow's gonna be worse than today."

>‹

Eedjia and I hike downhill through the woods. Jays screech at us and we startle a hare. I imagine we'll tromp far, far away and I'll have to set snares for my dinner, but we march near the compound most of the morning, wading through drifts. At noon, Eedjia hands me a chunk of bread without stopping.

So, today's to be the opposite of yesterday, I think. I'm almost smug 'til she leads me down the steep trail toward the secondary compound set well away from the river. A creek as wide as my arm is long rushes past us, too swift to fully ice over. The terrain steepens until I'm clutching tree branches to keep steady. Eedjia leaps from a ledge, but when I follow I land in the swift creek. Three buildings lie in the distance.

"You just keep running around that compound 'til I say you're done. Gimme your pouch and knife."

After I hand her all my gear, she flicks her fingers at me. I jog along a well-trod trail, more mud than snow from all the feet that have walked over and over that path. Alternately jogging and sprinting, it doesn't feel like discipline to run in fresh cold air with the sun shining. At its farthest, the path's maybe 10 metres from the buildings, but in other spots it hugs the rugged stone and concrete structures. Windows are either papered over from the inside or so dirty I can't see into them. One rusted metal door is shut. A generator hums.

I run around the path in less than a half-hour. Eedjia flicks fingers at me as I pass her, so I run a second circuit, then a third. On my fourth, I slow to grab another handful of snow to lick while I run.

The pile of muddy snow wasn't there on my previous three circuits. I veer around it but slip, sliding down into an open hatch and then into a cellar. The lights hurt my eyes and I leap up, ready to fend off Bug Eaters. As my eyes adjust to the light − electric light − several people stop work to study me for a minute. Me, a bedraggled, wet, stinking Baby Rider who got too prideful.

They resume their tasks. Three stir a vat, two sort jars of precious seeds, another helps Eedjia down through the opening I fell into. A couple haul a barrel across the room. They heft it up and ease its contents into the vat: a pinkish slurry that might be thawing ice. Ruby Ice.

I sniff, but no smell like blood fills my nose. Berries maybe, but probably some long-ago made chemical used to turn food red.

I eye the people one by one. I spot a woman in a dim corner carrying an armload of wood.

Rejeanne! But she's different; her face harder. She steps into the light. Her face is wrinkled, her eyes lighter than Rejeanne's, and she's taller.

Not Rejeanne, of course. Rejeanne's not here.

Eedjia plucks my sleeve to lead me up rickety wooden slats that pass as steps to outside.

"All this fighting just to eat some made-up pink stuff?" I say to Eedjia. "So, maybe Bug Eaters don't eat bugs and we don't drink blood? Does Gemini get to see that, too?"

Eedjia frowns. "Ten more laps. Get going."

>‹

Three weeks later I wake when the river ice breaks with a roar. I'm dressed and outside before Eedjia fetches me. We run through the moonless night to the river in a pack. The river's still frozen here, but the break upriver rushes toward us. I'm on the ice with everyone, running, running.

Was it this fast when Rejeanne rode the Floes? Did it wake her up or was she crouched by the bank, waiting?

The ice beneath me shatters. I hunker down to keep my balance.

Then I ride. Shadows pass me: deer, wolves, other Baby Riders, I don't know. I leap to a wide floe and ride it until the river curves north, where I leap again. The ice jams at the next turn where Baby Riders pile onto the bank and fall into the water. I race across bobbing ice like it's solid land.

If I could step back to watch myself, I'd be surprised I'm not scared. I waited my whole life for this day.

Ruby Ice, real or not, I'll taste you before morning. I grin like a wolf in a fairy-tale picture. No one can beat me.

Except the Baby Rider who jumps past me. Gemini, I think, but it's not. She's smaller, but swift. Like me.

The river curves downstream where I saw the Bug Eater steal ice. I catch a smaller floe to ride it, then run to catch the other Rider.

She's smiling. Even in the dark I see her face, like a saint in an old painting. She just loves to ride the floes and she maybe doesn't even see me beside her.

When Gemini shoves me into freezing water, I scream.

That's a penalty for her, the fool. If anyone sees that, she's outta the race.

I roll in snow, then catch the next chunk that sails past me. I'm behind Gemini and the other.

I know Ruby Ice is nothing special. I know Rejeanne won't be there to see me win. I know I'll be a Rider anyway because training's done and I'll patrol forests and save anyone – even Bug Eaters – who's lost, broken, frozen, or drowned.

The rapids are jammed. Two shadows hop over rushing water between dangerous floes. I hunker down on what seems like a shard – sharp, slippery – and ride the rapids like a pro.

The river spills onto the banks, flooding the south slopes where we'll later plant gardens. Floes pile up like a mountain, creating an impasse in the river ahead. The two shadows climb them and I leap over open water to catch up. I dig fingernails into snow, then ride the churning ice.

Behind us, a boom from the next break echoes downriver.

I see the small Rider. So quiet, almost invisible, I never bothered to learn her name. She was nobody; just another Baby Rider. She's over the ice jam and hopping onto a floe ahead of everyone.

I jump ahead to a spinning floe and hang on. The river veers south and the tiny Rider ahead of us leaps from her ice. And misses her target.

I don't even think. I ride so close I can touch her, struggling in the water.

If one of you falls into the water, you don't see her.

But I do. I grab her hands to haul her onto the floe with me. She spits out water, stares at me like I'm a Bug Eater stealing ice, then grabs the next cube.

My floe thuds to a standstill where the river splits. The Rider I helped is behind me, shivering but upright. Gemini's floe crashes into us.

I don't see how many Riders made it this far when hands pull us onto the banks.

It's done.

We now-real Floe Riders limp up the banks over to where a fire blazes. Seven remaining little girls who never really ate blood still learned how to tromp through frozen forests and ride dangerous water.

Doyenne presses a bowl into my hands. With the rising sun and the growing blaze, I see spectators' faces clearly: the trainers, the old woman from the trailer, even Xan.

But not Rejeanne. Rejeanne will never know I won. Rejeanne, the fool, didn't want to simply patrol forests and squabble with a few Bug Eaters. She went south to the real war instead of staying north in the forest she knew. Rejeanne wanted a real enemy to conquer.

I'm crying before I realize it, holding the cold bowl filled with ruddy mush. I have to eat it, no matter that it's not real; no matter that it's no victory.

I wipe tears with a frozen sleeve and dig my bare dirty hand into the bowl.

My tears stop.

Ruby Ice tastes like childhood: one cup of precious cream, one cup of cold milk, one cup of preserved strawberries, one spoonful of salt mixed into one bucket of fresh snow. Stir and stir then eat before it melts all over your hands.

I recall the recipe scrawled across that yellowed card smudged with ancient ruby streaks from years of red berries.

Doyenne gives everyone bowls filled with sweet, creamy ice that tastes like long-ago. In mine though, a shard of red ice glints in the firelight: Ruby Ice. It's real. I pluck it out and chomp like a wolf. It tastes like victory.

Snow Ice Cream

Ingredients:
- I cup cream
- I cup very cold milk
- I cup preserved strawberries (or finely chopped fresh)
- One pinch salt

Preparation:
• Mix into one bucket of fresh snow, stirring until firm.

THERE ARE NO CHEESEBURGERS AT THE END OF THE WORLD

Tapanga Koe

They've been travelling for a week and walking for days. At least the old junker had gotten them across the northern B.C. border – but they still had a long way to go. The Alaska Highway stretches endless. Despite sharing a sleeping bag, the April nights still chilled.

Charlotte traces two fingertips down Cliff's back; his thin skin stretches taut over each vertebra. Feeling each bone is like seeing him from the inside out. His thinness sets her more at ease, as if she knows him better, each bony knob and ridge. But also, it annoys her.

She wonders where all the food goes when he eats. Having grown up poor, her body is wise to the ways of starvation and knows how to hold onto the fat. She can live off less, so she gives him more, but it's as good as throwing calories into the fire, watching them turn to ash and blow into the ether.

Daytime is warmer but still cold. Keeping moving helps. Charlotte would walk steady, day and night, but Cliff cannot. He goes in fits and spurts, resting often, and then hurrying to catch up. This often creates a fair distance between them, and she is grateful. More space is better. At night, he cries and moans, saying he wishes he were dead like the rest. Sometimes, she wishes, too – that she were dead; that he were dead; that things were like before. But she'd never say it. What's the point?

She speaks very little now.

><

The first thing she sees is the smoke – a black column in the distance. She speeds up, thinks she hears Cliff shout something from behind, but keeps going. Where there's smoke, there could be people! It's been so long since she's seen anyone, so long, even, since any vehicles have whipped past. The handful of homes from which she's pilfered food along the highway have been occupied only by the dead.

"Liard River Hot Springs Lodge, open all year," the metal road sign reads. The lodge is a sprawling, two-storey log building with a red tin roof. No chimney: the column of smoke comes from somewhere behind the building. Charlotte glances back, but she has lost sight of Cliff due to the bends in the highway. He'll catch up – figure it out – or he won't.

She crosses the lot with its half-dozen dusty cars. No one waits outside the entrance. Not like in Whitehorse, where public places had been guarded; that is, until the guards themselves had fallen ill, or fled. Maybe this place is empty – maybe the smoke is just some random bushfire. But Charlotte doesn't want to think that way – can't – there have to be others alive, here, and other places. Here, and back home.

A rush of blessedly heated, moist air hits her as she steps inside. It warms a face she's almost forgotten she has. She is enveloped by scents of fried onions, garlic, and meat. Smells that remind her of her grandmother's house, where something always simmered on the stovetop. She needs to get back there so badly, the ache in her bones pulls her south. But right now, the rumbling in her stomach is a more pressing need.

She passes tables and chairs, tracing her fingers along the raw wood. Feeling throbs back into her icy hands. The restaurant isn't huge but could probably seat the remaining population of Whitehorse. She shudders off the thought, looking into the glass eyes of the foxes and bears and moose heads decorating the walls.

Something at the back of the room catches her eye – a washroom, its doorway shining with yellow light. The ventilation fan whirrs, an electric purr that draws her in. Her dry, tired eyes sting with watery gratitude.

She shuts and locks the door, drops her pack on the floor, and stands with her eyes closed. The moment transports her back in time – to a place where the steady hum of electricity is taken for granted – where plague and death aren't all the world has ever known.

Someone is knocking on the door. "Char?" It's Cliff. Guess he figured it out.

"Just a minute!" she answers.

"Okay," comes his muffled reply. She hears him shuffle away.

The girl who meets her eyes in the mirror has Charlotte's wild, open gaze, but she is gaunt, with dark circles under her eyes, and cheeks smudged with campfire ash and roadside dust. Her hair is choked with it, untended curls starting to dreadlock into thick mats. Her face is thin, pointed, and dangerous.

Charlotte turns on the tap, puts her mouth to the flow, and drinks until she can't breathe. She washes her face and arms and neck with loads of hand soap. It's pine-scented and slimy but feels good once it's rinsed off. She considers finding her makeup bag – it's in her pack somewhere – a vain indulgence, taking up space and adding weight, but one she has yet to regret. Just imagining applying lipstick, eyeliner, mascara, brings her a humanizing comfort she is yet unwilling to give up.

Plus, it wouldn't hurt to put a little flirt on whoever was cooking.

"Charlotte?" Cliff calls again.

With one last, longing look at the taps, she feels the fleeting sensation of imagined water running through her tangled hair, then unlocks the door.

Part of her hopes he'll be angry at being left behind, that he'll be as fed up with her as she is with him. But when she opens the door, his puppy-dog eyes convey only a loving worry.

"Can you smell that? I'm *so* hungry." He wraps his arms around his wasting middle.

Charlotte picks up her pack and brushes past him, gritting her teeth – bone on bone – a recent habit: her jaw is tiring of this, the muscles twinge. "Sit down." She drops her pack at a booth, and, without looking back, goes toward the double doors that must lead to the kitchen.

>·<

The man stands over a gas range with a massive, stainless steel pot. Seems like a big pot, for just one man.

"Hi... I was wondering if you got anything to spare...?"
It's tempting to bat eyelashes or jut out a hip, but her face
isn't made up, and her hips barely exist anymore. So, she
hopes the pathetic card plays, keeping her head tilted down,
eyes peering up from sunken sockets, body tucked back and
unimposing.

He looks her up and down, as though trying to decide:
animal or human; worthy or un- ; sick or well? The silence
stretches, and she feels an icy prickle of doubt – though she
bears no signs of the illness, no pocked skin or thinning hair
– if this man, for some reason, decides otherwise, he may
just shoot her on the spot. He seems like the kind of guy
who'd have a gun nearby.

"There's oatmeal," he says, turning his attention back to
the pot; he lifts the lid, and begins stirring. The meaty,
oniony vapour rises. Crossing the room, it sticks to her, a
magnificent, thin veil – it feels as if calories have travelled
by air, sinking into her cells via osmosis. Her stomach rum-
bles.

He stirs the pot for a long time, staring into it, before he
replaces the lid, then turns and fills a large, metal kettle at
the double, stainless steel sink, and places it on a burner.

"Maybe...maybe if you could spare two bowls?" Charlotte asks. Her thoughts race as her eyes travel the room, but
if there is a cache of food here, it isn't stored in plain sight.
Her eyes catch on a knife block – her hunting knife is with
her pack, but she could just as easily use one of these. He is
alone. How hard would it be to cut his throat? Could she
move quickly enough to plunge a blade into his heart? How
fast would he die?

"What's your name?" he asks.

"Charlotte." She blinks back the strange, murderous thoughts, uncertain where they've come from. "My boyfriend, Cliff, is out in the dining room."

"I'm Wilbur, but my friends call me Burr."

"Where are they, your friends?"

He sighs and shakes his head. "I guess I meant that's what they 'called' me."

"They go south?"

"South?" He cocks his head. "No, that's not where they went."

"Oh. Well, that's where we're headed, we're going back home."

Burr shrugs and starts reaching around in the cupboards, moving slow, pulling out bowls and spoons, lining them up on a plastic tray. "Listen, why don't you wait out there? I'll bring it when it's ready."

"Yeah, Okay, sure. Thanks."

Burr starts stirring the pot again. His eyes lose focus as he stares off. Charlotte wonders if he's always been a bit odd, or if, like her and Cliff, he's been changed by the emptying of the world.

>·<

She finds Cliff sitting in the booth where she left him and slides into the seat across. She is tired – all this waiting exhausts her. She'd rather be out walking, moving toward… toward…toward what? She isn't sure, doesn't want to think about it, but it has to be better than what they've left behind. She takes a shaky breath, trying to settle her nerves. She has to sit. Has to wait. They have to eat. And somehow, they –

no, *she*, has to convince Burr to part with some of his food before they go.

She pulls the map from the side of her pack. At first, she'd felt clever, remembering to take it from the glovebox. But now, she isn't sure it matters much. More than once, she's almost used it for kindling, when the ground was wet and the night was cold – it might be kindling, yet.

She traces a finger down the winding highway. Black eyeliner marks where they've been, and a much longer, yellow line, where they still have to go. "We're never going to make it walking. Where's the next town, even? There's nothing but lakes and parks for ages." She resists the urge to crumple the useless paper and fling it across the room.

Cliff reaches out. His long, knobbed fingers encase her wrist. She presses her lips together, glances away; it is all she can do not to shuck him off.

"Did you get us something to eat?" he asks.

"Cliff, are you even listening?" She yanks her hand away and pokes a finger into the map. "What are we going to do?"

"Sorry," he says.

She lowers her gaze, not wanting to see his sad, frightened eyes pleading for forgiveness.

"It'll be okay," he says after a long pause. "We'll be able to catch a ride. I mean, the farther south we go, the more traffic there'll be, right?"

"What makes you think that?! We've hardly seen anyone on the road since we've left. And even when we did, no one stopped."

"Well, what do you think we should do?" His voice isn't challenging, or angry, merely questioning. Somehow, this angers her more.

"We need to find a car!"

"You mean *steal* a car?"

"Are you fucking kidding me? What about all that food I've been getting from those houses while you just hang outside 'keeping watch.' Was that stealing? I didn't hear you complaining then."

"I..."

At the back of the restaurant, the doors to the kitchen bang open. Burr brings a tray with three bowls of steaming oatmeal and a little pot of brown sugar. Cliff's eyes widen at the third bowl, but his greedy look turns to one of disappointment when Burr pulls up a chair and takes a seat at the end of the table.

Burr picks up a spoon and begins, slowly, to stir his oatmeal.

Charlotte spoons out a little of the brown sugar, careful not to over-do it; she doesn't need the sweet but empty calories – tempting as they are. They will only burn out quickly and leave her aching for more. She knows it's protein she's sorely lacking, but for now, oats will have to do.

She offers the sugar pot to Burr. He declines. Cliff takes the sugar from her hands and dumps it all into his oatmeal, then begins shovelling the food into his mouth. He eats noisily, smacking and slurping and breathing heavy.

Charlotte glances at Burr, wondering what he makes of Cliff's rude behaviour, but Burr is too absorbed in his stirring. She digs into her own bowl, taking it slow, enjoying the contrast between the sweet, sugary bites and the wheaty, salty ones. They are good, steel-cut oats with a bit of crunch. She remembers her grandmother's bread pudding, miraculously rendered from the heels of plastic-bagged, economy bread. It didn't seem possible that something so simple could taste so good.

The pain of the memory bunches, a hard knot in her stomach, and she winces, sure she would have vomited had she been fuller. She blinks back tears and glances up to see if anyone has noticed. Cliff's bowl is to his face, he's licking it clean. Charlotte cringes, looks to Burr, he is watching her, his eyes dull and steady. "What were you thinking about?" he asks, his voice soft.

Charlotte pushes everything back, buries it deep, presses it down. She hasn't broken yet, and she isn't about to. "Economy bread," she says. "You know, I always hated the stuff – the way it smells when you open the bag, all plastic and bleached – but when my grand..." her voice falters; she clears her throat, swallows. "It's just, well...I guess I just miss the idea of it all. To be able to just pick a bag of bread, or whatever, off a shelf." She shrugs. "Even gross bread."

Burr's eyes check out for a moment. Then he blinks and starts to chuckle. Then laugh, throwing his head back. Charlotte feels something within her loosen a little – a place that's been tightening since this whole thing began. She starts to laugh, too; the tears that she had only a moment ago been biting back stream freely down her face.

Cliff's spoon clatters in his empty bowl. "What's so funny?"

Charlotte wipes her cheeks. "Nothing."

Cliff shifts in his seat. His hand starts toward Charlotte's, but this time, she casually shifts away before he can latch on.

"Thanks for the oatmeal," Cliff says. "I could eat a hundred bowls, easy."

Charlotte cringes again, but Burr doesn't seem to take offence at Cliff's clumsy, fishing remark, instead leaning back in his chair. "Yah? You got trade?"

"Trade?" Cliff asks, cocking his head.

Charlotte's full belly sinks. "I'm afraid we haven't got anything."

"No gas?" Burr asks.

"No," Charlotte replies. "We're walking."

Burr shrugs, stands, and begins collecting dishes. His oatmeal is fairly untouched, and Cliff is eyeing it, licking his lips, about to ask. Charlotte kicks him under the table and mouths for him to shut it. Until she can figure out how they can be of some use to the man – or until she can find and slip into his larder undetected – she doesn't want Burr to know how hard up they are, or to upset him with greedy requests.

Charlotte helps clear the table. She follows Burr into the kitchen, casting a warning look for Cliff to stay put.

"You have power," she says, nodding at the light overhead.

"Not for long, the genny's running out of juice."

"Can't you take the gas out of the cars in the lot?"

"Already have." Burr sets his tray down beside the sink and starts running the water.

"Let me," Charlotte says, nudging him out of the way.

He shrugs and goes to peer into the pot on the stove, stirring. After a minute, he turns off the burner and says, "Finish them up, I'll take you down to the hot springs." He doesn't wait for a reply, setting the spoon across the top of the pot and wandering out.

When she is sure he is gone, she steals over and looks into the pot. It is depressingly empty, with only an inch or two of brown liquid, a tantalizing, fatty sheen on top. Her body craves the protein and fat; she imagines the steel rim at lips, the warm, oily broth sliding down her throat. She reaches for the spoon, hand trembling. She can hear her grandmother humming in the living room, tapping her feet to the radio, the steady click-clack of her knitting needles.

"Don't," Burr says.

His voice startles her back to reality. Burr holds a stack of towels and a plastic bag is hooked on his wrist. His face is a storm, violent and foreboding. Charlotte takes a step back.

"Come on," Burr says. "I'm sure you could use a soak."

They get Cliff. Charlotte insists they bring their packs. Cliff complains. Burr takes them out the back, down a staircase, and onto a wooden walkway that leads into the woods. She can see the fire at the back of the cleared lot, can tell from what remains – blackened boards jutting into the sky, crossing in the vague outline of a doorway, a window, that this was once a small house, or large shed, set on a raised, cement foundation.

"What's the fire for?" she asks.

"My friends," Burr replies.

"Smoke signals – smart," Cliff says. "We saw the smoke from kilometres off."

Burr does not reply.

><

At the hot springs, Burr strips, descends the wooden steps, and wades in. Like them, he is too thin, but his body still holds some muscle; he has a pleasing, hard, masculine shape. Cliff rests a hand on her shoulder. "We can leave. Just keep going," he says quietly. "If you want."

"Are you kidding? You want to go now?" Charlotte drops her pack and begins to undress. "Well then go, if you want, but I'm getting in."

Burr is pulling little bottles of soaps and shampoos from the bag, lining them up in neat rows along a step. Charlotte walks down into the steaming water.

"I'm going back," Cliff says.

"Oh, come on, it's sooo nice," Charlotte beckons.

Cliff hesitates. His eyes ping nervously between Charlotte and Burr. His face is twisting with indecision and apology.

"Fine, whatever," Charlotte grumbles. She submerges herself to the neck; her muscles weep relief as the heat sinks in.

"I'll wait for you at the restaurant, okay?"

Charlotte nods. She doesn't watch Cliff leave. She closes her eyes and feels nothing but the water, her own buoyancy. It is quiet here, but not empty-quiet, not like she's used to, with nothing but the sounds of her footfalls on the highway – here is a freeing sort of quiet – a quiet that is *supposed* to be. It is clear alpine air and sentry pines that have stood on through the ages.

When she opens her eyes, she sees Burr floating with his eyes closed. She remains still, so as not to disturb him. He's not bad looking, when his face is not so pinched, and his brow unfurrowed. When he opens his eyes, she smiles. His face flashes, she catches a glimpse, a flicker of something; how he might've looked, in a happier time. Then it is gone. He swims back to the line-up of bottles, and she joins him.

"You know, you're not supposed to use soaps and things down here," he says, handing her a shampoo.

"Oh," she says, looking at the bottle in her hand with some confusion.

"That was before, though." He laughs, harsh and loud. Whenever he laughs, it isn't a smile so much as a grimace. As if laughing hurts him. "I don't think it matters anymore." He pops open a bottle and squirts it into his hand. "Nothing matters anymore. The two of us aren't going to make a spit of difference."

She shrugs. "Probably not, it's just this once, right." She lathers the shampoo into her hair, starts pulling apart knots. "So, did you use to work here, or…?"

"It was only supposed to be a summer job. I came up last year. To see the mountains, do some hiking. But I met a lot of cool people, so I stayed on. The owners are…were…the owners were super…everyone was…I'm glad I got to see it in the winter. It was really beautiful, you know."

When he spoke, it was as if he'd already left this place. Or as if it no longer existed. In a way, Charlotte supposed, it didn't. "Whitehorse was nice in winter, too."

"Is that where you're from?" he asks.

"Not originally, no. I'm from Vancouver. Up here for the same reasons, just wanted to travel, you know."

"And now you're going back."

It isn't a question, so Charlotte doesn't give an answer, instead working at her hair. She manages to rip a bunch of the larger tangles apart, but the mini-bottle of shampoo is no match for her mass of curls. Giving up, she leans back, floating with her face to the sky.

"You never caught it, did you?" Burr asks.

"No. Not me or Cliff."

"So you and Cliff, were you together before or…?"

"Yeah. What are the odds, eh? Everyone we knew either caught it and died, or else took off."

"Not everyone here caught it. But most."

"You didn't," Charlotte says. "You're not marked up."

"No," Burr whispers. "I didn't."

"You know, I don't think it happened for any reason or anything," she says. "I mean before things went ape-shit, I mean *really* ape-shit, there were loads of people on the radio and stuff, talking about the 'chosen few' and, like, 'genetic superiority,' but I think that's a load of crap."

"Survivors' guilt."

"Maybe, yeah… I wonder, you know, if maybe they were right about one thing, though – like, maybe it *is* somehow linked to genetics – not that I'm better than anyone, but, like, maybe…" Charlotte's throat starts to pinch with tears. It's something she's thought about a lot but never managed to give voice to.

"I couldn't reach my family either," Burr says softly. "Before the lines went down."

And then she is sobbing, and he is holding her, his hands resting lightly beneath the bony wings of her shoulder blades.

>ı<

They finish bathing. Burr helps comb out some of the tangles with an extra dose of conditioner. They are focused and methodical, and it is soothing to have this one task – this small thing, this singular goal.

When Charlotte climbs out of the hot springs, the chill spring air bites that much harder against her warmed and heat-softened body. She wraps herself in one of the big, fluffy towels, and Burr drapes the one meant for Cliff over her shoulders.

She looks at her heap of clothing and shudders at the thought of pulling on the cold fabric, slick with filth.

"Leave them," he says. "I'll get you some clothes up at the lodge."

"Okay…well, maybe I won't put them on, but I'll take them with me." She slings her pack over her shoulder and gathers the wad of clothing to her chest.

He winces, throws his head back and laughs until tears run down his cheeks.

"What?"

"You wouldn't…" He gasps for breath and wipes his eyes, "wouldn't want some bear traipsing around in your hoodie and jeans."

"Har, har." Charlotte tries to shift a hand to her hip, but it doesn't come off as very imposing, with all the clothing, and trying to hold up the towel, and the heavy pack on her back. She settles for narrowing her eyes and casting an annoyed glare, but can't help grinning a little at the image.

"I think you're right," he says, as they begin the walk back.

"About what?" she asks, though it doesn't matter, she's just happy he thinks so.

"I don't think you're special."

"Oh." Charlotte frowns.

"I mean not *you* specifically…and not me, not Cliff – not anyone who didn't catch it. And just because a person survived the sickness, doesn't mean they're built to survive what came…what comes after."

Charlotte nods, thinking of Cliff, thinking of how they used to be. Who he used to be. Or maybe Cliff hasn't changed; maybe she is the one who's changed. Or is it that circumstances have merely brought to light who he's really been all along? "It's all too fucking complicated," she mutters, and Burr grunts in agreement.

They pass the burning outbuilding and walk back into the restaurant. Cliff is sitting at a booth, his hands folded over his stomach. His face is grey and tight with agony. An empty bowl and the big, metal pot are on the table in front of him.

"Jesus! What are you doing?" Burr cries. Springing forward, he peers into the pot. "It's empty," he whispers.

"Cliff! What the fuck!" Charlotte shouts.

"I'm sorry." He groans and leans forward. "I was just so hungry. You seem like you have so much, I didn't think you'd mind."

Burr falls into a booth, slumping, hiding his face in his hands.

"What were you thinking?" Charlotte snaps.

"Sorry, I said I'm fucking sorry, okay! I just can't do it anymore. I can't keep up. All I want is a hot, *private* shower and to watch a shitty fucking sitcom. Eat a cheeseburger. This… it's all too fucking much, Char!"

Charlotte slides into the booth and holds him as he sobs. The vinyl is cold and sticks to her naked skin where the towel doesn't cover.

Burr gets up and storms into the kitchen. When Cliff stops shaking, sniffs hard and wipes his nose on his sleeve, Charlotte follows after Burr.

>‹

"Fuck, fuck, *fuck!*" Burr paces the kitchen, pausing to slam his fist into the stove. Overhead, the lights flicker and dim. "It's my fault. I left...left it out...was left..."

"Shit, yeah, I'm sorry. Cliff, he's...well, he's not handled any of this particularly well."

"I can fix this!" Burr pounds the stove again, then starts rummaging through drawers.

Charlotte returns to Cliff, who is lying down in the booth.

"Nice going," she whispers. "You've really pissed him off. Fat chance we'll get any food out of him now. The guy's going psycho back there. In fact, I think maybe we should leave. Now."

"Ugh, I really don't feel good, Char. I think I ate too much. Just give me a minute."

"Come on." Charlotte tugs on Cliff's arm.

"I can't, Char."

Burr comes charging out, wielding a metal serving spoon. "I couldn't find anything else!"

"Holy shit! Cliff, get up!" Charlotte jumps to her feet. "We gotta go!"

But it's too late. Burr pushes past Charlotte and starts pulling at Cliff.

"Leave him alone!" Charlotte cries, banging on Burr's back. "It was only stew, for fuck sakes!"

"It was poisoned!" Burr shouts, elbowing her off. "Those who didn't die from the sickness, those left behind, they made it and ate it and... Get up, buddy, come on, you've got to throw it up!"

"Poison?" Charlotte whispers. Her vision blurs as she crumples to the ground, all sound is sucked from the earth and she exists in a vacuum, feeling nothing, hearing nothing. Cliff's arms and legs flop as Burr pulls him upright; he sticks the handle of the spoon down Cliff's throat. Cliff starts to retch, his whole body trembling and seizing. The hum of electricity builds to one final, buzzing crescendo, and the lights go out.

>·<

Burr reaches out from a pool of candlelight and touches her cheek. She blinks.

"Charlotte?" His voice is loud. It breaks her open and allows sounds, and the memory of sounds, to return. She presses her hands to her ears to block out those memories – Cliff puking, his wheezing, laboured breaths, and her own, wretched sobs, as she held him.

Burr sets the candle down and sits on the floor beside her. "You should get dressed now. You're shivering."

She lets a hand fall onto the stack of clothes that have mysteriously appeared on her lap. Not her clothes. Someone else's. She shudders, but begins to dress, slowly, one leg, one arm, at a time. The flannel shirt smells like dryer sheets and is soft and warm. Electrically dried. She's forgotten how soft things can be. It makes her want to cry, but she has no tears left.

"Where is he?" she asks.

"Just out back, by the door. We'll take him to the fire…when you're ready."

"Thank you," she says quietly. "I think I'm ready."

Burr nods.

It is night, but Burr has lit the way with torches. It is a waste of precious resources, though Charlotte is ashamed of thinking about such things just now. Burr has wrapped the body in a sheet. She takes the feet and Burr the head. Together, they carry Cliff across the yard.

When they get to the fire, they have to swing him back and forth a few times to get him up onto the pyre. The sheets he's wrapped in burn away quickly. Charlotte steps back and stares at the shadow of a body she once knew. She once loved.

The breeze wafts with the smell of charred meat; memories of barbeque make her mouth flood with saliva, and, realizing its source, her stomach heaves. She swallows hard at the searing bile pushing at the back of her throat, struggling to keep her meagre stomach contents contained – calories she knows she cannot afford to lose.

Burr clears his throat. "Another has been taken from us today. He joins Ruth and Mika, Jim, Rhonda..." His voice catches, and he clears his throat again. "Cliff, you do not go into this dark night alone. Some of us were taken, and some chose to follow. Cliff, you didn't have a choice, I couldn't make a decision to follow, and my weakness, well, it killed you and... I'm... I'm sorry." Burr falls to his knees; strangled sobs come between long silences.

Charlotte fights the impulse to reach into the fire and stroke those bony ridges of his vertebra one last time. Instead, she rests her hands on Burr's shoulders. "We keep going," she says. "Because we have to. Because, whether we like it or not, whether we're better or not, *we* are the ones who accept that the last of the cheeseburgers are gone."

Grandma's End of the Line Stew
(Liard Lodge Hodge Podge)

Ingredients:
- Butter – Sniff test for rancidness.
- Flour – Keep the weevils/mealworms for added protein and texture!
- Onions, garlic – No? Try the spice cupboards for flavoured salts and powders. Check fancier houses for something extra nice.
- Bouillon – While you're digging around in those dead folks' cupboards, remember to grab some bouillon, and possibly that *extra special* ingredient (see below) Oh, and might as well raid the liquor cabinet, eh? (Note: keep alcohol away from open flame.)
- Rice/ noodles – Should be an easy find!
- Potatoes, carrots, turnips, yam – Whatever you got, throw 'er in the pot. (Don't worry if they're a little spotty or soft, once you've boiled them down, you won't even notice.)
- Beef? Pork? Chicken? – If you can't hunt up any fresh stuff, check for roadkill – Not a lot of traffic in your area? Lentils, garbanzos, kidney beans and other legumes are all excellent sources of protein and come in dried or canned form.
- Forest nearby? Forage for mushrooms – if you have the strength. Bonus! No worries if they're poisonous or not!
- Extra special ingredient: Grab up whatever toxic household chemicals you can find. Cleaners, pesticides, herbicides. Mix and match, keeping an eye out for those deadly symbols. Bonus if you can get your hands on some fatal-sounding prescription medications. There should be lots of these lying around. Don't worry, it's not really stealing.

Preparation:
- Stoke the fire. (Map as kindling, optional.)
- Mash up butter and flour. Fry until browned. (Now's a good time to add the meat if you got it.)
- Sauté onions, mushrooms. Add water, bouillon, chopped veggies. Simmer. • Add rice/noodles. Stir. Have a drink! Stir some more while you remember those lost. Shed a tear or two of relief and longing.

• Pour in that final, special stuff you've scrounged up. Moderate amounts, now, don't be shy. Simmer, stirring, until: you've lost all hope; are ready for the end; you're sick of it all; desperation wins out.

Do not leave unattended

PLUMCAKE

LYNN HUTCHINSON LEE

Eat, eat, baby Charleen
The plums are ripening over the green

It was the eve of the great conflagration, but nobody had a clue what was about to happen. Corn in the fields, plums on the trees, hens in the yard, honey in the hive. All good.

Before the cities went to rack and ruin, and the Manager brought his fist down upon the lands, before the Ottawa River glowed green beneath the bones of the nuclear plant, Mrs. Lorbetskie from the hill farm hollered up to her granddaughter, Charleen, who'd been sleeping in, "The plums are ready." Out they went with the basket into the orchard, where the hornets dive-bombed the branches and rollicked in the plumflesh, and Charleen got juice on her dress, the one she was still wearing from Trixie Kubishak's party last night. Grandmother Lorbetskie stopped picking long enough to sink her teeth into the juiciest plum she could find, rolling each morsel around in her mouth. "A cake without plums," she said between bites, "is like a child without a mother."

Charleen pretended not to hear. The whole story would get told again that night, usually after two glasses of plum wine, with tears running down Grandmother Lorbetskie's cheeks. The story was about Charleen. About her being a babe in arms when her mother, Eulalia May, the sweetest mother in all the valley, got drowned in the Ottawa River. Here, Mrs. Lorbetskie would stop and cross herself. Eulalia's truck flew over the guardrail and off the bridge because of her texting on her cellphone and not seeing the slaughter-house truck, with 25 of the Kubishaks' pigs, coming at her till it was too late. Mrs. Lorbetskie made a great sigh. There wasn't no dad in the picture, he'd took off. In the upstairs bed – the very bed she now slept in – Charleen was born, small as a rat, a month too early, and hardly breathing on account of almost being strangled by the umbilical cord, so they wrapped her up like a moth in a cocoon and kept her near the warming oven. At four months she had her first taste of plumcake, opening her mouth like a new starling. *Keep on truckin, baby Charleen*, went Eulalia in her sing-song voice, two hours before she ended up in the Ottawa River.

>‹

Mrs. Lorbetskie could make a plumcake out of thin air. The plums leaped from the tree into the basket, the eggs rolled themselves from the henhouse to the kitchen table, and the butter was brought by the cow herself from Kubishaks' barn. And Charleen told anybody who'd listen, *It's true, I seen it with my own eyes*, even though this was a flat-out lie.

The rest of the story was that Mrs. Lorbetskie's plumcake could mend a broken heart, banish the evil eye, guide the dying into the next world, and restore the near-dying to life. And – more lies – when life was hanging by a thread and the need was greatest, all the Old Ones, the long-dead, gathered in the kitchen to cook, set the world right, and drink themselves under the table with Mrs. Lorbetskie's plum wine. Charleen's best friend, Trixie Kubishak from down the hill, laughed at this, but Charleen's mouth hung open and she told Trixie she believed every word.

><

Mrs. Lorbetskie set the brimming basket down on the kitchen table. She told Charleen the recipe like she was telling a story, and Charleen was careful to follow her directions exactly, except for spilling flour on the floor and getting eggshells in the batter. While the plumcake was baking you could smell it down the hill and across the bridge to where the corn was ripening in the fields. And when it came out of the oven, that was the beginning of the sweetest torment, for the cake had to lie there all night as the tart juices of the plums embraced the sweetness of the batter, and they surrendered to each other, melting into a silken pudding.

While the cake spent its quiet night on the table, Charleen was tossing and turning with the nightmare of Eulalia May's truck leaping and spinning into the Ottawa River. In the morning, the clouds locked themselves over the hills, rain came in torrents, and the stream swelled into a raging river, flooding the bridge and all the fields. The sky poured itself over the land for 30 days. After it stopped, the sun came out and burned ferociously down for 30 days more. The trees dropped their leaves, hung their branches, the stream dried up, the dirt cracked, and the corn withered in the fields.

Then up came the storms again, with lightning dancing its way through the whole valley, and the nuclear plant up at the other end of the Ottawa River got hit. Next thing they knew there was a meltdown, with hydrogen explosions shooting steam, and forest fires on account of all that lightning. "You sure could roast a nice pig over them flames," said August Kubishak, and everybody slapped their knees and howled with laughter.

The jaws of the Manager's army ate through the valley, leaving ashes and bones in their wake. New fires rained from the sky, and people dived into their cellars or escaped to the abandoned mines or the caves along the Bonnechere River. The drones darted and swooped like bats as Mrs. Lorbetskie took herself and Charleen along the Opeongo Line, sleeping by day and walking by night. "Charleen," said Grandmother, "you gotta walk faster," and Charleen tried, but it was hard keeping up because of wearing her new party shoes with the wedge heels.

Little flocks of the living trudged along the roads, feet lifting through the ashes. Charleen cried and cried, and as they made their way across the Opeongo ridge, Mrs. Lorbetskie started handing out imaginary pieces of plumcake. They tasted the bloom of it in their mouths, holding its tartness and its sweetness against the bitter air, walking toward the memory, up ahead like a road sign showing them where to go.

At the mouth of the Bonnechere Cave, they stood looking in at the darkness.

"It's scary in there," Charleen said.

"Too bad," said Mrs. Lorbetskie, shooing her inside, while she went out to do her business under a tree. Then it came: a fresh rain of fire shooting itself from the roof of the sky. It found the tree, Grandmother Lorbetskie under it, and the fire unfolded in a scarlet bloom.

>·<

Locked in the most terrible grief, Charleen lay beside the little crater that held the dust of her grandmother. Trixie Kubishak, arriving with her parents and brothers that very day, scrounged for tasty leaves and wild onions, and fed Charleen like a baby.

There came a sort of winter, but no snow fell. There were no spring frogs, no smell of the earth, no sightings of birds or of the green sprigs and shoots that should be pushing themselves through the black dirt. Then came the day when Charleen stood herself up and said, quaking and shaking at even the thought of it, "I'm going home." She asked Trixie to go too, but Trixie stood at the mouth of the cave and looked outside and said no, maybe next week, maybe the week after.

Charleen, in her bare feet, set out alone under the pounding sun. Every cornfield was crammed with high grasses, their leaves like knives, and the trees were budding dayglo-green. In the middle of the road a crack appeared, and she thought, *What if the road opens up, and I fall through the crack and down into the arsehole of the world?* And if Grandmother Lorbetskie was beside Charleen right now, what would she say about that? *I'm picking the plums,* she'd say. *I'm beating the eggs; now I'm adding the sugar.* Charleen stirred the air, bending to put the imaginary plumcake into the oven and take it out again. How it filled her stomach and her heart! It was more real than the sky and fields and the road she walked upon.

On the second day, Charleen entered her childhood valley. It was nearly dark when she came up the hill through the leaves and ashes. There was Grandmother Lorbetskie's house above her, and beyond it the orchard. The trees were still standing, the leaves full against the darkening sky. She pulled down a branch. How could this be? She'd never seen so many plums, still new and hard as acorns.

>‹

Run, run, fast as you will
The shell-beast is coming over the hill

Her knees gave way to the sudden stink of metal and meat-rot, a grinding noise like the gears of hell. He, for it was a he, crashed over her like a nightmare, body a hard shiny shell, one sunken eye, and one red light in a swiveling socket. His gun was the big kind you had to hold in both arms. "This here's my orchard," came out of the swiveling jaws, "and these here's my plums." The red eye started to pulse. It happened so fast, his beetle arms shooting out around Charleen, that she couldn't even run. He opened wide his one real eye but there wasn't no human in there. Another kind of thing looked back out at her from a shady cave, and she couldn't turn away from that eye, and it kept pulling and pulling at her till she fell right in.

She woke up on the kitchen floor. The night was black as roofing tar. Her wrists were pinned together and her ankles tethered to a chair. She screamed Grandmother's name till she had no voice in her throat or breath in her lungs. *I'm alone,* was her only thought, *alone in this crappy dead world.* It was like that crack in the road, but with her on one side and Grandmother Lorbetskie's spirit, or whatever it was, on the other, and the crack getting wider.

Charleen floated in and out of sleep. She dreamed they were over at the kitchen counter with the plums, the sugar, the clouds of flour all dancing round Grandmother Lorbetskie like she was the moon and they were the stars. The next morning there was a raw egg in a dish, a piece of bread and a glass of water beside her on the floor. How can you eat with both hands tied together? But she found it could be done.

"I'm gonna trade you to the Manager," the beetle-man said, and when she started crying he fired two flaming shots out the door. "If you don't shut up, the next one's for you." Later she heard him talking, and made out some words. He'd escaped from somewhere or something. AWOL, it sounded like. Was he on a cellphone? "I'm gonna trade that girl for my freedom, plus I want my own farm." A silence, and the beetle-voice went on, "Yeah, she's nearly ready."

Trade and *nearly ready* scared Charleen more than the empty eye a mile deep. After that there was nothing but the mice in the walls and the hot raging winds that came over the hills. The bare boards of the kitchen floor ground against her bones, and she got to turning from one side to the other, twisting her leg where it was attached to the chair. She lay looking at Grandmother Lorbetskie's ratty old horsehair lounge, remembered them sitting there together, and then like a bird on a spit turned herself over to the wood stove, with the oven and the firebox and the ash reservoir. Again her mind went to Grandmother Lorbetskie, who in that one split second had collapsed into a pile of ashes like the ones in the stove, and where was she now? Not the ashes, but the rest of her?

>‹

Charleen couldn't believe how hard she was shaking when she spoke, not even daring to look at the beetle-man. "You ran away," she whispered, "didn't you."

"I'll shoot you," he said, "like the pigs down the hill."

"You ran away," Charleen said again. "From that grody-awful army." Let him shoot her. She didn't care.

"You don't say nothin against my army," said Beetle-man. "The Manager, he's lookin after us like he's our own dad." Out there the plums would soon begin to swell against the brightness of the leaves, and here was Charleen trapped by this stinking shell-beast who couldn't stop talking on his phone. Maybe it was his only friend.

"They said they'd give us a job. Yeah. A job. They took us to a camp and they built this here armour around us. It's never comin off, that's what they said." He craned his neck like it was stuck. "So they shot us up with stuff and stuck wires in our heads and we came out like super-heroes, better than real people." She wasn't sure if he was talking into the cellphone or to himself. "When I get enough girls for the Manager, then they won't put me in the hole for takin off, they'll give me a farm, see." After a while he shut up, tucked the phone into a hole in his chest and started pulling at the metal shell around his body, like it was too tight or something. "This is really startin to bug me," he said.

> **>**‹

The winds were something fierce. It felt like a week, 10 weeks, 100 weeks down on this floor, calling for Grand-mother Lorbetskie, and the heat like an oven it was, and always Charleen woke to the bread, the egg, the water, only sometimes there was no egg.

The plums were getting bigger. Softening at the tip end. She felt it.

At night she heard a scuffling, then a ripping sound out in the orchard, a muffled cry. An owl, maybe? A fox? She couldn't sleep, trying to figure out what it was, and waited for more, but there was only silence. "Your girlfriend," said Beetle-man in the morning, "from down the hill." Charleen went cold as ice. "Yeah. Trixie. She's in the shed. You plus her is two girls I got for the Manager."

In the afternoon Charleen dreamed about the day Byron Yantha told her he didn't love her no more, he loved Gloria Crowshank instead, and Trixie holding Charleen's hand and mopping her eyes and saying, *it'll get better, just wait.* Then Charleen mopping Trixie's eyes after Trixie got pregnant with a carrot farmer two hills over, and had the abortion on Mary-Lou Horgan's kitchen table.

Beetle-man was at the door. "What about my friend?" Charleen said. "Is she alive?" He was picking at his shell again, twisting his neck inside it and shifting his belly around. "What about my friend?"

He brought out a screwdriver, and she sickened. But he said, "What you're gonna do is unscrew the shell from my neck and my shoulder and you're gonna lift the shell right off. So I can, like, breathe." It was hard holding a screwdriver with her two hands tied together, and she nearly dropped it. "Get a move on," he said. But when she brought the screwdriver to the metal, he howled like she was digging into his very skin. She tried to pull the piece of shell off, but the shell and his flesh, they'd grown into

each other, and he was screaming and crying and screaming and crying.

Just shove the screwdriver in right now, she thought, *just
shove it in*, but didn't have the nerve.

"I never used to be like this," Beetle-man whispered.
"What'd they do with my feelings? They carved me up like
one of the pigs, and stuck everything back in the wrong
place, and then they put things in there that aren't supposed
to be in a person. But I'm still a person, aren't I? I used to go
and pick cherries with my Auntie Mary after my dad died. I
used to catch frogs down the stream and there's no frogs no
more, I don't hear them at night, but maybe it's because of
them things clankin around inside my brain." He was picking away at the shell like crazy. "Tell me!" Beetle-man said,
"tell me I'm a real person," looking at her with his real eye,
like he wanted to make sure she saw a person in there.
When it got dark and everything was in shadow, the eyelid
dropped. The chest rose and fell. He seemed to have fallen
asleep, but then the shell ruffled itself and closed over his
body. "Just because I'm talkin to you doesn't mean I'm gonna
let you go," he went.

He was right. He wouldn't let her go. Here he was, a
shell-beast with a glowing light for an eye and putrid armour
and a gun that shot flames. And her, well, she was just
Charleen, fastened to a chair, eating, sleeping, shaking on
the floor till the day he traded her to the Manager. *Please
don't let that day come. Let there be something else.*

And the air around her, it opened. Had she caused the
opening? Or had it been there all along? Through the opening came a whisper, not exactly words, but she knew what
was being said, the way you know in a dream.

The plums are softening, they're nearly ready. Wait. Was that Grandmother Lorbetskie? *A cupful of flour, a teaspoon of baking powder, a pinch of salt.* Charleen thanked her grandmother in a kind of prayer.

>·<

Time stretched itself out across the kitchen, through the window and over to the orchard and Trixie Kubishak in the shed, and then snapped back. Charleen turned over the last of the day's bread in her mouth, called up Grandmother's voice in the silence, and waited. *A cupful of sugar. Half a cup of butter – always use Kubishaks' and give them a plumcake as thanks – and two eggs from the henhouse.* Charleen held the bread under her tongue. The bread, soggy, started to taste of the batter. Could she send this taste to Beetle-man, melt his skin and bone and the metal crust till he was nothing but a puddle on the ground? Or to Trixie Kubishak's empty belly over in the shed?

As the plumflesh quickened and the fragrance drifted from the orchard, Beetle-man grew quiet. He stopped charging around with his cellphone, came and knelt on the floor beside her. "Please," he said. He brought the tips of her fingers to the shell on his body. "Oh please," he said. The whole shell shuddered at her touch, and was pouring tears.

In the middle of the night, Grandmother's voice came again. *You'll need two teaspoons of lemon juice, half a teaspoonful of vanilla, and don't forget the zest, the lemon zest, and we never measured it, did we, but that didn't matter, because the plumcake came out tasting different every time, a nice surprise because of not measuring the zest.* Would Trixie be able to taste the lemon bright in her mouth? The soft richness of vanilla?

Beetle-man went from one end of the yard to the other, his voice coming and going. Was he back on his cellphone again?

Now the plums. Fresh-picked, are they? Twelve you need, more or less. Grandmother Lorbetskie's words were shredding his, even as he came up the porch steps. He was doing a kind of dance. "Guess who was talkin to the Manager's Lootenant? And know what he said?"

And he started breaking up under Grandmother's voice bright in her ear. *No touching your plumcake till tomorrow, not even a crumb.* Charleen wished Grandmother's mouth could be with hers in that tomorrow, them eating together, their mouths inside the cake.

In the morning she could smell the plums hanging heavy and hopeful on the branches. The sun came through the window and across her arms.

><

Dark. It sounded like Kubishaks' pig truck straining up the hill. Then it stopped and she heard Beetle-man lonely and quiet on his cell. "The truck's ready, I got the two girls here, and I found three more. Yeah. Totally ready. Tomorrow."

All night, she thought how she, the runt, the scaredy-cat half-strangled at birth, would drive the screwdriver into Beetle-man's throat, or his heart if he had one, bury his body behind the barn, get herself out to the shed, and there'd be Trixie Kubishak, waiting.

Sometime in the late hours she dreamed of her life before the lime-green Jell-O of the Ottawa River. Grandmother Lorbetskie was over at the mixing bowl. *Plumcake banishes the evil eye, fulfills all desires,* and her dream laughter got high and scary because of what Charleen was about to do.

>·<

"If you get me some of them plums from the orchard, I'll make you a cake."

He stopped. "Is this some kinda trick?" he asked.

Charleen looked back up at him, her hands tied together like hands in prayer, and waited. After a minute, she said, "Do you like plumcake?"

He started jabbing the gun at her, and made a terrible noise, and over him Charleen went, "I need 12 plums," and again waited.

He wasn't budging. She waited. Then he left, finally, and after the longest time, brought back 12 of the ripest plums, and Charleen could feel their lively juices like they were running through her own veins.

"I can't make a cake when I'm flat on my back with my hands stuck together and this thing around my leg," she said, and he freed her so she could shake the pain from her legs and arms, start rummaging for the mixing bowls and spoons, get the fire going.

The oven has to reach three fifty, and remember to keep feeding it the exact amount of wood so it doesn't get too high or go too low. The dry ingredients, mix them together. Use one bowl for the dry and another – that white one with the blue rim

– for the wet. The sugar, yes, the sugar was there in its canister, but how did the butter and the eggs appear? *Beat the sugar and butter till they're all fluffed up.* Out the window she saw the corner of the shed where Trixie was trapped.

Beetle-man watched Charleen's every move.

Add the two eggs, and beat everything till it's a nice creamy yellow. And no lumps.

"What's goin on? Where'd them eggs come from?" said Beetle-man. "And that butter?" He'd sneaked up on her, his stink at her shoulder.

Now you gotta be careful. Add the dry to the wet, don't mix too long, just till everything comes together. Yes, that's enough. As she brought the wooden spoon to the bowl with its blue rim, Charleen saw how the bowl was like Grandmother Lorbetskie herself, holding the valley, the harvests, the people. And the lemons, bright as suns, appeared on the table like the eggs had done, and she squeezed their juices and grated their peels into the batter.

"You seen them, didn't you," she said, "comin out of nowhere." He was looking at the lemons like he was in some kind of bad dream.

"Yeah."

"Not everybody can see them," said Charleen.

The batter's stiff, and it goes in nice and even into the springform pan, the nine-inch one, greased with butter, just a bit, mind. And the plums, now put them skin-side-up in the batter. Sprinkle them with sugar, and set the pan into the oven, for 40 or 45 or 50 minutes, depending.

Later, when the smell of the cake filled the kitchen, she saw the beetle eye glaze over, and the red light flicker. "I never smelled nothin so good as that," he said, pulling at his shell something awful. When she brought the plum-cake from the oven, and set it down before him, she heard a sigh.

The next night Charleen took Grandmother Lorbetskie's carving knife and cut four pieces. One for Beetle-man, one for her, one for Grandmother, and one for Trixie Kubishak. And then, as an after-thought, a piece for long-gone Eulalia May. The shell-beast ate slowly, like the cake was pulling him into a dream.

Was that a tear she saw in the cave-black eye? "Georgie," he whispered. He was twisting and turning inside the shell where it joined his flesh. A bare place had opened at his throat. "Little Georgie." The knife was waiting on the table. "I never even seen him go in the water." Beetle-man shook his head. "I was drunk and foolin around with Sherry-Ann Cybulskie on the shore, and then he was gone." He got up and started crashing around. "You and Sherry-Ann are the only ones know I wasn't watchin him." He asked, "Why am I even tellin you this?" He was up close with his breath all over Charleen's face. "It just about killed our mom. You know how old he was? Three."

Charleen wanted to touch Beetle-man under the shell, touch him softly for just a second. His body didn't seem to know how to hold his little drowned brother and the drinking and the river, and he just kept saying *three* till he was down on the floor and crying like he wanted it to open up and pull him in.

On the last night, he gave Charleen the carving knife, and again she cut five pieces. And he ate. It must have taken him 20 minutes to finish off one piece. His voice was getting drowsy and thick. He turned to her. "I don't wanna be in this prison no more." He picked up another piece of cake. "I want this to be the last thing I feel," he said, and he put the cake in his mouth and she swore its softness melted the metal of his jaw, of his throat, even as the shell pierced the flesh.

She didn't have to pick up the knife. "You just keep on eating," she said. "Eat till you can't eat no more." He ate and ate and then the beetle-body pitched forward onto the table. Charleen got her arms right around the hot stinking metal and held him like she would've held her own dying grandmother if she'd had the chance. Like she would've held her own Eulalia May. She couldn't think of anything to say but, "It's okay to go now," and just before the shell-beast took his last breath, he went, "What's your name?"

>۰<

Let not your sorrowful, tender heart break
For Grandmother's coming to make you a cake

As the sun went down and the moon came up on the other side of the sky, Charleen lifted Trixie, shrunken and light as a sparrow, onto the horsehair lounge in the kitchen, and fed her the leftovers from the plumcake. Trixie ate till everything was gone, even licking the crumbs from Charleen's hand. "Remember when you fed me in the Bonnechere Cave," Charleen said, "till I stood up and walked myself out into the world?"

And as she said this, a shadow gathered itself into an old woman shape, and more shadows started sliding through walls and floating down from the ceiling. They talked in voices that came from their bodies in a whooshing sound. Some of them were arguing.

"Trixie, look. Can you see all them Old Ones, shimmering and shifting all over the kitchen?"

Trixie got out a whisper. "Yeah. Wow."

What they were arguing about was Charleen.

She had no right. That was my cousin Paulina's great-grandson.

She did so have the right, picking up a rolling pin and threatening the other. *She saved herself and my Trixie, and what did he do? Killed his kid brother, that's what.*

Accident, went another, and they started fighting.

"I didn't have no choice," said Charleen, "no choice," more for herself than for them. They heard, though, and milled around her, clacking their gums, and she thought some of them would've bared their teeth if they'd had any. Then the darkness flew apart and the fighting stopped, and they began to dance. The one belonging to Beetle-man stomped her feet the loudest, and the most bedraggled and bent ones, with their hunched-over backs and collapsing knees, out-danced all the rest.

There you are! Grandmother Lorbetskie came barging through the door, followed by none other than dear sweet mother, Eulalia May, hair long and green as the river, holding out her arms and calling *Baby Charleen* in a voice that filled Charleen's whole body. Eulalia swooped Charleen into her arms, crooned her a song, the truckin song, and stroked her hair till she fell into the sleep of the dead. And the shadow women, the women of her blood, the women of the hills and valleys, they carried on soothing and arguing, sniping and loving, spinning paring knives and spoons, plucking from thin air baskets of plums and eggs, bowls of honey, clouds of flour.

Who knows how long Charleen slept, but when the sun had set over the western hills, and the women were gathered at the table, Grandmother Lorbetskie raised her knife, the arguing stopped, and the cutting of the cake began. The women lifted their glasses of plum wine, and the whispering sounds that came from their bodies and hair and mouths said, *This is the food that holds the flames and ashes of the world at bay, the food that banishes the evil eye, grants death and restores life, the food that's prepared by our hands, the hands of the ancestors, when the need's the greatest.*

"Did you see them?" asked Charleen. "Did you see my mother? Did you see my grandmother? How they made the cake? Out of nothing?"

"Yeah, I seen it all," whispered Trixie, who no longer had the look of a starveling about her.

Eulalia May drifted over to Charleen. She was holding a piece of plumcake in her hand and whispering, *Eat, eat, baby Charleen,* and Charleen ate.

Plumcake

Preheat oven to 350°F.
Ingredients:
- 1 cup unbleached pastry flour
- 1 teaspoon baking powder
- ⅛ teaspoon salt
- 1 cup sugar
- ½ cup unsalted butter, room temperature
- 2 large eggs, room temperature
- ½ to 1 teaspoon vanilla

- 12 purple plums, halved and pitted
- 1 teaspoon lemon zest

Dry ingredients:
- Sift together flour, baking powder and salt.

Wet ingredients:
- Cream together butter and sugar until fluffy.

Preparation:
• Add the eggs one at a time.
• Add vanilla and lemon zest.
• Add dry ingredients to the wet, mixing until combined. The batter will be slightly stiff.
• Spoon batter into a lightly greased 9-inch springform pan; smooth top with spatula.
• Arrange the plums, skin side up, to cover the batter.
• Sprinkle with sugar.
• Bake on middle rack of oven until cake is golden and a toothpick inserted into the centre comes out clean, about 45 to 50 minutes. Remove from oven and gently loosen springform edge with knife, removing the edge and allowing cake to cool on the springform pan base.

Best not eaten right away: keep covered at room temperature for 8 hours or overnight (allowing juices to marry batter, making a silken custard), after which the plumcake can be eaten.

FERRY BACK THE GIFTS

KATE STORY

My mother's setting traps for me. Yesterday I found a jingle bell rolling around in my underwear drawer – apparently severed from the cotton-ball head of my Yule angel, one of those mangled juvenile crafts long consigned to the dump – rolling around in my underwear drawer. A week ago, my Award of Excellence for Minor Divination (Category: Card Reading) showed up at the bottom of my button box. A slip of the knife and a deep cut to my thumb; could be coincidence, but I wonder. And smells, with no warning or obvious source, lingering for hours: freshly sharpened pencils, wet wool, my ex-boyfriend's body odour (slightly sulphurous); she never liked him. And just once, her perfume – Magic – mingled with cigarette smoke and rye. It hung around for days, that one.

The climax was, of course, the car accident. Brakes, just tuned, suddenly failing. Putting my foot on the brake and encountering that… looseness… I was both light and terribly heavy, all at the same time, mind moving fast as a red squirrel, slow as a turgid river. I ended up in a lake. Remembered how she always kept a hammer in her car for just such an incident (she had enemies and she knew it).

Only the powerful have enemies. I don't keep a stinking hammer in my stinking car.

I managed to escape because a window happened to be open. Yes, I know it's winter, but the window was broken and

I couldn't afford to fix it. Couldn't really afford a car, either, but that decision was made for me. The old beater's at the bottom of Twenty Mile Pond.

She's been dead for almost ten years. Why is she reaching across now?

In any case, I'm presently and for the foreseeable future carless, thus restricting my employment opportunities still further. I keep body and soul together through various odd jobs: cleaning people's houses; sporadic personal care work; brief employment as a production assistant on the hit TV show *Republic of Foil*; and party tricks – card reading, etc. The work trickles in ever more slowly these days, and it's not enough.

><

Deck the halls with boughs of holly, fa la la la la…

I'm surfing for jobs.

"Wanted: Charmers! Successful social media networking a plus!!!!"

Tis the season to be jolly…

"Curses R Us! Subscribe to our newsletter, or you'll be sorry!"

Don we now our gay apparel…

I don't want a newsletter; I want to be employed. I'm a low-level charmer at best, able to guess at a hidden card, to blow out candle flames by staring at them. As a child I showed some promise as a healer; I can still tell when there's something wrong with a person, communicate fairly effectively with cats, and find lost objects. My Tarot readings bring in a little, here and there. But shamanizing as a full-time activity? No, no. To make a living, one needs weather management, high-level divination or, at the very least, a good clear cursing ability.

But if I knew how to "brand" myself – as a psychic entertainer, say – I think I could make enough to get by. Surfing Virago brings up hundreds of low-level charmers, shamans, witches and wizards.

My mother hated marketry, those trading in fake shamanizing and professional bamboozlement. On her deathbed – literally, she was near the end of the wasting sickness that carried her off after an awful fight of years – she pronounced, "If you ever join one of those plastic witch outfits, I'll come back from the grave and kill you."

People came to my mother through word of mouth, because she was good. Mind you, her career was well-established before the net, before Virago and the other Big Three. My mother, she was the real deal.

>i<

As early on as I can remember, I was an adept gleaner of wild foods in season, my mother's pantry, and other people's kitchens. My little friends' parents nicknamed me the Southside Locust, and nobody could beat me for my ability to pick (and eat) vast quantities of blueberries, chuckley pears, brambles, and crowberries during Newfoundland's short, sweet summers. I had knowledge of a rich patch of bakeapples, and they still grow there, and I will never tell. It's still hard for me, at parties, not to stand over the hors d'oeuvres tray making an unseemly pig of myself. As soon as I enter a building, I become immediately aware of all possible food sources: a vending machine, a café, a chip wagon across the street. It never ceases to amaze me when others display obliviousness to food. But then, I am usually hungry.

My first memory consists of making a meal for my younger brother and myself. We were hungry, she was elsewhere. I had been told I was not allowed to drag a chair into the pantry, and we weren't allowed into the fridge (for reasons which still remain opaque to me). So I prepared a meal from what I could reach on the lowest shelf of the pantry: a small handful of golden raisins, two dried apricots, Shirriff Instant Mashed Potato Flakes, and two pink, heart-shaped dog biscuits. They weren't bad, the biscuits. Better than the potato flakes, which dried your tongue to a husk. I put everything on plates to make it look like a real meal. Gave the dog one of the beige bone-shaped biscuits, because she was begging.

Within days I was dragging the chair around despite the prohibition and using milk from the proscribed fridge to make Jell-O Pudding on the forbidden stovetop. As long as I kept the handle of the saucepan turned inward so my little brother couldn't grab it and upend the boiling pudding onto his three-year-old head (an image that transfixed me with horror) I figured we'd be okay. My mother realized what I was up to as boxed Jell-O Pudding levels, which she had bought on sale and then hoarded, dropped precipitously, but she just gave me a tight and brilliant smile. "Good for you, then." And the next time she remembered to go grocery shopping (likely prompted by a dip in her stores of cigarettes and rye, or the need for an ingredient for a spell), she started supplying the house with pre-sliced bologna and Kraft Singles. I don't think she realized about the dog biscuits. We never spoke of it.

She was otherwise preoccupied.

>·<

Newfoundland specializes in plain old charmers, probably a last remnant of the gifted of western England and southwest Ireland. Also known as "toad doctors" and "girdle measurers," the charmers specialize in healing, possession, and cursing. Throw in a little weather-manipulation and some legendary flyers, and you have a nice healthy tradition that – while wiped out in Great Britain by the Renaissance, and further decimated by what one could simply call modern corporate capitalism – survives on this colonized island. It's mostly a woman's skill, although there was a male charmer acclaimed for his knot magic; his ability to control winds made incalculable contribution to the great success of pirate Peter Easton back in the early 1600s.

My mother worked on skill-building with my brother and I, as the mood took her, but like most men he learned contempt for it early and turned away, even though I believe he is more gifted in this regard than I.

But indeed, what real use are my skills?

I know few professional charmers. I can spot those with the talent, those other women and the odd fella. They are marked by a love of cats, and seedy crackers; an overly amorous relationship to brooms, and barely-suppressed rage at people who refuse to eat the perfectly edible rinds of aged cheeses. They guess at numbers and often do well at lotteries (a skill, alas, that eludes me). They sense when you are trying to conceal something. They adore sugarplums and eat vast quantities of them at Yule.

>‹

Hours pass and I realize it is 3 a.m., and I have gone down the internet Rabbit Hole. From charmer employment sites to healer claims for childhood disease cures to a new study on the damage toxic stress does to a child's developing brain to finding six other new studies, and finally sinking to the low of taking, myself, the online Adverse Childhood Experiences Test. ACEs, as they call them, are "stressful or traumatic events, including abuse or neglect." A high-ish score, they assure me, is an indicator for all kinds of adult diseases and behavioural issues, from arthritis and heart disease to STIs, alcoholism, jail time, and unemployability. ACEs. Ace in the hole. Ace that test. Pass that eye of newt, will ya, ace?

The site reassures me more than once that the study was conducted for the most part on white, middle-class subjects. I am bemused by this insistence until it occurs to me that they are trying to prove that an immense amount of damage has been done to children across the board. For me, say, there was the neglect as touched upon above, which extended to periods of unwashed clothing and, quite simply, looking funny in school. The alcoholism and contempt. I was molested, by a teacher and next-door neighbour. Nothing out of the ordinary, really; an ordinarily uncomfortable childhood.

Even a score of one puts you in the shade. One knocks years off your life; 19, they estimate. What kind of estimation is that? How did they derive it? Nineteen years, snuffed out, just like that. It's laughable. I mean, but laughable. I laugh.

The score's out of 10.

I get a six.

>·<

I sit at my kitchen table staring at a candle flame. My laptop lies next to me, closed. The room is dark. The entire apartment is dark, the city is dark.

What is the night?

Almost at odds with morning, which is which.

Time was I could have snuffed it with a thought. I stare, and the flame burns a twin into my retina. It flickers, arcing across my vision. Minutes pass. My concentration wavers. The candle burns.

I sense another in the room, a dark presence, and cold. And that smell: Magic and cigarettes and rye.

There's a sharp *click*, like the mandibles of a beetle snapping together. The candle goes out.

It will have blood, they say. Blood will have blood.

Stones have been known to move, and trees to speak.

Something runs up the curtains behind the table then, a lick, a tongue of light and heat. It takes a moment to understand what I am seeing. By the time I lurch to my feet the whole window is in flames, fabric dropping to the floor, blackout liners fusing and melting in the heat. I have a brief, incoherent thought that the flames must look very pretty reflected on the snowy porch roof outside.

Augurs and understood relations have
By magot pies and choughs and rooks brought forth
The secret'st man of blood.

My apartment is on the second storey; I must get down the stairs. I grab my laptop, start to crawl under the table for the cord, realize how fucking stupid that is, and run from the room. Go back for my phone. I reach through the flames for it. *That will hurt later,* I think. Flee the room, calling for Betty. Fuck, where is she? Oh, there, a big black comma on the bed, silhouetted against the white coverlet. Surely my mother won't kill Betty? She loved cats. No time to wonder, no way I'm chancing it – I fling open my closet, grab the cat carrier, and toss Betty inside. She has only time for an indignant *Mrow!* and we're out the door. Whole kitchen in flames, now. Last thing I see is the silhouette of a woman. It could be me, just my reflection, I tell myself. Tall, wreathed in flames, wearing a dark cloak and standing in front of the window.

>·<

The fire brigade comes promptly and the fire is doused without much trouble. The fire fighters – all men – start to flirt, then something about me (this often happens) occurs to them and they stop. The eldest of them, probably close to my age, has some grey in his hair and kind eyes. He tells me it's safe to go back into the apartment, but it'll probably smell bad. "You could ask your landlord for some paint to fix up the kitchen. He'll have insurance." There's no way Mr. Snelgrove will be offering me free paint. "Thanks," I sniff. Betty growls from her cage.

"Better get that kitty inside," the fire fighter says.

Betty growls again, and hisses. She hates being called "kitty."

"And take care of that hand. You want some ointment? Hey Mac, get this lady some antibiotic ointment." Mac gives me a tube from the firefighters' own first aid kit and some gauze and tape. The nice guy tells me to keep it clean and dry, and wrap it up.

I and the other tenants – Josh and his new girlfriend, and Bob in the basement – all troop back inside. There's no damage to their apartments, not even a smell of smoke. The damage is entirely confined to my place, and even there it is merely cosmetic. Nevertheless, they don't look at me or speak. They'll hate me even more, now. There'll be a complaint to Mr. Snelgrove.

Thanks, Mom.

The apartment stinks. I leave the kitchen window open and fall into bed. Betty curls around my head like she used to do as a kitten; we're both upset.

I dream, that night, of my mother. As always, she is big, big as a giantess, or I am small. Yes, it's more that I am small.

We are in the kitchen of my childhood; she is making the sugarplums. She wants me to help, but I can't remember what to do. Always when I dream of her it is like this: me, small as a parrot, and my voice is too quiet for her to hear. No need to go to Dr. Freud for analysis.

I wondered, all the time I was trying to take care of her during the last cancer, if the dreams would change after she died. They haven't. I am having trouble with the sugarplums. She has asked me to roll the balls in the sugar, but they keep sticking to my hands, unravelling and smearing to nubbins.

"Just roll them in ointment and keep them clean and dry," she says, exasperated. "Didn't you learn a damn thing?"

>·<

Cleaning the kitchen takes time, especially since my left and dominant hand is the burnt one. It features blisters and stinging redness. I scrub and scrub, right-handed. Every cobweb is outlined in soot. It's amazing how many there are. I smudge the walls and make more work for myself. I tack some old sheets over the window to replace the curtains. It depresses me. Really, the room needs a fresh coat of paint. I can't afford fresh paint.

Betty is still stirred up, and keeps alternately almost killing me by winding around my ankles when I least expect it, and staring at something on the sideboard shelf and growling.

"What is it?"

Her green eyes fixed on the shelf, she arches and hisses.

I sigh. She sees something, that's for sure. I go over to the shelf and start moving my hand around. "This?" I ask her. *Joy of Cooking*. "This?" *Middlemarch* – how did that get there? My hand falls on my mother's old recipe box. "This?"

She shoots across the room like a rocket and knocks my hand from the box. The box falls to the floor. Betty exits the room with a yowl.

I stare down at the box. The recipes have spilled across the linoleum, fanned like a vast hand of cards. The box is a tole-painted tin, orange, red, gold, and green flowers on a black ground. I've always adored it. The cards are all the same, formerly-white index cards now yellowed on the upper edges from the life-long tide of cigarette smoke. They are all written in her beautiful cursive, an old-fashioned, clear, decisive script. Her domesticity was weird, given her other proclivities, and sporadic. Molasses bread baked in clean clay flowerpots. Molasses cookies, spread out as big as a tea saucer on the baking sheet. Blueberry muffins with the bounty I brought down from the Hill, or even, sometimes, pies, the crusts dusted with coarse sugar that sparkled like fairy dust or snow. She used that same kind of sugar for the sugarplums too. It'd be about this time of year that she'd make the sugarplums, what with Yule coming up and all. I've been trying to ignore the holiday, not having much to celebrate.

"Happy Yule, Betty."

Betty refuses to come back into the kitchen; I can hear her growling in the hall.

I shuffle the cards, wondering if they're in any particular order. I haven't opened the box since Mom's death, I realize, even though ideas about making one of her recipes have floated through my mind; even though I had to fight my brother for the box and ended up just sneaking out with it. Low of me.

But the recipes aren't there. What I see is a heading unfamiliar to me: *Filicide.*

Filicide?

Over 500 children are murdered by their parents annually in the United States, the card reads.

The next card, bearing the heading *Filicide: Canadian* notes that *In Canada, estimate 30 children each year and kill.*

These cards aren't written in the shaky hand of her last year. This is my mother's writing, my mother in her prime.

One in five filicides are killings of adult children, the next card continues, with a touch of grim humour, or am I imagining that? *making filicide a lifetime risk.*

Of course, the true number of filicides are unknown, for many parent murderers manage to conceal their work.

Seriously, Mom, is this your idea of a joke?

Serotonin is the heading for the next card. *A significant proportion of filicidal parents experience depression and/or psychosis as well as personality disorders, and particularly borderline personality disorders.*

The next card is the recipe for sugarplums.

And the next.

And the next.

Sugarplums, to the back of the box.

Sugarplums are adored by women, despised by men and children, and made only for Yule. She never made just two dozen – always more, giving them away as holiday gifts to all her women friends. Your hands get sticky rolling the balls between your palms; it helps to keep your hands a little wet, and she'd keep a bowl of tepid water at our elbows for just that purpose. She used to put them in little gold foil paper cups so they didn't stick together, and packaged them in wee round flat tins, twelve to each tin, two layers with wax paper between.

The first sugarplum recipe card is marked with cocoa-ed fingerprints; a crystal of coarse white sugar sparkles, stuck to the thick creamy paper. Without thinking, I reach out my finger, dislodge the crystal, and put it on my tongue. The sweetness melts. I can't resist; I crunch down. I realize then that it probably came from her hand, the last year she was well enough to make the recipe.

>·<

I end up buying some white paint after all, and repaint the window frame and the upper cabinet doors. While I'm at it, I slap a white circle on the outside of my apartment door, about the size of one of Mom's molasses cookies. It works to keep ghosts away when painted on the doors of barns and fishing stages – maybe it will keep her off here, too?

Naw, b'y.

She used to lay on the Newfoundland accent when dealing with mainland clients, or even some of the people from town. There was no harm in it. It pleased people to think they'd hired themselves a genuine Newfoundland witch. Often, the ignorant would express disappointment that she didn't wear a pointed hat or brandish a dog-eared spell book. "It is not written," she'd snap. And indeed, it never was. I have no spell book from my mother, no spells. They have to be taught.

You have to go through the initiations. You have to go over the edge. You have to give in.

I had a roommate years ago, a woman given to disastrous affairs with married men. Oh, she loved a married man, and she was prone to doing things like leaving her thong lying around the lover's marital bedroom. I liked her, despite all this; she had other qualities that recommended her; like a strong stomach for Jameson and a loyal heart for her friends. The affairs all ended after a time, naturally, married men not being prone to leaving their comfortable situations if they can get away with it. One of the endings took her particularly hard. She literally took to her bed, and there she remained. I remember being genuinely worried that she would die. She stopped eating entirely and became so dehydrated that the skin on the back of her hands, on her face, looked like paper. I finally, reluctantly, called in her mother. She, a normal maternal sort, came over at once and started cooking and cleaning, tsk-tsking at our squalor. She got food and drink into my roommate, and slowly, as her body recovered, so did her heart.

I remember feeling mingled awe at her total letting-go, and contempt, which I tried to conceal. Awe because I knew I could never let myself fall like that. Contempt because she could. I am like the Ugly Duckling, swimming around and around the wintery pond to keep the ice at bay. A Lady Macbeth who never goes to bed.

Stop moving and go mad or die.

To bed, to bed, there's knocking at the gate…
What's done cannot be undone.
To bed, to bed, to bed!

Communication with beyond is fraught with difficulty. The messages are liable to misinterpretation, even for one with that gift. My mother could see ghosts and talk with them, although she never – to my knowledge – called anybody from the other side.

Now that she's there – well, what is she doing?

I go online. *Homicidal ghosts, vengeful parent, countering malevolent spells.* The searches only pull up flashy ads for plastic witches – one only finds the real deal through word of mouth. If I could afford it, I'd engage a Dukun from Indonesia. Or a Mongolian Udgan, or maybe one of the Obeah women from Jamaica, or (if they would consent to work this far north) a Sangoma from the south of Africa. An adept in any of these traditions could – if willing – tell me what to do.

But another thought strikes me, a cold finger down my back. She's acknowledging – as she never did in life – her illness.

I remember hearing the story – not from her, but from friends' parents, teachers, even a profile in the newspaper that touched upon it. Her plunge off the emotional cliff. The coma in which she lingered for days. The pronouncements in some ancient language, perhaps Celtic, perhaps Anglo Saxon. Her slow coming back, her change. She crossed over to the underworld. And so she could ferry them back, the gifts. The wounded healer becomes sick to understand sickness.

Not me. I never underwent the so-called initiatory crisis. My resistance to succumbing – my drive to live – prevented my journey to the underworld.

Envy is thought to bring bad luck to the one envied. I think this marked me early: fear of being harmed because people might be envious of my famous parent. I became a class clown as soon as I learned that I could make people laugh and concealed my high marks in school. Even now—

I give myself a shake and turn off the computer. There's no way I can afford a spirit-world worker. Those people are high-level, big bucks.

I'm on my own.

>·<

I dig through boxes containing old horseshoes, and nail them over every door frame and window, U-oriented to catch the luck. I hammer a board full of nails, and lay it points-up before my front door. I find a skirt with small round mirrors sewn into the embroidery around the hem, one I procured years ago and never wore. I wear it now, by Hecate. And then, as another wet howler of a winter storm shakes the city, I pour myself a glass of cheap red wine and set out to make the sugarplums.

Sugarplums are marked by the triangulations of colonization. Cocoa from Jamaica, figs grown in the uplands, cinnamon, and, of course, sugar. Salt cod from Newfoundland went to feed slaves in Jamaica who laboured in the sugarcane fields; the plantations sent us sugar and molasses, from which we made rum. And it was from the Turks and Caicos islands that the salt came with which to cure the fish: more salt than sugar came to Newfoundland from the Caribbean in those days.

Yule cooking reflects the old relationship: sugar, spice, and blood. The bitter, the salt, and the sweet.

Pus seeps through the gauze on my hand, so I wear a rubber surgical glove for sanitation's sake. I toast the almonds in a small cast-iron skillet from my mother's kitchen, usually hung from the mantelpiece and dusty with lack of use. I burn the first batch and have to throw them out; I'm not paying attention. I pour a second glass of wine and cut the hard bits from the stems of the figs because as a kid I hated finding them inside my mouth. That takes some time. And I have to be careful, remembering the other accident with the knife. My food processor is so tiny I have to do the work in three batches. In the days before food processors there would have been more chopping, fine as peppercorns. I eat the orange slices after zesting the orange, even though I rather hate oranges. But this one surprises me, juice bursting over my tongue like a last meal.

I top up my glass rather than pouring a whole third cup. It's going to be one of those nights when I surprise myself by drinking the whole bottle, is it? I lift the glass to the air. Here's to you, Mom.

Could there be anything like altruistic filicide? I suppose some parents might believe they are saving the child from a cruel world or relieving the real suffering of the child. Yes, one could imagine that; in fact, there have been cases. But since filicide is also sometimes linked to the parent suffering from a serotonin-related illness such as schizophrenia or depression, one could also postulate such suffering on the part of the child as being imagined by the parent.

Frankly, as small and possibly disappointing as my life is, I want to stay on this side of the ground.

Just because my mother is dead doesn't mean she's not still mad. She holds the poison apple in her hand. She always has.

I roll the sticky mixture into balls, then roll those in a shallow dish of sugar. I imagine what it would be like if the sugar still came from slave plantations. Would it have blood in it? No, of course not, not literally, I'm making things up. I pour more wine. My glass is sticky with fingerprints.

I don't have any foil cups. It's too bad. But they still look pretty on the plate.

I sit down, strip the surgical glove from my hand, lift a sugarplum to my mouth, and bite it in half.

The rich flavours of the cocoa and toasted almonds hum under the fruit like a bass line, the almond extract and orange sing a high note. The sugar melts and crunches.

The inside oozes with blood.

It's a heart, a heart the size of a partridge's, a rabbit's. Half of it bitten out, covered in sugar, it still beats and pumps blood.

I scream, flinging the thing from me. It lands, rolls, and stops. Betty, alerted by my scream, comes running to the kitchen (not, as would an ordinary cat, hiding, dear thing). She sees the thing on the floor, stops short, then cautiously stalks it. She touches her nose to it, looks at me, and miaows.

It's just a sugarplum. My teeth marks are plainly visible, and my mouth is not bloody, and Betty is winding around my ankles asking for dinner. Just a sugarplum, that's all.

I feed the cat and turn back to my wine. As I reach for the glass, I think, right, I should get that sugarplum off the floor, and the thought makes me clumsy and I knock the glass over. It shatters on the floor, red wine spraying out like a blood spill. And my left hand, the burnt hand, bursts into flame.

It doesn't hurt. It burns blue as a rum-soaked Yule pudding.

Now my right hand is afire. *Double, double, toil and trouble.*

The sugarplums have left the plate and sail around the room like wee comets trailing glorious fiery tails. They constellate around my head, setting my hair afire, and also my clothes. *Fire burn and cauldron bubble.*

I hear the small mirrors drop out of my skirt and onto the floor, *plink plink*, one after another. Everything I see, I see through blue, cold flame.

She stands before me, then, in her black cloak. It's not her as she was at the end – she's in her prime, the mother I remember from the dog biscuit days.

"I got six on my test," I tell her.

"Out of what?" she asks.

I can't remember what the top score is supposed to be. "Eleven," I hazard.

"That's rather poor, dear," she says.

"It's not a test you want to do well on."

"You can do better," she says. "You always could."

"Would you just please stop trying to kill me?" I manage.

"Kill you? Who's trying to kill you?"

"You are!" I sound like a teenager.

"Don't be ridiculous."

Her voice! Oh, I've missed it. The contempt, her quick and dismissive rejoinders – I've even missed those. But there's something odd here, and it takes me a minute to fix upon it as the blue fire plays over my body. Then I have it. We're eye to eye. I'm not a pigeon, a wee creature with a squeaky voice. We're talking as two women talk.

"I hope Betty can find her way out of the apartment before the whole place goes up," I sulk.

"Burn your house down?" Her voice drips with contempt. "With *ignis fatuus*? Are you actually going to let that happen?"

How maddening she is. Rage filling me, I run my hands over my body in a scooping motion and fill my palms with it. I bring my hands to my mouth and drink in the flame like water, eyes never leaving hers.

Ah, now that hurts. My throat is burnt with it, my mouth. But there is less fire on me now.

"What was it? Was it your narcissism, your alcoholism, that made you great?"

"What are you talking about?"

"Your psychosis?"

She laughs. "Oh, dearie, I'm not psychotic. I'm just very good at what I do." She keeps laughing, and it goes on, too long.

I run my hands over myself again, catching it, drinking it. With every agonizing swallow, my mother grows smaller. She keeps laughing, but the pitch gets higher and higher, like a child's, like a cartoon. I drink every drop until my body is clean of the stuff. My last glimpse of tiny her, I think I see her wink at me.

There's no more fire. She is gone.

My clothes are gone too, all except the little mirrors lying in a circle around my feet.

I rub my hand over my head and face and feel nothing but stubble where my hair and eyebrows used to be. Nothing else in the room has been touched by fire. Betty munches contentedly at her bowl. I am not scarred, and there's no pain on the outside of my body.

My mouth and throat, now, that's a different matter.

I would scream, but I cannot seem to make a sound.

><

It takes some time. My voice never returns. I am able to speak, but in a grating whisper, and it costs me. I also lose my sense of taste. Ironic, isn't it?

But something is unleashed inside me after surviving that night of fool's fire. I won't tell you the exact parameters of my powers, for it isn't done, and besides, I am still discovering them. But my life has become a great deal more comfortable. I am very busy. At times I find it hard to remember that I once couldn't afford new curtains.

Sugarplums

Ingredients:
- ½ cup slivered almonds
- 4 ounces dried figs
- 2 tablespoons unsweetened cocoa
- ½ teaspoon ground cinnamon
- 3 tablespoons honey
- Grated zest from 1 orange
- ½ teaspoon almond extract
- ¾ cup coarse granulated sugar

Preparation:
(No plums are harmed or even involved in the making of this recipe.)
• In a small skillet over medium heat, toast the almonds. Remove from heat, cool.
• Combine figs, cocoa, cinnamon, and almonds in a food processor. Pulse until peppercorn-sized balls form.
• Add the honey, orange zest, and almond extract. Pulse 3 or 4 times until well-mixed.
• Spread the sugar in a shallow dish. Form the sugarplums into 1-inch balls and roll in sugar.
• Makes about 2 dozen.
• Tightly-covered, these keep for about 2 weeks at room temperature.

CHEWING THROUGH WIRE

CHRIS KURIATA

Each evening, Auntie Paula washes her muddy feet in the same bowl she eats her dinner from. The clean bowls stacked in her kitchen cupboard are reserved for company only. Auntie Paula needn't say so, but it's been painfully long since the bowls last served company. The deep, wooden basins rumble like empty bellies after a long journey.

"She's a darling."

Auntie Paula's ancient arms strain, about to snap like dry branches under Emery's weight, but she finds a reserve of strength in her ailing body and hefts the baby over her head. Sunlight beams through a hole in the roof, warming Emery and making her smile.

Pucks of dried mud in the shape of boot heels litter the front hall. I locate a broom and sweep them out into the acreage's breeze. "When do the neighbours visit?"

Auntie Paula makes faces at the baby. "Every goddam day."

>‹<

Auntie Paula welcomes us with tea. "Keep an eye on him," she warns of the great lizard who lies basking on the stone windowsill. He looks too lazy to take an interest in Emery, but given the circumstances under which he and Auntie Paula met, he cannot be trusted around a baby.

More years ago than I've been alive, during a routine walk to the fences, Auntie Paula kicked a pile of hot dust, wanting to see the individual grains sparkle in the red setting sun, unaware the lizard was sleeping within. As payback for her inconsiderate act, the lizard bit her ankle and would not let go, no matter how much Auntie Paula sweet-talked him. She told her funniest joke but got not so much as a giggle. Only a switch to sad stories set the lizard's jaw quivering until he finally released the grip on her ankle.

Instead of returning the bloody lipped lizard to the ground, Auntie Paula tucked him into the apron of her dress. If he wouldn't apologize for biting her, she'd put his mouth to good use. Ignoring her swollen ankle, she made her way to the fences, where the neighbours had forbidden her to go. There, she used the lizard's mighty jaw to snip through the wires dividing the land. Unfortunately, a lizard is too small a tool to take down those obscene barriers.

"After biting through a dozen wires his teeth bleed. I press milk out of the tall weeds to rub along his mouth, but who can tell if the balm provides relief or not. Lizards are notoriously secretive."

Under Auntie Paula's care, the lizard has outlived its normal lifespan many times over, and grown to a size Auntie Paula can barely lift – heavier than a newborn baby. The lizard looks to me like some breed of monitor, whose ancestors must have been carried a great distance to settle here. *Invasive species* is the official term.

The fences are tall and stretch farther across the land than Auntie Paula can walk. She uses the lizard to chew gaps in the wires in the hope travellers may squeeze their way through. She ties bones to these openings so the wind whistling through the hollows will guide folks to where they can pass. Unfortunately, Auntie Paula's bone sirens also alert the neighbours to where she has snipped the fences, and they quickly assemble to repair her alterations – re-stringing the barbed wire as efficiently as spiders in a damaged web.

"If only you had a million lizards," I said. "You could chew up all the fences."

"If I had a million lizards there'd be no room on the acreage for anyone."

>ı<

The travellers are exhausted when they arrive at the fences. I can only imagine how long they've journeyed. I'm sure people are left behind; buried along the way or given up to the birds in the sky when the land is too rocky to dig.

Those who find Auntie Paula's gaps follow the light of her house, where she waits to feed them, filling those bowls that are reserved for company only.

In the morning, with fresh strength, the travellers always cook for her.

"It took time to understand my purpose out here," she says. "When I was younger and stupid, I used to knock the pots and knives out of their hands. I'd yell in their faces, *You don't have to do this!* In my selfish way of thinking, I assumed the travellers believed they owed me a debt and were cooking to repay my hospitality."

Recalling those early years yelling at the travellers clearly pains Auntie Paula. She keeps private about nothing. From her bowel movements to her glorious reminiscences of the handsome men who shared her bed, she speaks candidly. Too much sometimes, bragging. Only about yelling at the travellers does she feel shame. She would rather keep this past private but feels it important I learn from her mistakes.

"Of course, they weren't cooking for me, they were cooking for themselves. After travelling so long through those barren, chilly passages, the act of cooking is an affirmation of hope. Cooking proves, yes, we can survive here. We can provide for ourselves and our loved ones. There is some adaptation. I see them scouring the acreage for herbs and roots that most closely approximate their preferred ingredients, but they make it work. How joyful to cook for your family after such a long journey."

Auntie Paula turns dour. It has been ages since any travellers celebrated their arrival in her kitchen. Season after season, the bowls remain empty. The neighbours see to that.

>⟨

Like cowards, the neighbours never visit Auntie Paula one-on-one, but always in groups of seven, sometimes more. The ones who enter her house (always without knocking, naturally) wrap chains around their waists and lock the ends to the chassis of their trucks, so at the first sign of trouble their buddies can rev the engine and drag them outside to safety. Thick nettles sprout along Auntie Paula's lawn, so if that ever happens the bastards will be picking stingers out of their backsides for weeks.

Inside her house, they poke through the cupboards and peek under the bed, searching for clippers or axe heads, anything they suspect she might be using to cut wires. She knows better than to hide the lizard. During these inspections, he sits in plain sight, watching the intruders with his wizened eye. The neighbours never guess the lizard is the instrument Auntie Paula uses to sabotage the fences, so they get real friendly and tickle beneath his scaly chin.

"What right do they have, acting like the big sheriffs of the acreage?" My outrage stirs sleeping Emery. "Are they afraid the travellers are going to rustle their cattle? They've been watching too much *Bonanza*."

Auntie Paula shows these bitter drunks far too much patience. Put me on the case and their shenanigans would end in a big hurry. Does she forget the army at her disposal? One letter from me will summon all my brothers. They'll abandon their jobs, leave their wives and children in the lurch. I know for a fact they have an arsenal of shotguns buried out here. Let's see how tough these men with chains around their waists walk when it's my brothers standing on Auntie Paula's porch, loaded for bear.

"Love your brothers," Auntie Paula says. "But don't mistake them for guardians of the acreage. Each of them is defending fences somewhere. They care not about the travellers, only the opportunity to shoot people."

I tell Auntie Paula I'll learn to hold a gun. I'll write my most trusted brother asking for a map to the buried weapons. I'm prepared to arm myself and threaten those varmints off her land.

"You're allowed to cut all the wires you want. The neighbour's days of taking things from you are over."

Auntie Paula chuckles as she lifts Emery and smells her cheeks, whispering, "Your silly mother. Talk about watching too much *Bonanza*."

>!<

We share the bed. Emery sleeps beside me, away from Auntie Paula, whose bones can be felt through her skin. They are both as fragile and cold as icicles. The baby would wake with a deathly chill sleeping beside Auntie Paula. We pile cushions on the floor to keep her from rolling off the bed in the night.

In the dark, Auntie Paula becomes confessional. "I think of packing up my little house and moving to the other side of the fences. Meeting the travellers and filling the bowls for them would be so much easier over there."

I picture her slipping through the wires. She has grown so thin the lizard would barely have to chew to allow her passage.

"Selfish thoughts," she says. "What are the travellers supposed to do then? Turn around and go back from where they came?"

Embarrassed, Auntie Paula purges her bad thoughts by writing them down on a piece of paper, burning it, and inhaling all the smoke so no one can discover her faulty thinking.

Auntie Paula's letter inviting me to the acreage came after she discovered a cluster of bloodied travellers. They had not been dead long. They had made a desperate attempt to scale the obstacle, climbing higher than the acreage trees, but the metal had buckled, rolling over, crushing the travellers and imprisoning their bodies inside a tight, spiked coil.

The fences were made treacherous by design; sturdy at the bottom but weak at the top.

"They died holding hands," Auntie Paula says. To cut the bodies down would mean separating their intertwined fingers, and Auntie Paula didn't want to do that. Better to leave them suspended. The birds will clean away the meat and the remaining bones will whistle a cautionary tale.

The neighbours grow frustrated with their inability to locate Auntie Paula's wire cutters, so they change their tactics. Now, they sink their hooks into her food supply, dragging her cured meat out into the dirt for the insects to infest. They smash jars of preserves against the rocks, and for fun they toss canned goods into the air like clay pigeons and take turns shooting them down. Most of the neighbours have embarrassing aim. Even with buckshot, they can't hit airborne cans. In the end, they have to shoot them set on the ground. Everything bleeds out into the dirt; soup, tomato sauce, even salmon oil and cake batter.

The neighbours pride themselves on their twisted benevolence. The sweatiest, smelliest of the louts puts his arm around Auntie Paula and tells her not to worry, they won't let her starve. Each day, they leave her a morsel of food: a bit of sweetmeat, a teaspoon of beans, and a square of bread pressed flat. Only enough food to feed an old woman; nothing for the travellers lucky enough to find their way through her snipped passages.

This new arrangement invigorates the neighbours. They feel they are making headway in their struggle to preserve the fences.

><

The lizard's wheezing keeps me awake, his whistling louder than hollow bones in the wind. The neighbours' food rationing leaves Auntie Paula too weak to carry the lizard across the land. Without wires to chew through, his teeth grow thick and long until he can no longer close his mouth.

In the morning, Auntie Paula cradles the lizard and I follow them outside to the flat rock.

"I offered my ankle, begging him to wear down his teeth on my bones, but he is tired now too. We've spent a long time together."

Auntie Paula lays the lizard down. She sings to him, and tickles his sides, and tells him all of her jokes, anything to make him smile. She succeeds. His tight skin crackles as his mouth curls into one of the biggest grins I've ever seen. Swiftly, Auntie Paula scoops him up and bashes his head against the rock.

"I'm so thankful to have received such a useful companion. I'm glad to know he passed while smiling."

We take the lizard to the kitchen and put him to good use. After Auntie Paula places the body into boiling water, I hold him while she scrapes the scales and skin away. She does so gently, as though shaving a bedridden lover. Once the body is nude, she slits the belly and pulls the lungs free as gracefully as a magician slipping silk scarves from their sleeve. She sets the liver aside, and once the body is hollowed, she chops the meat into mouth-sized squares. I cringe at how close she swings the cleaver to her fingers. The amount of meat in the tail astonishes me.

From the garden, I fetch thyme and celery leaves. "The neighbours thought them weeds," she tells me. "If they knew these had use in the kitchen they would have torn them out."

The pot of lizard meat simmers. We tie tall grass together, cut the ends, and press the sweet milk into the pot. I don't think we'll have enough to make a proper sauce so I offer milk from my own breast, but Auntie Paula assures me we have all the ingredients we need. There is no need to steal food from Emery. Years of observing the travellers have taught her how to adapt.

I carry Emery outside, taking a moment of respite from the sweltering kitchen just as the neighbours' trucks rumble onto the acreage for today's inspection. Auntie Paula's stories of the neighbours' cruelty anger me, and I expect them to be skulking giants, but they look no different from our neighbours back home. Their monstrousness is not visible from the outside.

Auntie Paula joins me on the porch. She welcomes the neighbours wearing a flowing dress that in its day would have been called scandalous. Standing on tiptoes, she holds her palms flat, displaying the lizard's head. For a moment, she reminds me of the painting of the dancing girl and prophet.

The neighbours drop from their trucks cautiously, assuming they are being set up for a trap. They take their time wrapping the chains around their waists, tugging on the rattling links, making sure they are secure before approaching.

"All this time it was the lizard," she confesses. "That's how I cut the wires."

The neighbours crowd around, poking their fingers into the lizard's mouth, prying the jaws apart. Their examination is rough. Disrespectful. Wire shavings are caught between the lizard's teeth, evidence of visits to the fences. The neighbours wink at one another, congratulating themselves on finally putting an end to Auntie Paula's disobedience.

"You starved me out," Auntie Paula admits, her eyes tearful. She gestures to me and Emery. "Now that I've mouths of my own to feed, I can't have you taking all my food away."

The neighbours celebrate having broken her. Back in town, they'll be heralded for finally securing the fences. At last, no more travellers. The acreage breeze pulls the smell of Auntie Paula's cooking onto the porch, and all of a sudden the neighbours aren't in a hurry to leave.

"You will eat with us, and then we will have a truce. Yes?"

The bowls from the cupboard, which Auntie Paula has saved especially for the travellers, are blown clean of dust and dead bugs so she may set them around the table. The neighbours' chain tethers stretch just as far as their place settings. An inch farther and they would have to suck in their beer guts to reach.

When Auntie Paula wrote asking me to help serve the neighbours dinner I felt excited to assist in their downfall. They deserved a gruesome final meal for all their meddling. Together, we'd wrap those chains around their necks and choke them to death. Make them die with their tongues bulging and eyes popped out, leaving behind corpses even less dignified than the crushed travellers on the fences. I wanted baby Emery to witness our retribution and grow up knowing her mother was a woman of action.

"So bloodthirsty," Auntie Paula says of my fantasy, but without judgment for, in her younger days, Auntie Paula also thirsted for blood. Throughout her life she found more than her share, until she nearly drowned in it.

"What do you plan to do?" I asked, disappointed not to see the life squeezed from the neighbours' wretched bodies.

"Something I hope will be more effective."

Auntie Paula bloomed all morning. She confides in me that cooking is the sole physical activity the aging process has not throttled.

"I can no longer dance on the points of my toes, or climb to the highest bough of a tree, or make passionate love to a darling young man." Yet her weak back, stripped throat, and lowered libido have done nothing to inhibit her culinary skills. While her other talents fell away, Auntie Paula's cooking only improved. "In the kitchen, I feel like a mighty ship whose crew is dumping their cargo into the ocean so I may travel lighter and faster."

I ladle generous portions of steaming lizard into the dishes. To prove there is nothing sadistic in the meal, I lick the ladle after each serving, tasting sweet milk and stray scales. Feeling victorious, the neighbours josh and chortle, dipping their fingers into the bowls to scoop up chunks of lizard meat. Auntie Paula placed linen serviettes on the table, but none of the neighbours wipe their hands, preferring to suck the hot juice from their fingers.

Auntie Paula dips her spoon into the same bowl in which she washes her dusty feet, and begins to eat.

At the start of the meal, Auntie Paula's kitchen sounds like a beer hall – rowdy laughter and the singing of old songs – but as the neighbours get closer to the bottom of their bowls they grow quiet. There is no more joking and back-slapping. The only sound is the rapid clanking of their spoons. I watch fascinated as the neighbours lift the bowls to lick the insides clean, the bottoms covering their faces like masks.

The tongue is one of the most sensitive spots on the body, capable of finding a single grain of sand tracked into the mouth. The neighbours have toughened their tongues with years of unfiltered cigarettes and bitter words, yet the tips remain delicate enough to read the names carved into the bottoms of the bowls.

Auntie Paula has fed the travellers for longer than anyone is capable of remembering, and in return each traveller has scratched their name into a bowl. The history of all travellers is stacked within her cupboard, always waiting to be added to. There is room for more names than Auntie Paula will ever know. The bowls rumble louder than ever before, shaking dust from the ceiling. They are angry, and demand to know why they've been starved for so long.

The neighbours leap away from the table and clamp their hands over their mouths. Their tongues recognize many of the names carved into the wood; names that stretch all the way back to the early pioneer days of the acreage, names claimed with great pride nowadays. Many of the neighbours' tongues find their own family name, written decades, perhaps hundreds of years, before by weary travellers thankful to be fed after crossing one of the ugly barricades that have long excluded people from the land.

Muttering excuses, the neighbours rise from the table. *Early day tomorrow. Must get going.* They file outside keeping their heads down, rattling the chains in which they've shackled themselves. Satisfied, Auntie Paula collects the bowls and stacks them in the cupboard, pleased she could see them used one final time after so much idleness.

"Do you think they'll be too ashamed to come back?" I ask.

Auntie Paula holds her arm over the fireplace embers before crawling into bed. She pulls her tattered blankets over herself with such finality they may as well be the lid of her coffin.

"Perhaps not those neighbours, but eventually, their children will come. Someone will always be here to preserve the fences." She sniffs the air, desiring a comforting whiff of Emery's baby skin as she prepares for a sleep that is growing closer and closer to permanent.

"When they do come back," Auntie Paula says, "don't be so quick to dig up your guns. Teach Emery there are other ways to keep the neighbours disarmed."

><

While Auntie Paula and the baby sleep, I strap on her old boots and go for a walk, tearing my jeans on the brambles whose thorns curve like fangs on a cobra. The acreage ground is uneven, full of dips. I marvel at Auntie Paula's persistence and stamina, amazed by how long she made the long and arduous trip to the fences – in the dark, no less.

Structures like these that Auntie Paula has spent her life battling don't stand this long without learning to be devious. More travellers will crash upon their barbs. The duty Auntie Paula passes on to me is difficult. I will fail more often than I will succeed.

In the distance, where the dawn meets the earth, the travellers are already approaching. I kick off my boots and use my bare ankle to fish for a lizard, but there is no one crawling along the ground who will help me tear an opening through the imposing barrier. I panic at the thought of soon being face-to-face with the new arrivals, forced to look them in the eye through twisted metal as I apologize for letting them down.

My remaining years are too great in number to spend in despair. Inspired by Auntie Paula's lizard, I lean forward and bite my first wire. Painful vibrations stab my jaw, but I persist. I grind my molars back and forth, encouraged when the wire begins to slacken, on the verge of breaking. At last, I've found my proper place in this world.

The wire snaps, and I wave my arm, encouraging the travellers to hurry, confident by the time they arrive I'll be prepared to welcome them to Auntie Paula's kitchen.

Recipe submitted by a reader of the Australian newspaper *The Western Mail* in 1938

Goanna (Lizard) Tail with Parsley Sauce

Skin tail and cut into small pieces. Place in a saucepan, and just cover with water. Cook till tender. Make parsley sauce as follows: Boil one pint of water, throw into it one tablespoon finely minced parsley and half a teaspoonful of salt. Then add two ounces flour, mixed to smooth paste in a gill of water. Stir over fire until it thickens. Break into it one or two ounces of butter. Put cooked tail into this. Serve hot.

PHỞ CART NO. 7

Kathy Nguyen

The Turning Wheels of the Food Cart

The college student sat at one of the many cypress picnic tables outside the bar, trying to comfortably situate himself away from the loud crowd currently cheering on the football game playing on the large plasma TV. Ever since the re-emergence of food trucks, the bar had been crowded. It was a humid night. The swirling, foggy smoke emitting from cigarettes, e-cigarettes and cigars, the crowd, the increasingly sweating bodies, and the now compressed space was making the evening more sultry.

He always hated the summer. It wasn't the heat. He was used to the heat. Before permanently relocating to the United States, he was always living in a humid atmosphere. The blistering heats in Vietnam were unbearable. It was like being in contact with fiery flames every single day. Those heated memories were some of his happiest and most miserable.

But tonight, the evening ignited a sense of inner agitation that he rarely experienced. The discomfiting intrusion began after his mother chose one of her favourite near-obsolete cassette tapes. She played it on an old Jensen cassette player his father had bought at the Salvation Army after their archaic player from the '70s finally broke down, having been repaired one too many times every decade. He always listened to those tapes as a kid, but as he grew older he found the songs written about the war repetitive and dull. The messages had the tendency to duplicate each other: soldiers serving their country, deaths, loss of country and identities, relationships broken up due to the war. They were just depressing.

After listening to one of his mother's favourites sing about the rain and the memories dripping from it, stress levels materialized that he didn't know he had. He'd heard that song multiple times and yet it was currently haunting him, the lyrics begging him to dig something from the recesses of his brain, though he shrugged it off as he always did. He shouldn't be bothered by something that couldn't really be remembered, but he was. If it was possible, he would store *all* his memories. The *forgotten* ones. The *former* ones. The *lost* ones. The *erased* ones.

It was just dismal that a song he was impartial to was sparking memories. He didn't care for them. Perhaps after growing up a bit more and immersing himself in different musical genres, he had decided that Vietnamese music was frozen, stuck at that one point in time. There was no progression. Much like his parents.

Food was a different story. Over the years, he witnessed Vietnamese food being co-opted and appropriated by the masses. His parents rarely ate out, thinking their cooking was more authentic and had more cultural identity than the current *food du jour*.

He sipped his Scotch, feeling the burn sliding down his throat. How fitting. Noting the burn abating, he looked at the long line of customers waiting to order food at the *Vietnamese Pickle* food truck.

He sucked in a breath, faintly smelling the fresh scents of toasted baguette and chicken. He was getting hungry. Maybe he would buy a *bá nh mì*. He hadn't eaten one for a while and the aroma was getting to him. The pickled, juicy vegetables were desirable for this season.

"Aren't you going to get any food?" one of his friends, Allen, asked, mouth full of Korean barbequed pork and crunchy lettuce.

He nodded. "I'm thinking of ordering a *bá nh mì*. Do you want anything?"

Allen swallowed, followed by a quick rinse of the mouth with some ice-cold beer. "I'm good. Thanks."

He nodded again and left the table quietly, avoiding bumping into other people as he walked away from his uncomfortable seat.

Just as he was about to approach the *Vietnamese Pickle*, an aromatic smell of spices and herbs pleasantly struck his nostrils. The sensation wasn't unwelcome, but it was indeed strange. He looked around to see which food truck was emitting the smell, but it wasn't coming from the food trucks or the bar.

The smell was coming from the streets, across from the food trucks, the strong fragrance directing him to the location. He found it strange, unsettling even. There were at least a dozen food trucks across the street, yet this bicycle was parked at a dimly lit corner of an alley. It was like a horror scene waiting to happen. Against his better judgement, he decided to approach the person, curious to know what the vendor was selling.

Once he was in proximity to the bicycle food cart, he noticed a white sign with bold red lettering:

Phở Cart No. 7

He observed his surroundings, momentarily wondering if there were cart numbers 1-6 here. He then observed the bicycle food cart. It was nothing special, nor was it overly decorative like the food trucks, but that may have been due to the size difference between the two. The bicycle food cart reminded him of the carts from which his father used to peddle when they were in Vietnam. His father had sold ice cream when he quit school to take care of his family. As he grew older, he began selling various popular cold drinks like *cà phê đá* [1] and *cà phê s a đá*.[2] On some special occasions, his father would let him ride along, helping him sell his drinks.

As with most Vietnamese bicycle food carts, a small cart was attached to the bicycle. The bicycle was rusty-looking, lacking the dull shine of a new bicycle, as if weathering the most extreme outside conditions. He saw an old silver pot, steam coming out from the lid. The smell was engulfing his nostrils once again, and he could feel his hunger increasing as the fire assisted in keeping the broth hot and alive.

He wasn't sure if the food cart was attended by anyone, so he walked around it and saw a waifish, pale person fanning the fire with one of those palm bamboo hand fans.

The owner of the bicycle food cart must have heard his shoes hitting the sidewalk gravel. She stood up from behind the cart, looking at him as if she expected his presence.

He observed the cart owner. She looked like a young school girl, especially with her all-white ensemble: a long

---

[1] Vietnamese iced coffee.
[2] Vietnamese iced milk coffee.

white skirt, a white T-shirt, black sandals, and a typical white apron. The image in front of him was haunting. It reminded him of one of his mother's old class photos, where the women wore tailored yet flowing white *á o dà i*[1] as their standard school uniforms. He marvelled that the girl – or woman – looked like a child, yet she had deep black bags under her eyes as if she was awake at every hour fanning the fire so its longevity would maintain the broth, and her black hair was salted with noticeable white strands of hair.

"Can I help you?" asked the woman, her voice surprisingly deep and mature for her stature, halting his appraisal of her.

He swallowed, the smell of the broth getting to him again. "Um, yes. If you're open now, I would like to order a bowl of *phở*?"

The woman smiled. "Yes, of course. I'm only making beef-based broth tonight. Will that be all right with you?"

He simply nodded. He'd eaten more bowls of *phở* than he could count, and though the fragrance of this broth had a unique scent that wasn't comparable to past bowls, he was questioning if this *phở* was actually different, especially as more *phở* restaurants were opening and it was becoming popular comfort food for the masses.

Did *phở* have its own identity? Or was it all the same now? He decided to ask. "Is your *phở* different than the others?"

She never looked at him, eyes and hand focusing on stirring the clear broth. "The recipe for *phở* changes. It's prepared based on the cook's preferences."

---

[1] A Vietnamese traditional dress women wore with trousers. The white *á o dà i* was a school uniform in many Vietnamese schools.

That's true, he thought. Before he could ask another question, she told him, "I have a special ingredient for each customer."

He didn't understand and read her ingredients list.

> *Phở Ingredients*
> *Chicken, pork, or beef*
> *Two gallons of water*
> *Big onion*
> *Ginger*
> *Two dried fructus tsaoko*
> *Four to five dried anises*
> *One big daikon*
> *Salt*
> *Sugar*
> *One package of dried*
>   *rice noodles*
> *Additional herbs or*
>   *special ingredients*

"For you," she began after stirring, "it's from the streams that collected rainwater from the river of Sông Hương."[1]

He still didn't understand; he had never visited Sông Hương. Either she was trying to be clever or she was just a strange person. He remained quiet, not wanting to disrespect her and her cooking process.

She began assembling his bowl, pouring a generous amount of the beef broth into a big black bowl, a striking contrast to her outfit. She then grabbed a handful of long strands of translucent rice noodles from another bowl and placed them on top, slowly allowing them to bathe in the

---

[1] A river in Thừa Thiên-Huế, Vietnam.

broth. She neatly arranged thinly cut strips of beef on top of the slowly soaked noodles; lastly, she added small layers of what seemed to be freshly picked onions, Thai basil, bean sprouts, and mint into the bowl.

She looked up at him and smiled, eyes dancing with mischief, and set the bowl on a small table near the cart, with an extra plate of side herbs and lime and bottles of hoisin sauce and chili sauce.

His hand was shaking in anticipation as he squeezed the juice from the lime. He added some chili and hoisin sauce and mixed the ingredients in his white Chinese soup bowl. He took a sip of the broth, immediately tasting the fattiness of the beef and the charred ginger, but then noticed a headache forming. It wasn't all that painful, but the tension increased as the broth dissolved into his system. After a few painful, tight bands formed around his head, he breathed and relaxed, trying to savor the taste. It worked; the tension headache disappeared momentarily. He picked up a piece of beef with his chopsticks, entangled it with some noodles and chewed thoughtfully.

Although he felt the tension headache again, he concentrated on eating. The sweet broth and the tender beef were delicious and he wanted to experience the flavours rather than his bodily pains. As he sipped his broth again, he closed his eyes, seeing multiple moving phosphenes. An image entered his line of vision. It was 1955, as indicated by the wall calendar, precariously hanging by a small hook, and he – though much older – was smoking a cigarette watching the rain, his other hand holding a pencil as he lightly tapped an oak desk.

Was that him?

His parents had always told him stories about reincarnation – parables he never believed. After death, if spirits are able to enter reincarnation, then their previous lives disappear as they are escorted to their impending new lives.

He opened his eyes, disconcerted. He knew better than to ask about her identity. Instead, he asked, "Why allow me to relive my former life?"

She fanned herself with the palm bamboo hand. "People, animals, and things are always migrating, or immigrating, if you will, to various locations. They're drifters, always moving and transferring themselves. Even after death, your spirit wanders to a different place, creating new memories. Why not just collect memories then and accumulate your various lives' memories? Can one grow and change from living different lives but maintaining their memories? Will things remain the same or change? And most importantly, why follow traditions and rituals when the world is always evolving?"

He couldn't think of an answer, but continued to ask questions. "So, is this a punishment?"

She shook her hand. "You came to my food cart and my job is just to make a bowl of *phở* to your liking. Food and memories will follow you, always lingering."

He noticed she didn't answer his question and promptly followed up with another question, "So why are you here?"

"To disrupt the cycle."

"With *phở*?"

"And why not? People drink a bowl of broth to continue the one cycle to which some of us acquiesce."

He didn't answer nor did he question her further. He looked down at his half-eaten bowl of *phở*, wondering if food today was made to recreate memories.

A Wandering Cat's Bowl

The tortoiseshell cat was sleeping under a stranger's car as the rain was pouring. She didn't know its exact location, but right now she needed to rest after running away from that shelter. She didn't want to end up like her friends.

The cat didn't understand her current predicament. She had never had a place to call home. She was found with a cut mouth as she tried to eat leftover wet food from an opened can from a trash bin, and taken to the shelter. Weeks passed, months flew by, and finally three years. People kept passing by, but never stopping for her, adopting other kittens and cats. Slowly, she approached the expiry date when she would be deemed unadoptable. It was especially difficult for her to witness her friends slowly disappearing from their cages. Some were happily adopted, while some slept forever.

She didn't want that – she wasn't given a choice – so she decided to escape when possible.

She woke up shortly after the last raindrop fell on the soaking ground. Hungry again, she decided to come out of hiding and hunt for food. Her last meal had been scraps of bread left for the birds at the park.

The cat slowly walked around the busy streets, carefully noting to remain calm as cars zipped past. She stopped near one of the strip malls in the area, most of which were closed at this time of night. Maybe there was food around the stores.

She found some soggy French fries on the ground and started nibbling on them, but was immediately alerted when she heard the heavy chiming of metal chains and pedalling. She immediately tried to hide under a nearby bench.

The sounds stopped, but the cat didn't dare come out of hiding. She saw a shadow getting closer and finally strands of long black hair became visible. She growled and hissed, hoping the unwanted intruder would leave her alone.

A pair of dark eyes stared back at them. "You're hairier than I remember," a woman commented as she tried to stroke her head, but she hissed again. The woman, undeterred, tried to coax her out. As the woman reached toward her, wanting to touch her head, she scratched the woman's pale hand, grabbing it, and biting it.

The woman did not seem fazed by the attack and dramatically sighed. "You hurt my feelings. Don't leave." Her face disappeared, as did her shadow. The cat, however, was distrustful, knowing she probably wouldn't give up. She saw the woman's shadow again and resumed hissing, only to stop when she smelled something delicious.

The cat knew the woman was trying to entice her, but it was effective. She could smell seafood! Begrudgingly, the cat crawled out from under the bench and saw the woman sitting on the ground with a bowl in her hand.

The woman half smiled, beckoning the cat to come over. At that exact moment the cat knew she could trust the woman – she had food after all – and excitedly trotted over, purring and rubbing her head on her knees.

"Now *you're* a lovebug. I wondered what *their* collective decision was, forcing you to take this form in your current life – excuse me, lives – wandering around the streets like this."

The cat didn't understand, but she meowed and purred. It was rare she received human affection. She couldn't even remember the last time she had been petted.

"I know you probably shouldn't eat this type of food in your form, but – you know me by now – here." She offered her some shrimp, which the cat gladly licked and chewed, savoring the taste. Freshly cooked fish was certainly better than the kibble and processed wet food she was given at the shelter. The cat licked her mouth and looked at the woman, eyes asking to be fed more. And she complied. After each bite of shrimp and lobster, the cat felt uneasy, eyes slowly blinking. She looked at the woman, who looked her in the eye and said, "The shrimp and lobster are from the night skies of the Mũi Né beach.[1] Especially caught for you."

The cat wondered what she was talking about. Instead of answering, the woman got up and got a black bowl of what the cat thought was water, but the hot, fresh smell of the broth told her otherwise. After multiple licks, the cat stared at the woman's eyes, observing their own reflection in her orbs.

The cat remembered being a hawk, preying on smaller animals. At one point, she took a child's small kitten away as they were running from fires and explosions, ignoring the animal's cries of fear. This became a repeated cycle for the hawk; he needed nourishment somehow.

She slowly blinked her eyes, recognizing the woman. She meowed, as if communicating to her that she finally understood her present predicament.

The woman looked at the cat and sighed, stroking her head. "I shouldn't do this, but I guess I can feed and take care of you until your ninth life is up. I guess this is the reason *she* and the rest of *them* believe that a new life should

---

[1] A beach resort/town in Southeast Vietnam.

begin with new memories. The emotional attachment to the previous ones can hinder the present, final conclusions." The woman smiled, but the cat noticed the forced tightness of that smile.

The cat didn't meow, understanding they'd meet again in the future. And she would be in different forms then. The silence engulfing them was welcoming and comfortable for now.

The Moving Gears of the Factory

Every Friday evening after her shift, the factory worker would go downtown to eat her dinner. She didn't enjoy the busy streets, the loud overplayed music, the constant chattering and shouting. It didn't matter, since she was used to shutting out sounds. The crushing humming of the rotors, stators, fans, and vibrating panels of the electrical machines permeated throughout the factory where she worked. She ignored the crushing, blasting, sounds of metal-cutting and the milling-machine grinders. She was slowly losing her ability to hear. She could feel herself slowly deteriorating, feel the aches and pains of her aging body.

The factory worker didn't mind. To her, the noises were similar to the blasts she had heard in the war. The metal of the guns, bullets falling to the ground. The noises she wished to forever forget but couldn't – but she could choose to shut out other noises that reminded her of those times. Which was one of the many reasons she didn't enjoy downtown, but she did enjoy one bicycle food cart, Phở Cart No. 7, operated by that odd woman.

She had discovered the quaint, charmless food cart by accident. A co-worker invited her to a late dinner at a local diner. The factory worker was chewing her savory spinach crêpes thoughtfully – it was rare she ate out – when she noticed a bicycle food cart – identical to the ones she had eaten from in Vietnam – outside. She didn't think much of it until she bid her co-worker goodbye and walked to her car. It was then she noticed the smell of *phở* and followed the trail of steam produced from the simmering pot.

After that Friday night, it became a weekly ritual for her to eat a bowl of the woman's *phở*. It was familiar, comforting, and nostalgic, even after she retired, satisfied that she could live out her years without extraneous noises that sporadically triggered nostalgia, maintained that ritual. She remembered the first bowl. Eating it, she had experienced hallucinations of another's life – a person doing something awful, something she would never do in this lifetime. But she had instantly forgotten the details of the flashback as soon as she scooped the bowl clean. She had also noticed the woman's surprised face, but she didn't inquire.

They rarely conversed anyway.

It happened every Friday night, though. She experienced a different sensation and flashback with each bowl. It was incomprehensible, frustrating even.

She finally made her way to the food cart, where the woman was always fanning the boiling *phở* broth. Her food cart was always parked in the same place, at the same position. It was easy to locate her. Why was she normally the sole customer there, during the night? Was *phở* not popular anymore?

The woman stopped fanning. "Hi," she said. "The chicken-beef broth is almost finished. Do you mind waiting for a few minutes?"

She mumbled a quiet yes. The only thing that kept time moving was waiting. She was always waiting, as was everyone else.

She observed the woman's actions. Her movements were precise and purposeful, as if the motions had been performed the exact same way for many years. She couldn't ignore the fact that the woman's movements and gestures were consistent. Her predictable rhythm never missed a beat, even as she chopped the daikon into the right sized pieces.

"What's the special ingredient tonight?" she asked the woman.

The woman sipped broth, nodding in approval of the taste. "Nothing special, just some *ngò*."[6]

She was disappointed. The woman prided herself on singular ingredients. Each bowl tasted distinctively different, yet carried her back to her mother's quaint kitchen in Sài Gòn, Vietnam. But tonight's special ingredient was nothing but some pieces of ubiquitous *ngò*, maybe plucked from the woman's garden or recently purchased from the farmer's market. Perhaps tonight's bowl would be her first bowl of disenchantment, that or the woman was losing her touch. Even so, her tongue slipped and asked, "Is that it? Just *ngò*?"

The woman finally looked into the factory worker's eyes; the emotions behind her gaze unfathomable. The woman

---

[1] Cilantro.

was difficult to read, seemingly robotic at times. She humorously replied, "Yes, just *ngò*. But *ngò* picked in a family's garden before it was destroyed in 1975."

She could hear her heart palpitating after hearing the woman's response. The words elicited disjointed memories from the last five Fridays. She just didn't know why. It was also absurd that the *ngò* the woman was using was from 1975. There was no conceivable way the woman could have preserved it for several decades.

"Here," the woman said, interrupting her rearranged memories as she arranged the *ngò* around the edges of the bowl, making sure the broth would not fully soak the leaves. "A bowl of chicken-beef broth."

She wordlessly took the bowl but bowed as a sign of gratitude. The glistening fat at the top was making her salivate. After putting in some chili sauce, she took a sip of the broth, that one spoon taking her back to pre-1975. Using the chopsticks to pick up a piece of brisket, she put it in her mouth, savoring the tender, chewy meat. With each slurp of noodles, she experienced a sort of tunnel vision, seeing images of a person that might have been her, wandering as a spirit in several locations. She ate a piece of fatty tendon.

Maybe it was the summer heat, but the hot bowl of *phở* created a sweltering environment, much like the factory she used to work in. She piled some noodles, broth, and meat onto her sticky Chinese soup spoon and slurped the contents. And each time, she remembered a ghost that resembled her, waiting in front of a figure – one who looked threatening and powerful – informing the ghost of their karma and human errors. After each transgression her life was cut short by half until her debts were paid in full.

She looked at the woman fanning herself as she stared at nothing, understanding her transaction was complete.

The next morning, the retired factory worker passed away in her sleep. Her spirit found its way back to the realm of the dead, waiting in line for her broth, a prerequisite for her to advance to a new life.

Oil Change

The robot found their way to Phở Cart No. 7. After the changes in the world, even though robots were emerging as citizens alongside humans, figures like them were discriminated against. They co-existed, even if it was compulsory. Alternative options were not given to humans.

Even if the skies were no longer clear, the world was encompassed in a perpetual mist, and robots and machines had taken over the job market, the woman and her bicycle food cart remained.

The robot recognized her. They always reunited, each time they changed their form. It seemed inevitable that they would meet again in this changing world. Even if the robot wanted to trace her whereabouts, the woman would always beat them to it. She was good at appearing near the end.

The woman wiped the familiar black bowl, set it down to dry, and watched the robot, stealthily and steadily approaching her.

"Hello," the robot greeted. "I am sure you remember me."

The woman blinked, a smile slowly forming. "Yes."

The robot looked at the recipe. It had stayed the same.

"I've taken many forms and yet you still look the same," the robot continued. "Is this our last meeting?"

The robot noticed the woman's smile was slowly disappearing. "I'm afraid so. Everything has changed so drastically. Some bodies are unable to go through the cycle again. Times are different now."

The robot had predicted this outcome. Though they were not sure why this current mechanized body was chosen for them in this life, they realized that once their system failed, their consciousness, too, would disappear. The company would no longer download their consciousness as newer prototypes and advancing thinking agents were more desirable than them.

It was 2072. Of course, everything – like them – was changing and replaceable. It was also the reason their body was oxidized; the brownish stains were not attractive. The robot's company dumped the obsolete forms onto a truck, driving them to a location to be crushed and obliterated. That still didn't deter them.

"Can I make a request?" the robot asked the woman.

The woman expected it. "Yes?"

"Can you preserve my oil, just in case?"

"I can."

"And can you make me my last bowl of *phở*?"

The woman nodded. Without having to speak, the two companions knew what the special ingredient for this bowl was: premium machine oil.

Conclusion: Mạnh Bà's[1] Broth

She closely observed Mạnh Bà as she gathered the herbs she collected earlier from the crystal-clear ponds. Mạnh Bà was measuring the exact ingredients, sprinkling the herbs in the boiling pot of broth. The broth was prepared for the souls who entered Vọng Hương Đài, awaiting reincarnation, to drink before they entered reincarnation. After drinking the broth, their memories would immediately be erased as they floated to the Vong Xuyên River.

She never understood why a person – in all their multiple incarnations – had to forget their previous memories just to forge new ones in a new life. It was a vicious cycle. Why did they not get to decide whether their memories should be removed? Why must it be a binding life sentence in hell?

Times and people will adapt and change; life cycles are structured pillars. As someone who was present without any form of existence or known identity, she hoped the unseen could live on through memories.

Phở

Cooking the protein bones:
• Choose any of the following proteins: chicken, pork, or beef – may be combined.
• Clean the proteins.
• Peel one big onion and garlic, grill them, and place them at the bottom of the stockpot. Add ground pepper.
• Cut proteins into large pieces and put them in a stockpot.

---

[1] In Chinese folklore, she is known as Mèng Pó, or the Lady of Forgetfulness.

- Add one-two gallons of water.
- Bring to boil at medium-high heat.
- Cover stockpot. Leave to boil on simmer for 3-4 hours.

Making the phở broth:
- Drain the stockpot that cooked the proteins — only contents are needed.
- Place bones, ginger, onion, along with 2 dried fructus tsaoko, 4-5 dried pod stars of anise, one big daikon, a pinch of salt and sugar, in stockpot.
- Add two gallons of water.
- Simmer on low for 4 to 6 hours.
- Occasionally taste to add more salt or pepper into stockpot.
- Strain sauce.

Rice Noodles:
- Place rice noodles in large bowl filled with room temperature water. Soak for 1 minute.
- Boil a large pot of hot water and place noodles in the pot for another minute. Simmer pot.

Serving:
- Put rice noodles into a bowl. Pour hot broth over the noodles.
- Add protein. Broth should still be hot enough to cook the protein. Serve with any herbs such as bean sprouts, cilantro, lime wedges, etc.

THE CATERER

JOE DAVIES

I ground out my cigarette on the sidewalk before I rounded the corner. I hardly smoke at all any more, but for some reason the hardest one to give up has been the one just before I go in for a job. The anticipation is nearly always worse than the reality. Once I'm in the thick of things, I'm usually fine.

The hallway leading to the shop is ridiculously long, especially since it's the last door. I could come in the back, through the parking lot and down the loading ramp, but now and then I get stuck talking to someone if I come in that way and, in any case, the office and holding room are just inside the hall entrance, so I usually enter that way.

In the holding room there were five others. Two I recognized, three I didn't. I gave my name at the window and I swear I'd barely settled my kit on the floor next to one of the chairs before my name was called. This happens quite often. Sometimes I think they're just waiting for me to come in. As I headed for the door with the frosted glass, I could feel the eyes of the others on my back.

The office was warm and Rita was there behind her desk, looking, as always, in complete control. It's a talent. She held out the hat and I reached in and drew out one of the slips of paper and unfolded it.

"Oh no," I said. "Not again. I had this one last week."

"What?" she said. "What is it?"

"Last supper! I hate them."

"Why? What happened last week?"

"It was very sad. One of those houses out in a subdivision somewhere. The mother had cancer and they'd set up a hospital bed for her right in the living room. I mean, it was nice they'd worked it so she could be around for her kids, but it was so hard to watch. She could barely make it to the table."

"Okay," said Rita. "I'll let you off this once. Have another shot. Put it back in. But if it comes out again…"

"I know," I said. "I'll do it. But it'd be nice to get something a little less intense. A retirement, something like that."

I reached in and pulled out another and unfolded it.

"Hey," I said. "This is okay. All right. I'll do this."

"Good," said Rita. "Go on in then."

I passed through into the change area and suited up, then went into the prep kitchen where about a dozen other cooks were busy getting their own projects ready to go: some, like me, just starting out, others already packing up or loading into one of the vans. I recognized almost everyone, but it was unusual, there wasn't one I knew well enough to talk to. Quite often, if I can get talking, everything seems to go quickly and I'm done and all set to go before I know it.

Sometimes I have to think for a while, wander through the walk-in coolers looking at all the food and wait for inspiration, but I knew the instant I'd seen the slip of paper what I was going to do, and it was easy. It would be magic. Still, there were a few things to pack up. I grabbed one of the crates and heaved in a cast-iron frying pan and a rubber spatula, and I tried three pepper grinders before I found one that cracked pepper the way I wanted. There are some things you can trust the average home to have, that is, if you're cooking in a home: stove, fridge, running water, that sort of thing. But surprisingly, or maybe not, you can't be absolutely certain about a thing like a toaster, so one of those went into the crate as well. Also needed were: a small mixing bowl, a whisk, juicer, dish towel, cloths, apron, serving tray (one with short collapsible legs), plate, knife, fork, glass, cloth napkin, a small cooler and a plastic bag for waste. As for the food: two eggs, milk, butter, salt, half a baguette, two strawberries and three oranges.

I was done before nearly everyone who'd been in the room when I arrived.

My favourite van was already out, the grey-green one, so I settled for bright orange. It was just in from an oil change, which I figured was a good sign.

I usually enjoy the drive. Once I've got everything together, once it's all in the van and I know where I'm going and how to get there, the drive becomes that interval when I can take a deep breath and settle myself, not so much taking stock of things as letting them coalesce or come together. If it isn't in the van, if I haven't brought it, it isn't a part of whatever will happen.

>·<

I knew the part of town I was going to. I knew it well. I'd lived there before and loved it, but still was surprised how small the house was. I'd forgotten how small they sometimes come.

There was no need to knock at the door. Three people were out on the front porch. Two elderly men, standing there looking out into the street, talking quietly, and a young woman sitting on the bottom step. She swung herself to the side as I began to carry my things into the house. Another woman, a little older, just inside the door, welcomed me and took me to the kitchen, saying, "He's here, the chef's here."

Three other women were seated at a small kitchen table, squashed into a corner. I was asked if I needed anything and said I was pretty sure I could figure it all out from here.

One of the women said that was good, since no one there knew the house at all, which I thought strange.

I went back out to the van to get the rest of my things, the cooler, my own kit, and saw another man standing on the other side of the street, shuffling about, also quite obviously absorbed by what was going on in the little house.

When I went back in, I was introduced to one of the midwives. The father was there as well, talking on the phone, saying how it was the most amazing thing. It'd all happened in the bathroom. He'd cut the umbilical cord himself and right away his new little girl was handed to him, all waxy and purple and remarkably quiet, eyes already wide open and alert.

Listening to him, it was hard not to smile.

But it was time to get to work.

First, I cleared a little space on the small kitchen counter and set out my things. I plugged in the toaster and put the pan on the stove, which unfortunately was electric instead of gas. I suppose I could have brought a butane burner, but it was too late now. I set out the mixing bowl and the juicer and got my cutting board and knife from my own kit. Then I started pulling things from my cooler. I mixed the eggs with a little milk and salt. I juiced the oranges and poured them into the glass I'd brought. I sliced a few pieces off the baguette and slid them into the toaster but didn't put them down right away. Once my pan was hot and the butter had melted and was starting to sizzle, I pushed down the bread to toast. The eggs went into the cast-iron pan, and using the spatula I slowly swirled along the bottom, keeping the eggs from becoming firm. I turned the heat down and removed the pan a couple of times and when I was satisfied with their consistency, the eggs went onto the plate. Up came the toast, right on time. I buttered it and arranged it on the plate. I sliced a strawberry and fanned it out on the plate in the crook between the toast and eggs. Then I unfolded the legs from the little tray, loaded on the plate, the cutlery, the napkin and juice, ground a little pepper over the eggs and asked to be led to the new mother.

>·<

She was in a tiny bedroom, upstairs. The bed took up nearly the whole room. And it was quiet. Momentously quiet. There, in the middle of all those pillows, the duvet and quilts and baby blankets, a new life and its mother.

The mother was on her side, staring at the little bundle next to her.

"Hello," I whispered, my entry into the room having seemingly gone unnoticed. "I've brought food."

The mother stirred and looked at me, then slowly worked herself into a sitting position and flattened the bedding around her. She looked tired and full of wonder; almost glowing with life.

I set the tray over her lap. She looked at the food as if it was something she'd forgotten existed, something wonderful. She forked some of the eggs into her mouth and closed her eyes and slowly said "Mmmmm," a sound every cook loves to hear.

I looked at the bundle nestled close to the mother. The eyes were open just slightly. Not looking, not seeing, but there, switched on.

"A little girl, is that right?" I said quietly.

The mother nodded.

"Any name yet?"

The mother shook her head, a piece of toasted baguette in her hand. "No," she said. "Nothing yet. But I can't imagine it'll be a problem."

I nodded.

"She's very pretty," I said, and excused myself.

><

Downstairs I tidied up. There were people everywhere. A midwife came up to me and said, "Eggs?" I nodded and she gave me a thumbs up. "Perfect," she said.

A moment later another woman leaned over and whispered in my ear. "Be careful if you have to use the freezer," she said. "The placenta's in there."

"Oh," I said. "It's okay. I won't have to. But thanks."

I took what I could back out to the van and saw that there was still the one man standing there on the other side of the road. He seemed somehow both out of place and to belong.

Back inside I was cornered by an elderly woman who wanted to know the best way to go about making Yorkshire pudding. I told her I couldn't say. I liked it but had never made it myself.

"Can't you guys make just about anything?" she said.

"Just about," I said, "Except for Yorkshire pudding, it seems."

I was warned twice more by two other people about the placenta in the freezer.

The new father shook my hand and said thanks. I offered him my congratulations and told him I supposed it was likely the place would never feel the same. "That," he said, "is precisely what we're counting on."

A moment later one of the many women came down carrying my tray. I'd been about to go up and get it myself but was grateful I didn't have to.

The woman handed it to me and said, "I've been instructed to tell you that that was the best meal ever cooked on earth."

"Thanks," I said, laughing. "Thanks for passing that on."

"No problem."

Quietly, I gathered the last of my things and slipped away.

But as I was about to start the van the man who'd been standing on the other side of the street came up to the van window. I rolled it down.

"Boy or girl?" he asked.

"Girl," I said.

The man nodded. "And where…. Where was it born?"

"I think I heard someone say in the bathroom."

"Really?" He looked grave for some reason. "Thank you," he said, and handed me an envelope.

When I first started this work, I was told I would sometimes be tipped, and to just smile and say thank you.

So, though I was a bit confused, that's what I did.

"It's my house," the man chipped in, for some reason feeling the need to explain himself. "I've no family. I...I just...Thank you."

And he wandered back to the other side of the street, once more taking up his spot on the curb.

I waved to him and pulled away.

>·<

I didn't look in the envelope until I was back at the shop. I never do. It's not superstition exactly. I just like to think of myself as having patience.

Inside was $200. Much more than I usually see. I have been tipped more, though. Still, it was a little surprising. Somehow the size of the tip didn't seem to go with the size of the house.

>·<

While I was changing I pulled open the wrong locker, someone else who didn't use a lock. There was nothing unusual inside, just clothes, and really I didn't look except to confirm it was the wrong locker. But unexpectedly intruding on someone's privacy like that, even though they weren't there, even though there was nothing to see, there was something unsettling about it. And I thought, isn't it weird? I brush up against all sorts of vulnerability in my work, but all it takes is one unlicensed glimpse into someone else's closet and I become all ashamed. Strange, the lines we draw in the sand.

Scrambled Eggs

Ingredients:
- 2 eggs
- I ounce milk
- Salt
- Pepper
- Butter
- 2 slices of any desired bread
- Strawberries

Preparation:
• Break eggs in a small stainless steel bowl. Add milk and salt. Whisk until blended.
• Begin toasting slices of bread. (The next step – cooking the eggs – is unlikely to take longer than this toasting.)
• Turn stovetop gas or stove element to high. Melt a judicious amount of butter in a cast-iron pan. Before the butter begins to brown, remove from heat, tip egg mixture into pan and stir vigorously with a rubber spatula, being sure the eggs do not adhere to bottom of pan. Reapply heat as needed to achieve the preferred consistency – the exact balance of firm and runny, the elusive gustatory ideal, is often hard to attain and some say can only be achieved when the cook is in love.
• Tip cooked eggs on plate, add black pepper as desired. Butter toast and arrange next to eggs along with slices of strawberry. Serve immediately.

OFFERINGS

Nathan Adler

I watch as Zilpah sets the spirit plate precariously on the edge of the deck railing and beats the welcome mat with a wooden spoon to shake off dust and debris. The spirit plate contains a small offering of what we'd had for dinner that evening, and a pinch of tobacco.

The branches of the willow tree sway gently in the breeze, drone of insects coming to life now that spring has finally sprung. Dragonflies zip by on iridescent wings, the metallic sheen of their bodies almost mechanical. Crickets creak. The sound of rushing water from the creek drifts from the back of our lot, high flow with the run-off from yesterday's thunderstorm.

"Why do you put that plate out every night?" I look up from *Tuck Everlasting,* the book I've been reading. I speak loudly so my great-grandmother can hear; Zilpah is now well into her eightieth winter, and she is a bit hard of hearing.

"For the manidook. The spirits. This is their land too. Better to have friends. Better not to make enemies. Mchi-manidoosh."

"Rats!" Zephyr exclaimed. "That's who she's feeding. Rats and squirrels, which are basically just rats with bigger tails." Zeph has her hair pinned up into two separate Bjork-like Princess-Leia buns, her sleeves rolled up like the *We Can Do It!* feminist propaganda posters to reveal a constellation of ink swirling across her skin. Ojibwe florals and geometrics reminiscent of my mother's beadwork. But only a simple diamond stud in one nostril. She is dressing down today. The spade flashes as she digs up the small herb garden she's taken to tending this last year. Basil. Rosemary. Sweetgrass. Sage. Grandmother Zephyr is proud of her status as a 40-something-year-old grandmother.

It's been over a year now since my brother Zachaeus drowned, leaving us a household of women. My mother Zoe, my grandmother Zephyr, my great-grandmother Zilpah, and me: Zaude. I wonder abstractly if there is something unnatural or witchy about being a family of women, although I suppose Uncle Zeamus still counts and he visits often. I helped him build the deck last summer; the wood is still green. It has a nice shingled awning that provides shade, and it has quickly become our new favourite part of the house during the warm months.

I watch a ladybug with black polka dots on a red lacquer sheen of nail-polish; it waddles across the green lumber beneath my lawn chair. Lady flaps her wings as if about to take to the air. I raise the old-school, 35mm film camera that is almost permanently strapped around my neck – never know when you're going to stumble across that perfect, impossible shot – and you never will unless you're ready. Lady rises into the air, and oddly seems to hover in place just long enough for me to adjust the focus ring and snap the shot. A flare from the sun arcs through the frame to create an interesting lensing effect, like a small halo, through the fragile under-wing that is usually protected beneath the harder shell of the elytra, the garden and sky a turquoise-and-lime blur in the background. I'll have to wait until the film is developed to see how the shot turns out though. Like I said. Old school.

I see the shadow of my mother through the screen door. Zoe peers out, but doesn't join us on the sunny patio, preferring to stay indoors. Can't say I blame her. Some days I feel the same way. Some days I refuse to get out of bed. Some days I think I'd be better off dead... I know my brother wouldn't want that though, for me to be so sad I can't even enjoy the beauty of the day. I don't call to my mother. I know that tomorrow it can just as easily be me, unable to face the beauty of the day, life going on even after one life came to a stop. Today I am determined to enjoy what joy there is to be had while the getting is good. Besides, we'll all be dead eventually, what's the rush?

>·<

Out on the lake, with Zeamus.

Paddling paddling paddling. Once we get out of the shallows, Zeamus drops the outboard motor and the engine propels us over the surface of the lake, cresting the peak of each wave. Beautiful day. Quintillions of ovoid refractions of light, sparkling like rising campfire embers in the sun. The wind whips my hair in a frenzy so I gather the loose strands at the back of my head, the stretchy elastic fabric of the band held in my lips. I've lost more than one Jays cap to the drink, and Zach's are too precious to me to risk losing – we've already lost so much to this lake. But this lake, it is our life, it is our home: intellectually I know the sparkling surface holds no malice; on the contrary, Auntie Zelda always says the land loves us.

"She is our mother. She loves us."

But maybe it is all physics? Atoms colliding like a game of pool, and if the angle is just right, the particle will sink. Math and geometry, no emotions required. Is a world of indifference less lovely than a world infused with relationality? No. It's definitely just as lovely. That doesn't make it any less painful. Or deadly. If you sink beneath the waves you'll drown. If it is -30 the blood will freeze in your veins. Facts. No gills. Physics. Not love.

Once we hit the open water past the floating islands off Drinker's Point, Zeamus cuts the engine and we drift with the islands, bobbing as the sunlight drenches us. Photons like a physical force. Zeamus pulls out his papers and rolls himself a doob with a rustling of dry organics. The heady smell of marijuana drifts across, pang-inducing, the way Zoe's savoury *mooz Bourguignon* elicits hunger. It's like *boeuf bourguignon* except with moose meat instead of beef. Mooz being the Ojibwe word for moose, basically the same word since the English borrows the word. Not many moose in Europe. I don't usually like pot, it makes me too anxious. It just doesn't have the same effects that Zeamus describes. Euphoria, relaxation, and calm. When Zeamus offers I take the smallest possible hoot and quickly pass it back. Microdose.

"Do you ever get tired of living here?" I ask.

Zeamus raises his hands, palms open, and twists as if to take in the surrounding beauty, his silver eyes looking over the edges of his purple-tinted John Lennon glasses, twist of greying goatee sprouting from his chin like a mini wizard-beard.

"I mean – don't you get tired of being the only one? Don't you want to live in the big city with all those city gays?" And Zeamus laughs.

"There's more of us around than you'd think."

"Really?" I raise an eyebrow. The Rez isn't exactly Gay Central Station. Though traditional values actually celebrate sexuality and gender-fluidity, Christian values hadn't left our territory entirely unmarked; there are enough close-minded folks both on the Rez and in the town of Cheapaye as there are in any other rural area.

"Don't worry about me, I do alright." Zeamus winks one eye over the top of his lenses.

"Really, who are you dating then?" I couldn't believe the beaders' circle hadn't kept me in the loop.

"Well, *dating* might be too strong of a word…"

"Who?"

"Well, there's that Fannon fellow." The skin at the corners of his eyes crinkled in crow's feet, silver eyes twinkling through purple lenses.

"Ogers? Edna's nephew?"

"Yep."

"Haanh. But not dating-dating?"

"Weeell. We'll see."

>।<

Zilpah passed. I miss her. I miss her blaring TV. So loud it makes the walls shake. I miss the way she shouted to be heard over her own deafness. The smudges emanating from underneath her bedroom door, and the home-made quilts she churned out with the output of a factory. Our home feels a lot quieter. A lot sadder.

My mother Zoe retreats into her own crafts, her beading and sewing, her online marketplace where her customers place their custom orders for earrings and moccasins and medallions and other assortments of beaded bling.

"*Land Back* and *Baby Yoda* are all the rage," she says with a close-mouthed smile.

After a month and a half, Grandma Zeph goes back to doing her nursing job at the hospital in Cheapaye. "I need to work" she says, "I need to keep busy – otherwise I just play those damn video games all day." Overnight Zephyr has become the new matriarch of our little witchy family; she has the goth part down at least, though she isn't used to being the one in charge. Zilpah had always been around, Zilpah knew everything, Zilpah always had a word or two of advice, an opinion to opine on any given subject.

Two months after her passing, Zephyr announces her need for a change, "There's a nursing conference in The City." *As if there is only one.* "It might be nice to have a change in scenery. Would either of you like to come with me? Zoe? Zaude?"

"It might be nice to get away." Zoe looks up from the gold and brown hummingbirds she is beading. "It's been a while since I've left the Jiibay."

"I don't know," I say, my eyes straying to the cherry blossoms in the yard. "I think I'd rather just stick around here."

I have the place to myself for two whole weeks. I can't remember the last time I've been this alone.

And me? I have my camera. Well, Zach's camera. What had been Zach's camera when he was still alive. I walk through the house taking pictures of anything and everything that reminds me of my aanikoobijigan, my great-grandmother Zilpah.

Her abandoned walker, still standing by the front door. The plants she would overwater until they turned brown. The ticking of the ancient wind-up clock she'd gotten from who-knows-where. The x's she'd drawn on the kitchen power outlets so it was easier for her to find the holes for the prongs on the cord of the electric kettle. The small shelf she'd screwed to the wall, on the underside of which she'd affixed the smoke detector so she could reach it without having to climb up a stepladder to reach the ceiling. Her adaptations and inventions were everywhere.

I slide aside the panes of the double-glass sliding doors and step out onto the porch Zeamus, Zeke, and I built. Trickle of water from the creek. Sway and shift of the leaves in the trees. There is the tarnished silver bowl balanced precariously on the edge of the railing, just where she'd last left it. The bowl is empty. I wonder if the spirits feel abandoned now that Zilpah isn't around to leave her offerings. Her twists of tobacco, and pinches from whatever she was eating on her plate. Do they wonder where she went? Are they angry that she no longer pays tribute. Those spirits. Those manidook?

Sunlight sparkles on the silver, the refraction of light causing a glow, like the lensing of light through a ladybug's inner wing. I raise the camera strapped to my chest and snap a photo. My mother had blinged-out the leather cord from which it dangles with beaded lightning. Purple, lime-green, and gold. Won't know how it turns out until I get the film developed. That's part of the fun. The excitement of not knowing and waiting to see the results. Photography is always an experiment. A revelation. ·

>·<

I sit in the den watching reruns of old horror movies. I've never seen the original version of *The Fly* before. What should I watch next? I click through some of my options. *The Burbs. Night of the Living Dead. Fright Night. Candyman. Creature from the Blue Lagoon.* I briefly consider inviting my cousin Zeke over, or his father Zeamus, but I dismiss the idea. This is my first chance in a long while to be really alone, and I don't want to go and spoil it out of loneliness. This is my first night to myself. There are still another 14 days if I really need to fill the vacuum with the sound of other living voices. For now the TV will keep me company. And Zilpah's quilts. And horror movie screams. And spaghetti.

That's when I hear it.

Clunk

It sounds exactly like a bird hitting the window. It's happened before, but usually at that twilight stage between day and night, dawn or dusk, when the glass hardly appears to be there at all. It had something to do with the quality of light, which was also the reason why it was the best time for still photography. Since then we've been careful to keep the curtains drawn, hang a few crystals and ornaments for visibility.

Then it comes again.

Clunk

Two birds? I wonder. How likely could that be?

One stone, my stupid brain immediately rejoins.

"OKAY, OKAY," I say out loud to myself. Throw off great-grandma Zilpah's quilt, grab an iron poker from the mantel before the fireplace, slip on my fur-trimmed boots at the front door, and head back through the kitchen to investigate the source of the sound. The curtain is drawn vetoing my two-birds theory. I flick on the exterior light, and peer out the sliding glass. Nothing seems out of the ordinary. But everything beyond what the light reaches opaques the backyard into an impenetrable sphere. Bugs instantaneously manifest, swirling about the exposed bulb. If I open the door I know those damned skeeters will get in and they'll be hounding me all night with their high-pitched whine. Zaagimeg. Bloodsuckers.

Feeling magnanimous, I slide the doors open, iron poker raised prominently like a sceptre. Whoever is around, I want them to know who they are dealing with, that I am armed, and I am a queen.

I eye the deck for avian corpses but don't any see any ruin of feathers. I grip my sceptre tighter. The night seems ordinary. Nothing seems out of place. Lawn chairs and patio furniture are in the same arrangement as when I last saw them. Hummingbird feeder is swaying. Hunh. Swaying. The hummingbird feeder is shaped like a spinning top, a bulbous round part to hold the sugar water, a cork plug in the top, and a curved bit of metal like the kind in a hamster cage but with a red-tipped nozzle that is meant to attract the eye. "Hummingbirds are attracted to the colour red," Zoe's told me.

I know the winged beings to be positively mad for the sweet stuff. Ziinzibaakwad. Zoe fills the feeder with some kind of faux nectar, at least when she remembers to keep the reservoir full. Wings beat so fast they blur. Faster than the human eye. Hovering like helicopters.

Are hummingbirds nocturnal? I don't recall ever seeing the hummingbirds come by after dark. I mull this over in my head, consider checking the internet, the encyclopedic answer for everything you've ever wondered. I pull out my cell and lean the iron poker against the brick wall. Punch out the question with my thumbs.

ARE HUMMINBIRDS NOCTURNAL?

Answer: Hummingbirds are diurnal. Meaning they are only active during the day, though they might also feed during twilight.

Hunh.

"Well, it's well after twilight now." I eyeball the rotating feeder. It wobbles from entropy as the energy available for continued momentum slowly unwinds.

I shrug, glare once more at everything within the field of my vision – deck chairs, haunted hummingbird feeder, and the overgrown grass in the backyard.

Could have been anything. Skunks. Raccoons. Squirrels. Wolverines. There are always plenty of animals around. And at least some of them are nocturnal and might have liked to test out the taste of the sweet water.

I slide the doors shut and lock them. Leave the security lights on. Head back into the den, my La-Z-Boy, and my quilted blanket.

Back to the debate: what should I watch? Should I abandon the whole enterprise of watching a horror movie alone – that's never really bothered me before. Usually they just make me laugh rather than frightening me. Twisted sense of humour, I guess. Sometimes I laugh at the most inappropriate moment. Sometimes I'm the only one laughing, and I think *maybe my brain just doesn't work like other people's anymore*. And so what? Maybe it doesn't.

Clunk

Thump

Thump

"What the actual fuck!" I know I am not imagining it this time. What am I, *living* in a horror movie? I throw Zilpah's quilt off my legs, jam my feet into my boots, sceptre ready. Peer out at the illuminated yard. Nothing. Step out the sliding glass doors. Crickets. Flowing water. Toads turning their raucous blurbs and blargs into a patchwork of song.

I reach back through the sliding glass to flick off the light, waiting for the spots to recede from my vision, and for my night vision to kick into gear. Waiting for my pupils to enlarge so they can gather in more of the available light. Light from the moon, and the stars, and whatever residual light pollution that might exist from our nearest neighbours who are all quite far away. The residential allotments. Zilpah had successfully campaigned for a lot on the river where her family had always made their summer camp.

"Zeke? Zeke is that you?" I make out the form of my cousin standing at the edges of Zoe's garden. My eyes seem to slide away from his face; I can't seem to focus in the darkness, the edges of things blurry. Without definition. But there is his omnipresent hoodie, basketball shorts, and flashy name-brand sneakers. He's even holding a basketball the exact same way as I'd last seen him. Though that had been in his driveway shooting hoops. "You little perv," I tease, "what the hell are you doing skulking around my backyard after dark?"

"Water finds a way. Water still flows." His voice is all buzzing and wheezing. Not at all like his usual baritone. Kid is only 14. Much too short for basketball. Should give up on his dreams of NBA and join the choir. That's what he is suited for. Too ugly for theatre. A voice for the radio.

"Are you high?" Jesus. I step closer to the railing, trying to make out his face, but his hoody is up throwing his features into shadow. His face is a dark hole.

"Raindrops. Creaks. Streams. River. Lake." Buzz. Buzz. Buzz.

"Ok, Zeke, I'm calling your dad!"

Zeke whirls around like an ancient Greek statue of an Olympic athlete throwing a discus and whips the basketball at my head. *What the Heck!* I duck, and the ball bounces off the brick wall of the house, bounces off the railing, and rolls out into the foliage of the trees surrounding the yard. I look back toward where Zeke had been standing, but he's gone. I scan the rest of the yard, but he's nowhere to be seen.

I flick the security light back on as I squeeze through the sliding glass doors. I've accidentally left it open a few inches. I know those zagimek are going to eat me alive and it's all Zeke's fault. Back in the den I sit in the comforting glow of the television, the movie poster artwork of *Fright Night* leering at me out of the clouds. Glowing green eyes and too many teeth. The house looks nothing like ours. *What had all that been about?*

I sit staring at my phone, wondering if I should tell Zeamus what happened. We've always been pretty close. Closer than Zeke and me, who is technically closer to me in age. Just entering his teenage years as I am leaving mine. Zephyr so proud of being a young grandmother; Zeamus continued the family tradition of having a child while still being a child himself, managed to knock up his girlfriend before he had all his sexuality sorted out. A father at 15, he is almost half a decade younger than my mother Zoe. Though Zeamus is my uncle, he is nine years older than me, and he's always felt more like an honourary brother. But I don't want to alienate the younger generation – I don't want to be that "uncool" aunt that tattles on her nephew. I want to be a cool aunt.

I click on Zeke's number instead and send him a text.

GETTING INTO YOUR FATHER'S STASH?

I wait. A few minutes later the dot dot dot, dot dot dot, dot dot dot … … … of a forming text message appears.

BORED ALREADY?

I GOT PLENTY TO SPARE

MY OWN GREEN

NOTHING ELSE TO DO ON THIS REZ

Kid was shaping up to be a lot like his father. I smile. I know he's been given all the same lectures on birth control.

WHAT WAS ALL THAT ABOUT?

HUNH?

WHAT WAS WHAT ABOUT?

THAT STUFF ABOUT RIVERS LAKES STREAMS

…

… …

… … …

???

AND THROWING BASKETBALLS AROUND MY YARD

DON'T KNOW WHAT YOU BEEN SMOKING [sideways laughing face emoji]

WASN'T ME

Hunh.

YOU WEREN'T JUST IN MY YARD?

…

TWASN'T I

Hunh.

GHOSTS

"Ha!"

MAY-BE

Ok. So maybe it wasn't Zeke. I never saw his face. It didn't mean it was a ghost necessarily. But still. Weird. Creepy. Spooky. I look back at the *Fright Night* movie still displayed on the TV.

"How about a comedy?" I click over to the titles listed under humour. Rom-Coms weren't usually my deal. Maybe an animated cartoon? "Something a bit more light-hearted." *The Last Unicorn. Coraline. The Dark Crystal. 9.*

"Something with talking rodents maybe?" *The Secrets of NIHM. An American Tail. Ratatouille.*

I scroll through more kids' titles. *The Peanut Butter Solution. The Goonies. Jacob Two Two Meets the Hooded Fang.*

Geesh, when did kids' movies become so terrifying?

Ping

I look up from my search.

"O-kay, what was that?" My ears are strained, listening. Waiting for the other pin to drop.

PING

There it is again. Louder this time. Like a wine glass that's been clinked against something. Or a heavy coin dropped on cement.

Cling

Ping

Ding

The quiet, irregular chime continues as I drag myself to the glass partition and peer out to the halo cast by the security light. Slide the double doors apart and step out onto the porch. Moths and other winged insects swirl about the bulb, casting shadows with their bodies.

I take an assessment of the scene. Lawn chairs. Patio furniture. Deck railing with Zilpah's silver offering bowl still resting precariously on the edge, and beyond that the freshly turned earth of the herb garden, and the rusted metal O-ring of an old tire rim that we use to contain campfires. Everything appears as usual.

At the very edge of the circle of light, where the shadows are too thick for the security light to penetrate, I see the outline of a shape. A figure. A boy standing at the edge of the light. Hood down, but it's too dark for me to make out his face. Jeans instead of basketball shorts. Not Zeke this time. But oh so familiar. The slant of his shoulders, the weight of his stance. No, not Zeke. ZACH. It looks like my brother Zaccheaus, but I know that's impossible. Zach is dead. He's been dead for over a year now. It can't be Zach. I'm trembling. The iron poker I'm holding up at a defensive angle is shaking. There's no strength in my muscles. Tears blur my vision, I feel wetness on my cheeks. My stomach has dropped. It's down at my feet. My blood sugar has dropped like I haven't eaten anything, like I skipped lunch and dinner and I just need the quick rush of sugar. I'm hunched. Curled in on myself. I can barely stand. Can't breathe. Barely speak. I'm gasping.

"Zach?!" I say. "Zach? Is that you?" I'm sobbing now. I can't believe my own eyes. There's Zach, my little brother, my little brother, my little brother, standing there in the yard. I can see him more clearly now, though he's still standing in the shadows.

"Tribute." The voice wheezes out. Buzzing. "Tribute must be paid. The river flows."

It's not him. It's not him. The relief is like a flood, a dam that's broken open, releasing all the emotions which have been held back, contained. That's not Zach's voice. That's not how he sounds. It's not him. It's not him.

He turns and I can see his ear. See where his ear used to be. It's all blood and pus with white maggots crawling around in the wound. Eating the dead flesh. When they found his body, he'd been missing an ear. He moves into the shadows and he's gone, erased.

My eyes fall on the silver tray. Zilpah's spirit plate for offerings.

I guess. Tribute must be paid.

A recipe to appease your neighbours:

- A pinch of tobacco
- A morsel from your own plate
- A drop of blood for good measure
• Pray. Give thanks.

KRACKEN

SANG KIM

Goo smeared across the sushi chef's apron leaves you with second thoughts, but after passing up both in-flight meals, you will try just about anything, even this. Pink tentacles swell around his gloved arm like sex organs. When he wrests it free, it is the same sound the tub mat makes when you yank it back for cleaning. The server seats you at the table overlooking the bridge, and for the first time since landing, your thoughts return to her.

The eulogy is short, perfunctory. According to the primer, you are not to betray the faintest hint of emotion; it is etiquette you are after, not empathy. There will be no mention of the video streamed online – of her arms crooked around suspension cables, her bare feet feeling tentatively for the ledge, and passers-by Snapchatting from the sidewalk. Nor will you refer to the last postcard she sent you, the one with Afro Girl metamorphosing into a giant sea slug. On the back, the familiar cursive: *we come and go in medias res*. And below that: *Love* – the bottom of the *e* looping over the stamp like a thrown javelin. You are not sure if she simply forgot to sign off with her name or if it was meant to stand alone this time – a directive.

The *sannakji* is served in a white nesting bowl, hacked into pieces and writhing in its own inky residue. The pattern reminds you of the Rorschach test her therapist conducted;

you saw axes pointed in opposite directions; she saw broken wings. Tentacles bunch together on the edge of the bowl like severed thumbs. You pick one up with chopsticks, dip it in sesame oil. Tiny suckers pinch the tongue. And because cephalopods regenerate lost limbs, you imagine fractals proliferating all the way down the digestive tract.

At the karaoke bar, you told her you didn't sing, so she invited you to play a drinking game instead. Three chances to answer a riddle, 30 seconds for each chance. *Which number between 1900 and 2000, when divided by three, leaves you with the highest quotient?* You gazed at snow eddying down the street, and guessed 1999, 1966, 1933 – in that order. The correct answer is 1998; the quotient, 666. She explained that 1998 was the year of one of the deadliest floods in South Korean history, that when the waters receded from Ganghwa Island, scientists discovered 666 new species of crustaceans. Later, you ate instant ramen from styrofoam cups and binge-watched the entire first season of *Yellow Larva: The Curse of Lucifer*. In between episodes, she told you about her twin brother, who disappeared after his third failed attempt at the national college entrance exam; the way her mother dug her nails into her thighs whenever her father mentioned his name. The one that really got you was about the preparatory teacher who forced her to swallow a page of the *Cassell's Latin-English Dictionary* after committing it to memory. The last term on the last page she crumpled into her mouth before she dropped out of school and went abroad: *in medias res*.

When you were 10, you read *Twenty Thousand Leagues Under the Sea* in your cabin while your parents watched passing icebergs from the deck of the cruise ship. On the cover: a giant octopus, its tentacles braided around the masts of a ship during a storm. Underneath, the caption: *KRAKEN* – the empty spaces within each letter cobwebbed like some forgotten corner of the basement. When your parents were asleep, you walked out onto the balcony and scanned the black sea with your binoculars for breaks that never came.

That first summer at the cottage, you followed a trail of her clothes to the dock. You sat on the edge, splashed the moon into her face with your feet, were surprised by the water's viscosity, and thought about the way nylons must feel around an old woman's calves. She explained how the Kraken was a kind creature, trying to save the ships, not sink them, during a storm. When you lost sight of her, you hopped from one slab of rock to another, calling out her name. Startled cleavers of light fell from neighbours' bedroom windows. You found her on a prickly patch of juniper, knees clutched to her breasts, arms gleaming with goosebumps. She pulled you to her, breath halting and short, and abandoned the full weight of her sobbing body into yours. *Oh, God, I am so sorry.* It wasn't the first time you thought she was holding onto someone else.

Cephalopods are solitary, disappear when the world becomes too much. They have three hearts and you wonder why Nature was not so merciful with your species. You pick up a big chunk, forego chewing on it this time, swallow. Suckers latch onto the walls of the esophagus, the trachea contracts. When you empty the contents of the beer into your mouth, the epiglottis sputters like an overworked ox.

So this is how you eat a live octopus, you think, as you are lying there on the floor, shouting. Glasses clatter on the server's tray. The fan's shadow creeps slowly over your face.

Diners stare at butchered limbs slinking across your table, chopsticks suspended in mid-air, words abandoned mid-sentence.

Tomorrow, you will recite platitudes the mourners are coming to hear. There will be nods of approval for your poise, your unwavering voice. They will not know what happened to you today or about the kraken that has long lurked inside you; will not have witnessed your belly giving birth to its bulbous head or its tentacles unfurling from your fingers and toes, stretched as taut as a trampoline under the bridge. They will not have felt her shirt slapping against her skin like a defective parachute or the *whoosh* of her body cutting through the air, or heard the name you kept calling out, again and again like a broken song, as you lay there under the indifferent blue sky, waiting.

Sannakji (Chopped Baby Octopus)

Ingredients:
- One live baby octopus from a trusted seafood vendor. Make sure it is still very much alive. Carry it home in its own saltwater container/bag.

Contingency Plan:
If hungry while caught in a traffic or during the Armageddon, remove from container and eat as is.

Preparation:
• Take the baby octopus out of the container/bag. Do not rinse or clean it. The salt on its flesh is critical to the overall taste experience.
• Hold the baby octopus down on a cutting board. You may need the help of others, family, or friends who are not squeamish. Usually eight hands are required to hold it down properly.

• Sever the head from the tentacles. Cut everything into small pieces and plate it in a rimmed bowl. Make sure it is still in wiggle-mode.

• A dash of sesame oil works to give it a round nutty flavour. If you want a bit of a citrusy finish to it, or just really want to get the sannakji fired up, squirt some lemon on it.

Eat it (before it eats you).

THE DANCE
OF ABUNDANCE

Colleen Anderson

In the great houses, the ambidextrous monks of Culinaria enacted a dance of abundance every three years. One for the sowing, one for the growing, and one for the harvest ever flowing: the last, the year of abundance. Everything began and ended at the temple, with the selection of the ingredients and the great baking. The pastry had to be perfection to ensure the cycle of abundance continued.

Pere Korpos had danced that dance 12 times, making lesser dishes, juggling bottles of ambrosia, carrying platters into the feasts, each time a little rounder, redder-cheeked, and sweating. This year the cadre of Chefs had anointed him the Grand Chef and this would be his last participation, the pinnacle of his life's devotion. But what would he do after this year? He so loved his devotions to St. Culinaria.

He glanced frequently to the great hourglass as he oversaw the mixing of the eggs, lard, and flour. Dribbling golden salt into his hand, he sniffed it, then tasted it. Arid, no hint of copper or other metal – he sighed, smiling. He used a glass cup to scoop up the salt and ascended the ladder to the bowl. As he dribbled the salt in, he looked up and noticed a monk cracking one egg in upon another. Pere Korpos shrieked, "No! No no no."

His brother and sister monks, hats firmly crammed to their heads, froze on ladders about the bowl's rim.

"This pastry must capture the essence of love and nurturing and all the bounty of the years since the last dance. You must crack each egg in its rightful place in the flour. No crowding. Now quickly, shift the egg into its own space."

An egg relay began to space the eggs. Pere Korpos held bright red silk in each hand and waved it, yelling, "Let the mixing begin!"

In a flurry, people stirred and Korpos waddled around, inspecting, directing some monks to speed up, others to slow down. Every stage had to be seamless – even if the fields had been yielding less, and the vines were producing inferior tasting fruit of late. He hoped that the taste would still excel beyond these limitations.

Finally, they prepared to roll out the pastry ribbon.

Someone dropped a brush glistening with oil and Pere Korpos stifled a shriek, bustling over to make sure nothing had splashed the dough. Everything for the sacred dish looked ready, but his brow creased. The great lords who kept the tenets of the Order of Culinaria had singled him out for a special role, something more than Grand Chef, yet no one spoke of it. How could he do his best without knowing what was required or when?

For weeks leading to this great day his companions had been avoiding him, ever since he found out he would fill a position that appeared only once every 39 years. When he had been a child, he remembered magnificent pastries but that might have only been the memory of a small boy since every third year displayed heavenly desserts of abundance.

But this year, he'd been telling anyone within earshot, "I'm to be the Transformationist. It's a great honour. Of course, I've danced every Dance of Abundance in the last 12 rounds, but I must have danced superbly to receive this position."

He didn't mean to go on about it but the honour elated him and made him a little nervous that he might make an error. In his agitation, he couldn't stop talking, causing the monks to work sombrely and quietly under his administrations. They stayed true to their devotions, as he did, and Pere Korpos talked less when idleness disappeared beneath the constant monitoring of every step. But still, he worried his earlobe trying to fathom what the role of Transformationist meant.

He puffed up and down the line of monks as they rolled out the first foot of smooth, creamy pastry, the Trimmers and the Boarders standing by with fine knives and the nine-foot board. "Stop, stop!" he yelled. The two Rollers lifted their white marble cylinders and waited.

Holding up the glass hanging from the cord around his neck, he bent over, inspecting the flat tongue of dough. Up and down the line, monks dressed in white pants and shirts, wearing the holy aprons of the Order of St. Culinaria, held their breath or bit their lips.

Pere Korpos pulled small shears out of his apron pocket and cut off a three-inch strip of the wide pastry. It draped over his hand. Feeling the texture, cool and slightly tacky, he sniffed it. Then he bit off a piece and let it rest on his tongue. Slightly salty, buttery. "It's perfect," he sighed, and everyone smiled. The Dance of Abundance would not be marred.

As Pere Korpos wiped his bald head, happy that the great pastry making unfolded as decreed, the Tasters entered the sacred ceramic-tiled kitchen, their grey robes swishing through the floury floor.

Pere Korpos gasped, and a chorus of inhalations joined him. "Wh-what are you doing here? You're supposed to remain hidden until the great pastry is baked."

A voice like parchment paper rubbing together came from the cowled darkness.

"You have other duties. The baking will be seen to by the Second Chef."

A myriad of unseen hands pushed Mere Gardo forward; though she looked as bewildered as Korpos felt, she squared her shoulders, straightened her white cap. and nodded to the Tasters.

"But, but, it's my sacred duty to complete the baking," Pere Korpos blustered.

"In all other years, yes, but the Transformationist has special tasks."

As two beefy Sackers, freed from carrying bags of flour and vegetables, escorted him from the kitchen, Pere Korpos wondered if he'd done something wrong.

Protest he did, and dig in his heels, but dancing in the festival, with movements that amounted to twirling, had not kept him in any semblance of fitness.

He was ushered into a large tiled room, where silent monks stripped and soaped him, then lathered and shaved his body, all while Pere Korpos protested and tried to wriggle away.

He realized in that moment that while he coveted some attention, this wholesale perusal by the Tasters bewildered and scared him. He preferred working on the holy confection to being isolated and honoured this way. He hoped the rolling of the pastry had gone well and figured they must be starting to fill it with crushed almonds, roses, and vanilla. He shuffled from foot to foot and, one moment when the monks had turned away to gather toiletries, Pere Korpos tiptoed silently toward the door, his skin puckering in dread. As his hand touched the door, it whisked open and two Sackers, standing shoulder to shoulder, looked down on him. He drooped and returned naked to the ministrations. He distracted himself with going through the steps for the great pastry.

Nine sacred spices flavoured the holy pastry, and only Pere Korpos and the other Chefs knew the secret. Sighing as more people with rough towels buffed him dry, he expected a special robe, but Pere Korpos went cold when they ushered him, wearing nothing but a linen loincloth, into a large white room with a great many pillar candles, and devoid of anything but four Embellishers, robed in the black of their order, preparing pots of inks and pigments.

He tried to run again but the Sackers held him still as two Embellishers drew out fine brushes, dipped them in red or black or blue containers, and began to ink his body. He squealed from ticklishness at first and asked, "Wh-what are you putting on me?"

The Tasters, standing quietly to the side, whispered, "We put on the holy writ of food preparation, the errors, so that all sacred recipes may be perfected by baking out the wrongness."

The Embellishers began to chant as the other two joined in with sharp needles that stung his flesh like a hundred bees. "Baste, or the meat goes dry. Two hundred and fifty degrees will cause the flan to fall. Failure to skim the fat makes the gravy oily. Without washing, the spinach is gritty. Too high a heat scalds. Not enough stirring will ruin the roux."

The endless litany frightened Pere Korpos, but the pain lessened as the inks seeped into his skin. He had been about to ask what they meant by "baking out the wrongness," a small worry that sank deep within him, slowly dissolving as he opened his mouth.

The brushstrokes and pinpricks turned to a soft vibration, as if he were being licked by the farmyard cats who greeted him every morning. Pere Korpos now stood placidly, swaying as the Embellisher etched the last symbols and phrases over his arms and legs, buttocks, and chest.

Voices sounded as though they were coming through bales of cloth. He hummed, warm, happy, watching a dream when the past Grand Chefs, ones he had thought long retired, walked into the room, carrying a nine-foot board with a thrice-folded pastry. Ah, the dough, 27 feet of faultless, six-inch-wide strips. Somewhere, where his mind still could think, he mumbled, "Why...pastry here?"

In answer, they began delicately unravelling the dough ribbon, spiralling it up his legs. Several hands gently pressed the seams together, and fingers patted the dough against him. Even with the calming effects of the narcotic dyes on his skin, his panic began to simmer and bubble. He knew he had overseen the making of a similar dough, but this pastry bore a more robust thickness.

Brushes dipped in egg white and milk swept over the pastry dough.

"I don't unnerstan. Wha's goin' on?"

The cowled Tasters began, first with one speaking softly, and each one joining in on a new sentence. "You are plenteous, Pere Korpos. You are honoured, and revered. Your flesh is abundant. Your words are abundant; your skills are abundant. Thus shall you be the dish served at the Dance of Abundance."

"Nooo," he moaned, but the lethargy held him too firm. "No, I'm sorry I talked sooo much, sorry I bragged. I didn't mean to." Most of his protests came out as a mumble.

"This is your last dance, Pere Korpos, in honour of St. Culinaria."

They fitted the last piece of pastry into place, blinding him, with just enough space for nose and mouth to poke through. Delicate blades cut designs into the dough, the same as used on the pies and tarts. Not one knife nicked his flesh.

Then strong hands grabbed him and laid him down on the board, just like a giant sausage roll, and they carried him carefully, though he felt he would be sick from the movement. Weeping softly, Pere Korpos wondered how this could be happening. He'd always been a devoted monk. Surely, he didn't deserve this.

Down the staircase, through to the sacred ovens: he knew where they carried him now. He pleaded and whimpered, but his words did not make sense, even to him. Then everything halted.

Loudly, but close to his head, someone intoned. "Three are the years for the cycle to return, and three times thirteen does the wheel complete its circuit. We must balance the sowing and the growing and the abundance ever flowing. We offer this servant so that our fields will grow hale and hearty again."

In the background, the litany began: *One for the sowing, one for the growing, one for the harvest ever flowing.*

Another voice, high and like a bird's melodic trill, reached Pere Korpos' ears. "Pere Korpos, you are honoured to be our

Transformationist. Do you believe in the power of St. Culinaria?"

"Yes," he squeaked.

"Do not fear," someone whispered, and louder, "Have you always believed in the Dance of Abundance?"

"Yes," he breathed and hoped that he had nothing to fear. The fire roaring in the great oven added an ominous tone.

"Then you will carry our wishes and receive the highest blessing." Someone held a tube to his lips. "Drink now of the sacred elixir of St. Culinaria."

He sucked, tasting the fiery liquid, with a perfumed hint of elderflowers and tart hibiscus. As the liquid coursed to his belly, heat rose in him. The warmth from the orange light seeping in around his pastry shroud did not seem so bad. Then they rolled him into the hot interior, where flames licked hungrily from the oven's stones.

Sound and thought and fear subsided, then disappeared.

>·<

Dull blades pierced the chrysalis, as a buttery light shone through. The aroma of fresh baked breads, succulent meats sizzling on spits, and the honeyed nectar of bees infused the air. Of sound, there was only that of a crusty, yet giving, surface breaking.

He awoke as if from a long hibernation. Something important that he should know tickled his mind. Was it day or night? Day, he thought, and wondered who he might be.

Slowly it came to him as hands pulled apart the flaking cocoon. A dance. Yes, the Dance of Abundance!

He'd played a role. Something important...frightening ...mysterious.

His name, it was Pierre? Pear? Pere! Pere Korpos!

His eyes opened and he sat up, then stood, wobbly yet feeling whole. The hushed crowd, monks and nobles alike knelt before him and bowed their heads.

"I don't underst – " He stopped. That was not his voice, but one of a youth. As he held up his arm he noticed the fine tattooed lines: herbs and spices listed on his left arm, fruits and vegetables on one leg, meats and cuts on another, various liquids and drinks down his right arm. The errors originally inked on him had been baked away.

"Why, I'm an Epicurean's delight!" he exclaimed. "What is this?" He felt the luxurious curls of hair about his head.

"You are the embodiment of St. Culinaria," said one of the Tasters. "Every 39 years we must rebalance. You will teach a new generation about delights passed down from our saint. If we ask about a food, you will develop new recipes, now that St. Culinaria's wisdom flows through you."

Pere Korpos only heard half of this, marvelling at his young firm limbs, the strength that coursed through his veins, the vigour that infused him. "And here I thought you were sacrificing me because I was no longer of use, because I had been a braggart."

"Holy vessel, we are human and we cannot be without flaws," the Taster said. "We chose you because you were the best and had served your years in faith. You will eventually move to a new position in another 39 years when we repeat the special dance. Then you, too, will become a Taster."

Pere Korpos laughed. The Dance of Abundance had unveiled a new path for him, just when he thought his life was ending.

"Now," he said, "let's eat!"

Pastry was the focus of this story, so here is a recipe for **Sweet Almond Pastry**

Preheat oven to 400°F

Ingredients:
- 2 eggs
- 1 tablespoon water
- 6 ounces almond paste
- 3 tablespoons granulated sugar
- ½ teaspoon vanilla extract
- ½ of a 17.3 ounce package Puff Pastry Sheets (1 sheet), thawed according to package directions (better yet, make your own pastry)
- ¼ cup sliced almonds
- 1 tablespoon confectioners' sugar

Preparation:
• Lightly grease baking sheet or line with parchment paper. With a fork, mix one egg with the water in a small bowl.
• Place the almond paste, granulated sugar, remaining egg, and vanilla in a mixing bowl and beat until smooth.
• Roll the pastry into a 12x10-inch rectangle. With the short side facing you, spoon the almond mixture on the bottom half of the pastry to within 1 inch of the edges. Cut several 2-inch long slits, about 1 inch apart, on the plain side of the pastry. Fold the pastry over the filling and seal the edges with a fork. Brush the pastry with the egg mixture. Sprinkle with the almonds and place the filled pastry on the prepared baking sheet
• Sip a fiery drink as you slide the pastry into the oven. Ouzo, Cointreau, or whiskey is suggested.
• Bake for 12 minutes. Reduce the temperature to 375°F. Bake for 20 minutes or until the pastry is golden brown. Cool on a wire rack for 15 minutes. Sprinkle with confectioners' sugar, if desired.

THE ONE
THAT GETS AWAY

Casey June Wolf

Carl lay on the grass, hands clasped behind his head, idly taking in the shaggy crowns of trees and the wash of cloudless blue above. A slender strand descended from the treetops in quick, punctuated drops, lengthening as, he guessed, the spider now coming into view was able to throw out more line. It landed in the grass and vanished from sight, the strand disappearing nearly as fast, and he was alone again.

That morning at the Port Renfrew Community Dock he had been alone, too, but he had not been idle. He'd assembled the sleek black fishing rod he'd brought with him three months before (when he came here for a job that never materialized), peered hard into the water, cast his line, and waited.

The guy who said his friend would hire Carl for his logging crew had also told him that people paid big bucks for fishing vacations on this unspoilt coastline, but Carl'd be able to fish for next to nothing 'cause he'd be there anyway. The guy had grown up around here so he knew what he was talking about. Carl had thought it over: big bucks, beautiful country, and free fishing, or little bucks, stressful city, and the continued joy of drinking on weekends.

He got in his car, got on a ferry, and drove to Port Renfrew. It really was an amazing place, so even though the job was a figment of that guy's imagination, he stayed on anyway, living out of his car on the savings he'd pulled together before quitting his car-detailing job and coming up here chasing smoke.

Since learning how to put his rod together he'd been spending a lot of time on the public dock. It was not that big and looked very touristy, but most of the time there weren't many people there. He'd sleep till his car got too hot then, just before the lunch opening, walk to the pub from wherever he'd parked. There, Sid, who was a friendly guy he'd got talking to his first day in town, would let him wash up in the restroom and get some clean clothes on. Then he'd stroll past the book and souvenir shop, the tour operators, and the luxury rental cottages, all of which were built of fine local lumber. (They were small and single-storied, and Carl guessed some architect hoped they looked like a fishing village. But they didn't; they were way too fancy.)

He'd smile at the woman in the shop and nod to the tour operator and so far no one ever questioned him, although by now they had to have heard of the mainlander living discreetly where he could, even if they hadn't observed him sleeping rough, themselves. It was that small a place, and though Carl generally kept to himself, and though he tried to keep everything copacetic so no one would have reason to complain, still, he knew that the tide could turn against an outsider quick as a wink.

But all that aside, honestly he didn't worry about it too much. He just kept an eye on his bank balance and went down to the dock. If it wasn't too busy he'd amble past the ragged foreshore, where bald eagles float silently overhead, crows hammer at who knows what forage among the barnacles, gulls and cormorants drift here and there on the tide among the fronds and air bladders of the bull kelp. On some days white pleasure boats moved in the mist hanging between Port Renfrew and the mountains up the coast. At the extreme end of the dock he'd stand out of the way of containers and chains and capstans, looking metres down into the unknown, his thermos beside him and a bag of sandwiches, and he would cast his line into the wild waters below.

He would wait. Watch the waters as they danced around the bay. Watch the hanging mists and unmoving, ever-changing mountains. Watch the people like dots appear and disappear from view on the long golden San Juan beach across the way.

He would particularly watch the shifting of the seaweed in the water below and the odd darting form of a fish.

Some of them would see the twitching endpoint of his line and rush to meet it, and it was these he lived for. Many days – and he came here most every day – there were no takers. The full of his thrill for however long he hung around was just the changing light, the constantly moving bay, and the occasional word with somebody who had business on the dock. Sometimes there would be fish but they would pass his line like shoppers in a mall, eyes ahead, always questing for a better bargain, and no matter how seductively he made his line dance, off they went.

Once he caught sight of the browny-orange mottling of a spiny-backed rockfish, moving along the soft bottom of the bay. Once he saw a weird little fish crawling on its fins – a sculpin, apparently. Once he saw a massive brute as long as Carl was tall, or nearabouts, with a big mouth and beautiful green spots. This one he learned was a lingcod (Sid did an off-site I.D.), and good eating, with a scary set of teeth. But Carl didn't see its teeth because the lingcod moved placidly onward, and besides, realistically, could he and his rod land a creature as big as that?

But other times he had better luck. He got a small cabezon – a mottled beast with a bright red eye – the fish nearly two feet in length and the first one of substance he'd successfully landed. He brought it up on the lower dock, climbed swiftly down a chain ladder, and then stood over the fish, dumb, as the light in its eye slowly went out, and the gills stopped moving, and the whole crazy creature grew still. He brought it up to Sid and asked if he could do anything with it and Sid said, "Absolutely," and later that night Carl was sitting in Sid's house for the first time, chatting with Shirley, his wife, while Sid cooked up the delicious flesh of the cabezon on the grill.

And once he got a little guy called a Red Irish Lord, but he threw it back because he couldn't imagine this scrawny red bulldog being edible. When Sid saw the photo on Carl's phone he shook his head woefully. "Never even tried that one, myself," he said. "I hear they're not bad." But he shrugged it off because after all, it wasn't like Sid was short of food.

The day he caught a shark, though, was the day every-thing changed. From the moment he captured the thing he thought of as a mud shark, but which Sid informed him was a spiny dogfish, he himself was hooked. It was a thing of beauty, long and slender and smooth-coloured like a polished stone. It thrashed and worried and fought so hard it cut a chunk several inches long from its own cheek, and it got away. Got clean away and yet it didn't streak out from the spot, but snaked its lovely body almost gently through the waters till it was swallowed in the murk.

From then on, Carl had little interest in birds, or waves, or mists, or sculpin, or any other fish. He was consumed by the desire to see, to catch another shark. If a shark had thrown a line down from the sky and Carl, glancing up, had seen its perfect, crescent mouth or glimpsed its muscular pectorals or its inky eyes, he would have thrown his hands around that line and hauled himself to heaven to take a better look.

He did see more; did catch more. Silent Carl became the guy with the long black fishing rod who would call to strangers on the far side of the dock, "Hey! Come look at this!" And they would run or saunter over, according to their nature, or turn away or act like they never heard, and maybe they didn't. The Great Shark mustn't call to all.

After that first one, he did better. Standing on the high dock he would draw them from the bay. Fighting and jerking they would swing at the end of his line and, once, twice, three times he would guide them over to the boards below, where finally he would land them and, in view of witnesses or entirely on his own, he would clamber down, and he would gaze at them. All the fight gone out of them, not even labouring for breath; he felt as if he could stare at them all day. Take his photos. Take a video. Search around for anyone who might see his skill and luck. Then he would walk cautiously toward the breathless creature. He'd pull out his cutters and hold the shark's frightened body away with his

booted foot and – now dealing with a struggling beast again
– he would argue with the line until it broke. The fish would
writhe. Carefully, carefully, always avoiding those nasty
dorsal spines, he would push it with his foot. Inch by inch,
closer to the edge. Then a last thrust, and into the bay the
shark would roll, and come to its senses, and swim beautifully away.

Sid had balked when he heard that Carl was throwing
them back. "Are you kidding?" he had asked. "Have you ever
eaten dogfish? Hell, I'll take them if you don't want them."

Carl shifted uncomfortably from foot to foot, staring into
the image on his phone rather than looking directly at Sid.
He knew it was strange to be throwing good food away, but
these guys were more than food for him. He couldn't express
it, not just because he was struggling to find the words, but
because his response was so visceral it wasn't even fully con-
scious. Just looking at them, just having them look back into
his eye and knowing that image they saw of him would be
going off to sea permanently imprinted on their brains, that's
what he was feeding on. Rescuing them from himself and
watching them being swallowed by the great grey comforting
sea, *that* was the nourishment he got from his captured
sharks.

That morning he had caught the biggest one yet. It must
have been more than four feet and its skin bore scars. Fighting maybe? Or hunts gone wrong? Or snagged on some
industrial debris buried in the water?

This time he had spectators with him on the dock, and
he was proud and jubilant and in awe. When he released
the shark, off it went, maybe never to hunt these waters
again. Maybe to Europe, maybe to California, maybe to

the Caribbean Sea. Carl didn't know how these things worked, how far the dogfish swam or where, but he knew they travelled farther in their lifetimes than he ever had in his.

This afternoon, lying on the grass with the sky circled round by trees, the lone line of the parachuting spider brought him back to that magnificent beast. Carl had hurt him, he knew, but he couldn't help it. He couldn't help the joy he felt in being near his sharky kindred. He couldn't help feeling like every time he let one go, it took a part of him with it. Out along the soft bottom of the coast. Far away from car camping, and jobs that never existed, and jobs he'd thrown away. Guys he barely knew who did him kindly or did him unkindly. Nowhere places and nowhere pasts and nowhere imaginable to go.

With the dogfish, he was free. He was happy.

Carl gazed long at the sky, hands clasped beneath his head, and thought of the night before him, curled up and just a little too chilly in his car. He thought of oats soaked in cold water and a sprinkling of sugar and powdered milk. He thought of sunlight slowly melting his rigid muscles. A walk in town. A sponge bath at the pub. A thermos of coffee. And the dock.

The dock. It brought a wide, slow smile, and with that smile came an idea. His breath quickened; a tingle ran down his sides, all the way to the tips of his toes.

What was stopping him?

He wouldn't wait for morning. He'd go now, beckon to the sharks in the restless waters, use his body, not his line, to call them in. He was ready to flex against the teasing, pulling tide, to find its hidden courses and let the currents take him. Forget his fishing rod, his clothes, his car – he'd leave them. Answer the great call.

Carl laughed, flipping over and stumbling to his feet. He rummaged in a pocket for his keys. He was going back, right now, and hope to hell he could find that four-foot beauty somewhere still around the bay. If not, he would follow them. He knew he could follow. He would smell them. Taste them. He knew, suddenly, exactly where they would be.

He felt it in every prickle of his skin.

How Sid Would Have Prepared Carl's Dogfish
(And How Shirley Would Have) Given The Chance

Ingredients:

- First, catch a dogfish. Buying it in a store won't be the same at all. Trust me.

- Gut and fillet your shark, or have someone else do it. Being sharks, dogfish can end up tasting like ammonia if you don't gut them as soon as they have been killed. Soak them for no more than ten minutes in salted water, approximately ¾ cup of salt in three litres of water. If left too long the meat will break down.

Prepare a breading. This recipe will give you a light, crisp batter.

• I cup wheat or gluten-free flour. A half-and-half mix of pastry flour and kamut or spelt is nice.

• ½ cup milk. Sid would use cow milk but Shirley is more adventurous and would use coconut milk (from a Tetra Pak).

• ½ cup water. (You can increase the liquids to ¾ cup. each if the batter's too thick.)

• 2 teaspoons baking powder.

• Salt to taste. Sid likes about a teaspoon, but some of us dispense with it altogether. Sid also likes to add black pepper and garlic powder, although that wasn't how he learned the recipe. But he doesn't go in for fancy herb mixtures. So play that by ear. (Shirley uses real garlic in her recipe.)

• Mix all the ingredients together and roll the dogfish in them.

• Turn on your burner to medium high heat. Heat a cast-iron frying pan big enough to easily accommodate the fish, with enough vegetable oil that it will come halfway up the side of the fillet when you place the fish in. When the batter begins to darken, turn the heat down a little.

• Cooking time depends on the thickness of the fish.

33 RAZ STREET

Elisha May Rubacha

By some combination of architecture and incantations, the stoop of 33 Raz Street hid Scry completely. Passers-by never so much as noticed her sitting there. Pillars on either side blocked the view at precisely the right moment. Seeing no one, people carried on, completely unaware that they might be watched. Nor was there any risk of being discovered from within. Since the HaTai district had been taken, many of the residences had been left empty. The Lab, however, looming over the neighbourhood, was newly occupied after years of disuse. Power had been restored to the machines, and she could feel the vibrations in the pavement, blocks away.

She had taken up her post during the extreme heat of the day while most of the city slept, at least on this side of the river. She drifted in and out of consciousness herself while basking in the brutal sunshine, waiting for night to overtake day so she could watch and listen as the Heralds made their way to work. Three nights passed uneventfully, and she longed to return to her favourite rooftop. Margot, her magpie, would watch over her when she slept there, and warn her if anyone approached. The rest of the time Margot flew, and fed, and stole at her leisure. Scry, growing impatient with the task at hand, found herself missing her companion, but knew even Margot could not find her on the stoop of 33 Raz Street.

Although there were other routes to the Lab, Scry had decided this was the best place to start her surveillance. She was desperate for information. Nobody had seen the massacre of HaTai coming. Even through her facemask, she could smell whatever work the bikes were powering. She regretted that it had not occurred to her to investigate the rash of bike thefts that preceded the slaughter, but it had seemed innocuous enough at the time.

It was difficult for Scry to spend so much time there so soon after. The Heralds had paid morticians from DurLel to clear the bodies from the streets, but many remained in the surrounding buildings. When Scry had done a sweep of 33 Raz Street the stench had been overwhelming. It had not, however, stopped her from looting. The previous tenants left behind a wealth of tradable goods. She filled her bag with cloth, tools, trinkets, and food. The stores of apples, canned tomatoes, and dried beans she would give to the Guild, keeping only a bottle of cider for herself. The rest, with the exception of a knife and a bobbin, she would trade for favours and information. Now, as she waited, she stitched the bobbin onto her jacket to mark 33 Raz Street on her map of ZarNik Jarr.

The underlings approached first, as soon as the suns were set enough to bear. The security guards, with their makeshift weapons, arrived earliest to relieve the over-day staff, followed by the low-level administrators, and the generators who powered the bikes. The senior staff would follow a full hour later and seemed to leave whenever they pleased.

Scry had no paper to write on or ink to write with, so everything she saw was committed to memory. She was literate, unlike so many since the Wall, and it was not unusual for her to spend full weeks in seclusion with only the company of Margot and stolen books. In her short life, she had become an expert in avoiding others. She was uniquely equipped for isolation.

Finally, two Heralds strolled up Urd, the cross street, engaged in conversation. Scry set down her sewing and peered out at them. The taller of the two she knew already as Jarek. She had seen him walk to the Lab each night, always talking to someone. On the second night, he mentioned that he had lived in HaTai, but moved to WarrN in the month before the attack. She was certain he had known it was coming.

The man he was with wore fitted clothes made from a single fabric. Where Jarek's clothes were also fitted, they were patched together from many different textiles, and in many different colours. What the other man lacked in height, he made up for in self-assurance, somehow dwarfing Jarek by his presence.

"As necessary as *this* was, Sendo, doesn't it make the campaign a little too hard to swallow?" Scry silently repeated the stranger's name to herself. "How can we possibly distance ourselves from *this?*"

"It's being handled. We're very well aware that it's impossible to proceed without the public will."

"I was out into the day over in Drink and heard there'd been a meeting in Appleseed. They've already started to organize."

"We've recruited better men than you to be paranoid, Jarek. It would be in your best interest to show up to work on time tomorrow. Which might be easier for you if you went home to WarrN at a reasonable hour rather than stumbling home from the Drink in the perilous light of day."

Jarek seemed to shrink further next to Sendo, before both disappeared completely up the road.

><

Scry had been at the meeting in Appleseed. She had arrived at the gathering uninvited, first tailing LinKun's messenger to the Dirt, then Ruth, who left the warrior farmers' territory shortly after. Scry followed her to the Owl's Eyelid and entered without drawing any attention to herself. The purpose of the meeting was plain, despite being outside the usual purview of the Guild. The threat the Heralds posed affected the whole city, and the loss of HaTai had disrupted the economies of every borough, as well as the delicate balance between them. Although they all agreed something had to be done, what that was remained up for debate. Several small clusters had formed to bicker or strategize while they awaited the other representatives.

Best, Duchess of the Four Legs, sat with her back to the wall nursing her youngest son Doreon while commiserating with her equally decadent counterpart from MukTa, the place of many names. The loss of her neighbours meant an almost complete loss of customers. HaTai had been one of very few places within the city that had the infrastructure and resources to cook, and without that resource her livestock was of little good to anybody.

Thrust, the representative from MukTa, did not have the same sort of authority over their borough as Best had in hers. DurLel had long been misunderstood as lawless, but it was only the place of many names that was truly ungoverned among the boroughs of ZarNik Jarr. Even there, in the furthest neighbourhood from HaTai, the disruption would be felt. The services they provided were luxuries, and in a time of fear and uncertainty those expenditures would be the first to go. With no agriculture of their own, their whole borough might starve, as the city had starved so many times since the Wall.

Baldur himself was there, Boss of the Drink, masked and hooded for discretion. He had crafted a reputation as a drunken scoundrel to disguise his unparalleled cunning. Scry had seen him scheming more than once before, usually with Grid, his right hand, and was under no illusions about what he might be willing to do. He sat silently as he waited for the meeting to start and was approached only by a brave barmaid who brought him a cider, unbidden.

LinKun, arguably Appleseed's brightest comrade, spoke with Ruth, one of the Dirt's most respected clan members. Without having properly met either, Scry had developed a special fondness for them purely through observation. In stark contrast to the likes of Best and Baldur, their motivations were always grounded in the good of their people. It was only within their lifetimes that the two districts had developed stable systems in which every denizen took an equal share of the produce, regardless of position. Scry had no people of her own but admired and even envied the selflessness of LinKun and Ruth.

"The other boroughs will care more about goods circulating than Heralds circling," Ruth said, keeping her voice low.

"But we must remember that it's much easier for *us* to focus on the root of the problem," LinKun said. "Is the clan prepared to donate its surplus? If we can assuage their fear of starvation, they may agree to a more effective approach."

She shook her head. "If Appleseed were hungry, there would be no hesitation. We are still cousins. But too many in the clan hold grudges against the other boroughs to form a consensus."

"Would they allow their resentment to stand in the way of preserving what we've at long last built here, after generations of suffering?"

"It's too early to tell. No one understands what's happened yet, or why. Or who these people are, or what they're trying to do. There's no strong defence or counterstrike to be made until we have intel to base it on."

LinKun nodded in agreement. Scry wanted to chime in then but preferred to maintain her anonymity a little longer. The meeting had still not begun in earnest.

They were about to say more when the Su, Chief of the LanSu of RuDen, entered in a robe of feathers, smelling strongly of fresh mint. The LanSu people had lived on this land well before the city had formed, but their numbers were few and the territory under their control was minuscule. RuDen was fertile and self-sufficient, but it was very near the Lab, and the history of their people was already too fraught with ruin. The Su would naturally align with LinKun and Ruth.

Everyone, even Baldur, bowed their heads to the Su before carrying on, with the notable exception of the three representatives from WarrN. Each belonged to a different mob and ruled over a different subset of the borough's corridors. Scry had been inside the massive haphazard structure, but never very deep, and never for very long. There was nothing that terrified her more in ZarNik Jarr than the prospect of getting lost or imprisoned in that dark labyrinth. On her jacket, the many blocks of her nightmare were marked simply with a stroke of black paint. Any room or stretch of hallway she had been in was recorded within that darkness. Her experience of the place was limited, so she knew little to nothing about the mobsters, but managed to pick up their names as they insulted one another. Duff seemed to be the most powerful, and the least obnoxious. FiShek ogled the barmaids, and spoke often and quickly, sometimes using language she did not understand. The third was called Rat Tree, which she assumed for some time was a WarrN-specific insult until the barmaid referred to him that way as well. He reeked of jasmine. All three men wore bioluminescent necklaces. Their light-emitting algae was one of the major exports of the borough, along with myriad drugs and a smattering of services. One of Scry's few trips inside had been to get a wisdom tooth pulled. She had paid with a pot of apple savoury, a popular dish of hot unsweetened applesauce with crushed garlic, onion, and herbs. It had been cooked in HaTai.

The Su found their seat quickly, and the perceptive barmaid doted on them. No one but the Su themself remembered the person who had fulfilled the role before them. This Su had served for over 50 years, longer than most lifetimes in ZarNik Jarr. Scry had spent hundreds of hours watching the LanSu and their trained birds of prey, but she had never heard the Su say more than a dozen words. She had seen them smile though, and eat nuts with thoughtful precision, and look at plants and bugs with the LanSu children.

LykuGosa, one of the three councillors of the Seam, glided in wearing a shimmering red dress. The Duchess was immediately and visibly covetous. The councillor's arms were tattooed right down to her fingertips, and she had two rings through the left side of her nose. The Seam bordered on the place of many names, and although the clothing made there was certainly more of a necessity than anything you might find in the adjacent borough, it was still not half as essential as food.

A messenger arrived, sent by one of the regular spokespeople of DurLel, the anarchist community between the river and WarrN. Ruth spotted her first, showed her to the centre of the room, and whistled between two fingers for everyone's attention.

"On behalf uh'Isra: Please fuh'give muh absence. Having had nuh'choice but to accept a contract tuh'serve HaTai, we fin'ourselves in an uncomf'tuh'ble conflick uh'interest. We fear tha' participation in talks may be puh'ceived as warmungerin' fuh'profit, so for the ti'being, I'll recuse muh'self. Tha' said, I wa'na be cle'uh that we in nuh way condone the beha'ver uh'the Heralds. Send word if yuh'need some'in from us."

Mr. Grackle, the owner of everything beyond the river KurShek, did not come, nor did he send a messenger to express his regrets.

LinKun took the floor and called the meeting to order.

"After the horrific events of yesterday, I thought it best we all gather face to face to discuss this common threat. Over at least the past two moons, the self-styled Heralds have been recruiting across the city." The way Baldur nodded to LinKun suggested to Scry that he had been the source of this information. "A handful of survivors from HaTai sought refuge with us, and by all accounts, the Heralds are responsible. Isra's message suggests the same. However, not a one of those survivors had even an inkling as to the motivation behind the attack. Other witnesses say that the blockades around the old Lab have since been torn away, and that they have been unceasingly busy inside. HaTai itself appears to be empty, but it's possible they have people stationed throughout."

Baldur cleared his throat. "I'll send in a party. We'll need to collect water from the KurShek soon one way or another. They'll be prepared to defend themselves, if necessary."

"Their reaction might be informative," LinKun said, considering it. "Other thoughts?"

"We cannot allow this to stand," Best said, her voice trembling. "My neighbours have all been murdered in their sleep. Any of us could be next. We must strike before their members slink back into our boroughs."

Ruth stood to speak. "Yes, we have a fight ahead of us, but we must fight wisely. Start with recon. Get eyes on the Lab, and ears in every district. I need to know what we're dealing with. We did not save the Dirt by rushing in unprepared."

"And while you do your research, how will the Four Legs eat?"

"Surely you have some stockpile you can ration or furs you can trade."

Best wrinkled her nose and LinKun jumped in to redirect the conversation.

"Hunger is no longer our enemy. The Guild's formation has returned ZarNik Jarr to the kind of stability that hasn't been known since the Wall. Everyone will continue to eat. The city's supply of food remains the same, indeed with fewer mouths. Although we may not have those foods pre-pared in the ways to which we are accustomed, we will not starve. You, Best, will not starve, nor will your people. As autonomous as we all prefer to remain, the Guild exists to unite us in a system of mutual support."

Ruth nodded.

The meeting went on like that for some time, LinKun mediating between the strongest wills in ZarNik Jarr to arrive at the best plan of action. LykuGosa offered to clothe the warriors if the time came to do battle. Duff promised to pro-vide lights whenever they were useful, but like Thrust and LykuGosa, he had no combatants to send in. The people who lived in WarrN were not fond of leaving WarrN. Best had an armed guard, but they were few and she was not will-ing to part with them. She did agree to donate meat – raw dog, cat, and rabbit – to the cause. The Dirt, the Drink, and Appleseed would take up the fight, and everyone would look within their communities for answers.

The Su had nodded assent here and there throughout the meeting but spoke only to LinKun after the other represen-tatives had left.

"Our birds will tell us what they see," they said, taking his hand gently in theirs, then parting. It was often treated as mere legend, but the LanSu's connection with their birds was in fact so profound that they had trained them to com-municate in the common tongue. Scry, ever the skeptic, had tested the claim more than once, and had found herself an inadvertent believer when confronted with the proof. She had scrutinized her own abilities with the same rigour. Scry was never one to trust what only seemed. When she left the Owl's Eyelid that night, Scry had gone straight to HaTai to see what she could find out for herself.

>‹

Before she could form an opinion as to the identity of the informant, a group of five strangers walked up Urd: the inky hands, the paint-stained redhead, the intact glasses, and the twins. Each seemed improbable and fascinating to Scry, as her gaze flitted frantically between them. Anything committed to ink or paint would be of the utmost importance. The young man with the intact glasses wore clothes finer than Sendo's. They seemed to be imbued, like the stoop, with some additional quality. Scry could sense that he was persuasive. And although she had seen twins in the streets of ZarNik Jarr, she had never known any. None of them uttered a word as they made their way to the Lab, but they made an impression.

She lingered at 33 Raz Street until she could leave under the cover of daylight, but as she dusted herself off and started to gather her things, two cloaked Heralds emerged. One carried a stack of posters, and the other carried a bucket of paste with a brush. Then another pair followed, and another, always with posters, sometimes with a hammer and nails. Scry had never seen so many people out in the daylight this side of the KurShek. Dozens passed her before the street cleared and she was able to leave the stoop.

Where it was possible, she made her way along rooftops, climbing down to street level only when necessary. It wasn't until they crossed into the neighbouring districts that they started to plaster the walls with the phrase, "A HERALD NEVER HUNGERS." She tore down the first poster she came across, rolled it up, slipped it in her bag, and quickly returned to the rooftops. It was easy to get ahead of them once she dropped down onto the crude structures that filled what had been oLios Street many years ago. The precarious panels were dangerous and unstable, but Scry knew precisely what to avoid, every pitfall sewn into her jacket and studied until manoeuvring around them had become second nature. She moved quickly through Appleseed, and went straight to uNomia Avenue, finally dropping down onto the fire escape of 42C, where she knocked on LinKun's covered window.

He pulled the curtain aside with caution, a knife in hand, and squinted out at her. She showed him her empty palms, and he slid the window open.

"Yes?" he said, beads of sweat already forming on his forehead.

She pulled her facemask down and let it hang around her neck. "I've been watching the Heralds for several days, and now they're on the move."

He peered down at the street, then up at the rooftop opposite, and finally gestured for her to come in. He sat down at his table in a room that had been a kitchen, several generations previously, and she followed suit.

"You're Scry, aren't you?" he asked.

She was taken aback, but nodded, and tried not to show it.

"And a thief, I'm told, who belongs to no district."

"I prefer to think of myself as a scavenger, thank you. A redistributor of resources, not unlike yourself."

"And why should I trust a scavenger who has no affiliation to recommend her?"

Scry took a breath and considered how best to answer him. Finally she asked, "Do you remember the storm in the lower market, maybe a moon ago?"

He nodded. It had been brief but severe.

"I was doing a bit of trade with Atsuko. First, the wind picked up a little. Enough that the stalls all shook, and I had to wait while she braced hers. We finished up our deal, and as I was turning to leave, the rain suddenly hit. Some ran for home, but most of us visiting the market that night ducked into the stalls, and held them down, or moved goods in from the downpour. I had never felt so... useful. That's an inadequate word, but you take my meaning."

LinKun smiled in the dim of his repurposed kitchen.

She went on, "And you. While I shifted crates, you ran from vendor to vendor in the rain, sending extra hands where they were needed." She paused to let the emotion rising in her dissipate. "It was something."

He got up to fetch an apple from his cupboard and offered it to her. Scry held it in her hands, admiring it. "But Appleseed has been an equitable district for some time now. I'm sure to you it's commonplace." She set the apple down decisively on the table between them. "Is it okay if I take some things from my bag?" she asked, still aware of his knife. She proceeded to take out the apples, canned tomatoes, and dried beans, placing them neatly on the table. "I've been staked out in HaTai for days. I took all of this from a house there, and I want you to have it."

"Why wouldn't you keep this for yourself?" he asked, as she knew he would.

"I have no use for it." Scry watched him move quickly from confusion to wonder.

"On several occasions, I've been told stories about you. And each time I speculated as to how it could be that you survive this place on your own. Admittedly, this possibility never occurred to me."

"Sunlight and water. Of course, I *can* eat if I have to, to keep up appearances, but the organs are vestigial and inefficient. It's uncomfortable, and I hate to waste food that could sustain someone else."

For a moment they sat in silence and Scry hoped that her secret was enough to win his trust.

"Ok," he said. "Let's hear it."

She told him everything she knew, sometimes repeating things for him as he took it all in. Finally, she unfurled the poster and said, "And now they're posting this."

The wheels were turning behind LinKun's eyes. "How un'the'suns are they feeding themselves…" he muttered.

"My gut tells me they're trying to form a centralized government, and the first thing they'll have to do is lie about what happened in HaTai. Somehow they're going to have to convince everyone that they were the good guys."

"Do you think they'd come after the survivors?"

"Jarek knew about your meeting. If the leak was from someone inside the Guild, it's possible the Heralds are looking for them. But they might not even be worried about loose ends if they're already on the ground spreading their story."

"We'll have to tell ours, and faster."

"Exactly. But it won't end there. If they had just wanted the Lab, I doubt anyone in HaTai would have stood in their way so long as it didn't interfere with business. If their bigger plan requires the public will, killing at that scale was a major risk. They took it out because they know it's a lynch-pin for the entire economy this side of the KurShek." LinKun was nodding. This had already occurred to him. "They're trying to divide the districts, to topple the Guild, while also taking a strategic position in anticipation of com-bat."

"Best wanted us to fight."

"In the spirit of honesty, I should tell you I was there, at the Owl's Eyelid."

"So, you have more than one secret…" he said, contem-plating by what means she was able to remain out of sight in the one-room pub.

"Unfortunately, the Duchess is most likely your mole. She was very keen to have you go to battle. But you shouldn't. I'm sure Ruth knows how high a risk you run of being flanked. Especially with Baldur losing folk to the Her-alds. If you attack, they could come into Appleseed behind you, or they might try to take the Dirt from the Four Legs. Stand your ground and hold the Guild together."

Outside, the primary sun had started to set. LinKun shifted in his seat.

"Can I get you some water?"

"Please."

When LinKun turned back around to offer her the glass, Scry was gone.

><

At last, Scry returned to her roost at the junction of Apple-seed, RuDen, and DurLel. She had several stashes and sleeping places throughout the city, but this was the closest thing she had to a home. Pressing back to brick she climbed, walking up the opposing wall like children walk up door-frames. Although the Lab had always been there, it was only when she had finally settled on the roof that she realized the Heralds could be looking down at her now. A nook formed by several old useless machines perfectly concealed her and her belongings, but the rest of the rooftop felt exposed. She ducked quickly out of sight and whistled for Margot. The magpie flew down to her, perching on her arm.

"Hi," Scry said.

The bird said "Hi, Hi, Hi!" in response. She was an excel-lent mimic but was not willing or able to truly communicate as the LanSu's birds did. Margot always seemed quite capa-ble of understanding her though. After spending a few min-utes stroking the bird, Scry told her to keep a lookout, and to wake her shortly.

But the bird woke her sooner than she had hoped. Scry peeked out above one of the lifeless machines and saw in the twilight what must have been every bird in the city flying the skies above the boroughs. All of them cawing, "Heralds Mur-dered HaTai, Heralds Murdered HaTai," over and over.

Scry descended from her roost. The streets were much more populated than they usually were at dusk, so she remained a storey or more above the commotion wherever it was possible. It quickly became clear that a great deal had happened during her short slumber. The Heralds' posters lined the walls but many of them had already been torn down or painted over with "INDEPENDENCE" and "THE HERALDS CANNOT GIVE US WHAT WE HAVE ALREADY GIVEN OURSELVES." LinKun had wasted no time. On DuRor Street, and again on HerUt, she saw a symbol painted of two people holding down a market stall, rain pouring down on its roof, obscuring the Heralds' message. A teenage girl stood below the emblem on HerUt, retelling Scry's own account of the storm in the lower market to a crowd, as though it were a parable.

"We will stand together!" she said. "We will not be deceived!"

She doubled back to DurLel and found criers every few blocks addressing assemblies of dozens.

"The Heralds are vilifying their victims!" one called out.

Another said in his deep resounding voice, "The Heralds among us have defended their misdeeds by accusing their HaTaiUn victims of standing in the way of ZarNik Jarr's salvation. DurLel, do we need saving?"

The crowd screamed "No," with fists raised in the air, the birds swooping down, still shrieking, "Heralds Murdered HaTai."

She went around WarrN to the Seam, then to MukTa, then the Drink, finding a growing resistance in every borough. In the place of many names, an entire play was being enacted on Kaimin Boulevard. Several actors posed as Heralds and pretended to murder those playing the sleeping HaTaiUns. As red ribbons unfurled from their victims' wounds, the fake Heralds stood and made outrageous claims. One pouted comically and said, "They *made* us do it." Another held an ancient baby doll by the throat and said, "This HaTaiUn stood in our way." Yet another kneeled, crouching over a body, and feigned eating its flesh, red bioluminescent algae smeared on his face. He tossed his head back and yelled out, "A Herald never hungers!" The performance continued on, all the way up the thoroughfare and into the Drink.

When she finally got out ahead of it, she stumbled on some locals in a narrow laneway, spreading the message of the resistance in their own custom. Four grizzled men had surrounded a Herald and were kicking the life out of him.

Scry very nearly carried on unconcerned, but when she heard the man on the ground pleading she recognized his voice from her time on the stoop of 33 Raz Street. It was Jarek.

She raised the hood of her jacket and dropped down into the alley.

Apple Savoury

Preheat oven to 350°F.

Ingredients:
- 6 apples, cored and chopped
- 3 tablespoons pan drippings
- 6 cloves garlic, minced
- 2 small onions, minced
- 6 sprigs rosemary, minced or ground
- ½ cup water

Preparation:
• Bake apples, pan drippings, garlic, onions, and rosemary.
• When apples are soft, mash, then add water and return to heat until edges begin to crisp.
• Mash again and serve hot or cold.

MY MOTHER'S GARDEN

SALLY MCBRIDE

I remember watching, as if it were his eyes I was looking through.

Shimmering heat makes the slope of land look enormous, though it's just a garden plot occupying a small part of our one acre. It's near the city, that's why it's good. We lived 30 miles out, before moving here, on a farmland that consisted of two pigs, lots of raspberry canes, and a cabin with no running water. Today it's the pale morning of Toronto's outskirts, hot already, my mother out there weeding before it gets even hotter and more humid. Back then no one had air conditioning, or a fridge lusty enough to produce ice.

He watches her bending, hunting, pulling green slivers of beans from under their leaves. He watches, and I can feel her hands, nimble as they search. The still-green tomatoes squatting on the ground, her plucking a fat, horned worm from among the twisting stems, stepping on it, moving forward. Shimmering thin and busy. She's going to stake those tomatoes up, later. Tanned shoulders, black hair held off her neck with tortoiseshell combs.

He looks at her for a long time and she doesn't see it, then he turns and leaves. He's gone for the usual three nights. I could help her in the garden, but instead I climb our elm tree and stay there for an hour.

The next time, he stands looking and she turns and sees him. It's later in summer, the tomatoes are ripe; the squash are ready. She holds one, a butternut, the best of a bad lot in my opinion as a 10-year-old who doesn't appreciate squash. It's in her arms like a newborn baby. They look into each other's eyes and I don't know if anything is being transmitted. *Sorry. Why. Please.* She bends down and puts the squash in a bushel basket, sees a weed and pulls it up. Not looking at him. He turns and leaves again.

Leaves with the fruit, hiding it. Leaves and leaves; I like to roll the words around in my head. The fruit of the soil is what matters. He needs to leave, or so she says to me, as in the evening we drop the tomatoes into a boiling pot, then dip them out into a bowl of cold water until they're cool enough to slip off the skins. We're going to freeze them; we have a freezer now. Things change.

He has clients. That's what she tells me. He goes to the city so we can get a new car. In the future lies an in-ground swimming pool, since the clients like him. I will find out about it on the walk home from school, the machines plucking away at the soil. I don't know what *clients* are. I get to help dip the bobbing red globes from their pot of bubbles and toss them, screaming, into the pan of cold water. I scream for them, as the tomatoes have no voice.

She freezes or cans everything. Makes pickles and sauerkraut. It's where I've gained my taste for sour things. Rhubarb, lemon, my mother's dill pickles. Though we prepare for it, we never seem to have winter, in my memory.

What she serves him is what she thinks he might like. Perhaps he does. He eats it. We have macaroni, mashed potatoes, pork chops fried into leather. Pale orange creamy dishes that involve soup cans. They drink instant coffee and Tang.

The next morning, she makes bread for the week. It's the same bread her mother made; white, sturdy, tasteless, though I love the smell of it in the oven. In a couple of days, when he comes back, he brings sliced store-bought bread, soft and even, its crust fragile as tanned human skin. Her bread has already petrified, and tomorrow is made into French toast.

She says to me, "I can't keep him forever. They told me that, after I figured out what was going on. I don't have what he needs. Isn't that funny?"

I didn't think so. What did she mean by "forever"?

We're in the kitchen, some other time in my memory. Evening has brought a little breeze. She has a glass of home-made wine beside her, made from our own grapes. She pulls a big enamel bowl out of a cupboard, locates her whisk among the wooden spoons in a drawer. She is moving deliberately, pouring more wine, taking eggs from the fridge. Dry mustard from a shelf. A lemon, which we get only for this particular operation, waits nubby yellow on the counter. The oil is last. It's kept in a room she calls the pantry but which is really just a nook in the cellar, dirt floored, a door of hanging cloth. But it's cool and smells like mud. Corn oil in a glass bottle. She measures two cups.

She's making mayonnaise. We all love it. I love it because it's like magic, and I think he loves it for the same reason. Or maybe because it's like some kind of art. Or like a story. It changes as you go, and someone has to watch it carefully and do just the right thing at just the right time. She can do it.

Once, when I was only eight I think, he came into the kitchen while she was making it. He had a shirt and tie on;

plus his good shoes. I do believe she was barefoot, pink with heat, her black hair frizzy around her neck. She was pouring out a long stream of oil as thin as a strand of spaghetti into the bowl of eggs and mustard, whisking like mad with the other hand. He watched, his eyes that strange blank grey, and then he put out a finger into the stream and caught a bit of oil. He looked at it, then licked it off his finger.

"It's really quite amazing," he said. "You doing this."

"It's just chemistry," she said, concentrating on the stream and the motion of her left-hand whisking, "It's just emulsification."

"Yes." He nodded as if she'd said something erudite or special. Clever. Perhaps, where he came from, they didn't have such a thing. Maybe they'd forgotten how it was done; how you made food. How you grew it, and boiled, and fried, and canned it. I didn't know what kept him alive. Not food. Not a wife. Not me. He was waiting, I think, for things to change, for beings such as him to be noticed. Then what? Would he teach us how to make the food he liked? He was hiding here, long years of growing old waiting for someone to come and change things.

Then he left, and her hand stopped moving. The oil was gone. The bowl contained creamy white piles of mayonnaise. She put in the salt and the lemon juice and a grind of pepper. One of her black hairs fell in, and I retrieved it, slid it out to drop on the floor, licking my finger.

We had both seen the slim, pale, jittering thing that flicked behind him, while the oil sped downward. It was waiting for him, impatient as summer or sickness. He had to turn to it and go.

She put the mayonnaise into the fridge with a plate on top to keep it from developing a skin, and we went to the garden for a tomato. We had to search for the perfect one, the biggest, the reddest, the most perfectly fat and wide. Beefsteaks. All three of us agreed on the mayonnaise, but only my mother and I loved the Beefsteak tomatoes. Warm from the sun, traversed by worms and rain, sliced thick onto homemade bread lavished with mayonnaise, salt and pepper. The smell of it all; the taste in our mouths. It was our world's perfect food, or so we told each other, red juice running down our chins.

Mayonnaise

Ingredients:
- 2 egg yolks
- ½ teaspoon salt
- ½ teaspoon dry mustard
- 1 tablespoon lemon juice
- 1 teaspoon white vinegar
- 1½ cups vegetable oil

Preparation:
• Whisk the yolks vigorously in a medium bowl, then add the salt, mustard, lemon juice and vinegar, whisking for about ½ minute.
• Pour in about 1/3 cup oil in a slow, thin, steady stream, whisking hard. In about a minute the oil should be incorporated and mixture should thicken. Add more oil, whisking fast, until it's all in. You can rest your arm every 30 seconds or so but keep pouring the oil in at a slow and steady pace till it's all gone.
• Refrigerate in a jar and use within a week or two.

(This recipe is adapted from what I remember of my mom's method, after making a few batches of my own.)

THE BAO QUEEN

Melissa Yuan-Innes

Mui Mui was born in 1980, which was too late for most things, including Lava Lamps, Pet Rocks, and most importantly, the Fairy Godfather.

Her brother, Trenton, was 7 years old when he defeated the Fairy Godfather who'd threatened their parents at Guandong Barbecue, their Toronto family restaurant. Mui Mui, who'd been only three months old at the time, couldn't remember one second of the showdown.

Trenton didn't like talking about it. "It was a long time ago," he said, stuffing paper napkins into the steel container on the counter next to the cash. Napkins were free at their restaurant, but they didn't give away too many of them. If you kept them next to the cash, people were so busy paying that they didn't grab extras.

"It was *six*, almost *seven*, years ago!" Mui Mui stomped her Mary Janes on the tile floor, in front of the counter that would soon be filled with food. "You were already older than me when it happened. You *have* to remember!"

Trenton shrugged. He was 14. He liked listening to Dire Straits and picking out "Axel F" on the keyboard, not talking about the Fairy Godfather, and definitely not helping out in Guandong Barbecue any more than he had to. He wasn't rude to their parents, but he wasn't spending all his free time asking Baba for his secret recipe for crispy pork skin.

"That guy's gone now, " he said. "Good riddance."

"I want to *see* him! I want to kick him in the tail!" One thing Trenton had let slip was that their Fairy Godfather had reminded him of a pig. That was kind of weird. Mui Mui had trouble picturing anything except the three little pigs in the Disney cartoon, which definitely wasn't right.

"He's already been kicked." Trenton smiled a tiny bit, the smile that drove her crazy because it meant he was remembering stuff she couldn't.

"I want to kick him again!"

"Look, Mui Mui. It's not worth bringing him back. He was bad luck for our family."

Mui Mui stuck her chin out. "And good luck. You think he might have helped Mama and Baba make the best pork—"

"Baba would have made the best pork anyway. That's why he spent so long bribing chefs with wine and trying to figure out their secrets in Hong Kong. That's why he spends so much money on the freshest pigs and ducks. They make the best barbecue in town. Just...leave it alone, all right?"

Mui Mui wrapped one of her pigtails around her finger. She used to suck on the ends, but her mother put hot sauce on them to cure her of the habit, so now she twisted them in her hands while she was thinking. "It's not fair. You get all the adventure, and I get—"

"To have fun," Trenton snapped. He stomped to the kitchen, which was also the back room, where Baba silently tended to the pig roasting. The meat sizzled, putting an end to their talking.

"It's not fair!" she yelled at his back.

Mama's weary steps clomped up from the basement under the kitchen. Usually, Mama minded the cash in the front room, but Mui Mui had gotten up early today because the July sun had burned so brightly behind the beige curtains of her bedroom, and because Trenton was trying to figure out "Money for Nothing" on the guitar he'd gotten for Christmas. He hadn't plugged it in, but still. They could hear everything in their tiny apartment above the restaurant, from the pipes rattling to the people coughing next door.

Mui Mui could tell from her mother's steps that she was carrying something heavy, probably a goose for dad to blanch and then roast. They never asked Mui Mui to do stuff like that. Usually, that was good because she didn't want to carry heavy, dead, smelly animals up from the basement. But sometimes it made her mad. She was just as strong and smart as anyone in the family, but because she was the smallest and a girl, no one ever got her to do anything!

"What is all the yelling?" asked Mama, sticking her head out of the kitchen. Sure enough, she held a dead duck in front of her. Her hair was tied in a neat bun and caught under a white hairnet.

Mui Mui tried not to look the duck in its staring, black eye. "Nothing, Mama."

"Well, then, why don't you make us a pot of tea?"

"Yes, Mama." Mui Mui hurried past her, so now the whole family was wedged in the kitchen. Baba smiled at her, letting her go by before he threw the latch to open the oven doors. Even though it was only 7 a.m., in July the temperature of the small room soared, and she could see his face light up with flames. Once, she had a dream that Baba burned to death, but when she'd screamed herself awake, Baba had laughed at her fears.

Mui Mui closed her eyes and forced that memory away, back where it belonged.

Trenton had his back to her, blanching the goose in a pot on the stove. She knew he despised the feel of the cold flesh on his hands. It gave him a rash. He was scared of scalding himself with the hot water, too. But he never complained to his parents, who worked harder than anyone else they knew, which was saying a lot in Scarborough, their tiny section east of Toronto crowded with Chinese immigrants.

Mama was tired a lot lately. Tea was one thing she trusted Mui Mui to do. Mui Mui jumped onto the counter and sat on it while she threw open the top cupboard.

Baba cleared his throat. Even over the rumble of the rail, as he slid the pig out of the oven, she could hear the rebuke in his throat.

"Sorry, Baba." He wanted her to use a stool instead of sitting on the counter. Mui Mui grabbed the tin of black tea and jumped back down to the ground. Mama usually wanted that one, not the green, yellow, or white tea. They had so many kinds of tea in their cupboards, and they never drank it. Kind of like the Fairy Godfather they never talked about.

Mui Mui plugged in the old steel kettle. Some of her friends had plastic ones, but her parents never bought anything new when they had something they could use for another 10 years. They said it was a waste of money.

Beside the kettle stood a mound of white dough in a white ceramic bowl, wrapped in a clear plastic wrap. "What is this, Mama?"

Mama sighed. "Mrs. Ma wants some *Char Siu Bao*."

Mui Mui wiggled with delight. She loved the white, fluffy steamed buns, filled with her own family's pork, in a slightly sweet sauce. They had them so rarely. "You're making them for her?"

Mama glanced at the front room. She was worried about getting everything done in time before the first customers arrived in three hours. "I'm going to try. Trenton can—"

"I'll help you!"

Mama pursed her lips before she nodded. "Yes, I think you're old enough now."

Trenton snorted behind them, so softly that only Mui Mui could hear him underneath the sizzle of pork and duck. He always said that Mui Mui got away with murder and that he'd been working in the kitchen as long as he could remember.

The tiny room was ferociously hot, even with a fan whipping the air around. They washed their hands before Mama wiped down the tiny table opposite the counter and unwrapped the dough ball. She poked her finger in the middle of it, making a hole.

"Can I do that?" asked Mui Mui. It was the palest dough she'd ever seen, as pale as a cloud.

Mama glanced at her watch, but she said, "Okay."

Mui Mui stuck her finger in the dough, an inch away from her mother's hole. She felt the dough give way, softer and more yielding than Play-Doh. She could smell the meat roasting and feel the humidity rising in the air, with a new sweetness on her tongue, and a voice in her ear seemed to breathe

— *Hello*—

"Hello," Mui Mui said back, automatically.

Mama looked at her out of the corners of her eyes, but said, "*Jo san,*" which meant good morning in Cantonese, and Mui Mui realized that her mother hadn't spoken.

The voice was quieter and more breathy than her mother's. More like the wind, Mui Mui decided. She poked the dough again.

She heard someone take a breath, like she was tickling Trenton, but no one said a word. Could she have imagined it?

Mama started pushing her fists into the dough, turning it around her knuckles. "Let's get all the air out."

— *Wait!*—

Mui Mui grabbed the short, stiff sleeve of her mother's green and white dress. "Did you hear that?"

Mama looked annoyed. "The sound of the dough?"

"No! The—" Mui Mui bit back the words. "Yes! It's talking."

Mama shook her head and kept pounding. "Mui Mui, we don't have time for you to play games."

"Sorry," said Mui Mui, more from habit than anything else. She glanced around the room. Baba was turning the pig so he could poke holes in its skin with a carpenter's nail, and Mama was punching the dough…

— *Ha!*—

Mui Mui stiffened and strained to fine-tune her ears.

— *Ha, ha, ha!*—

After a second, she realized that the dough was laughing. It wasn't scared of Mama or getting hurt. She could relax again and learn how to do it. She stuck her hands in the dough and started pushing at a corner.

"Your hands are too small," said Mama, but she added, "Do you see the honeycomb texture of the dough? See how it looks like bees' honeycombs?" She dug her fingers into the dough and pulled the top part aside.

Mui Mui knew what honeycombs looked like, partly because of the cereal, but the dough just seemed like rough dough to her. She nodded anyway and joined in with her small fingers. She thought the dough might be getting firmer and harder to push around.

Mama clucked her tongue. "What is wrong with this? I bought the special bleached flour, and I used a bit of milk."

"Baking powder?" said Baba.

"You know I did. The yeast, I bought specially from You Dun. Oh, I don't have time to make a new batch for Mrs. Ma!"

Mui Mui's hands slowed. She didn't want to be accused of messing up Mama's dough.

— *I like your fingers*—

It was the first time anyone had expressed approval of anything Mui Mui did in the kitchen, so she thought very hard. *Thank you.*

She didn't hear any response, no matter how she tried.

Meanwhile, Mama said, "It's getting cold in here. That's no good for the dough. The yeast has to rise."

Mui Mui realized that the usual blast of the oven had died down. In fact, she had goosebumps on her arms. Was this because of the dough spirit?

"This dough might be garbage," said Mama, standing up and grabbing the bowl. She was going to pitch it in the garbage.

Baba slammed the oven door shut. The sound thundered through the room.

"Wait!" Mui Mui called. Her heart thudded. She didn't know what was going on, but she knew that was wrong. "Could I have it?"

Mama frowned. "I thought you wanted to learn how to make *Char Siu Bao*."

"I do! But could I try with this? Even if it's not perfect?"

Baba's mouth jerked into a grin. Although he didn't say anything, Mui Mui knew he was on her side. He liked that she wanted to play in the kitchen.

Mama threw her arms in the air. "You want to waste your time, fine. I have to make a new batch for Mrs. Ma." She reached into the cupboards overhead and grabbed a bag of Chinese bleached flour, the special kind that even Trenton wasn't allowed to touch, and grumbled as she poured it into a blue plastic bowl.

Meanwhile, Mui Mui shaped the dough, tickling it, making it chortle, until its sounds grew fainter and fainter, and Mui Mui knew that it was done. She set it aside, rubbing her fingers together so that bits of dough came off them, almost like pieces of her skin. She dropped them back in the bowl. She didn't want to lose a crumb.

After her hands were clean, she realized that Mama was standing over her shoulder. Mama had finished her next batch of dough and joined her, asking, "Do you still want to use this dough?"

Mui Mui nodded. "I think it will be delicious, Mama."

Mama sighed, but then she smiled. The air around her felt gentler. Warmer, somehow. "All right, Mui Mui. Let's give it a try." She oiled a new bowl and placed the dough ball gently inside before covering the bowl with a damp cloth. "I'm sure Baba can spare a bit of meat."

Baba laughed. "Always enough for my family."

That wasn't true. He usually sold out of meat before the end of the day, because their restaurant was so popular, and they had to eat the *tofu* or other leftovers. But it was true that if Mui Mui wanted a piece during the day, all she had to do was stand beside him, and he would slip her a piece.

Baba sliced off a chunk of pork belly almost as big as Mui Mui's head and handed it to Mama with both hands, smiling. Mama opened her mouth, and Mui Mui waited for her to scold him for wasting meat. Instead, after a moment, Mama closed her lips and kissed Baba on the cheek.

Even Trenton stopped slicing green onions, so Mui Mui was sure he'd noticed something strange was going on. But after a moment, his knife started up again.

Mama made short work of the meat. She got her own wooden chopping block and used a cleaver to chop it into even cubes smaller than the dice Mui Mui played with. She added some of the green onions Trenton had sliced, after asking him to chop them even finer, as well as a tablespoon of water from a cup on the counter.

"Why do you need water?" asked Mui Mui, standing on her toes.

"For the ginger taste." Mama lowered the cup to show her the piece of peeled ginger that had been soaking in the water.

Mui Mui thought that was a good idea. She hated eating a stir fry and accidentally biting into a big chunk of ginger, like at their neighbour's house.

After Mama mixed the pork belly with the seasonings, she washed her hands and sprinkled flour on the fake wood table before she reached for Mui Mui's ball of dough, which was now so big that it looked like a pregnant belly underneath the cloth.

Mui Mui held her breath, but the dough spirit didn't speak.

Mama's quick hands rolled the dough from a ball into a baguette, a longer and thinner shape. The table wobbled on its metal legs as she worked.

Mui Mui didn't hear the dough object, so she relaxed until Mama picked up a butter knife. "What are you doing?"

Mama frowned. "I have to cut it up for the *bao*."

"Can't we use our hands?"

"It will take too long. Look."

Mui Mui screeched, but it was too late. The metal blade swung through the air and sliced through the dough, cutting a circle that fell on the table. Mui Mui snatched it up, thinking, *Can you hear me? Are you okay?*

Mama clucked her tongue. "What is wrong with you?"

"You killed it!" Mui Mui started to cry.

"Killed what?" asked Mama, but she was already slicing up the rest of the dough. Chop, chop, chop. More circles of dough that didn't speak. "Honestly, Mui Mui, I don't have time for this."

Trenton materialized by her side. "It's okay, Mui Mui. Let's go in front. I think I hear a customer."

Mui Mui allowed him to tow her out of the kitchen by her elbow, although she dragged her feet and tears dripped down her face.

When they were alone, behind the cash register, Trenton said, "It's still alive."

She stopped crying and eyeballed him suspiciously. "What is?"

"That thing. The one that was talking."

Her heart fluttered. "You heard it, too?"

"A little bit. I felt it."

"Like...the Fairy Godfather?"

Trenton laughed. "No, that was a big, fat man. This was different."

"But where is it? Mama cut it up—"

"She cut up the dough, but that spirit didn't die. I can still feel it."

"Where is it?"

Trenton jerked his thumb backward, toward the kitchen. Mama was singing now. She hardly ever sang in the kitchen, or even at night. Her voice rose and fell, telling a story of a girl who dressed up like a boy and fought in her father's stead, bringing honour and riches to her family, before she found true love.

They stood frozen, listening to every note, until the last one faded into silence.

Mui Mui tiptoed to the doorway. Baba was still wearing his apron and his white hat, but he had his arms around Mama, and she had her hands on both sides of his face, kissing him like they were in the movies!

Mui Mui gulped. She turned to look at Trenton, who had come up behind her, before he pulled her back to the cash register.

Mui Mui's lips trembled. Finally, she got the words out. "The dough spirit..." She couldn't finish the sentence.

Trenton nodded. His hands twisted. Finally, he said, "The Fairy Godfather went to her first, too. It's like she attracts them." He gave Mui Mui a sharp look, and she jerked to attention. The dough spirit was inside Mama. Forever? Would it hurt her?

No, that was impossible. Mui Mui twisted her braids, not caring if she got bits of dough in them. "But she didn't hear it! She didn't talk to it!" Mama could have been faking deafness, but Mui Mui didn't think so. Mama cared about work. That was what she did. She wasn't thinking about spirits.

"I don't think that matters. It's in her anyway. I haven't heard her sing since you were a baby."

Mui Mui's heart thumped twice. "We've got to get it out of her."

Trenton didn't say anything. They sat in silence, Mui Mui yanking on her braids so hard that they hurt, before Mama laughed in the back room.

It was a laugh Mui Mui had never heard before, a low and teasing laugh. Baba's voice floated in the air, too soft for them to hear the words, but it was like a comforting bear growl.

Mama emerged from the back room, holding a bamboo steamer containing two *Char Siu Bao*. Her face looked flushed, and Mui Mui thought she'd never seen her mother's eyes gleam so brightly. "You have to try these, Mui Mui. I think they're the best I've ever had."

Mui Mui was scared. She didn't want to, but Trenton grabbed his and peeled the wax paper off the bottom of the bun before he took a hearty bite. "Mmm!"

Mui Mui trusted her brother enough to reach for a bao, which looked like a white ball with a flattened bottom while the char siu peeked out a hole in the top. Mama had once told her that the bao were considered good luck because they looked like money bags.

The warm dough indented under Mui Mui's fingers, and she waited for it to speak, but when it didn't, she closed her eyes and licked the top.

Trenton didn't lie. Her mouth flooded with saliva, and visions washed through her brain. She saw Mama elbowing her way toward a food stall strung with paper lanterns. Baba offered a glass of wine to a man wearing a white hat and apron just like the one he wore now. Finally, a red-faced man in a Hawaiian shirt that barely contained his enormous belly leered at one small, scared Trenton, who gulped but squared his skinny shoulders.

Mui Mui gasped, and the image faded. She opened her eyes. A much bigger Trenton frowned and set down his bao so he could talk to her, but Mama was already smoothing out Mui Mui's bangs and touching the ends of her braids.

Mama said, "You have flour in your hair, silly," and kissed her on the forehead.

Mui Mui clung to her bao. The dough squished under the pressure, but the filling didn't squirt on to the floor. She would eat every crumb and lick the sauce from her lips.

Mui Mui wasn't afraid anymore. Maybe Mama would attract a dozen more spirits to Guandong Barbecue. Some might be evil, like the Fairy Godfather, but the dough spirit was gentle and funny and stronger than she had imagined. Cutting it and cooking it had only transformed its powers.

And Mui Mui would be at the centre now. Trenton could feel the dough spirit, and Mama could swallow it, but Mui Mui was the only one who could talk to it and use it to slip into her family's memories. Was that because she was a girl, or because Mama had passed the gift on to her? Maybe Mui Mui would find out when she was older, like Trenton. Especially if she ignored the guitar and spent her time learning how to make bao and barbecue pork with her parents, in their kitchen.

"Thank you, Mama. I love you." She was talking to her mother, but she knew that Trenton, Baba, and the dough spirit could hear her, too.

Char Siu Bao

(adapted from the BAO restaurant, London, England, and Zoe Liu at bakeforhappykids.com)

Ingredients:
- 3 cups bleached white bread flour (more if required to adjust the dough's consistency)
- 3 tablespoons sugar
- ½ teaspoon salt
- ⅘ teaspoon baking powder
- 1 ¾ teaspoons instant yeast
- ¼ cup lukewarm water
- ¼ cup milk
- 1 teaspoon vegetable oil, with some extra for greasing
- ⅔ pound char siu (barbecued pork), cut into ½ inch cubes

Preparation:
- Mix the flour, sugar, salt, baking powder and yeast. Next, add the water and milk to make a rough ball.
- Move the ball on the countertop to knead it by hand, past the honeycomb texture, until it is smooth and doesn't stick to the counter. This will take 10 or 15 minutes. If a dough spirit giggles, you must be Mui Mui.
- Gently place the dough ball in an oiled bowl. Cover the bowl with a damp towel and let the dough rise until the dough doubles in size, which will take about an hour.
- Take the doubled dough and roll it into a baguette shape.
- Cut or pinch the dough into 15 equal portions, which will each weigh about 2 ounces. You'll roll these 15 pieces into balls before using a rolling pin to flatten them into circles.

• Place them on a baking sheet with room to grow. Cover them with a cloth and let them rest for 20 minutes.

• Place 1 tablespoon of filling in the middle of the circle. Make six pleats and then bring the pleats together to make a ball. Remember, you want enough filling because that's the best part, but not so much that it spills out of the bao.

• Now the steamer. You have to line the steamer with oiled baking paper. Turn up the heat until the water is simmering, not a rolling boil.

• Place the bao in the steamer with room around each. You don't want them to mash together, so you may have to do multiple batches. Let them steam for 15 to 25 minutes, depending on your steamer. They should swell up and have a smooth surface that bounces back from a light touch.

Makes 15 buns. Serve warm. Eat lots.

TRENCHERMAN

Liz Westbrook-Trenholm

The oil and mud slime in Ed's boots squished as he stamped his numb feet, listening for any stealthy sounds from No Man's Land. From the back of the trench came murmured calls on a poker game. Silence, otherwise. He stole a quick glance over the top. Nothing but black stumps, churned mud and the waft of Foul Fritz rotting on the edge of the shell hole where he'd copped it. Nothing for days now but rain and boredom. Sunny today, but the trench still ran like a ditch, filling his boots whenever he stepped down from the fire step. Oil held off the trench foot so far, at least. Time for rotation back soon. Hot food, time to dry his boots, maybe a letter from Marsa waiting. Nothing 'til then but scratching his cootie bites and trying to stay safe.

A loud clank ducked him low, rifle gripped, peering about for the threat. Bert the Brit, helmet propped atop his giant ears, squatted over an empty wire spool on his sleeping ledge, bashing on a hard biscuit with his trench club.

"Jesus, Bertie, I thought you were the damn Hun." Bertie seemed to be making little impression on the biscuit. "What good'll that do, dingbat? It'll still be inedible."

Bertie threw him a gap-toothed grin. "Boil it up in a bit of tinned milk and I've got a lovely Wipers pudding."

"I'll wait for dinner," Ed said. "Horse stew, if we're lucky."

"More likely boiled bully beef and cabbage again, with tepid tea tasting of boiled beef and cabbage. My piss tastes better than that tea."

"Where *is* our bloody dinner? I'm starving." Ed sneaked another peek toward the rear.

"Head down and move around, Ed you id-jit," Bertie said mildly. "Foul Fritz's cousin Jerry will be notching you on his stock, you keep popping up same bloody spot every time. What would you do without Uncle Bertie to look after you, you daft bugger?"

Ed moved along the trench and looked again. He froze. A bank of yellow-green rose above the broken land. Even as he watched, it gained height, billowing toward their lines.

"Bertie, what is that?"

"Head down, you fool!" Bertie leapt up on the fire step, but stopped still at his elbow, staring. The others, noticing, set down their cards, rising to look. The mist oiled most heavily toward the French on the left flank. As it reached the front trenches, figures staggered up over the top, dropping weapons and backpacks in a desperate haste to escape. A machine gun krug-krugged and men dropped like puppets with their strings cut. Ed ducked down below the level of the trench, eyes stinging, breath catching.

A man in the turban and brown pantaloons of the Algerian Spahis tumbled blindly into their trench, gagging and coughing. More followed, pushing and shoving to get to the communications trenches to the rear.

Their lieutenant drew his revolver and blocked their passage. "Hold up, you cowards, or I'll shoot you where you stand." A soldier halted, clutching his chest, eyes bugging in his brown face. He retched as if trying to expel his own lungs and collapsed onto his face. Another fell on top of him, writhing and clutching his throat.

"Stretcher crew!" someone shouted. The lieutenant yelled for the signalman. The trench grew chaotic with officers and non-coms shouting orders to hold position, soldiers jostling into place and the gurgles of dying Algerians.

"Back on the line, soldier!" Someone pushed Ed hard on the shoulder. He found his way back up onto the fire step and peered through the stinging mist, eyes burning and blurry. He held his bunched up handkerchief to his mouth and nose with one hand, aiming his rifle one-handed as he blinked away tears. Gunfire chattered steadily from out in the Salient, poking like a fist into the German line, with the occasional whump of a grenade. The mist was thickening. He shuffled along the fire step, trying to find a position where it might be thinner, where he could see. *I only wanted to be safe,* he thought. *I only wanted Marsa to be safe.*

He misstepped and slid down the muddy trench slope, steeling himself for cold water. Instead, he felt solid floor under his feet. He blinked tears away. Sun shone in his eyes, filtered through a lathe lattice onto a broad verandah, diamond shadow and light patterns falling on unpainted planks. It felt familiar and yet strange, as if he should know the place. The sun was warm but the air taut and cool; one of those surprise days that pop up in the midst of early spring in Alberta.

A wrought-iron table and chairs stood by a door open to the dark interior of a house where he glimpsed a staircase, a grandfather clock standing on the landing. On the table was a tray laden with flowered china cups, saucers, plates, napkins, and, oh lord, a basket of scones, jars of honey and raspberry preserve, neatly labelled in handwritten script, and a cake, already cut, golden yellow with eggs and butter.

Marsa stepped heavily through the door and crossed the verandah to set the teapot on the table. She was hugely pregnant. With a sigh she sank into a chair and along came her two sisters, fussing over her and chattering like birds as they always did, a waterfall of noise. Ed felt an intruder in his mud-caked uniform and smelly boots, but they seemed not to notice him, not even when he poured himself tea and filled a plate with scones and cake. He burnt his mouth on tea, ate and ate, and ate some more. Layers of buttery scone, piled with home-churned butter, thick cream and jam, and huge, hungry bites of moist, sweet cake.

"You were hungry!" said Esme, the older.

"She's eating for two," declared Agnes, patting Marsa's shoulder. They went off to make more tea, always a duo those two, and, alone with his beautiful, strong pregnant wife, he didn't know what to say. So he knelt at her feet and laid his hands on her belly. Marsa closed her eyes, soaking in the sun and his touch.

"Albert if it's a boy," he whispered. "Alberta if it's a girl. Because it's where the baby will be born. And because it's the name of the man who tried to keep me safe."

She nodded.

"I suppose I'm dead," he said.

"You ought to be, wonder of wonders and no thanks to you, you daft bugger." Bertie's voice sounded oddly muffled. "Did you not hear the orders? Piss on your hankies, they said. But you? You had to have Uncle Bertie do it for you."

Cloth was wadded over Ed's face, tied tight at the back of his head. The stench of urine choked him.

"I'm suffocating," he said. But, by damn, it was working. The chlorine gas wasn't getting to him anymore, except for the eyes. He could just make out Bertie's big-eared profile, lower part of his face hidden behind a wad of white.

"No whingeing, Ed. I was saving that lot up for my afternoon tea. Be appreciative." Bertie hauled him upright and back into position on the fire step. Just in time.

A monster with goggle eyes loomed out of the mist, running straight for him. German helmet. Ed shot the bastard, and the next, thinking of brown faces turned blue, of Marsa, big on her verandah. When the Huns pulled back for a bit, he and Bertie stripped the masks off the dead ones, wiped off the blood, put them on and didn't talk about it, right through that night's push to take the line vacated by the Algerians.

Still wearing a dead man's mask, he and some others snatched a nap between bouts in the Algerian trench while Bertie stood watch.

Ed saw a little child in an embroidered smock, blonde curls escaping from the brim of a lacy bonnet. He recognized the verandah where she sat. The child toiled herself upright, arms out and up for balance and staggered one, two, three steps, all the while looking right at him. She laughed. She looked past his shoulder, as if catching sight of something. Her eyes widened and her face crumpled, fearful.

Ed was up shoulder to shoulder with Bertie, firing at the advancing enemy almost before he was awake.

"Where do you get your energy?" Bertie asked.

And again, two days in, waiting to be relieved, waiting for water in a tin to boil for a drink of Oxo, he glanced up and saw a slim girl in dress and pinafore standing on the verandah steps. She was urging a horse that looked huge beside her small frame closer to the verandah railing. It clomped through a patch of nasturtiums and settled by the rail. The girl clambered up on the rail and onto the beast's back. Leaning down, she scooped up a lard tin he hadn't noticed that was sitting on the same railing. She glanced once at him, grinned, and rode away. He wanted her to stay.

"What the hell are you looking at?" Bertie demanded.

Ed shook his head. "Just thinking of home." Bertie made a confirming noise and they sipped, side by side.

"Your wife's in the family way, isn't she?"

Ed nodded. "Happened just before I left. Due in May."

"Least you're leaving someone to follow in your foot-steps."

"No, thank God. No war for her."

"Her?"

"It'll be a girl."

Bertie laughed uproariously. "You daft beggar, it'll be what it wants to be."

They held the salient, he, Bertie and the others who'd scavenged German gas masks doing better than the others caught in the first attack. A lot got led back, eyes bandaged, hand on the shoulder of the next as they shuffled away from No Man's land and battle.

>‹

A shell blew close enough to pop eardrums. Bertie, stirring his inevitable hard biscuit mash, affected not to notice.

"No hot meal coming in this noise, Ed." He handed over a mess can. "Get some of this into you. I added Oxo and tinned bully. Washed down with your tot, it's just like stew and dumplings."

"Just like shit," Ed said, but scooped out a share. The liquor burned his near-empty stomach.

As so often and uselessly over the last months, the order came to attack. Like a well-oiled machine, Ed and Bertie wiped their mouths, lifted their packs, and fixed bayonets.

"Canajuns to the rescue of the useless Brits," Bertie remarked.

Ed grinned. "If you were any more English you'd wear a monocle and bowler."

"I'm Canajun!" Bertie exploded with indignation. "I have a chin. And a spine."

Over the top, they ran zigzag and low, protecting their heads, limbs, and genitals, not necessarily in that order.

Their own guns pounded a creeping barrage in front of them, ostensibly forcing snipers down.

They avoided the inviting defiles through the wire. A Hun gunner certainly sighted along them. A glance back showed men following parallel to their path through No Man's Land.

"Babies to mind, Bertie," he muttered.

They cut wire, edged around the top of a shell hole and wriggled in low to do it again a yard on. The guns let up. Bertie hollered, "Heads and arses down!"

A gasp behind them: "I'm hit," as the rifle report hit their ears.

"He didn't listen."

"Stay put! Fritz's pinned us." The barrage started up again, providing cover.

"Shall we twinkle our toes toward the Hun, chaps?" said Ed.

"You bugger." Bertie in the lead, they zagged well to the side of their first position. Rain began, icy, slanting, weighing down the wool of their uniforms. Mud sucked at their boots, each step stirring up the stench of decomposing corpses.

They stuck fast short of a cluster of what might have been buildings once. Shelling and gunfire so heavy they could only keep low and hope.

"Courcelette," said Bertie.

Ed pushed up on an elbow. "I'm impressed—" A hot-cold punch threw him onto the verandah. A girl, Bertie, older now, holding up a half-empty tin of shrivelled saskatoons, face too adult for her age. The air baked.

Back to the mud and guns pounding. "There's a drought!"

"Jesus, Ed, it's pissing down."

"I have to get back. She's so thin. Getting older too fast."

"You stay with Uncle Bertie, Ed."

Dizzy falling sensation. Distant call, "No, Ed!"

Two men and a couple of youths in dust-caked overalls drooped on either side of him around a low wicker table dappled in light falling through the hop vines. They looked as exhausted as Ed felt, as disheartened.

Marsa, slim and lovely, eased sideways out the door of the house, laden down with a wide tray heaped with sandwiches and an impossibly tall white cake.

"Angel food!" She began laying things out on the table. "The hens are laying like crazy."

"Chicken sandwiches!" crowed one of the boys.

"Not *all* of the chickens are laying, Pete." The men laughed and dug in, Ed stuffing as fast as the others. He felt the strength of the food flow into him with every bite.

"So? How was *your* hay crop, Dad?" Marsa's strong brown arms and freckled hands placed custard yellow-rich with egg yolks beside bowls of stewed saskatoons and raspberries. The sound of her voice filled him with as much warmth and comfort as did the bread, moist and fresh from a morning's baking.

Marsa's father, aged more than Ed remembered, slurped tea, the delicate china cup disappearing in his heavy-knuckled paw.

"Been better. Been worse." He dragged fingers through his hair, disturbing particles of dust and chaff. "Spring rain helped. Grasshoppers didn't. We'll have to buy feed before next spring."

"What for, Dad?" A man with blonde hair thinning above his sun-roughened face leaned in, bunching his fists. "Why feed steers when we can't afford to ship them? Bill Kennan away. Tried to sell the farm. No one to buy. Even the bank doesn't want it."

The older man's broad shoulders sagged. "Least we don't have the dust like out east."

"I wish we could do something!" Ed glanced up at the sound of such youthful passion. His heart did a double flip. Squeezing the young Marsa in a hug was another Marsa, older, heavier, but undoubtedly his strong, handsome wife.

"We'll get through, Bertie," she said to her daughter. "We've got chickens. They love the grasshoppers. We've got berries galore this year. We've got a good well and our own strong backs. We'll get through this year and then we'll see."

"What year?" Ed said.

"Bloody 1916 you git." Bertie's voice strangled with effort. Bertie's shoulder dug into Ed's belly, Ed's head and arms dangling. Blood dripped down the fingers of his left hand onto the back of Bertie's boot sunk in the mud. The boot hauled free and a jerk shot fire through Ed's shoulder. The fingers on his left hand felt numb.

"Let me walk."

Bertie slid him off his shoulder and searched his face, panting, eyes haunted.

"I had chicken sandwiches, Bertie."

Bertie's face broke in an incredulous laugh and he hooked an arm around his waist. Ed's tale of angel food cake got them to the medic station.

The medic poked the wound in his shoulder.

Bertie leaned over a white, tiered cake beside a young man in an unfamiliar uniform. Their hands joined over a knife handle, cutting the lowest tier. Ed felt a jolt of jealousy. Bertie smiled up at him. Her veil was the one Marsa had worn when she floated to meet him on the arm of her father up the aisle of their log church. Bertie was as lovely.

"Bertie, you are beautiful."

"He's off his noggin. Pay him no mind." Bertie's face swam into focus, alongside the medic with raised eyebrows. "What are you grinning for, you daft bugger. You've taken a hunk of shrapnel straight through you."

"All out," said the medic. "You'll be back in the fun in no time."

Ed felt terribly tired, but happy. "I was at her wedding. My Bertie, married."

The medic exchanged glances with Ed's friend, who shook his head.

"More cake and chicken sandwiches?"

"Wedding cake. But I didn't get any before I got back."

"Good thing I saved you dinner, then," Bertie said. He disappeared from Ed's view. The medic checked Ed's ears, felt his scalp and asked, "How many fingers am I holding up?"

"Don't get your knickers in a twist," Bertie called from somewhere. "He's always travelling off into the future, like Jules Bloody Verne. Knew he was having a daughter before he got the letter. Comes back full of bread and jam. Never brings any with him, selfish bugger."

The medic shook his head. "Guess I've heard stranger stories." He helped Ed into a sitting position. He was in a trench bunker. Other men lay about on stretchers and pallets. Medical station, then. Safe from fire.

"Your chum hauled you halfway across No Man's land," said the medic. "Fire all around, but he kept on."

Bertie swam into sight. "Ha. A thick twit like you, better than plate armour. Here, get this into you. Turnip bread, boiled bully of course, and tea like dishwater. Bloody feast." He pushed a mess tin between Ed's limp hands.

"Thank you, Bertie," said Ed.

"I don't want to eat that swill," said Bertie. "Next time you head home, bring me back a tea." He stood up. "Well, back to it." Ed tried to watch him go, but his eyes wouldn't stay open. Eyes shut, he called, "Keep your head and your arse down, Uncle Bertie."

Bertie's profane response sang him to sleep.

>‹

"March here. March there. Survived Wipers. Survived Vimy. Survived Passchendale. And now have us bloody tiptoeing back of the line like the lodger visiting the missus in the night. Where to? Nobody tells us PBI." Ed couldn't see Bertie in the dark, but he could certainly hear him, even above the incessant rumble of the big guns all up and down the front, and the growl of the tank they were following. He shifted his rifle as he picked his way through confusing moon shadow criss-crossing the road. His shoulder ached from the wound he'd got at the Somme. Bloody useless battle that. But after that one, he'd noticed that even the Brits started treating them with respect, like equals.

"Shut it, you two. Orders!" The lieutenant wasn't a bad one, but jumpy as a cat right now. "You're on a secret raid, not doing a bloody vaudeville act."

"Does he mean us?" Bertie asked.

Ed snickered. "Nah. He means you."

A barrage like a thunderstorm started off back of them, some poor bloody infantry about to go over the top somewhere. Why are we marching away from it? Ed wondered. Nothing up this end of the line but the usual sporadic shell blast, passing the time of day with the Hun. He caught a scrap of German drifting on the warm August air. Close to the front line, then. The voices sounded near peaceable, unsuspecting. Ed remembered a time when he'd have felt uneasy about killing ordinary men, sons and husbands alive one minute, extinguished the next. Even as the thought flickered alight, he snuffed it. Them or me. Survive. Keep safe. Head and arse down.

Even Bertie shut up.

They stood down, sitting or napping silently in a ditch by the side of the road. They chewed some hard rations, no talking, Bertie skipping the menu recitation. Ed tried to sleep, but it wouldn't come. No raid this, he could feel it. Officers tense, keeping everyone orderly and silent. Big push then. A heavy fog rolled over the ditch, faintly luminous. Dawn coming. No barrage as yet. He waited, gut twisting. Come on, come on. Get it over with.

Bertie woke up, stretched and went off to relieve himself.

When he returned, he gathered his equipment, checked his rifle and shook his flask with a satisfied nod. "Arse and head down," he whispered.

The guns and orders came at the same time. The fog flashed with explosions from the creeping barrage a hundred yards or so in front of them. They ran, fast and low, waiting for the return barrage. Tanks flanked their section, firing ahead of them.

"When are they going to start shooting back?" Bertie yelled over the bellow of the guns.

The man next to them dropped, and they hit the turf. A machine gun blindly sprayed bullets above them. They crawled forward. The gun fell silent, reloading maybe. Ed stood up, ran and fell into a trench. A scared kid in a German helmet, mouth wide in shock, fumbled with his rifle. Ed rolled and lifted his bayonet. The soldier dropped his weapon and raised his hands. "Kamerad!"

Ed ran him through. In seconds what was left of their group piled into the trench, stabbing and shooting at close quarters. In the thick of it, teeth bared and revolver smoking, the lieutenant shot every Hun in sight hands up or not. "Keep your Kamerad, you murdering bastards!" Ed pushed into a dugout. Three officers stood around a table, stools tipped over as if they had just leapt up. They stared at him, one with a cup still clutched in his fingers.

"Breakfast!" Bertie crowed at Ed's shoulder. He rushed toward the officers who cringed back, raising their hands. Bertie ignored them, turning over items on the table. He tossed down a biscuit in disgust.

"Their rations are as crap as ours." He jerked his head. "Come on then, Krauts. Food this bad, you don't deserve to be shot."

As the German officers exited the dugout, the lieutenant raised his revolver.

The verandah was empty. The usual teapot and cups stood beside a plateful of drop cookies. This time he'd get some for Bertie. He grabbed a handful and stuffed them in his blouse pockets.

"No!" Marsa shouting inside the house. He started guiltily. "I won't let them have you."

"The WACs didn't kidnap me, Mother. I joined up." Bertie sounded impatient. "And being stationed in England means I'll get a chance to see Taylor. My *husband*, Mother." A long pause, heavy with emotion that thrust into Ed's belly. "And…I have to do something for the war effort. Mom. I have to."

"And what will the war do for you? What did war do for your father?" Marsa's voice came harsh, bitter, striking like a bayonet.

Bertie blew out onto the verandah, straight and crisp in a blue jacket and short skirt that barely passed her knees, a peaked cap firmly set on her head. She paused, eyes wet. "Goodbye." A mere murmur.

Marsa stumbled across the verandah, tears streaming down her face. "Bertie! Bertie!" The young woman checked, turned, and ran up the steps into her mother's arms. They parted, Bertie waving and waving as she headed toward a strange vehicle with a bulbous snout, idling on a gravel pad where the horses used to tie up. Marsa stood on the top verandah step, hands clutched to her chest. "When will it ever end?"

"Soon," Ed said. "We've got them on the run."

"Please be safe," Marsa said.

"Sir! Sir!" Bertie helped Ed hold the lieutenant, who was screaming, bug-eyed. "They surrendered, sir! We've won the objective." The tension drained out of their officer. He straightened and stared meaningfully at their restraining hands. They let go of him and he lowered his revolver.

"I'll overlook this," he said, not meeting their eyes. They shoved the German officers and their few surviving soldiers out of the trench, leaving the dead where they lay.

As they waited at the rally point, Bertie said, "You were off again. I swear to God, it's like you fade out a bit, not quite gone, not quite here. It's bloody eerie."

Ed nodded. "There's a war."

Bertie's uneasy expression broke up into laughter. "You noticed, did you, you bloody eejit? I say, lads, Ed's noticed there's a war on." That met with laughs and profane suggestions as to where his head had been. Bertie leaned in more closely, lowering his voice. "What was there to eat?"

Ed fumbled in his blouse pocket and pulled out a mess of crumbs and raisins. "Sorry, Bertie, they got crushed."

The laughter died out of his friend's face as he stared at the broken cookie. "Take me with you next time." He turned sharply away, not waiting for a reply.

The numbers of surrendering Germans swelled over the day, columns of them shuffling toward the allied rear.

"Out of it, lucky sods," Bertie commented as they trotted after their lieutenant toward the sound of fighting.

The real resistance hit them after dark eight miles in. Machine-gun fire pinned them below a rise. Shell tracers streaked the night sky like fireworks. Corpse stench melded with the acrid bite of cordite. They tucked in, sentries posted, and tried for a bite and some rest. Just as Ed drifted off, a sentry screamed. Once.

"Here we go," said Bertie. Ed was already up and looking for something to shoot at in the dark. Something punched him. Familiar hurt.

"Damn, I'm hit." Another punch. Down. Pop-pop-pop of shells off enemy lines. Familiar and dreadful. He fumbled on his gas mask and dragged himself up the rise. Better to get shot to death than burn slow from the mustard gas. Another blow. More. Shattering pain and numbness in his hip.

Marsa sprawled on the verandah, screaming and pounding the planks, a cream slip of paper crushed in her hand. The two blonde youths crouched over her, crying and begging her to stop, please stop.

"I'm sorry," Ed said. "I'm so sorry. I didn't mean to leave you."

"Oh, you're not gone yet, son." A sister in a starched veil held his hand. "You'll be fine. Five bullets we dug out of you but you'll pull through. Doctor saved your leg. You Canadians are a hard lot to keep down." She said it the way Bertie did, with a 'j' sound.

"Who *is* dead, then?" Ed whispered.

A mess in the shape of a man, nude torso blackened and blistered, head turned away, coughed on the bed next to his.

Ed met the sister's eye.

"Mustard gas," she whispered. Ed asked the question with his eyes. She answered with a faint head shake that rustled her veil. "We could have helped him if he'd come when he was told. He wouldn't leave until they took out the gun nest that hurt you."

The man turned his face, shockingly clean and unmarred, given the devastation of his body.

"Damn it, Bertie! Heads and arses down, you fool. Why didn't you keep safe?"

Bertie coughed. "More apple tart, please."

"Yes, Bertie," Ed said. "Eat, get strong, come back."

"Staying on a bit, I think," Bertie said. "Nice company here."

Shock roared through Ed, searing in his chest like a bullet to the heart.

The verandah. Empty. Still under a night sky, moon casting sharp edged shadows through leaves. A shadow passed across one end. A slim figure in a short skirt and peaked hat sank into the wicker arm chair at the back corner, one leg up over the arm and swinging. No. No. She's just a baby, a little girl, a bride.

>·<

Ed woke to Marsa's lined face hanging over him, concern deepening the wrinkles on her brow. A magpie squawked in the pines that towered now over 30 feet on the north end of the verandah. A breeze ruffled the hops' leaves. Ed's shoulder and knee joints throbbed, arthritis and old war wounds drumming a familiar tattoo of discomfort.

"You cried out."

"Ache all over," he said. "I'm an old man."

Marsa's mouth pulled down in a fond smile. "I shouldn't have let you fall asleep in that chair. But I hated to wake you. You put in a long day."

"But the hay's all in," Ed heard himself say. He was a soldier, but he was an old farmer, a young husband and father, but a great-grandfather. A history of joys and sorrows paraded through his memory. "This verandah has seen a lot over the years."

"She'd be a grandmother herself now, but it feels like yesterday we got that awful telegram." Marsa turned on him her blue gaze, experienced and a little sad. "Ah well. We've made it through. Pretty much."

"You pulled us through, Marsa. You *and* your cooking. Saved me more times than I can say."

She laughed, eyes lighting up. "I can take a hint!" She leaned in, flirtatious as a bride. "Scones, butter, cream, and lots of jam."

Rising, Marsa kissed him on his bald patch and headed into the house.

"Scones and cream! Bloody marvellous." Big-eared Bertie leaned back in the armchair in the back corner of the verandah. He patted his stomach below his gas-mask satchel.

"Heavenly." Lovely, slim Bertie sat with her sensible lace-ups resting on the low table beside her blue WAC cap. She glanced past Ed and smiled, eyes sparkling with welcome.

Marsa swept past, dumping her tray on the worn table. "What a wonderful surprise!" Ed's son, Pete, and his wife, middle-aged now, followed their own son and daughter-in-law up the verandah stairs. A little girl, blonde-curled, and chubby, staggered determinedly ahead of them only to dump in a heap at the last step.

Marsa gathered up the wailing toddler, hugged her and plopped her on Ed's lap. "There you go, 'Berta." She reached out for the bundle in their granddaughter's arms. "And this is young Ed."

The last Bertie in Ed's life exchanged cries for giggles as Uncle Bertie knelt before her, pulling his ears out and making faces, while Aunt Bertie gave her a dollop of cream to lick off her finger. Ed pressed his cheek to wee Berta's curls, inhaling the sweet aromas of child and scones and peace.

Scones

Fire up the wood stove or preheat oven to 450°F.
Ingredients for a dozen or so scones:
- 2 cups flour
- 3 teaspoons baking powder
- ½ teaspoon salt
- 1 tablespoon (more or less) sugar
- ½ cup shortening (or half butter, for nice flavour)
- 1 egg, broken into measuring cup
- Milk on top of egg to make up to ⅔ cup

Preparation:
• Sift together dry ingredients. Blend with shortening/butter to consistency of coarse corn meal.
• Make well in centre of dry ingredients. Add milk and egg.
• Work with hands until blended. It may be quite soft.
• Sprinkle flour on counter top or marble slab, turn dough onto it and roll out once, fold up, and roll out again to about a ½ to ¾-inch thickness, sprinkling rolling pin and dough with just enough flour to keep it from sticking.

• Using a glass or biscuit or cookie cutter, cut scones and place them well-spaced on ungreased cookie sheet.

• Bake about 15 minutes until well puffed and golden-brown on top.

YOU ARE EATING AN ORANGE. YOU ARE NAKED.

Sheung-King

Gender is a kind of imitation for which there is no original; in fact, it is a kind of imitation that produces the very notion of the original as an effect and consequence of the imitation itself.

—Judith Butler, *Imitation and Gender Insubordination.*

0

You just started a new job as a writer and photographer for an independent cultural magazine. Ever since you quit your marketing job, you've been reading more. It is a Sunday in July and we spend the day eating, talking, taking baths, and smoking weed. That night you decide that you would like to go to visit Taiwan.

1

"What the fuck?" You put down your book. "What is the point of having such a loud car?" You look at me, expecting an answer.

"I think loud engines make the car accelerate faster and whatnot."

We are sitting on the patio of a café a few steps from our apartment building.

"What's the point of that? Look! He's stuck at a red now."

"I don't know. Some people really like the two seconds of going really fast."

"That's not true. If that's true, then we'd see people yelling and sprinting on the street."

"Maybe they like the attention? Or maybe they think it's attractive to have a loud car."

"There's nothing attractive about that. I think if you're a sensible human being, you would never drive an obnoxiously loud car with only two seats."

"Maybe some people like loud cars."

"It's selfish. Unless there is something attractive or sexy about being selfish. Do you think there's anything sexy about being selfish?"

"Maybe."

>·<

The loud car is nowhere to be seen, but we can still hear it.

The café we are at also sells weed. After you order your coffee, you walk up to the barista, give him a little chin-up nod, and follow him to the back room to buy some weed before sitting down to read your book.

You manage to finish half of *The Unbearable Lightness of Being* over the course of a large coffee. I, on the other hand, over the course of drinking my coffee, manage to reply to an email regarding my tax return.

>·<

"Strip," you whisper. You are sitting next to me. You are wearing a purple silk kimono with detailed flower patterns. I find out later that you're wearing nothing underneath. "Strip," you whisper again. This time even quieter. I don't know how to react. I look over at you.

"Let's just head home. Reading this makes me want to have sex." You don't look at me when you say that. You simply stand up and leave, expecting me to follow.

2

We fall asleep immediately after. In my sleep, I come to the conclusion that Sunday afternoon is by far the best time to have sex. We wake up. I look out the window. The weather is the same as it was this morning. It is three in the afternoon, but for some reason, it feels like a different day. You ask if I want to take a bath with you. I fix us a bath. Our bathtub isn't especially large. We barely fit in it.

"Why'd you whisper 'strip' to me at the café?" Steam is rising from the water. Your eyes are closed. You give me a little shrug. Your slender shoulders are starting to sweat a little.

"I thought it'd be fun," you say.

"How?"

"In the book I was reading, the main guy – Tomas – would utter the word 'strip!' and the women he was seducing would listen."

"They would just strip for him on demand?"

"Yeah." Your eyes are still closed. You rest your head on the edge of the bathtub. I imagine you picturing scenes in the book. "You know about Nietzsche's idea of the eternal return?" you ask.

"Kind of."

"Nietzsche believes that all things in existence recur over and over for all eternity."

"Yeah."

"Existence is inherently weighty because it is fixed in an infinite cycle. So, everything that occurs takes on an eternally fixed meaning. And when we are born, we are born into a world that is filled with already-fixed meanings that we need to live by. As Milan Kundera puts it, 'We are nailed to eternity as Jesus Christ was nailed to the cross.'"

"Do you think people naturally want the power to change and shift the meaning of things? I mean, Jesus never tried to change his fate."

"Right. In the book, the concept is inverted. Wait. Hold on. Let me go get it." You leave the tub and without drying yourself off, you run to get the book. The floor is wet. "All right, here we go." You get back in the tub. "'Life that does not return is without weight...and whether it was horrible, beautiful, or sublime...means nothing.' See? Without weight, each life is insignificant and every decision does not matter. And that is a relief." You toss the book on the toilet seat and look at me. "If one does not consider the eternal return to be true, then every decision we make will be under the premise that we, as individuals, are not important. That is, when we die, we leave nothing behind. We don't matter. And that is unbearable. So, one of the main questions the book is asking is, which should we choose? To live life dutifully and heavily, or freely and lightly?"

"I don't know. All of that sounds so self-centred. I think I'm not that important, and I don't think that that's unbearable. That's just how life is. But anyways, tell me more. How does the whole 'strip' thing tie into this?"

"Living lightly bears the burden of constantly reminding the self that it doesn't matter, and the constant thought of self-insignificance becomes a burden of its own. So, the characters in the book are trying to find some kind of balance between lightness and weight. And here's when the stripping comes in."

"Finally."

"Because every sexual encounter of Tomas, who is married, is 'light' and without emotional attachment. The women he has sex with also tend to be 'light.' Over the course of every sexual encounter, there is an overwhelming amount of lightness, so the women seek a sense of weightiness to balance the situation. Thus they develop a longing to be tied down." You pick up the book from the toilet seat. The book is now wet. "The women are 'Intoxicated by the beauty of submitting completely to another person's commands.' That is why they take off their clothes when he simply utters the word 'strip.'"

> ı <

The water is getting cold. You want to keep talking in the tub, saying that you are too lazy to move. You run more hot water in the tub and turn your back toward me.

"Shoulder massage, please."

I start massaging your shoulders. I guess I am also, in a way, intoxicated by the beauty of submitting completely to your commands. Hot water fills the tub once more. Your hair is wet and beautifully dark. You reach for the book and from between the pages, you take out a joint. You light it.

"When did you roll that?" I ask. Instead of answering me, you pass me the joint. I take a drag.

Some time passes. Out of nowhere, you stand up. You take the towel to dry yourself off and leave the bathroom without saying a word. I am left alone in the bathtub.

3

I find you sitting on the red couch in the living room with legs crossed. You are naked. You are eating an orange. Above your head hangs a black and white photograph of Ai Weiwei giving the Hong Kong Harbour's financial district the middle finger.[1] I take out the Polaroid camera and take a photo of you. In the photograph, you are naked, a piece of orange is sticking out of your mouth, and you are giving me the middle finger. You like the picture. A week later, you slip it into my wallet without me noticing. I will carry it around from then on.

4

"I want Chinese food," you say. We are on the balcony. You are trying to dry off your copy of *The Unbearable Lightness of Being* under the sun.

"Sure."

You leave the book on the balcony.

)ı(

---

[1] The photograph was first exhibited in Ai's exhibition – *Fuck Off*, at the Third Shanghai Biennale in 2000. The exhibition was very controversial. Ai exhibited a series of photographs of him giving "important" monuments around the world the middle finger (including the Tiananmen Square, the Eiffel Tower, and the White House). He was flipping off historical buildings in other parts of the world, but when he went to Hong Kong, he decided to flip off buildings of big corporations and offices instead.

We go to a Chinese restaurant at Yonge and St. Clair. We don't usually go there for dinner. The restaurant is famous for its dim sum, and dim sum is food for the daytime.

"For two?" asks a man with a moustache.

"Yes."

"Over here."

We sit down.

"Tea?" he asks

"Water," I answer.

"Other drinks?"

"Not right now."

The man walks away.

At night, the menu is slightly different. You decide to have soup and tofu. I decide to order a dish called Taiwanese Three Cup Chicken.[1]

"Water," the man returns with a white pot of hot water. "What would you like?"

"I'll have the pumpkin soup and the tofu pot, please," you say.

"Okay." says the man. I order my chicken.

"Anything else to drink." His tone is without a question mark. For some reason, that makes me feel like I need to order something to drink.

---

[1] Taiwanese Three Cup Chicken (*sānbēijī*) originates from the Jiangxi province of southern China but has become especially popular in Taiwan. There are many legends explaining the origin of the dish, one of which takes place during the Song Dynasty. National hero and commander in chief Wen Tianxiang was captured by the Kublai Khan's army during the war. He was tortured for four years. But Wen held his head high and not once did he beg to be set free. A warden of the Kublai Khan army admired Wen's persistence. The night before Wen's execution, the warden mixed three kinds of leftover sauces in the kitchen and made Wen the simple, yet surprisingly delicious dish – Three Cup Chicken. Wen was grateful and died with a full stomach.

"Want to share a Tsingtao?" you ask.[1]

"Sure."

"One Tsingtao," the man tells himself, and leaves.

"You know why I like Chinese restaurants?"

"Why?"

"They make me feel like I'm in a Wong Kar-wai[2] film." You close your eyes and start humming Nat King Cole's "Te Quiero Dijiste."[3] "If there's an extra ticket, would you go with me?"[4] you ask.

The man comes back with a Tsingtao and pours it into two thin glasses. You drink quickly. You finish your glass before the food arrives.

><

We finish our food. "You want dessert." Again, the man's tone is without a question mark.

---

[1] Though Tsingtao is widely regarded as a Chinese Beer, the Tsingtao Brewery was actually founded by Anglo-German settlers of Hong Kong in 1903.

[2] Wong Kar-wai is our favourite filmmaker. He is an internationally renowned auteur who has won awards at almost every major film festival around the world. Most of his films are about Hong Kong and feature Hong Kong actors. Because Hong Kong is a corporate and profit-oriented city, his films are often dismissed within the city and considered "too artistic" for people's taste. However, his films are extremely popular in Europe, Mainland China, and Japan.

[3] Nat King Cole's "Te Quiero Dijiste" was one of the songs used in the soundtrack of In the Mood for Love – one of Wong's most successful films. The film explores the relationship between two neighbours who share the mutual knowledge that their spouses are having an affair. Summarizing Wong's films is kind of pointless. His films are explorations of feelings and ideas, less focused on a dramatic plot. Perhaps that's why they tend to fail commercially in places like Hong Kong.

[4] This, perhaps, is the most famous line in In the Mood for Love. By the end of the film, the two characters who share the mutual knowledge that their spouses are having an affair involuntarily fall in love. The man has decided to leave his unfaithful wife, and to leave for Singapore for a job. On several occasions, he asks the woman, "If there's an extra ticket, would you go with me?"

"Sure," you answer.

"What do you want?" He does not give us a menu.

"Do you have any *tong sui*?"[1] I ask him in Cantonese. I ask him this because I remember that when we visited Macau, you really enjoyed this one particular *tong sui*. I want to see if they have it.

"No, we don't make that here," answers the man with a moustache. "Canadian people don't eat that stuff. Order some mango pudding."[2]

"Sure," I answer.

"I want myself some good *tong sui*, too," the man continues. "There's a small dessert place in Chinatown that has it, but it's nothing like what I eat at home. The job of a Chinese restaurant in Toronto is to serve customers the idea of Chinese food rather than actual Chinese food." After saying that he walks away to get us the pudding.

"What did he say?" you ask.

"The job of a Chinese restaurant in Toronto is just to serve customers the idea of Chinese food, rather than what that really is."

"The idea of Chinese food?"

"Yeah."

"Do you agree?" you ask.

"I'm not sure."

"I guess we can't deny what we ate was an idea of Chinese food – a Westerner's idea of Chinese food, that is. Which is actually a little healthier – less greasy, don't you think?"

---

[1] *Tong sui* is a collective term used for any sweet, warm soup or custard served as a dessert at the end of a Cantonese meal.

[2] Mango pudding originated in India, but became especially popular in Hong Kong.

I come to the conclusion that maybe Chinese food is nothing more than just an idea, and that there is no such a thing as *original Chinese food*.

>‹‹

"What difference exists between an idea and a metaphor?" you ask.

"Huh?"

"Metaphors are sexier than ideas," you say, ignoring me.

"Bill." The man with the moustache places the bill on our table, cutting you off. We pay.

"Have a good night," says the man.

5

The time is 8:00 in the evening. The sky is still bright. We are full. From St. Clair Avenue, we decide to walk down Yonge Street to Bloor. Whenever I'm out with you, I notice people turning their heads to check you out. You don't seem to notice. Or maybe you're just used to it.

"All right. Here's why metaphors are sexier than ideas. Are you ready for this?" you ask.

"Yup."

"Metaphors are sexy because they can give birth to love."

"How?"

"Tomas was what we might call today 'a player.' He was married once but left his family and felt great about it. He was also a top surgeon in Prague. He had met Tereza when he was visiting a small spa in a village. Tereza was a waitress at a restaurant Tomas visited before he returned to Prague."

"Hold on, I need to tie my shoelace," I say.

"One stormy night, Tereza, without any explanation, decided to go to Tomas' apartment in Prague. They had sex." You are standing next to me in black high heels. You continue talking while I am on my knees tying my shoelace. "To Tomas, Tereza seemed like a child someone had put in a basket and sent downstream for him to fetch at the riverbank of his bed. Because Tereza seemed so vulnerable, the player let his guard down. And the more Tomas thought of this metaphor, the more he felt like he could not let the child keep floating down a stormy river."

"Okay. Let's go." I get up.

"Tomas did not know that metaphors were that dangerous. So just like that, Tereza entered Tomas' poetic memory."

"What's that?"

"Love begins with a metaphor. Which is to say, love begins at the point when a woman enters her first word into our poetic memory. Tereza entered the player's poetic memory in the form of a metaphor and gave birth to love. So that's what makes metaphors sexier than ideas." You put your arm around mine and your chin on my shoulder.

"Remember how we met?" I ask.

"Yeah. One day I woke up and you were sitting in a little basket next to my bed."

6

The time is 9:00. You say you don't want to go home yet because we spent the entire afternoon at home already. We decide to visit the small dessert house the man with the moustache was talking about.

"I have a question," I say. "Is Tomas really in love with Tereza or is he just in love with the idea of playing protector in the metaphor he created for himself? I mean, he's a player, right? So, he must be 'light.' And according to the whole Nietzschean thing, the role of a protector is a 'weighty' one. So, is he 'in love' with her just because he longs to be weighted down?"

"Let's not talk about that book anymore. I'm sick of it.

"I think the book tries too hard to make sense of shit," you continue. "I don't think everything happens for a reason, and I don't think about whether things matter or not that much. Most of the time shit just happens by chance."

7

"I have a story that doesn't try to understand what love is at all," I say.

"Can we order first?"

"Sure."

The Taiwanese dessert house is quite small. However, the menu is not. There are over seventy kinds of desserts to choose from. You had *dùn nâi*[1] for the first time at a dessert house[2] in Macau and loved it. We order two.

>‹

---

[1] There are many variations of this dessert, including the original steamed milk pudding; steamed milk custard; double boiled steamed milk; double-skinned milk; and steamed milk with egg white. The dessert is simple, yet hard to make. The texture of it is smooth and the taste is not too sweet.

[2] We visited an old dessert house that made both Portuguese and Cantonese desserts. There, we had the best steamed milk pudding.

"Once upon a time in the Mountains lived White Snake and Black Snake. Both snakes had magical powers."

"What kind of story is this?"

"A Chinese folk tale," I say.

"All right, go on."

"They wanted to visit West Lake for its beautiful scenery. White Snake metamorphosed into a very beautiful girl – Lady White. And Black Snake turned itself into a lovely maiden as well. While they stood on a bridge to admire the beauty of the lake, Lady White noticed a young man walking toward her from the other side of the bridge. Lady White immediately fell in love with the young man."

"What?"

"It gets even weirder. To help her sister, Black used her powers to make the young man fall in love with White. The two got married. However, the Abbot of a remote Buddhist temple sensed that something was wrong and he pledged to the gods that he would expose White Snake and capture her. After the wedding, the three of them, that is White, Black, and the man, moved to the city and opened an herbal medicine store."

"This is quite good," you say.

"The dessert or the story?"

"Go on."

"White wrote out the prescriptions while the man and Black gathered and dispensed the different herbal medicines. They were kind people – or snakes. Patients who were unable to pay were given free treatment and medicine. The store became well known and popular. The Abbot, however, still found the relationship between White and the man to be problematic. So, he approached the young man while he was delivering medicine to a patient and warned him that his wife was a snake. Did I mention that by the time this happened, White was already pregnant with the young man's child?"

"No."

"Well, she was. The Abbot told the man that if he gave White the festival alcohol drink during the Dragon Boat Festival, her true self would be revealed."

"Wait, hold on. How young is this young man?"

"I have no idea. Anyway, the man did not believe the Abbot, but figured that there was nothing wrong with having a drink with his wife, so the man brought home the festival alcohol to celebrate with Lady White. White had no reason to refuse a drink with her husband. She took a sip and immediately fell ill and retired to her bedroom."

"Are you sure that's not because she's pregnant?"

"I'm sure. Anyway, the man went into the bedroom to check on Lady White, but she was no longer there. In her place was a large white snake coiled on the bed. The man was so shocked that he fell to the floor and died."

"He died?"

"Yup, dead cold, on the floor, by the bed."

"That's not the end, right?"

"Of course not. When the power of the alcohol had faded, Lady White resumed her human form. She was heartbroken to find the man lying dead beside the bed. But she knew of a magical Ganoderma – a celestial herb which grew in the Kunlun Mountains – that could restore him to life. Using her magical powers, she flew to the Kunlun Mountains to pick the celestial remedy. But on her way back, she encountered the White Crane, who was responsible for looking after the Ganoderma. The White Crane attacked Lady White. Lady White, who was pregnant and had just flown for thousands of miles, was too tired to fight, and she lost the battle. Just as the White Crane was about to kill her, a voice from the skies commanded the White Crane to stop. It was the voice of the Immortal Southern End."

"What's that?"

"In the story, it's just a voice that comes from the skies. It has no form."

"Interesting."

"Lady White begged the voice of the Immortal Southern End to help her. Impressed by her sincerity and perseverance, the Immortal Southern End commanded the White Crane to spare White's life and grant her the Ganoderma. Thanks to the celestial herb, the life of the man was restored. But when the man woke up, he still remembered that his wife was a snake. He left the house, went to the temple where the Abbot resided, and requested a divorce from his wife. The Abbot felt that the man should now devote his life to the temple to atone for having had a relationship with a snake, and forced the man to become a monk."

"You can force people to become monks?"

"Yes. The Abbot trapped the man in the temple and shaved his head. Lady White, along with Black, went to the temple and begged the Abbot to let Lady White's husband go. The Abbot refused. In anger, Lady White and Black gathered together a great army of underwater creatures to attack the entire monastery, and they used water to flood the temple. But the Abbot had the power to make the mountain grow higher than the water level, and so he was able to keep the temple safe. The Abbot also had the magic ability to command heavenly soldiers. Soldiers came from the heavens and defeated all of the underwater creatures."

"Want to share another one?" you ask.

"Are you that hungry?"

"Yeah."

"All right. Go ahead and order one more."

"Go on with the story."

"Lady White, again with child, could not possibly fight any longer. So, Lady White and Black fled to West Lake – the place where they had first met the man. Black was very angry at the Abbot for his cold-heartedness and pledged to kill him the next time she saw him. But little did they know that while the Abbot was fighting Lady White and Black, the young man had been secretly released by a young monk who worked at the temple. And by sheer chance, the man wandered back to West Lake. Black and White saw the young man walking across the same bridge. Black, wanting to capture him, went for her sword."

"Why would she do that?"

"Because Black loved White, and saw the man as the source of all of White's sufferings."

"Okay…"

"But Lady White held Black back and, instead, told the man the truth about how they were snakes. With a full understanding of each other, the two were able to fall in love again – this time without the use of seduction by magic. They went back to their home and started a family. Lady White gave birth to a son and the four of them lived happily together."

"Is that the end?"

"Nope."

"This story is kind of long."

"Should I stop?"

"No! I don't want to hear half a story."

"All right."

"Keep talking, I'm going to eat this."

"The Abbot, unhappy to see the family living together so happily, went to heaven and asked the Jade Emperor for help. A powerful fighter with a magic lantern was commanded to assist the Abbot.

"One day, the man went to the market to buy a hat for his son. Both the man and son were drawn, for no good reason, to an ugly straw hat. They bought the hat and returned home. It turned out that the hat was actually the powerful fighter's magic lantern in disguise. Just as White had transformed into a human, the fighter had transformed his lantern into a hat – and just as Black had used magic to seduce the man into marrying White, the fighter used his magical powers to seduce the man and his son into buying the hat. When the son brought home the hat, it made Lady White physically weak. Lady White was then captured by the fighter and imprisoned under the Thunder Peak Pagoda by West Lake. Black, however, was able to escape. She returned to the mountains and practised magic. Several years later, Black's magic became strong enough to take revenge for her sister. She managed to destroy the Pagoda and she rescued Lady White. Lady White reunited with her husband and her son. Black then defeated the Abbot, and before the Abbot could ask for help from the heavens again, Black had him swallowed by a giant crab. The family of four lived happily ever after."

"Interesting. I have no idea who the hero is," you pause for a bit, "but I guess that's okay."

I cannot help but contextualize this story within the ideas of lightness and weight. I know you don't want to talk about the book anymore, so I decide to keep that thought to myself.

"I finished all of it!" You show me the empty bowl.

8

We leave the dessert house. The time is 10:30. We start walking home.

"If I hear a loud car on the way home, I'm going to slap you."

"What?"

"Each time I hear another car with a roaring engine, I'll slap you in the face."

"Why?"

"Because you're a man."

"So?"

"I've realized that it is the fault of men that there are so many loud cars on the street."

A loud car passes by. You slap me in the face and continue walking. I know this is actually going to continue until we get home. I decide not to walk home anymore. I wave for a cab.

9

We are back on the balcony. You are standing next to a familiar basket, big enough for a snake to curl up in. The book is dry but you decide that you're not going to read it any more. I pick it up. I decide to read it in the morning.

"The moon is kind of red, isn't it?" you ask.

"It is. How strange."

Our apartment faces the Toronto Islands. The moon is large and the lake is lit by the moon's brightness.

"We have to work tomorrow," you say.

"We do."

"When do you have some time off?"

"I'm not sure. Why?"

"If there's an extra ticket, would you go to Taiwan with me?" you ask. "I hear they have beautiful lakes there."

How to make Taiwanese Three Cup Chicken

Ingredients:

- ¾ cup sesame oil
- One 3-inch piece fresh ginger, peeled and sliced into 12 to - 15 thick discs
- 12 to 15 whole cloves garlic
- Four whole scallions, trimmed, cut in 1 inch pieces
- 2 to 3 small fresh red chilies, halved or sliced
- One cup of rice wine
- One cup of light soy sauce
- Two tablespoons of sugar
- Two cups of basil leaves
- Pieces of thinly sliced chicken breast

Preparation:

• Heat sesame oil in a pan over medium-high heat, and then add ginger, garlic, scallions, and chilies, and cook for a minute. Add chicken pieces, stir for two to three minutes. Add rice wine and soy sauce and bring to a boil. Reduce to a simmer and cook, uncovered until the chicken pieces are cooked through. Stir in the sugar. Remove from the heat and stir in the basil. Eat it.

SPAM® STEW AND THE MARM MINAMALIST BEDROOM SET FROM IKEA®

GORD GRISTHENWAITE

sx̣ay̓wih (sh AYE wee) husband
xeʔɬkʷúpiʔ (ka ASH kwoopee) the Creator
snúye (SHNU ya) money
qéck (hechk) older brother
c'eweteʔ (shaw WET eh) Indian celery
tetúwn'(ta TOON) Indian potato
skʷóześ (sko LE) son

So this story tells about the time the old lady's sx̣ay̓wih came home for SPAM® stew, his favourite meal. Pretty good trick for a dead guy. You might not think a stew made of SPAM® worth pulling your dead bones from your grave, through town, and up that mud-slick, two-mile trail to the house, but you haven't tried the old lady's SPAM® stew.

The old lady never measured ingredients when cooking.

"Ach! Maybe I could write it down. But I couldn't read it."

"But, Mum. I could read it. We don't want your recipes to die with you."

"Have I up and died on you?"

"You know what I mean."

Now the old lady chooses to drop the whole thing. Her daughter, Violet, got back from treatment a week ago. Violet stays with her mother. She doesn't leave the house for anything: "Oh, Mum. Cos everything's a trigger."

The old lady's question: "So whose finger's on it?"

Violet answers: "Everyone I ever known, Mum. You can't joke about stuff this serious." Before her mother can snark an answer, "But not you, Mum. Not you and Walter, for sure. You always watched out for me."

"Anyways, I told you a million times: you want to cook like me, work with me in my kitchen, and learn by watching and doing it."

So despite the triggers, or because of them, Violet will learn to cook with her mother. To can, and make pickles. To make wimmin's bread, but not for a while, cos stringing them two words together gives her a minor breakdown. She cries for days, curled up in an unshowered fetal ball. She won't talk about it. Violet falls apart, but doesn't console herself with wine, or whiskey, or mouthwash, or vanilla extract. She doesn't crave it. Not even a beer, or ginger beer, or root beer. The old lady lets her alone. Under six wool blankets, Violet sweats, shivering like she has the TB, or pneumonia, or the DTs, or has withdrawal again. But no.

The old lady kisses the blanketed lump where Violet's pillow shows.

She knows that sometimes body memories – flashbacks – look like things they aren't. She won't talk about it, not in a way that makes sense to her own self. But she tells Violet – all of her kids, nieces and nephews – to sit with it till it can't sicken you the same way. She puts out hot tea for her three times a day, and she keeps fresh ice in the jug of water beside Violet's bed. Sometimes Violet drinks the chicken broth, despite its sickly yellow colour. Sometimes she sits beside Violet's bed, telling her stories, singing healing songs.

She kisses the blanketed lump where Violet's pillow shows.

She cackles that old woman cackle. "Better not be your ass I'm kissing, Daughter."

Then she rests a hand on the lump. "Sorry you got to go through this shit just to stay alive."

Taking care of fragile Violet's like annealing a knife blade, i'nit? Too much will ruin it, make it brittle and useless. Not enough and it won't work like it's supposed to.

She says, "Two more days of this. Two days and no more, then you go for a sweat bath. Steam with the grandfathers, not your own stink."

The lump of Violet under her blankets shakes and rattles like Regan MacNeil's bed. The old lady starts, "Ai-eee!"

Then the bed bucks like a frisky calf, wobbles off the floor, rising three feet, then five.

Lump of Violet stills.

Bed vibrates, bucks, and spins.

Violet, not so much a still lump now, whimpers like a roller-coaster-scared kid on El Toro. She hangs her head over the bed's raging edge, and vomits, but not green-pea-soup-projectile vomit. But vomit is vomit. The old lady mops up the mess on the floor, sponge baths Violet, daubs her neck and forehead with cold cloths. Maybe two more days of this not enough, after all.

Gonna be a long, long night.

Another long night, the next one. Bed bucks and spins. Violet vomits, whimpers, and cries. The old lady mops up the mess.

Next morning, after taking green tea with lemon, they sit on the porch and watch the melons and peas grow.

Five days and nights the same. The old lady catnaps while beading or crocheting. Violet stares at the old water stain on her bedroom wall so long it performs a healing dance. Each time that stain's fan goes up, a bit of happy air tingles away some of the ugly shivers Violet shoots out.

Fifth night as ugly as the last four.

Sixth dawn and Violet sips nettle tea, nibbles on toast with sour cherry jam, and picks at two eggs scrambled. Bacon would've been nice, too, but the old lady says Violet's guts can't handle it now.

When they finish tea, the old lady washes Violet's hair, draws her an Epsom salt bath, and cleans her like a newborn. She sings prayers so low, like whispering to xeʔɫkʷúpiʔ.

Then she puts Violet to work in the garden. All morning pulling weeds, feeding, watering, pinching back oregano, basil, and dill.

The old lady uses her good shears to trim greens off some scallions. "You know what today is?"

Violet counts days on her fingertips. The arithmetic would be easier if she had a start date. "I dunno. The ninth?"

The old lady laughs. "It's your dad's birthday."

They laugh. Violet shakes her head: "The ninth. Sheee-it."

Violet now knows what date and what month, but not what day of the week. But no job waiting, so the day doesn't matter. (It's Thursday.)

Heavy wheels flick rocks like bottle caps off the under-carriage of a truck down the road a ways. Dust hangs in the air like a wind-borne feather.

Violet perks up. "Sounds like Walter."

The old lady nods. "Could be. He said he might stop by today."

The old lady knows Walter's on the way home for his father's birthday, and he has a huge surprise for his baby sister.

Yeah, Walter drove all the way to Big Town to get that MALM minimalist bedroom set from IKEA®. (Maybe the only two things Walter hates: Big Town and IKEA®. Those are two stories I might tell one day, but not now.) He gets lost. Drives by the airport three times. The fancy-schmancy GPS they put in his shiny new truck knows the city as good as Walter. Good thing his cousin Mildred gives good direc-tions. One phone call to her, and Walter finds his way again.

Sure enough, some minutes later Walter backs his truck up close to the front door.

Violet steals a peek under the tarp. "You moving back home, qéck?"

"Something like that."

The old lady swats Violet's hand. "Get your nose out of your brother's business."

The three of them sip tea and eat baked bannock. They only eat it baked cos the old lady's blood is mostly lard. She has to eat it dry. Can't even sweeten it up with a little sour cherry jam. Violet learnt to make it in rehab. They printed recipes on little cards, three a week for all but the first week. (She cooks good when she has a written recipe to follow. But who doesn't, hey?) Therapy they called it. Violet and the women called it indentured labour, even them who wanted to cook for a living after they got all cleaned up.

The old lady gently pats the gooseflesh bubble-wrapping her forearm. She sighs, half-smiling. Blows a little kiss at the ceiling.

So they sip tea and talk, the three of them. Four if you count the old man hovering above the kitchen table. So stealthy that old man, he sneaked away from his shadow. And that shadow stand in a field of bitterroot. And it passes for a gnarled old apple tree. But not so stealthy that he could sneak up on the old lady.

>·<

The old lady wobbles off into the bush with a hatchet and machete so sharp that cedar boughs fall to the ground when she nears a tree.

Violet and Walter dig a fire pit about two feet deep and five feet in diameter. Another foot deeper and they could roast a hindquarter of moose in it. If they had one. But the fire will wipe the spirit haunting Violet's bed away and out of her life. Maybe for good.

They smudge, the three of them. The old man hovers above them inhaling that sweet smoke. He envelopes himself in it. He smells the memory of it. He bathes in the memory of it.

Violet chops kindling. Walter chops seasoned pine and spruce. Nice logs they dragged from the bush two, maybe three years ago. On a bet, Walter whacked out a cord of it one-handed. On another bet, he whacked one out left-handed. Yeah, that one hurt. Walter's a lot like that Chuckie when it comes to wagers. Neither of them two loses a bet. But people keep trying, like a stubborn slot machine – they expect it to pay out big-time one day.

So Violet stacks kindling, wads up pages from the Sears and Eaton's catalogues, then stuffs it into the stack of kindling.

Walter laughs, and pokes his sister in the ribs. "Look atchoo. Away for a coupla years and forgot how to make a real fire."

"Ah, you. I could do it easy. I just love the colours them catalogue papers make when they burn."

"Yeah, sure. You just keep telling yourself that."

Pretty quick, that fire crackles and pops to life. Flames tinted with colours you don't see in nature. Pop and crackle like the old man pushing himself out of his chair at bedtime. But he doesn't pop and crackle any more. Just one bonus of death, I guess.

Two at a time, Walter hands Violet chunks of wood. Two at a time, she places it over and around the kindling.

Pretty quick that fire flare, too hot to throw smoke.

The old lady hands Violet a cedar bough.

Violet places it on the fire. It fwooms fire, crackles and spits fiery embryos into the smoke plume it spews.

The old lady, two-stepping around the fire, sings healing prayers.

The old man, two-steps alongside her, singing healing prayers.

The old lady doesn't think it strange that gooseflesh pop like burning spruce and pine.

Walter helps Violet haul everything from her bedroom. Everything except the plywood floor, ceiling, and walls.

Dresser. Dresser drawers. Dresser and drawers burn un-earthly colours. Bed frame. Bed rails. Bed burns in unearthly colours. Nightstand. Nightstand drawers burn unearthly colours. Box spring throws black smoke. Mattress pukes black smoke. Sheets. Black smoke. Blankets. Black smoke. Pillow. Black smoke. Pillowcase. Black smoke.

Black smoke shrieks pain.

One piece at a time, they put it on the fire. And after every piece bubble, shrivel, or snap in the flames and smoke, either black or unearthly, the old lady shakes a handful of sage mixed with juniper berries onto it.

So that fire burns good and long. Violet watch that fire, poking it with a stick, tossing pine and spruce into it. That fire has to burn to ash, and the ash has to burn to dust, and the dust has to stay buried.

Violet concentrates. She looks at how her life will unfold from this day onward. She sees good stuff in it, like a job with the band, as its D & A counsellor. Her three-year cake is a confetti angel cake. She graduates with a degree in Social Work four years after that. If the band funds her.

No.

They will.

The band will fund her.

They will.

>·<

Violet, all covered in soot, smoke, and dirt, sweats beside the fire, feeding it all night long. Her father squats beside her, wafting in and out of visibility in the white smoke drifting on the rise and fall of Wind's lazy lungs. He spins stories of his brother as a boy, how he's not the same since falling from that apple tree. Lands on his head. Not the same since. Not always wrong in the head. He don't come around no more. He don't drink no more. Keeps pretty much to himself, living in a shack way out on Crown land. Couple times a year a nephew takes out a sack of flour, tins of coffee and tobacco, a box of tea, and a pail of lard. Brings back a stack of hides and pelts. Sell it all. Put enough cash aside to get next season's supplies. Put the rest away for the girl's schoolin. She need a lottta of *snúye* for D'n'A school, i'nit? Enough in them savings to pay for a coupla years of college now. Maybe four, if she live cheap. Maybe get some from the band. Maybe a few more from INAC. Who knows, hey?

You could blame his broken head. You could blame his drinking. He does still. So I guess he gotta stay in the bush till he sees it different. Like you, i'nit? He's my brother. You're my daughter. My baby. You could have a good life still. You will. Glad to see you leave the bush, my baby. An old man couldn't ask for a better birthday present. You gived it to yourself. Good. I tried. I did.

Violet jolts alert. Three a.m. crickets sing like old man laughter. She tosses two more logs onto the fire. Old man drapes an arm around Violet.

She shivers in the 3:00 a.m. cold.

><

Walter builds a fire near the tall yellow cedar the old lady uses for her sweat baths. Soon the fire burns brighter than sunrise. He shovels in the grandfathers and sings under his breath.

Violet's seventh day starts with sunrise. Her eyes burn red. Her hands cramp like the old lady's. Her back aches. Her ass as numb as when she gets so lost in a book that she forgets she's sitting on the shitter. Not too different from walking out of a blackout drunk, just a few steps short of oblivion, back into that foggy reality you spent the last six days trying to escape.

The old lady helps Violet to her feet. Guides her to the sweat bath.

"Can I change outta these clothes first?".

The old lady purses her lips. "No. Start your bath with it on. Maybe take it off before the third round."

Violet laughs. "What makes you think I'll last three rounds, Mum?"

"I'll bring you clean ones to put on."

Walter clenches his jaw. He says, "You better."

"Last thing I need's to see you running bare across the yard."

"Ha. Qéck, you think you're funny."

"Naaaaaaaaaaaaah. I know it."

> ‹

After her sweat bath, Violet paints her bedroom ceiling cerulean, and its walls dusty rose. She and Walter fit the floor with pink granite lino.

The old lady nods in the doorway. "Hang some pretty curtains, and I'll have to charge you 25 bucks a night to sleep over, i'nit!"

For nearly a whole breath, Violet takes the old lady serious.

Windows and doors open. Ellen blasting from the TV
the old lady protested having in her home. She hasn't turned
it off since Walter screwed it onto the wall. He and Violet
got her a clicker that listens, and automatically switches to
Moosemeat & Marmalade, and *North of Sixty*, whenever it's
on.

"That TV's not so smart. I say find me something good to
watch. It don't do nothing. Or it tells me it can't find it."

"Maybe it's smarter than you give it credit for, hey? Never
anything good on it. 'Swhy they call it the boob tube."

"Thought they called it that for all the smut it plays after
midnight."

>·<

While the paint dries and the glue under the lino hardens,
Violet and Walter build the IKEA® MARM minimalist bedroom set. Walter bets they will have three bits left after
they're done. Violet bets one. The old lady says none will be
left, and she backs up her word by tossing a dollar onto the
fancy-schmancy saucer Walter brought back from Victoria.
It came with a cup. Turns out the cup could fly – once – but
the saucer could not. Violet put in a buck. Walter put in a
buck. A pool is not a wager, or Walter would have raised
them 20, to make it interesting. Both wish they had whiskey
in their teacups. Both think it would be faster to make and
season boards and then build furniture from it.

No extra parts this time.

Nearly dark by the time they get it done and slid into
place. Curtains from the Sahali Superstore. Bedding from
the Sahali Superstore. Too many ghosts in used bedding,

used curtains. Sometimes got to wash it five times to get them ghosts and old smells out of it, too. And really not too much cheaper than new from the Superstore. Harvesting other people's junk not quite the same as picking berries, c'ewete?, or tetúwn'. But finding a good used one sometimes more fun. Sometimes.

Sun's moved behind Mount Shasta, taking 10 degrees of warmth with it.

"Hey, Mum, when's supper?"

"When you make it."

"When I make it? Holy! We don't even have enough bread for sandwiches."

"C'mon. Wash up and I'll show you how to make SPAM® stew and bannock."

"I already know how to make bannock."

"Mine?"

"Well, I would if you wrote it down."

The old lady shook her head. "Yeesh."

Walter finds a ball game, says over his shoulder: "Be nice, you two."

><

The old lady, her arms crossed, stands behind Violet. "Open two cans of SPAM® and pour it onto the cutting board."

She slides the eight-inch French knife from the blade block. "Now chop it into squares about this big."

"You mean like one-inch cubes, Mum?"

"'Swhat I said, i'nit? Get them two onions off the window ledge. Peel it. Then chop it into small squares."

"You mean dice it small?"

"Whatever. Geez, you. Just chop it into small bits, so it don't feel all slimy in the mouth when you eat it."

Now you might think the two women will start scrapping at the cutting board, but nah. Mostly, it's all in fun.

"Get that big pot from the pantry. Wipe it out real good. I don't want no spider shit or fly eggs in it.

"And while you're in there, bring out the deep frying pan for the bread."

"Wimmin's bread?" The words just blurt from Violet's mouth, kind of like a ketchup bottle fart. Though instead of spraying all over your best tee-shirt, Violet laughs.

"Your father would smack you upside the head if you dared put raisins in his bannock."

Walter shouts over Dan and Jim (who marvel at how Miggy's knees have recovered), "So will I!"

"Now grab two sticks of celery. Make sure you wash it up real good. Then chop it up into tiny bits, like the onions."

Violet preps the celery. The recipe writes itself onto a card her brain files.

"Now scrub a half-dozen medium-size potatoes. Just like you scrub your nails after working the garden all morning. And pick out the eyes. And chop out every dark spot."

The old lady looks them over. She takes one, slices it in half lengthwise. Slices each half lengthwise again. Lays it flat and slices each half in half the other way. Then chops it crossways into chunks.

"Now you hack the rest of it."

After chopping up the spuds, Violet pours a solid glug of oil into the hot stew pot, whooshes it around before tossing in the onions. "Stir it fast. Stew will taste ugly if you let it brown."

Next Violet adds the potatoes and stirs it in real good.

Next Violet adds the celery and stirs it in real good.

Next she puts in the tomatoes, water, and broth. Mixes it all in real good.

Next she adds three hard jerks of Tabasco®.

Stirs it in. Adds three more.

Pretty soon that stew boils. Violet stirring it up all the while.

Last, she shakes the SPAM® chunks in and gently stirs them into the bubbling vegetables.

The old lady takes the stirring spoon and slurps a mouthful, swirls it over her tongue, smacks her lips. She nods. "Pretty good for your first time. Turn the fire low and cover it up. It'll be ready by the time the bread's fried."

Violet grabs the dry measuring cup from the back of the bottom drawer, the flour and lard from the pantry. The lard can has a tin cup tied to the handle.

The old lady puts the measuring cup in the sink. When Violet pulls out the measuring spoons, the old lady puts them in the sink.

She rolls up her sleeves and counts four handfuls of flour into the mixing bowl. Four handfuls and a little bit more. She pours salt into the palm of her hand, then dumps it onto the flour.

"Let me show you a trick. How much salt you think I put in it?"

"I dunno. Maybe a tablespoon or two?"

The old lady pours about the same amount of salt into her palm. "Now hand me them spoons."

She shakes the salt into the teaspoon measure. "Don't matter how big your hand is, that much salt always make a teaspoon. I put in two. Now you put in two."

"That's a lot of salt, i'nit?"

"Not for your father. He'll shake another spoonful onto it."

Violet heebie-jeebies. Salt always makes her think of tequila. And thoughts of tequila give her dry heaves. Or they did before she left rehab this last time.

"Stir it up real good. Yeah, like that."

The old lady presses a fist-sized dip into the mound of flour. Now she taps a tin cup of lard into the dip.

"You could heat the bread pan and lard it good while I work the dough."

With both hands she kneads it into a ball, adds some water, and kneads it some more.

"You want it soft enough to shape. And you want it about this thick. Too thin and it gets hard enough to break teeth. I'nit, skʷóze??"

Walter waves his uppers over his head. "Ha ha, yeah."

"Anyways. Make it too thick and it don't cook through."

"Like Uncle Don's creamed-filled bread?"

"Yeah. No amount of salt and jam could make it taste good."

The women laugh and shape the dough into palm-sized balls, moosh it down into a T-bone shape, dust it with flour, and stack it on a chipped enamel plate by the spattering lard.

"I tried making dumplings one time. Dumplings instead of bannock. Your father refused to eat it, none of it. Not the dumb-things. What he called them: dumb-things."

Laughs. "Dumb-things, really?"

The old lady nods and cackles.

"Chicken broth stained it all yellow. He says, 'How you 'spect me to eat this shit, old woman? Looks like someone pissed on bull balls.'"

"'Try it,' I says. 'Just try it. It's dumplings. Like bannock. Just boiled with the stew.' So he pokes it with his fork. Pink, pink, pink, like that. Pink, pink, pink. And it's a little sticky. And it's a little spongey. And it's a little yellow. He goes, 'Dumb-things won't stick to my damn fork.'

"I don't wanna eat it, but I made it, so I got to. I made it after all. So I cut into one. Show him inside of it's just bread. Not fried. Not baked. Boiled bread.

"Kinda slick on the outside. Kinda slimy.

"And I bite into it. And chew. And chew. And chew. Like I popped a whole pack of Hubba Bubba® in my mouth."

"Oh, Mum. Gross!"

"Tch. I know, hey! So, it gets caught in my throat and won't go down when I try swallowing."

She pinches a dough, and carefully places it on the boiling oil. Then another.

"This pan holds two at a time. But you got to make it this size. You don't want it touching, and you want it cooked at the same time.

"And you put it in gentle so you don't start a grease fire, and you don't burn your hands. Oil burns ugly."

"How long's it take?"

"When you see it bubble up in the middle like that? Turn it over. Should be golden. Not too dark. Not too pale. Golden. Like this one.

"Now grab that big bowl off the table. Wipe it out good."

After inspecting the bowl, the old lady says, "Yeah, like that. Now take about six squares of paper towel. Lay it in the bowl like this."

She tongs a bannock and shakes oil off of it. Pats it down with paper towel. Folds another one over it. Grease stains the paper almost invisible.

The old lady hands the tongs to Violet. Violet mimics her mother's moves. Something she could do since she was maybe five. But how could she learn when her own gums are too busy flapping? That's what Dad would say, i'nit? Stop flapping your gums, girl. And listen.

"Check your stew. Make sure none of it's sticking to the pot."

The old lady takes the spoon from Violet.

Sometimes you eat it with rice.

Sometimes you eat it with a can of niblets.

But always with Tabasco® brand red pepper sauce. Always.

The old man's birthday has passed. Just like him, I guess.

But they put out a bowl of stew and two chunks of bannock for him, like they do every Sunday.

Violet tips her water glass in her father's direction. "Happy birthday, Dad."

Walter tips his can of Pepsi in his father's direction. "Happy birthday, Pops."

The old lady tips her glass of water in her husband's direction. "Happy birthday, my sx̣aẏwih."

The old man lifts the bowl of stew to his nose and inhales noisily.

The three living ones gawk at him like they see a ghost. (They do, of course.)

"You don't set out my meal just so I could look at it!"

"Sx̣aẏwih, I put one out for you every Sunday, and every birthday since you died. Something wrong?"

"Geez, woman, I want to share a meal with my family. Like I've done every other time."

"But you don't usually talk. And you don't look so alive."

He pats Violet's hand. He imagines brushed denim heat rising from her. Gooseflesh paints itself up her arm. "Today's special. My baby girl cooked it."

"Oh, Dad. I helped a little."

"You did morren that. You'll sleep good tonight. Maybe every night from here on out."

The old man shakes salt on his stew and on his bannock. He splurts Tabasco® on his stew.

Then spurts a little more.

He eats loud for a dead guy. But he eats.

SPAM® Stew

Ingredients:
- 2 cans of SPAM®, cut into one-inch cubes. (Do not use SPORK® or canned corned beef hash, or the old man will have something to say to you!)
- 2 small cans of diced tomatoes.
- 2 small cans of water.
- 1 small can of chicken broth.
- 2 medium onions, diced.
- 2 stocks of celery, diced.
- ¼ to maybe ½ cup vegetable oil
- 6 medium potatoes, cut in one-inch chunks, give or take.
- Salt to taste.
- Tabasco® sauce, and plenty of it. (Use only Tabasco® brand red pepper sauce or the old man will have something to say to you.)

Preparation:

• Prepare vegetables and set aside.

• Pour tomatoes and broth into a mixing bowl. Fill the tomato cans with water, then stir it into the mixing bowl. (Note: for a thinner broth, add a little more water.)

• Heat a large saucepan over medium heat. Add cool oil. Stir in onions and cook off volatiles. Do not let the onions brown, or the old man will have something to say to you!

• Stir in the celery and potatoes. Add the liquid. Stir well. Make sure stew doesn't stick to the bottom of the pan, or the old man will have something to say to you!

• Cook it till the spuds is mostly done, maybe 40 minutes.

• Gently stir in the SPAM®.

• Add Tabasco®.

• Bring to a simmer, cover, stirring occasionally, until it's finished, maybe 15 minutes.

• Add more Tabasco®.

• Serve it with bannock – fried, not baked, or the old man will have something to say to you!

• Or serve it over rice. If you want the old man to eat it with you, use long grain white rice. If you don't, use any rice you like. Add Tabasco® brand red pepper sauce to taste. Enjoy it!

'TI POUCE
IN FERGETITLAND

GEOFFREY W. COLE

On the last Somday in Novembuary, 'Ti Pouce pulled the stunt that set us to starving. Pers and Mamons and we seven and also 'Ti Pouce was lined up outside Lor Gerol's palazzo to procure vittles. The smerf fam ahead of us, distant cousins of Mamons, was giving their gifts to Lor Gerol's cliquo, when 'Ti Pouce leaned in to us at Danley.

"Watch close, my brothers and sisters," our wee big brother said. "Today I will secure enough vittles for the journey across the Fergetitland."

"To what place?" we said.

"Think of any place," said he, and we did. "That place is better than here."

"Quiet, children," Pers said. "'Tis our turn with the cliquo."

Pers sent we seven hopping up to the cliquo Gerol with what we scavenged from the waste: a block-o-cinds, a tire, pillow stuffing, an action figure, one bucket, a rake handle, and a ratty corpse. All good rawmats we could have turned into vittles, but we gifted them to the cliquo Gerol instead.

"Seek you a blessing?" the cliquo Gerol said.

We said what Mamons always taught us: "We're blessed as we are."

The cliquo laughed at that. "Little spider thinks they're blessed. They live in a hovel!"

"Our hovel suits us finely."

That seemed to stoke their mirth further.

"Ignore them, my brothers and sisters," 'Ti Pouce whispered to us at Margerine. "'Tis the last time you'll go begging from them."

"Be cautious here," we whispered back, and he stepped up ahead of us.

"Generous cliquo Gerol," he said in a voice five times larger than his slight stature. He reached into his pockets and took out a big clod-o-ground in one hand and a lovely if stale cakelet in the other. "I offer thee this fine clod-o-ground."

He gifted the clod to the cliquo Gerol, then he lifted the cakelet to his lips.

"We could offer a much finer blessing if you were to gift us that cakelet," the cliquo Gerol said.

The cliquo smacked their seven fat mouths. They were surrounded by fine gifts that could be transformered into vittles, enough for hundreds of those cakelets.

"I can see you are ahungered," 'Ti Pouce said. "And I know 'tis a hardship for a cliquo to walk to the fabupot for your vittles. I think I see a remedy. Trade me what my brothers and sisters gifted you, and this cakelet is yours."

The cliquo Gerol tossed everything we gifted them right back at 'Ti Pouce and soon were fighting over the cakelet.

"Don't know about this, 'Ti Pouce," Pers said.

"Squarefair was the trade," 'Ti Pouce said.

'Ti Pouce dragged all the regifted gifts through the door into Lor Gerol's throneplace. Pers and Mamons and we seven followed him in.

Mamons' cousin was getting vittles from the Lor. The cousin dropped the rawmat he'd brought into the fabupot and Lor Gerol rized up from his throne and had to scrunch so his headbone didn't crack the ceiling. Fingers like mallets punched the codes and the fabupot beeped like a happy animal. The rawmats rattled and splorked as they was transformered and out the other end slopped twin bowls of icyscreamy, a mound of cakelets, a bucket of poulet frittes, a bottle of medicinals for the cousin's sickly wife, and a sack of wine slurpee. Lor Gerol punched codes to make the fabupot stop, and he kept the slurpee to himself. We seven's bellies grumbled as the smerf fam walked away with that fine haul.

It was our turn.

"Vittles please, your Lorship," 'Ti Pouce said. He opened the bag with all the regifted gifts, plus the rawmats we brought for the fabupot.

The door to the throneplace opened behind us and the cliquo Gerol waddled in, all seven of them covered in cakelet crumbs, them wailing like one of their heads was dead.

"Whatever's the matter, me darling cliquo?" Lor Gerol said.

"The weency one tricked us, Dada," the cliquo said. Fourteen fingers accused at 'Ti Pouce. "He made us give up our gifts for a lone cakelet."

"This true, Pers Moyer?" Lor Gerol said.

Pers dropped to his kneebones. "Your cliquo traded squarefair with my 'Ti Pouce."

Lor Gerol roared like a waste train. "I ask so little for providing the vittles. No tithe, no tax, only gifts for my darling cliquo. Yet your runt tricked them." Lor Gerol pounded the ceiling with a fist like a boulder. "From this day and each one after, you are barnished from this here palazzo, Pers Moyer. Step feet on this stone again, and your kin will be wiped from this Earth."

The yellow light atop the palazzo shined dim and sickly against the grey of smoglight. Pers whipped 'Ti Pouce in front of the other smerf fams waiting outside. We thought he deserved more, it was his fault we was ahungered, but Mamons had enough and told him to cease. The palazzo sits atop the tallest hill in the waste, and on most Somdays while we walked home we seven admired the fine views of the trenches and the excavations and the Clavement waste rail line and the scattered hovels that fill the valley Lor Gerol renamed after himself, but that Somday the view was of a deadland, and we was doomed to soon add our grave to the countless graves below.

On the walk home, we seven fell into a hole where other smerfs had excavated rawmats too close to the road and Pers and Mamons and 'Ti Pouce had to pull us out. After, 'Ti Pouce said it remembered him of the day we septuplets was spawned: all of us spilling out of Mamons, one after the other, each conjoinered to the next at the kneebone, five sharing a shinbone and foot with the next so we only had eight legs between us to trod this ruined Earth.

"The nursing went on morn, smoglight and dark," Mamons said as we got to walking again. "A cliquo of seven. You were adored."

She grew quiet then, but we knew the story well. We was the first clique-de-sept anyone ever heard of, and for a while we was famous. Smerfs from across the valley would come and gift us in exchange for a touch. Blessings of health and fecundity, Mamons said those touches profited upon the gifter, until a month after we was spawned, when Lor Gerol announced one of his wifes had spawned his own clique-de-sept. They were a more perfect cliquo than we: they were conjoinered at the hipbone, each with a chubby pair of legs and arms to call their own. He declared his cliquo to be the only true provider of blessings, and the gifters ceased their pilgrimages to our hovel. We was first, though. We thinks Lor Gerol had a hate on for us ever after.

Mamons had some vittles tucked away in the hovel for just such an occurrence. Dryish cakelet, molded frittes, battered butter, and handfuls of chewing gum. Filled us up, it did, but the next morn we was ahungered again. Mamons begged round the neighbouring smerfs but none obliged. Lor Gerol had sent the crier out: any smerf fam spied feeding Moyers would be starved out same as us. With no soda or latte to bev, we got mighty thirsty too.

Pers had heard of another town other side of the Lorenshen Fergetitland that had a fabupot, so he packed sacks for travel.

"Let me adjoin yourself," 'Ti Pouce said to Pers. "I'm useful."

"Unambiguous no," Pers said. "You are the speaker for the Moyers until my return."

Pers returned two days later with a crusty stump where his left arm used to hang. "Cancanlupan took it," he said as he tumbled to the floor.

We knew some medimangling from some paperwords we regandered once, and with the medicinals in the hovel, we patched Pers up. Three days after that, Pers was feeling well enough to swear, and we was all so ahungered that we ate dirt. He and Mamons was in conference all day and well past dark. We seven slept on our stitched together mattresses and 'Ti Pouce lay lengthwise at our eight feet.

Pers shook us awake with his one remaining hand. "Up get, me cliquo, and me runtling 'Ti Pouce. The stork-o-fortuna flied by in the dark."

"We're leaving for a new place, aren't we?" 'Ti Pouce said.

"'Tis what you've been waiting for, me runtling," Pers said.

"Why doesn't Mamons join us?" we said. We didn't like that Mamons hadn't packed a thing.

"She'll join us before dark," Pers said. "She wants to say goodbye to her cousins."

He had us pack what we hadn't traded to Lor Gerol for vittles and marched us into the gloom-o-morn. Mamons waved from the window of the hovel, she holding a rag facewise.

"We're going for the Fergetitland?" 'Ti Pouce said.

"The stork-o-fortuna showed me the way," Pers said. "We going Oowest."

We gripped the hand of our wee big brother.

"Picture it, my brothers and sisters," 'Ti Pouce said. "No Lor to bend knees to, no queue for vittles. 'Tis the day we been waiting for."

"'Tis the day you been waiting for."

We walked for hours, Pers saying nothing, 'Ti Pouce telling every joke he knew. His excitement couldn't infect us, and the laughter from Pers sounded false. For a shortish while we knew the landscape – trenches cut into the waste for rawmat, hovels like the hovel Moyers, bones of old buildings, graves and graves and graves – but soonish it changed. Spindly black things sprouted from the dead earth. Fogclouds seeped up from slick pools. Things like living

ropes twined and teased along the ground, tripping us up.
The Fergetitland.

Near dark we arrived at a riverlet flowing with clouded
waters. The slopes steepened on either side of us and then
they grew sharpish and cliffy, and the waters went from
clouded to clearer.

"Take a pause and breathe a bit," Pers said, "while I regander ahead."

Pers disappeared round a bend in the creek. A cancanlupan howled its code.

"Danley, Staniel, Raggity Anne, Allan, Paul, Saul, and
Margerine," 'Ti Pouce said, singing our names like he always
does.

"Oui?"

"What for does the cancanlupan howl?"

We shrugged our seven pairs of shoulders.

"Wouldn't you be crying if you was living in Fergetitland?"
He howled at his joke.

"Nothing about this is amusing, 'Ti Pouce."

"We're going to a new place. Cheer yourself!"

"Then why is Mamons still homewise?"

Pers showed his headbone from the top of the cliff.

"Me cliquo, 'Ti Pouce," he said, his voice aquivered. "Me
and Mamons is regretfilled, but we got nothing more to feed
you. Better to try out here then see you starve at home. This
be your place now and evermore. Bev the water, mash the
growing tings. You're better off here."

That flat headbone disappeared. 'Ti Pouce climbed up
the cliffside while we seven hollered bellow.

"There's no track nor trace of him," 'Ti Pouce said. He slid
down the cliffside. "But badness isn't the entirety of it. We're

free, my brothers and sisters. We can find some better place as we please!"

We started crying, first Allan, then Danley and Staniel, then it caught all around.

"What for's the matter?" 'Ti Pouce said.

"Our hovel."

"What of it?"

"At the palazzo Gerol, when you told us to think of any place, that's the place we thought of. We want no other."

'Ti Pouce paced upstream a ways, and for the moment between the howl of a cancanlupan and the answer of its echo, we thought he might leave us, but he returned.

"Your brother will right things," he said. "Regander this." Metalbits glinted on his grubby palm. "I left the metalbits so Mamons could find our path. Looks like we'll require them now."

'Ti Pouce showed us his trick: during the long walk, he dropped metalbits through the Fergetitland. The metalbits shined frosting-like in the moonglow.

"'Twill guideline us home."

Homeward we walked. 'Ti Pouce reconnoitred ahead, collecting the metalbits as he did, and we seven followed as fast as our legs allowed. We was still enfuried with him, but he was making things right. We whistled as we went. Our brother tried to hush us but we said we read paperwords that proclaimed whistling kept the cancanlupan and the lion-o-iron from murdering your body, so he whistled likewise. The Fergetitland did not seem so terrifraiding while whistling, until 'Ti Pouce quit his whistle.

"This be a tragedy for which I am unprepared," 'Ti Pouce said. He scuffed the ground.

"What's wrong, brother?" said we seven.

"The metalbits are gone."

"Where for now?"

He gazed into the fogclouds and up at the moon and scratched his wee headbone.

"This way," he gesticulated to the left of the moon. "I think."

We followed. His whistling was different. Rattylike. Our mouths too dry to make an accompanying whistle. We clasped our hands and his.

"For a bit of positivity," he said. "The cancanlupan no longer howls."

But we heard other things in the Fergetitland: snappings and breathings and moanings and then there was the smells, all fungicide and oil and metalblood. After a while we found a dark creeklet that smelled like the one near our hovel. We followed it, the banks slick, the mud sucking at our eight feet. 'Ti Pouce whistled, and it sounded bravish now, fierce and certainlike.

The coyoodle leapt on our backside and got Margerine in its toothvice. We hollered and struck it, but the steel dentition only sunk deeper.

"They lust after metals," we shouted. "Lure them off us!"

"Hey 'oodle," 'Ti Pouce said. He shook the metalbits he'd recollected at the coyoodle. The creature looked up from where it was mauling us, beady glasseyes following the metalbits. "Want them, 'oodle? Come get em."

'Ti Pouce tossed a few metalbits at the ground and the coyoodle leaped off us to gobble the metalbits. We seven sobbed. 'Ti Pouce tossed more metalbits into the dirt by the creeklet bank, and coyoodle gobbled those up too. 'Ti Pouce tossed the last of them metalbits into the creeklet and coy-oodle jumped in after them. That critter screamed like a waste train unrailing, the creeklet stripping the furs right off its bones.

More yips behind us. Three more coyoodles slinked out of the spindlies, eyes aglow, teeth slickened with bile, head furpuffs quivering, tail furpuffs wagging.

"Run, cliquo," 'Ti Pouce said. "We don't have no more trinklets to distract them."

We ran as well as we could. 'Ti Pouce broke off a basher from a spindly and bashed the coyoodles when they got close. He splashed creeklet waters at them, and that slowed them, but still they followed. We hurt at Margerine, the blood clotty on our rags. They chased and chased us, the moon dropped lower, and when the biggest coyoodle bit through 'Ti Pouce's basher, we knew we would soon end up as coyoodle poop.

"This way, cliquo," 'Ti Pouce said.

We ran with him to the edge of a trench; it was the waste we was in! 'Ti Pouce held us there and whispered, "Drop when they pounce."

"Advance upon us, 'oodles," he screamed at the three beasts. "Discover what Moyers is made from."

All three jumped as one. 'Ti Pouce tugged us earthwards. The coyoodles soared above us and clattered into the trench below. They howled and yipped as 'Ti Pouce helped us up, but they could not climb the trench walls.

"We're saved," 'Ti Pouce said.

"Not remotely," we said. We sniffed the wound at Margerine. "That'll turn to gangrene if we don't care for it soonish."

"We got medicinals at home to fix it."

"We used all the medicinals on Pers's stump. There is only one other place with medicinals."

A lone light shone in the dark of the waste: a sole yellow glimmer upon the tallest hill. With the coyooldes crying in the trench behind us, we walked toward the palazzo Gerol, bellies afull of hunger and fearbile.

The waste is almost as terrifraiding a place as the Fergetitland come dark. It was here the Dead Folks dumped all they no longer required: autos, coldboxes, metals, fakerock, mirrors, all that stuff they knew how to make and we didn't. They devoured the world, Mamons said of the Dead Folks, and left us nothing but bones. Well, not just bones. A few of their interventions survived. The fabupot was one of them. It let us turn their bones into vittles.

The palazzo light was made by the Dead Folks too. The yellow glimmer drew us up there just like a ratty corpses draws blackbills. Up and up we walked, us hurting more and more at Margerine. Many a time we considered just sitting there and dying. Hadn't we suffered enough to earn a nice long sleep in the dirt? But 'Ti Pouce wouldn't let us.

"You are Moyers," he said. "Four hundreds years our fam been mining the waste, and we never gave up then. We sure aren't going to start now."

At the top of the hill, 'Ti Pouce harangued us over to a fakestone bowl bigger than our whole hovel and had us lie deadlike beneath it.

"You seven stay quiet. I'll slip inside, steal the medicinals, find us some vittles, and then we scamper home. Give Pers and Mamons a knock on the headbone for abandoning us. Once you are healed we can find a new place."

We listened through the sounds of the dark. Yips of coyoodles, the slow gurgle of creeklets, the moaning of collapsing trenches. 'Ti Pouce could be quiet as sleep, if he wished to. There was hundreds of times he slipped out of our bed without us awakening to go commit some prank on Pers and Mamons: bedclothes tied to mattress coils, moustache facepainted onto Mamons with sooties, Pers's wig replaced with a ratty corpse. It was just like one of those nights, we told ourselves even as we moaned at Margerine.

The roar must of awakened all the smerfs in the valley. The palazzo's front door opened and out ran 'Ti Pouce, arms full of vittles and medicinal jars. 'Ti Pouce was halfway to the fakestone bowl where we quieted when a huge shadow rolled out of the palazzo. Lor Gerol stood upon his seguer, another contraption of the Dead Folks, and he raced down upon 'Ti Pouce. The Lor snatched up our brother in a fist almost as fat as 'Ti Pouce was tall, took back his vittles and medicinals, and stuffed 'Ti Pouce in a sack. We stayed dead-like, even as Lor Gerol rolled around in front of his palazzo, sniffing at the air like a cancanlupan.

He was rolling back into the palazzo when we whined at Margerine.

"Do you misunderstand the meaning of barnished?" he said as he scooped us up at Danley and stuffed us into the sack with 'Ti Pouce. "I gave you a chance, you wretched cliquo. Now you are mine."

He dragged us into the pallazzo, the smell all frosting and frying fat and chocolate and sugarcake and citrus treats.

"'Tis all your fault, 'Ti Pouce," we whispered.

"Hushem," he said. "I'm working on listening."

Lor Gerol dropped us onto the ground hard enough to make each one of our mouths yowl.

"Awaken, me darlings," Lor Gerol's vocals roared. "And see the toys your loving father has procured for your enter-tusement."

The sack shook and out we tumbled onto the polished fakestone floor. A cut of light appeared as Lor Gerol pulled back curtains. The Dead Folks' light shone yellow and into that wedge of sickly illumination slipped seven fat faces.

"These seven plus one are yours until the first crow of the blackbill," Lor Gerol roared. "Come morn, they'll be break-fast for the whole clan. The little one I won't even feed to the fabupot. Him I'll pickle in slurpee and suck his meat off his bones."

Doormetal locked behind Lor Gerol. Those fat faces squealed with delight. We tried to axesplain that we was injured, that we required assistance, but they cared none. They started right into their fun. They had we seven do jigs for them, while they stuffed their faces with cheesiepuffs and cakelet. They made 'Ti Pouce swing from the curtains.

"Kindly cliquo Gerol," 'Ti Pouce said after his perform-ance. "'Tis the last night of repose my seven brothers and sis-ters will ever see, and they never slept on a true bed. Could you find it in your seven beating hearts to offer them this one terminal kindness?"

The Gerols thinking looks awful like the Gerols eating, probably on account of they were eating while they were thinking.

"We've come upon our conclusion," they said. "Tell us seven jokes, cliquo Moyer, and provided each joke be fun-nier than the previous, you shall sleep your last upon our bed. Don't think we need to axesplain what'll be the out-come should laughter not be tickled from us."

"Would it be impertinent of me," 'Ti Pouce said, "to ask to serve you vittles while my cliquo amuses you?"

"'Twould be impertinent for you not to feed us."

'Ti Pouce served vittles while we tried to remember what jokes 'Ti Pouce had favoured us with over our years, and then to rank them in order of hilarity.

"What for does the cancanlupan howl?" we said, starting with the unfunniest.

"Dunno."

They groaned at the puncher.

"Better be funnier next one," the cliquo said around mouthfuls of cakelet.

Next one was this: "Why did the blackbill fly over the creeklet?"

"Unknown to us."

"'Cause if he'd waded through his legs woulda melted off."

That seemed to tickle them.

"How about that longish joke," 'Ti Pouce said. "The one about the waste miner who discovers a magic auto?"

We knew it, but it was long, longer than it takes for the moon to transverse our bedroom window, but if 'Ti Pouce asked it, there was a reason.

"There was once a waste miner name of Orfeo," we started, and on we continued with the long joke. The cliquo Gerol had their 14 legs dangling sidewise from their bed, the legs swinging and kicking. They was still beving slurpee and mashing vittles, but as we unspooled the joke, they slowed. Each mouthful took minutes to swallow. Six of their 14 eyes was closing, and we was terrifraid they would find this joke no funnier than the last. Our telling slowed too, but 'Ti Pouce whipped us on with: "And then?" and "Whatever happens nextish?" and "Continue, cliquo!" So on telling we went.

Now we arrived at the puncher: "The magic auto drove off and left Orfeo's head at the crossroads."

Not a chuckle or guffaw to be heard. Nought but snoring. Our marrow ran cold. Then a laugh did start in the dark, the laugh of our wee big brother.

"You done it, my brothers and sisters!" he said. He pulled back the curtains and the yellow glimmer shone on seven faces asnoring on their huge bed. 'Ti Pouce held up a cakelet: a single medicinal pellet was pressed into the thick frosting. "Now out we go!"

We started for the door when out on the waste a blackbill squawked. Our telling had taken too long.

"Yer time is at an end, cliquo Moyer!" the Lor roared. "Finish up, my darlings. I'll porridge them soonish."

'Ti Pouce stood by the door terrifraiding. "We're to be transformered."

"Maybe not," said we, for an idea had been passing between our seven brains and we spoke it now. 'Ti Pouce laughed again and we went to work, going as fast and as quiet as we could. We dragged the cliquo Gerol to the floor where the Lor had tossed us. 'Ti Pouce shredded their bedsheets into ropes and we tied their legs together, transformering the cliquo Gerol from a 14-legged creature to an octopod like us. We then climbed onto the bed, a more comfortable experience we never knew, while 'Ti Pouce snapped off bedposts and headboard and we added six leggies to our eight. He stuffed raggies into the mouthbits of the sleeping cliquo Gerol.

"But the yallow glimmer," we said. "The Lor will see 'tis his cliquo on the floor and us bedwise."

'Ti Pouce crawled out the window and in a blink it was dark all round the palazzo Gerol.

He squirmed back into the bedregion and shuttered the window as the Lor's footsteps echoed outside the door.

"Hide under the bed, brother," we whispered.

'Ti Pouce shook his head. "The Lor is expecting a weency one as well as a clique-de-sept. You hear the fabupot, you run. Your brother will caretake of himself."

That door opened and the stink of Lor Gerol, all glazing sweet and slurpee-wine sour, filled up the bedregion.

"For the sake of all the Christlings," Lor Gerol roared, "what has happened to my yallow glimmer?"

"Take them away, Dada," 'Ti Pouce said, throwing his voice so it seemed to come bedwise. "We hate having the mean cliquo with us in the dark."

"Hushem, me darlings. Dad will erase your troublings."

We listened, feeling sick in all seven of our bellies, as Lor Gerol stuffed 'Ti Pouce and his own cliquo into the sack. He dragged the sack out of the bedregion. We waited until we heard the beeping of the fabupot before we sneaked out of the bed, and for a moment we considered running into the throneplace to assist our brother, but then all the children Moyers would be vittles, so instead we ran out the big door of the palazzo.

A pale misty had arisen over the waste. We clattered down the road, the whole time considering whether we would ever see our wee big brother again. He'd saved us, he had, and here we were, running away from his demise. How we hated ourself.

Down we tumbled into the dust and started weeping.

"Onward, cliquo," our wee big brother said as he ran by. "Before the Lor uncovers his error."

Overjoyed, we ran after him. 'Ti Pouce carried a great mound of vittles and he dropped a pie or biggiemac on the road behind him as he ran. We wanted to eatum, but by then we knew to trust the strange exertions of our wee big brother.

"Me darlings!" the Lor roared clear enough for us to hear a klick away, and it was coming closer. "Me darlings!"

We was too slow. Our wee big brother was doomed because of our cruddy pace.

"Continue without us," we said. "We will only get us all killed."

"Never," he said. "We Moyers stand together."

We found a nearby trenchlet and tossed ourself in. "Run, big brother. Find yer better place."

He considered for long moments. The Lor's roaring was upon us: "He'll pay, the runtling will."

"I'll return for you," 'Ti Pouce said, and he ran.

The Lor roared on: "I'll flay the flesh from his bone and turn it to pork rinds."

The grind of the seguer wheels crunched down the hill and ceased near us. The sky was blotted by the vast shape of the Lor.

"Where for is your runtling brother?"

"We'll never say."

He roared out laughter. "He's dropped his vittles, the greedy creep has. Don't move, cliquo. I'll return for you once I've turned his testicules to gobstoppers."

The sky unblotted and the seguer wheels resumed, and soon the Lor Gerol's roaring disappeared toward the Fergetitland.

We waited in the trenchlet all through smoglight, but he never returned. 'Ti Pouce neither. It was dark when we climbed out and returned to the hovel Moyers. Pers and Mamons were overcome with weeping when we approached. Mamons kissed us on all of our cheeks while Pers checked us over from the footbone at Danley to the headbone at Margerine. Both of them was terrifraid of the wounding at Margerine, and they forced us to the mattress, where Mamons dabbed hot raggies on the wounding while Pers digged out on the yard, and returned with a vat of medicinals.

"Where for is my runtling?" said Mamons.

"Unknown," we said. The medicinals were pushing us slumberwise. "The Lor chased him to the Fergetitland."

We awakened next morning to find the hovel afull of vittles. Frittes of all kinds, cakelets, chocolates, sacks of slurpee both boozed and virginian.

"The fabupot's been running morn, smoglight, and dark," Pers said as he mashed icyscreamy. "Lor Gerol must not have stoppered it in the haste of his departure."

We feasted like never we feasted before, but it was no happy feast, for we couldn't share it with our wee big brother.

Weeks passed, then months, then seasonings. The fabupot transformered Lor Gerol's palazzo into vittles, and then started on the hill on which it stood. The days was filled with feasting on account of our liberation from the tyrant Gerol, but that was no consolation, for the Lor took 'Ti Pouce with him. Pers and Mamons tried to cheer us with jokes and vittle combinations, and they enfattened like we never seen them, but it was no use.

A year to the day of the Lor's disappearance, the smerf families in the Valley Gerol organized a festival to celebrate the overdue arrival of the stork-o-fortuna. Pers and Mamons begged us to join them, but we wouldn't go.

From the hovel, we could see what remained of the hill where the palazzo Gerol once stood. Now it was just a pile of vittles. Pers and Mamons walked down the road, her fat arm on his stump.

A coyoodle yipped in the Fergetitland. It made the old wound at Margerine ache. We returned bedwise and lay there, entroubled, when we heard a sound we could never unremember: seguer wheels on hard ground.

It was Lor Gerol, we knew certainlike, return to devour us.

The raggies parted and a wee figure stepped in.

"My brothers and sisters!" said a voice five times larger than its owner.

We leaped from bed and snatched our wee big brother up in all our arms. Near crushed him and soggied his fine new shirt with our weepings.

"Where you been?" we seven said.

'Ti Pouce told all.

When Lor Gerol dumped the sack containing his own asnoozed cliquo into the fabupot, 'Ti Pouce danced and quirmed to stay out of the transformering hole. The Lor returned to his bedchamber, and only then could 'Ti Pouce slide out of the sack. He scooped up medicinals and vittles that had once been the cliquo Gerol and ran until he found us. After we jumped into the trenchlet, Lor Gerol followed the trail of medicinated vittles 'Ti Pouce left for him into the

Fergetitland. When 'Ti Pouce dropped his last vittle, he hid way up in a spindly. Lor Gerol rolled in on his seguer not long afterwise. The Lor leaned that machine up against the spindly where 'Ti Pouce was acowered, and sat his giant sitbones in the dirt. "Turn your blood to slurpee wine," was the last thing Lor Gerol said before he stuffed another medicinated donut mouthwise and aslumbered.

'Ti Pouce waited longish, then hopped down from the spindly and stole Lor Gerol's seguer. 'Ti Pouce is wee and Lor Gerol hugish, but the seguer's controlpole shrunk right down for 'Ti Pouce and off he rolled into the Fergetitland.

"Why didn't you return to us?" we said.

"Why was you aslumbered upon my return?" he said. "It was the night after we fled the palazzo. You was sleeping on your stitched together mattresses, Pers and Mamons weeping over you. Everything regandered correctish, so I departed."

"Where for?"

"The world, me cliquo." And with that, 'Ti Pouce gifted us a sack. Inside was orange stickies and reddish lumps. "Carrots and apples. Real vittles, not fabbed. Eatum."

The carrots was dry, but the apples crunched and juiced most wondrously. 'Ti Pouce stood still in the door raggies.

"You're departing, aren't you?"

"Come with me," he said. "There's so many places and things to show you."

We regandered around our hovel: the chair where Pers sat to think, the washbasin where we washed ourselves, Mamons's stack-o-magazines, all our paperwords on a rack, and at the base of our stitched together mattress, the weency 'Ti Pouce-shaped indentation.

"Here is where we belong."

"I was affeared to hear it, but 'tis not unexpected. I'll return at least once yearly. I'll bring gifts for my brothers and sisters."

"And tales. Bring us tales."

We regandered from the hovel as 'Ti Pouce rolled into the Fergetitland. The wind had never felt so cold, nor the waste so empty.

We was still there some time later when a smerf fam wandered up the road from the festival. The young patron and matron carried a waifish child with a stunted leg between them.

"You the cliquo Moyer?" the matron of the smerf fam said.

"Seen any other clique-de-septs around here?"

They placed some vittles from the festival and a hand-wound rope at our feet.

"Could we ask your blessing?"

The cold still afflicted us, but the wind didn't seem so frigid.

"Take up your things," we said. "We are blessed as we are."

We touched their child upon her stunted leg and gave her blessings of health and growth, then gave them instructions to care for the girl we remembered from old paperwords.

It was dark when Pers and Mamons returned from the festival. We never told them of 'Ti Pouce's visit, not that one, nor the others that followed over the years. They asked about the gifts he gifted to us, but we said it was from the fams who pilgrimaged to our hovel for blessings and medi-mangling.

As the seasonings change, we sit out front of the hovel on a special chair 'Ti Pouce brought for us, listening for the sound of seguer wheels in the Fergetitland. We have to listen hard, for further down the valley the fabupot churns and churns as it transformers the world into vittles.

Cakelet with Slurpee and Frostings

These are the paperwords Mamons made for us in the event of she should perish. She wrote this years ago, before 'Ti Pouce filled the valley with vittles, so it's more for history than real usage, but we keep it beneath our mattress and regander it on occasion to remember how bad things could be were it not for our weency big brother.

How to Acquire the Vittles:

Things for the pot:
- Clod-o-ground
- Ratty (preferable deadlike)
- Nucklebones
- Coyoodle puffs
- Any old things

Directives:
• Get out to the wastes earlyish, before full smoglight. 'Tis cooler then, and the dark has a way of filling up the wastes with all sorts of gifts. Regander about for the simplest pickings – there's no sense going too far out in the waste and having coyoodles savage yer hamstrings – so stay near our hovel. Fill a sack or bucket with the things you scrape from the waste.
• If it is not a Somday, wait. If it is a Somday, haul that sack up the hill to the palazzo Gerol. Get yer weency brother to help.
• Give yer tithe to the cliquo Gerol, those most wretched of creatures, and march yer hides into the throneplace. Be quiet, be smart, be grovelly. Do whatever is required to keep the Lor content, my loves. Ask him for

what you please (not too much cakelet now, remember to eat your frittes and biggiemacs), and say many a merci.

• Take the vittles home and eatum only little at a time. We never know when the Lor's fury might choke us off from the bounty of his fabupot, so 'tis prudent to always tuck some vittles away for the day the stork-o-fortuna flies Sud.

• Make sure yer weency brother eatums too. 'Ti Pouce sometimes fergets to eat when one of his enthusiasms take him.

THE SOUP OF FORGETTING
AFTERWORD

Heute back ich,
Morgen brau ich,
Übermorgen hol ich der Königin ihr Kind;
Ach, wie gut ist, daß niemand weiß,
daß ich Rumpelstilzchen heiß!

What was *Rumpelstilzchen* baking today (*backen heute*)? Holy thrice-folded pastry with its unusual filling as in Colleen Anderson's "The Dance of Abundance?" Scones such as those in Liz Westbrook-Trenholm's "Trencherman?" Or Pink 'n' Red Pie, the pie in "Red Like Cherries Or Blood," in which Rumpelstiltskin is the protagonist? We had so many submissions in which *backen* figured that I joked more than once to my co-editor, Candas, that we could have changed the theme to *Cake of My People*. The baking stories showcase recipes for European baked goods as well as from Asian communities including Chinese bao as in Melissa Yuan-Innes's "The Bao Queen."

A German immigrant, my mother read us *Kinder-und Hausmärchen* (first published in 1812) in the original. When I started school, my parents switched to English at home and my German is now little more than a kitchen language. I was in Berlin over the summer of 2017, visiting family and friends, and boned up before I left. It made a difference; rereading *Grimm's Fairy Tales* would also help.

During the early '40s my maternal grandmother, Regine Faust, was an active member of the German resistance group Rote Kapelle, and we remain good friends with the son of her comrades who were murdered by the Nazis for their involvement. Hans Coppi was born at Barnimstraße Women's Prison in Berlin. His mother, Hilde, was allowed to nurse her son until shortly before her execution when Coppi was just eight months old. How strange for the Nazis to privilege breast feeding over the life of the mother! Researching this piece I discovered there are folk tales from around the world in which a sorceress's breast milk is poisonous. If I'd known about this trope beforehand, I might have been inclined to commission such a story or, really, any story at all about our first food.

Dr. Coppi works at the Berlin Resistance Museum now, and while we were there, was chairing a conference on the rise of white supremacy in both Germany and North America. We went out for smoked trout and fermented beets on a barge moored in the Spree. I missed my grandfather, Peter, who used to order us *himbeergeist* after dinner.

Pleasant (or horrifying, as the case may be) as it was to fill our days with museum visits and dinner dates, I quickly realized I needed a way to structure my time. My sister and our artist friend/host both slept late. Even if we'd been out for *döner* followed by a *Kneipe* or *Ratskeller* the night before I got up early and, tablet under arm, went out in search of coffee and Wi-Fi. I often ended up at St. Oberholz, which, while trendy, was close to our friend's Mitte apartment. The signal was strong, and as it's a co-working café, no one minded me reading anthology submissions for hours over little more than coffee.

Döner is as ubiquitous in Berlin as shawarma is in Toronto: the vertical stacks of meat are the Turkish rather than the Arabic version. Turks came to Berlin in the early '60s as part of the *Gastarbeiterprogramm*, but are now able to apply for citizenship, and many are second generation. Today, throughout Germany – and not just in multicultural Berlin – Turks are the second largest ethnic population after Germans. In the GDR, many of the temporary foreign workers were Vietnamese, and to this day there are excellent phở restaurants in the former East. The signature Vietnamese soup is pivotal to the plot of Kathy Nguyen's story, "Phở Cart No. 7." It's an emigration story too, but the border that is crossed is the spiritual one, from life to afterlife and back, from animal to human to machine life. Marking the end of each incarnation, the protagonist returns again and again for a bowl of Mạnh Bà's phở, the soup of forgetting. If we didn't eat it, we'd be overwhelmed by memories of our past lives. In Ojibwe author Nathan Adler's story, his protagonist's grandmother, Zilpah, leaves a plate of spirit food out on the deck railing, and Zaude is left thinking about what this tradition means. It's perhaps not surprising that food often has spiritual undertones; we feed spirits with the same food with which we nourish our bodies, and eat soup in order to forget previous incarnations.

Nguyen's story ends in a science-fictional future, but others, while also taking place farther down the timeline, inhabit a devolved Weird world – more than one – in which science and technology have saved us from ourselves. When we emigrate, food becomes both symbol and substance, hearkening back to all that was left behind. Chris Kuriata looks at this question in his New Weird piece, "Chewing Through Wire," in which he writes about a family who disguises travellers' culinary herbs as garden weeds, so they won't be pulled by xenophobic neighbours. In Geoff Cole's Riddley Walkeresque "'Ti-Pouce in Fergetitland," only-a-little-bit-futuristic printing technology provides survivors of the apocalypse not an Instant Pot but a "fabupot" with which to create food, or a reasonable facsimile thereof, out of landfill, the one resource remaining in large enough quantities to be exploited. Lisa Carreiro's world in "Ruby Ice" is also a post-apocalyptic Weird scenario in which young women undergo grueling training with the goal of becoming rangers in a re-wilded world. As our own world becomes more and more science fictional, I pondered the ways in which Weird has become an increasingly legitimate writerly response.

Candace and I received more *Soylent Green*-type tales than expected, but we probably should have known they were coming. The anthrophagic stories, Casey June Wolf's "Eating Our Young" and Tapanga Koe's "There Are No Cheeseburgers at the End of the World" echo the cannibalistic themes of earlier tales, "Jack in the Beanstalk" and "Hansel and Gretel." We had a back and forth conversation about which recipe to include with Wolf's opener (beyond the *über*-disturbing obvious choice!) and, to my mind, her final recipe is brilliant in its pathos.

This book has been a long time in the making. We pitched it in 2015. At the end of the summer of 2017 I returned from Berlin to Eastern Ontario, to Treaty 20 Michi

Saagiig territory, to begin the editorial process. We returned to the book in 2020 to expand and finish it (only to then have the pandemic delay the release to autumn 2021).

We are grateful to our authors for sending us their beautiful stories from Turtle Island and around the world, and for their patience. Thank you also to my lovely and clever co-editor, Candas Jane Dorsey, whose witty and thoughtful emails were much looked forward to, particularly during the early days of the pandemic, and whose amazing short story was our original inspiration. Thank you also to those at Exile Exiltions, for publishing not just this book but the entire collection of themed speculative fiction anthologies that are a part of the *Exile Book of...* series.

We wish this anthology to be used as a cookbook as well as reading material. Shall it live on the night stand or in the kitchen? I would like copies of *Food of My People* to become spattered with lizard broth, *gochuchang* sauce and plumcake batter as all my favourite cookbooks are. (Well, maybe not the lizard broth.)

Richard Van Camp, in his beguiling story-poem "Widow," shares traditional northern recipes, including the burial in the "hallowed earth" of a caribou head, allowed to bake all morning beside a fire. It's a fitting opener, as we are reminded that all food comes from the hallowed earth, and that our bodies will one day return to it and be food for other beings, whether animal or vegetable.

Ursula Pflug

ABOUT THE AUTHORS

Nathan Adler is the author of *Wrist* and *Ghost Lake*, and co-editor of Exile's *Bawaajigan: Stories of Power*. He has an M.F.A. in Creative Writing from UBC, is a first-place winner of the Aboriginal Writing Challenge, and a recipient of a Hnatyshyn Reveal Award for Literature. He is Jewish and Anishinaabe, and a member of Lac des Mille Lacs First Nation.

Colleen Anderson of Victoria, British Columbia, has been nominated twice for the Aurora Award in poetry and longlisted for the Stoker Award. As a freelance editor, she has co-edited *Tesseracts 17*, and Exile's *Playground of Lost Toys*, which was nominated for a 2016 Aurora Award. *Alice Unbound: Beyond Wonderland*, for Exile, was her first solo anthology. She writes fiction and poetry, which has appeared in *Grievous Angel*, *Futuristica*, *Starship Sofa*, *The Sum of Us*, *On Spec*, and others. She is currently working on an alternate history/dark fiction novel and a poetry collection. *A Body of Work*, a collection of her dark fiction, was released in 2018, and the poetry chapbook, *Ancient Tales, Grand Deaths and Past Lives*, can be found at kelpqueenpress.com/colleen_anderson.html/. www.colleenanderson.wordpress.com.

Lisa Carreiro rises before dawn to spin the chaos in her head into stories before morphing into a humble office drone. She hiked in the mountains years ago during summer when bears were all there was to worry about. Her short fiction has appeared in Exile's *Playground of Lost Toys*, as well as *On Spec, Tesseracts Eleven,* and *Strange Horizons.* She lives In Kitchener, Ontario, but moves often.

Geoffrey W. Cole of Oakville, Ontario, has had his delicious short fiction appear in such mouth-watering publications as *Clarkesworld, On Spec, New Worlds,* and the Exile anthologies *Playground of Lost Toys* and *Cli-Fi: Canadian Tales of Climate Change.* He is the 2016 winner of the Premi Ictineu for best story translated into Catalan. Geoff has degrees in biology, engineering, an M.F.A. in creative writing, and a doctorate in cappuccino. He is a member of SF Canada and SFWA.   www.geoffreywcole.com

Joe Davies' short fiction has been published mostly in Canada, but also in England, Ireland, Wales, India, and the U.S. He lives in Peterborough, Ontario.

Candas Jane Dorsey is the internationally known, award-winning author of the novels *Black Wine, Paradigm of Earth* and *The Adventures of Isabel*; the short story collections *Machine Sex and other stories, Dark Earth Dreams, Vanilla and other stories* and *ICE and other stories*; four poetry books; several anthologies edited/co-edited; and numerous published stories, poems, reviews, and critical essays. She has been an editor and publisher, teaches writing and communications studies, and speaks widely on SF and other topics. She was founding president of SFCanada, and has been president of the Writers Guild of Alberta. Among her other awards, she received the Province of Alberta Centennial Gold Medal and the WGA Golden Pen Award for Lifetime Achievement in the Literary Arts, and is in the Edmonton

Arts and Cultural and the Canadian Science Fiction and Fantasy Halls of Fame. She is also a community activist, advocate and leader. A Treaty 6 person of settler stock, she lives in Edmonton, Alberta.

Gord Grisenthwaite from Lytton, British Columbia, is a member of the Lytton First Nation. He holds a University of Windsor M.A. in English Literature and Creative Writing, and currently resides in Kingsville, Ontario. His stories and poems have appeared in *ndncountry, Offset17, The Antigonish Review, EXILE Quarterly* (which nominated his story for a National Magazine Award, resulting in his being a finalist), and *PRISM International*, among others. Some of them have earned prizes and awards, including the 2020 FreeFall short story contest, 2014 John Kenneth Galbraith Literary Award, and the 2007 *PRISM International* short story prize. His first novel, *Home Waltz*, was published in 2020.

Sang Kim of Toronto is an award-winning chef, writer, and food literacy advocate. He has been behind some of the best-known Asian restaurants in Toronto. He is a CNE Celebrity Chef; LCBO's Chef of the Month; winner of the prestigious "Best Dish" at the International Food Competition in Chengdu, China. He is a regular food correspondent on CTV's *Your Morning* and *The Social*. His own cooking and culture show, with director Francis Mitchell, will be launched in autumn 2021. He received Exile's 2013 Emerging Writer $10,000 Carter V. Cooper Short Fiction Award for his story "When John Lennon Died" and looks forward to the eventual publication of his memoir, *Woody Allen Ate My Kimchi*, with Exile.

Tapanga Koe of Hastings, Ontario, has had short stories and poetry published in the anthologies *They Have to Take You In* and *That Not Forgotten*, as well as magazines and e-zines like *Capricious SF, Asymmetry, KZine,* and *Mystery Weekly.*

Chris Kuriata has edited award-winning documentaries about murderers, faith healers, and hockey. His fiction has appeared in publications such as *The Saturday Evening Post, The Fiddlehead, Gamut,* and the Exile anthology *Playground of Lost Toys.* He lives in (and often writes about) the Niagara Region of Ontario.

Lynn Hutchinson Lee is a multimedia artist living and working in Toronto. Her artworks have been exhibited in Canada, Latin America, and Europe. Her stories, creative non-fiction and poetry have appeared in Exile's *Cli-Fi: Canadian Tales of Climate Change, Romani Women in Canada: Spectrum of the Blue Water, Romani Folio, Bridges and Borders, Jane's Stories Anthology IV, Sar O Paj,* and an anthology of poetry by Romani women. Her spoken word poem, *Five Songs for Daddy,* was one of four works in chirikli collective's sound installation *Canada Without Shadows* at the Roma Pavilion, 54th Venice Biennale, Italy, *bak (basis voor aktuelle kunst)* in Utrecht, Netherlands, and Romania's National Museum of Contemporary Art.

Desirae May is a queer artist living in landlocked Alberta and dreaming of the ocean. She has an interest in cross-genre fiction and wants to be Terry Pratchett when she grows up.

Sally McBride was born and raised in Canada, and now divides her time between Toronto and the mountains of Idaho. Her stories have appeared in such venues as *Asimov's, Amazing, Realms of Fantasy, Descant, Northern Frights, Tesseracts, On Spec,* and other magazines, anthologies, and best-of collections. She has won Canada's Aurora Award, and received Hugo and Nebula nominations. She has published the fantasy novels *Indigo Time* and *Water, Circle, Moon,* and she has other novels and stories in progress. She learned to cook good hearty food from her mother, and loves to discover edible native plants wherever she goes.

Kathy Nguyen of Fayetteville, Arkansas, is a Multicultural Women's and Gender Studies doctoral candidate at Texas Woman's University. She has taught/teaches Gender and Social Change, U.S. Women of Colors, Asian-American Diaspora, and Exploring the Humanities courses. Her work has appeared in *Kartika Review, FIVE:2:ONE, diaCRITICS, Fearsome Critters,* and elsewhere. Her article, "Echoic Survivals: Re-Documenting Pre-1975 Vietnamese Music as Historical Sound/Tracks of Re-Membering," was recently translated in French. She is also a Short Fiction Section Co-Editor at *CRAFT.*

Ursula Pflug of Peterborough, Ontario, has had her award-winning short fiction appear in *Lightspeed, Fantasy, Postscripts, Leviathan, Strange Horizons,* and elsewhere. Her sixth book, the near-future YA novella, *Mountain,* was released in 2017. Her latest novella, *Down From,* was released in 2018. Her third story collection, *Seeds,* appeared in 2020. She didn't like to cook till she moved from Toronto to eastern Ontario where she embarked upon a decades-long adventure in foraging, organic gardening, and procuring pastured meat and poultry from her friends. Suddenly it all made sense.

Elisha May Rubacha was born in Lanark County, Ontario, but lives and writes in Peterborough, Ontario. She was a finalist for Peterborough's Outstanding Emerging Artist Award in 2018, and shortlisted for the *PRISM International* Creative Non-fiction Contest in 2016. Her poetry chapbook, *too much nothing,* was published in 2018, and her first stage play, *Waiting for Real Jobs,* was produced during the Precarious Festival in 2019. She is the founder, editor, and designer of *bird, buried press,* which has published 20 books of fiction and poetry since 2016.

Sheung-King (Aaron Tang) was born in Vancouver and raised in Hong Kong. He holds a Bachelor's Degree in film studies from Queen's University and is now an MFA candidate at the University of Guelph. His debut novel, *You Are Eating an Orange. You Are Naked.* (developed from his story in this anthology), was longlisted for CBC's Canada Reads 2021, and named one of the best book debuts of 2020 by the *Globe and Mail.* He teaches creative writing at the University of Guelph.

Kate Story is a writer and theatre artist from Newfoundland, living in Peterborough/Nogojiwanong, Ontario. She is the author of novels *Blasted* (receiving the Starburst Award's Honourable Mention), *Wrecked Upon This Shore,* *This Insubstantial Pageant* (tipped by the *Toronto Star* as a "top science fiction read... exotic, funny, and very sexy,") and the YA fantasy duology, *Antilia*. Her short fiction has been published in *World Fantasy* and Aurora Award-winning collections, and in *Imaginarium 4: The Best Canadian Speculative Writing*. Kate is a recipient of the Ontario Arts Foundation's K.M. Hunter Award for her work in theatre. Coming up is a new YA novel, *Urchin*, and in 2022 her first collection of short fiction, *Ferry Back the Gifts*, with Exile.

Richard Van Camp is a grateful Tlicho Dene from Fort Smith, NWT. He is the best-selling author of 26 books over 26 years. His novel, *The Lesser Blessed*, is now a feature film with First Generation Films. You can find him on Facebook, Twitter, Instagram, and at www.richardvancamp.com.

Liz Westbrook-Trenholm of Ottawa has published or aired mainstream and speculative short fiction, most recently in *Neo-opsis Science Fiction Magazine*, the Prix Aurora-winning anthology, *Second Contacts*, Laksa Media's *The Sum of Us*, Bundoran's *49th Parallels,* and Exile's *Over the Rainbow*. She also writes comedic murder mysteries for Calgary entertainment company, Pegasus Performances, with over 80 scripts produced.

Casey June Wolf of Vancouver writes poetry, and occasional, mostly speculative stories. Recent publications include "Delta Marsh" in *Reckoning 2*, and "All-Giving Sun" in *Harp, Club, and Cauldron: A Harvest of Knowledge*. Her book, *A Brigit of Ireland Devotional: Sun Among Stars* (under the name Mael Brigde), was released in September, 2021.

Her speculative fiction collection, *Finding Creatures & Other Stories*, was published in 2008.

Melissa Yuan-Innes, who lives outside of Montreal, wrote this story as a companion to "Fairy Tales Are for White People," which appeared in *Fireside Magazine* and was selected for *The Year's Best Dark Fantasy & Horror 2017 Edition*, edited by Paula Guran. Her stories have appeared in Exile's anthologies *The Playground of Lost Toys* and *Dead North*. She has had her award-winning stories appear in *Weird Tales*, *Nature*, *Writers of the Future*, *Tesseracts 7 & 16*, and the Aurora-winning anthology *The Dragon and the Stars*. Three of her stories earned honourable mentions in Gardner Dozois's *Year's Best Science Fiction* collections. As a mystery writer, she was shortlisted for the Derringer Award.

ANTHOLOGIES IN THE SERIES

AND SOME PREVIOUS PRAISE

"*Bawaajigan* is the Anishinaabemowin word for dream, but the struggles and, as the title also suggests, forces of power narrativized in this anthology are very present in waking life too... In each story, the author's unique prose lays bare the complex time frames of violence, events, and wisdom – the long, long course of things. It's a tough but refreshing look at the different way spiritual and cultural power can adapt and surprise, even in the echoes of the darkest struggles." —*Broken Pencil*

"*Those Who Make Us*, an all-Canadian anthology of fantastical stories, featuring emerging writers alongside award-winning novelists, poets, and playwrights, is original, elegant, often poetic, sometimes funny, always thought-provoking, and a must for lovers of short fiction."
—*Publishers Weekly*, starred review

"In his introduction to *Clockwork Canada*, editor Dominik Parisien calls this country 'the perfect setting for steampunk.' The fifteen stories in this anthology...back up Parisien's assertion by actively questioning the subgenre and bringing it to some interesting new places."
—*AE-SciFi Canada*

"*New Canadian Noir* is largely successful in its goals. The quality of prose is universally high...and as a whole works well as a progressive, more Canadian take on the broad umbrella of noir, as what one contributor calls 'a tone, an overlay, a mood.' It's worth purchasing for several stories alone..." —*Publishers Weekly*

"The term apocalypse means revelation, the revealing of things and ultimately *Fractured* reveals the nuanced experience of endings and focuses on people coping with the notion of the end, the thought about the idea of endings itself. It is a volume of change, memory, isolation, and desire." —*Speculating Canada*

"*Playground of Lost Toys* is a gathering of diverse writers, many of them fresh out of fairy tale, that may have surprised the editors with its imaginative intensity... The acquisition of language, spells and nursery rhymes that vanquish fear and bad fairies can save them; and toys are amulets that protect children from loneliness, abuse, and acts of God. This is what these writers found when they dug in the sand. Perhaps they even surprised themselves." —*Pacific Rim Review of Books*

"In *Dead North* we see deadheads, shamblers, jiang shi, and Shark Throats invading such home and native settings as the Bay of Fundy's Hopewell Rocks, Alberta's tar sands, Toronto's Mount Pleasant Cemetery, and a Vancouver Island grow-op. Throw in the last poutine truck on Earth driving across Saskatchewan and some 'mutant demon zombie cows devouring Montreal' (honest!) and what you've got is a fun and eclectic mix of zombie fiction..." —*Toronto Star*

"*Cli-fi* is a relatively new sub-genre of speculative fiction imagining the long-term effects of climate change [and] collects 17 widely varied stories that nevertheless share several themes: Water; Oil; Conflict... this collection, presents an urgent, imagined message from the future."
—*Globe and Mail*

"[*The Stories That Are Great Within Us* is a] large book, one to be sat on the lap and not held up, one to be savoured piece by piece and heard as much as read as the great sidewalk rolls out...This is the infrastructure of Toronto, its deep language and various truths."
—*Pacific Rim Review of Books*

"*Yiddish Women Writers* did what a small percentage of events at a good literary festival [Blue Metropolis] should: it exposed the curious to a corner of history, both literary and social, that they might never have otherwise considered." —*Montreal Gazette*

THE EXILE BOOK OF ANTHOLOGY SERIES
NUMBER EIGHTEEN

BAWAAJIGAN
STORIES OF POWER

EDITED BY
NATHAN NIIGAN NOODIN ADLER
CHRISTINE MISKONOODINKWE SMITH

BAWAAJIGAN:
STORIES OF POWER

CO-EDITED BY NATHAN NIIGAN NOODIN ADLER
AND CHRISTINE MISKONOODINKWE SMITH

"This is, overall, a stunning collection of writing from Indigenous sources, stories with the power to transform character and reader alike…the high points are numerous and often dizzying in their force… This is an inspiring and demanding collection, and that is by design. The stories challenge readers on numerous levels: thematically, narratively, and linguistically…" —*Quill & Quire*

"The range of stories in this anthology is remarkable, and so are the many themes explored: discovery and recovery, whether of oneself or of ancestral knowing and ways of being; journeying to other worlds; experiences of residential school; the fates of murdered and missing Indigenous women; and gifts that were once commonplace and are now misunderstood or misused." —*Malahat Review*

Richard Van Camp, Autumn Bernhardt, Brittany Johnson, Gord Grisenthwaite, Joanne Arnott, Délani Valin, Cathy Smith, David Geary, Yugcetun Anderson, Gerald Silliker Pisim Maskwa, Karen Lee White, Sara General, Nathan Niigan Noodin Adler, Francine Cunningham, Christine Miskonoodinkwe Smith, Lee Maracle, Katie-Jo Rabbit, Wendy Bone.

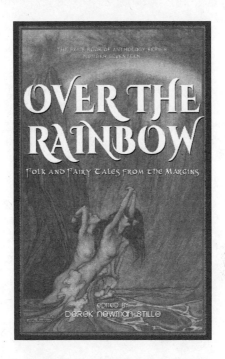

OVER THE RAINBOW:
FOLK AND FAIRY TALES FROM THE MARGINS

EDITED BY DEREK NEWMAN-STILLE

Fairy tales tell us the stories we need to hear, the truths we need to be aware of. This is a collection of adult stories that invite us to imagine new possibilities for our contemporary times. Collected by nine-time Prix Aurora Award-winner Derek Newman-Stille, these are edgy stories, tales that invite us to walk out of our comfort zone and see what resides at the margins. *Over the Rainbow* is a gathering of modern literature that brings together views and perspectives of the underrepresented, from the fringe, those whose narratives are at the core of today's conversations – voices that we all need to hear.

Nathan Caro Fréchette, Fiona Patton, Rati Mehrotra, Ace Jordyn, Robert Dawson, Richard Keelan, Nicole Lavigne, Liz Westbrook-Trenholm, Kate Heartfield, Evelyn Deshane, Lisa Cai, Tamara Vardomskaya, Chadwick Ginther, Quinn McGlade-Ferentzy, Karin Lowachee, Kate Story, Ursula Pflug, and Sean Moreland

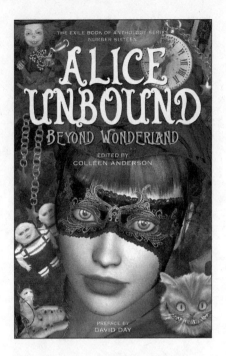

ALICE UNBOUND:
BEYOND WONDERLAND

EDITED BY COLLEEN ANDERSON

"This tremendously entertaining anthology…will delight both lovers of Carroll's works and fans of inventive genre fiction." —*Publishers Weekly,* starred review

A collection of twenty-first century speculative fiction stories that is inspired by *Alice's Adventures in Wonderland, Alice Through the Looking Glass, The Hunting of the Snark*, and to some degree, aspects of the life of the author, Charles Dodgson (Lewis Carroll), and the real-life Alice (Liddell). Enjoy a wonderful and wild ride down and back up out of the rabbit hole!

Patrick Bollivar, Mark Charke, Christine Daigle, Robert Dawson, Linda DeMeulemeester, Pat Flewwelling, Geoff Gander and Fiona Plunkett, Cait Gordon, Costi Gurgu, Kate Heartfield, Elizabeth Hosang, Nicole Iversen, J.Y.T. Kennedy, Danica Lorer, Catherine MacLeod, Bruce Meyer, Dominik Parisien, Alexandra Renwick, Andrew Robertson, Lisa Smedman, Sara C. Walker and James Wood.

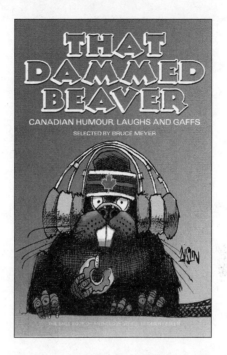

THAT DAMMED BEAVER:
CANADIAN HUMOUR, LAUGHS AND GAFFS

EDITED BY BRUCE MEYER

"What exactly makes Canadians funny? This effort from long-standing
independent press Exile Editions takes a wry look at what makes us laugh
and what makes us laughable." —*Toronto Star*

Margaret Atwood, Austin Clarke, Leon Rooke, Priscila Uppal, Jonathan Goldstein, Paul Quarrington, Morley Callaghan, Jacques Ferron, Marsha Boulton, Joe Rosenblatt, Barry Callaghan, Linda Rogers, Steven Hayward, Andrew Borkowski, Helen Marshall, Gloria Sawai, David McFadden, Myna Wallin, Gail Prussky, Louise Maheux-Forcher, Shannon Bramer, James Dewar, Bob Armstrong, Jamie Feldman, Claire Dé, Christine Miscione, Larry Zolf, Anne Dandurand, Julie Roorda, Mark Paterson, Karen Lee White, Heather J. Wood, Marty Gervais, Matt Shaw, Alexandre Amprimoz, Darren Gluckman, Gustave Morin, and the country's greatest cartoonist, Aislin.

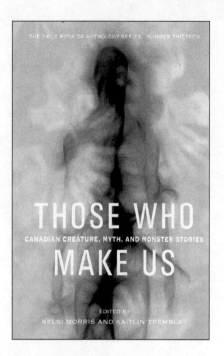

THOSE WHO MAKE US: CANADIAN CREATURE, MYTH, AND MONSTER STORIES

EDITED BY KELSI MORRIS AND KAITLIN TREMBLAY

What resides beneath the blankets of snow, under the ripples of water, within the whispers of the wind, and between the husks of trees all across Canada? Creatures, myths and monsters are everywhere…even if we don't always see them.

Canadians from all backgrounds and cultures look to identify with their surroundings through stories. Herein, speculative and literary fiction provides unique takes on what being Canadian is about.

"Kelsi Morris and Kaitlin Tremblay did not set out to create a traditional anthology of monster stories… This unconventional anthology lives up to the challenge, the stories show tremendous openness and compassion in the face of the world's darkness, unfairness, and indifference." —*Quill & Quire*

Helen Marshall, Renée Sarojini Saklikar, Nathan Adler, Kate Story, Braydon Beaulieu, Chadwick Ginther, Dominik Parisien, Stephen Michell, Andrew Wilmot, Rati Mehrotra, Rebecca Schaeffer, Délani Valin, Corey Redekop, Angeline Woon, Michal Wojcik, Andrea Bradley, Andrew F. Sullivan and Alexandra Camille Renwick.

CLI FI:
CANADIAN TALES OF CLIMATE CHANGE

EDITED BY BRUCE MEYER

"In his introduction to this all-original set of (at times barely) futuristic tales, Meyer warns read-ers, '[The] imaginings of today could well become the cold, hard facts of tomorrow.' Meyer (*Testing the Elements*) has gathered an eclectic variety of eco-fictions from some of Canada's top genre writers, each of which, he writes, reminds readers that 'the world is speaking to us and that it is our duty, if not a covenant, to listen to what it has to say.' In these pages, sci-entists work desperately against human ignorance, pockets of civilization fight to balance morality and survival, and corporations cruelly control access to basic needs such as water….The anthology may be inescapably dark, but it is a necessary read, a clarion call to take action rather than, as a character in Seán Virgo's 'My Atlantis' describes it, 'waiting unknowingly for the plague, the hive collapse, the entropic thunderbolt.' Luckily, it's also vastly entertain-ing. It appears there's nothing like catastrophe to bring the best out in authors in describing the worst of humankind." —*Publishers Weekly*

George McWhirter, Richard Van Camp, Holly Schofield, Linda Rogers, Seán Virgo, Rati Mehrotra, Geoffrey W. Cole, Phil Dwyer, Kate Story, Leslie Goodreid, Nina Munteanu, Halli Villegas, John Oughton, Frank Westcott, Wendy Bone, Peter Timmerman, Lynn Hutchinson Lee, with an afterword by internationally acclaimed writer and filmmaker, Dan Bloom.

Edited by Colleen Anderson and Ursula Pflug

PLAYGROUND OF LOST TOYS

EDITED BY COLLEEN ANDERSON AND URSULA PFLUG

A dynamic collection of stories that explore the mystery, awe and dread that we may have felt as children when encountering a special toy. But it goes further, to the edges of space, where games are for keeps and where the mind plays its own games. We enter a world where the magic may not have been lost, where a toy or computers or gods vie for the upper hand. Wooden games of skill, ancient artifacts misinterpreted, dolls, stuffed animals, wand items that seek a life or even revenge — these lost toys and games bring tales of companionship, loss, revenge, hope, murder, cunning, and love, to be unearthed in the sandbox.

Chris Kuriata, Joe Davies, Catherine MacLeod, Kate Story, Meagan Whan, Candas Jane Dorsey, Rati Mehrotra, Nathan Adler, Rhonda Eikamp, Robert Runté, Linda DeMeulemeester, Kevin Cockle, Claude Lalumière, Dominik Parisien, dvsduncan, Christine Daigle, Melissa Yuan-Innes, Shane Simmons, Lisa Carreiro, Karen Abrahamson, Geoffrey W. Cole and Alexandra Camille Renwick. Afterword by Derek Newman-Stille.

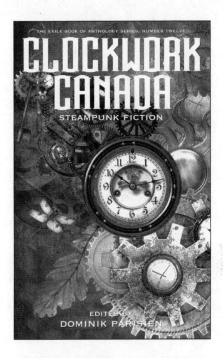

CLOCKWORK CANADA: STEAMPUNK FICTION

EDITED BY DOMINIK PARISIEN

Welcome to an alternate Canada, where steam technology and the wonders and horrors of the mechanical age have reshaped the past into something both wholly familiar yet compellingly different.

"These stories of clockworks, airships, mechanical limbs, automata, and steam are, overall, an unfettered delight to read." —*Quill & Quire*

"[*Clockwork Canada*] is a true delight that hits on my favorite things in fiction — curious worldbuilding, magic, and tough women taking charge. It's a carefully curated adventure in short fiction that stays true to a particular vision while seeking and achieving nuance."

—*Tor.com*

"...inventive and transgressive...these stories rethink even the fundamentals of what we usually mean by steampunk." —*Toronto Star*

Colleen Anderson, Karin Lowachee, Brent Nichols, Charlotte Ashley, Chantal Boudreau, Rhea Rose, Kate Story, Terri Favro, Kate Heartfield, Claire Humphrey, Rati Mehrotra, Tony Pi, Holly Schofield, Harold R. Thompson and Michal Wojcik.

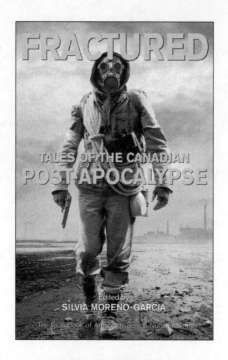

FRACTURED:
TALES OF THE CANADIAN POST-APOCA-
LYPSE

EDITED BY SILVIA MORENO-GARCIA

"The 23 stories in *Fractured* cover incredible breadth, from the last man alive in Haida Gwaii to a dying Matthew waiting for his Anne in PEI. All the usual apocalyptic suspects are here – climate change, disease, alien invasion – alongside less familiar scenarios such as a ghost apocalypse and an invasion of shadows. Stories range from the immediate aftermath of society's collapse to distant futures in which humanity has been significantly reduced, but the same sense of struggle and survival against the odds permeates most of the pieces in the collection... What *Fractured* really drives home is how perfect Canada is as a setting for the post-apocalypse. Vast tracts of wilderness, intense weather, and the potentially sinister consequences of environmental devastation provide ample inspiration for imagining both humanity's destruction and its rugged survival." —*Quill & Quire*

T.S. Bazelli, GMB Chomichuk, A.M. Dellamonica, dvsduncan, Geoff Gander, Orrin Grey, David Huebert, John Jantunen, H.N. Janzen, Arun Jiwa, Claude Lalumière, Jamie Mason, Michael Matheson, Christine Ottoni, Miriam Oudin, Michael S. Pack, Morgan M. Page, Steve Stanton, Amanda M. Taylor, E. Catherine Tobler, Jean-Louis Trudel, Frank Westcott and A.C. Wise.

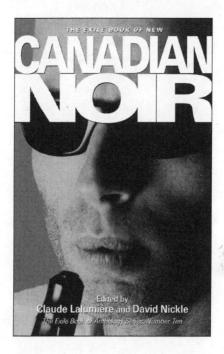

NEW CANADIAN NOIR

EDITED BY CLAUDE LALUMIÈRE AND DAVID NICKLE

"Everything is in the title. These are all new stories – no novel extracts – selected by Claude Lalumière and David Nickle from an open call. They're Canadian-authored, but this is not an invitation for national introspection. Some Canadian locales get the noir treatment, which is fun, since, as Nickle notes in his afterword, noir, with its regard for the underbelly, seems like an un-Canadian thing to write. But the main question *New Canadian, Noir* asks isn't "Where is here?" it's "What can noir be?" These stories push past the formulaic to explore noir's far reaches as a mood and aesthetic. In Nickle's words, "Noir is a state of mind – an exploration of corruptibility, ultimately an expression of humanity in all its terrible frailty." The resulting literary alchemy – from horror to fantasy, science fiction to literary realism, romance to, yes, crime – spanning the darkly funny to the stomach-queasy horrific, provides consistently entertaining rewards." —*Globe and Mail*

Corey Redekop, Joel Thomas Hynes, Silvia Moreno-Garcia, Chadwick Ginther, Michael Mirolla, Simon Strantzas, Steve Vernon, Kevin Cockle, Colleen Anderson, Shane Simmons, Laird Long, Dale L. Sproule, Alex C. Renwick, Ada Hoffmann, Kieth Cadieux, Michael S. Chong, Rich Larson, Kelly Robson, Edward McDermott, Hermine Robinson, David Menear and Patrick Fleming.

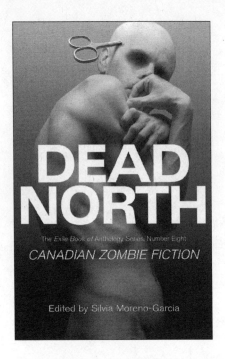

DEAD NORTH:
CANADIAN ZOMBIE FICTION

EDITED BY SILVIA MORENO-GARCIA

"*Dead North* suggests zombies may be thought of as native to this country, their presence going back to Indigenous myths and legends…we see deadheads, shamblers, jiang shi, and Shark Throats invading such home and native settings as the Bay of Fundy's Hopewell Rocks, Alberta's tar sands, Toronto's Mount Pleasant Cemetery, and a Vancouver Island grow-op. Throw in the last poutine truck on Earth driving across Saskatchewan and some "mutant demon zombie cows devouring Montreal" (honest!) and what you've got is a fun and eclectic mix of zombie fiction…" —*Toronto Star*

"Every time I listen to the yearly edition of *Canada Reads* on CBC, so much attention seems to be drawn to the fact that the author is Canadian, that being Canadian becomes a gimmick. *Dead North*, a collection of zombie short stories by exclusively Canadian authors, is the first of its kind that I've seen to buck this trend, using the diverse cultural mythology of the Great White North to put a number of unique spins on an otherwise over-saturated genre."—*Bookshelf Reviews*

Chantal Boudreau, Tessa J. Brown, Richard Van Camp, Kevin Cockle, Jacques L. Condor, Carrie-Lea Côté, Linda DeMeulemeester, Brian Dolton, Gemma Files, Ada Hoffmann, Tyler Keevil, Claude Lalumière, Jamie Mason, Michael Matheson, Ursula Pflug, Rhea Rose, Simon Strantzas, E. Catherine Tobler, Beth Wodzinski and Melissa Yuan-Ines.

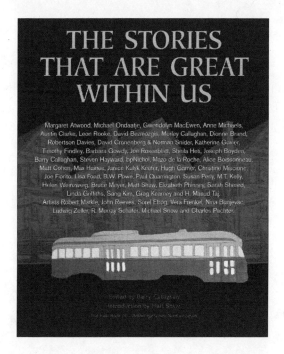

THE STORIES THAT ARE GREAT WITHIN US

EDITED BY BARRY CALLAGHAN

Among the 50-plus contributors are Margaret Atwood, Michael Ondaatje, Gwendolyn MacEwen, Anne Michaels, Austin Clarke, Leon Rooke, David Bezmozgis, Morley Callaghan, Dionne Brand, Robertson Davies, Katherine Govier, Timothy Findley, Barbara Gowdy, Joseph Boyden, bpNichol, Hugh Garner, Joe Fiorito, Paul Quarrington, and Janice Kulyk Keefer, along with artists Sorel Etrog, Vera Frenkel, Nina Bunjevac, Michael Snow, and Charles Pachter.

"Bringing together an ensemble of Canada's best-known, mid-career, and emerging writers…this anthology stands as the perfect gateway to discovering the city of Toronto. With a diverse range of content, the book focuses on the stories that have taken the city, in just six decades, from a narrow wryly praised as a city of churches to a brassy, gauche, imposing metropolis that is the fourth largest in North America. With an introduction from award-winning author Matt Shaw, this blends a cacophony of voices to encapsulate the vibrant city of Toronto." —*Toronto Star*

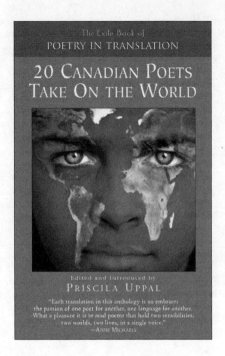

The Exile Book of
POETRY IN TRANSLATION

20 CANADIAN POETS
TAKE ON THE WORLD

Edited and Introduced by
PRISCILA UPPAL

"Each translation in this anthology is an embrace:
the passion of one poet for another, one language for another.
What a pleasure it is to read poems that hold two sensibilities,
two worlds, two lives, in a single voice."
—ANNE MICHAELS

20 CANADIAN POETS TAKE ON THE WORLD

EDITED BY PRISCILA UPPAL

A groundbreaking multilingual collection promoting a global poetic consciousness, this volume presents the works of 20 international poets, all in their original languages, alongside English translations by some of Canada's most esteemed poets. Spanning several time periods and more than a dozen nations, this compendium paints a truly unique portrait of cultures, nationalities, and eras."

Canadian poets featured are Oana Avasilichioaei, Ken Babstock, Christian Bök, Dionne Brand, Nicole Brossard, Barry Callaghan, George Elliott Clarke, Geoffrey Cook, Rishma Dunlop, Steven Heighton, Christopher Doda, Andréa Jarmai, Evan Jones, Sonnet L'Abbé, A.F. Moritz, Erín Moure, Goran Simić, Priscila Uppal, Paul Vermeersch, and Darren Wershler, translating the works of Nobel laureates, classic favourites, and more, including Jan-Willem Anker, Herman de Coninck, María Elena Cruz Varela, Kiki Dimoula, George Faludy, Horace, Juan Ramón Jiménez, Pablo Neruda, Chus Pato, Ezra Pound, Alexander Pushkin, Rainer Maria Rilke, Arthur Rimbaud, Elisa Sampedrin, Leopold Staff, Nichita Stănescu, Stevan Tontić, Ko Un, and Andrei Voznesensky. Each translating poet provides an introduction to their work.

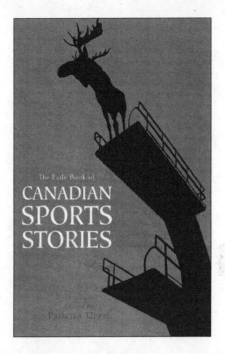

The Exile Book of
CANADIAN
SPORTS
STORIES

Edited by
PRISCILA UPPAL

CANADIAN SPORTS STORIES

EDITED BY PRISCILA UPPAL

"This anthology collects a wide range of Canada's literary imaginations, telling great stories about the wild and fascinating world of sport... Written by both men and women, the generations of insights provided in this collection expose some of the most intimate details of sports and sporting life – the hard-earned victories, and the sometimes inevitable tragedies. You will get to know those who play the game, as well as those who watch it, coach it, write about it, dream about it, live and die by it." —*Toronto Star*

"Most of the stories weren't so much about sports per se than they were a study of personalities and how they react to or deal with extreme situations...all were worth reading" —goodreads.com

Clarke Blaise, George Bowering, Dionne Brand, Barry Callaghan, Morley Callaghan, Roch Carrier, Matt Cohen, Craig Davidson, Brian Fawcett, Katherine Govier, Steven Heighton, Mark Jarman, W.P. Kinsella, Stephen Leacock, L.M. Montgomery, Susanna Moodie, Marguerite Pigeon, Mordecai Richler, Priscila Uppal, Guy Vanderhaeghe, and more.

CANADIAN DOG STORIES

EDITED BY RICHARD TELEKY

Spanning from the 1800s to 2005, and featuring exceptional short stories from 28 of Canada's most prominent fiction writers, this unique anthology explores the nature of the human-dog bond through writing from both the nation's earliest storytellerssuch as Ernest Thompson Seton, L. M. Montgomery, and Stephen Leacock, as well as a younger generation that includes Lynn Coady and Matt Shaw. Not simply sentimental tales about noble dogs doing heroic deeds, these stories represent the rich, complex, and mysterious bond between dogs and humans. Adventure and drama, heartfelt encounters and nostalgia, sharp-edged satire, and even fantasy make up the genres in this memorable collection.

"Twenty-eight exceptional dog tales by some of Canada's most notable fiction writers... The stories run the breadth of adventure, drama, satire, and even fantasy, and will appeal to dog lovers on both sides of the [Canada/U.S.] border." —*Modern Dog Magazine*

Marie-Claire Blais, Barry Callaghan, Morley Callaghan, Lynn Coady, Mazo de la Roche, Jacques Ferron, Mavis Gallant, Douglas Glover, Katherine Govier, Kenneth J. Harvey, E. Pauline Johnson, Janice Kulyk Keefer, Alistair Macleod, L.M. Montgomery, P.K. Page, Charles G.D. Roberts, Leon Rooke, Jane Rule, Duncan Campbell Scott, Timothy Taylor, Sheila Watson, Ethel Wilson, and more.

NATIVE CANADIAN FICTION AND DRAMA

EDITED BY DANIEL DAVID MOSES

The work of men and women of many tribal affiliations, this collection is a wide-ranging anthology of contemporary Native Canadian literature. Deep emotions and life-shaking crises converge and display Indigenous concerns regarding various topics, including identity, family, community, caste, gender, nature, betrayal, and war. A fascinating compilation of stories and plays, this account fosters cross-cultural understanding and presents the Native Canadian writers reinvention of traditional material and their invention of a modern life that is authentic. It is perfect for courses on short fiction or general symposium teaching material.

Tomson Highway, Lauren B. Davis, Niigaanwewidam James Sinclair, Joseph Boyden, Joseph A. Dandurand, Alootook Ipellie, Thomas King, Yvette Nolan, Richard Van Camp, Floyd Favel, Robert Arthur Alexie, Daniel David Moses, Katherena Vermette.

"A strong addition to the ever shifting Canadian literary canon, effectively presenting the depth and artistry of the work by Aboriginal writers in Canada today."

—*Canadian Journal of Native Studies*

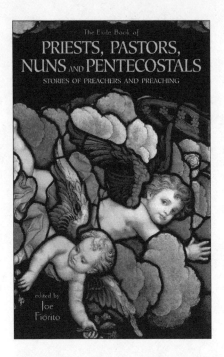

PRIESTS, PASTORS, NUNS AND PENTECOSTALS

EDITED BY JOE FIORITO

A literary approach to the Word of the Lord, this collection of short fiction deals within one way or another the overarching concept of redemption. This anthology demonstrates how God appears again and again in the lives of priest, pastors, nuns, and Pentecostals. However He appears, He appears again and again in the lives of priests, nuns, and Pentecostals in these great stories of a kind never collected before.

Mary Frances Coady, Barry Callaghan, Leon Rooke, Roch Carrier, Jacques Ferron, Seán Virgo, Marie-Claire Blais, Hugh Hood, Morley Callaghan, Hugh Garner, Diane Keating, Alexandre Amprimoz, Gloria Sawai, Eric McCormack, Yves Thériault, Margaret Laurence, Alice Munro.

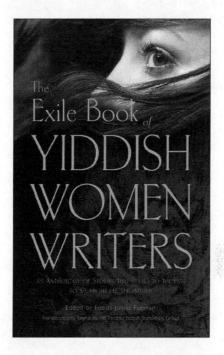

YIDDISH WOMEN WRITERS

EDITED BY FRIEDA JOHLES FOREMAN

Presenting a comprehensive collection of influential Yiddish women writers with new translations, this anthology explores the major transformations and upheavals of the 20th century. Short stories, excerpts, and personal essays are included from 13 writers, and focus on such subjects as family life; sexual awakening; longings for independence, education, and creative expression; the life in Europe surrounding the Holocaust and its aftermath; immigration; and the conflicted entry of Jewish women into the modern world with the restrictions of traditional life and roles. These powerful accounts provide a vital link to understanding the Jewish experience at a time of conflict and tumultuous change.

"This continuity...of Yiddish, of women, and of Canadian writers does not simply add a missing piece to an existing puzzle; instead it invites us to rethink the narrative of Yiddish literary history at large... Even for Yiddish readers, the anthology is a site of discovery, offering harder-to-find works that the translators collected from the Canadian Yiddish press and published books from Israel, France, Canada, and the U.S."

—*Studies in American Jewish Literature*, Volume 33, Number 2, 2014

OVER $100,000 AWARDED TO CANADIAN WRITERS

Through Two Literary Competitions That Support Emerging Talent And Writers With An Established Publishing History

(SEE OPPOSITE PAGE)

14 Winning and Shortlisted Authors have also gone on to Full Book – or First Book – Publication with Exile Editions (covers on following pages):

Silvia Moreno-Garcia*[1]   Christine Miscione*[2]   Matthew Loney*
Darlene Madott[3]   Veronica Gaylie   Linda Rogers   Leon Rooke
Martha Bátiz*[4]   Hugh Graham*[5]   Rafi Aaron   Austin Clarke[6]
George McWhirter[6]   Jeff Bien
Autumn 2021: emerging winner Katie Zdybel's* collection, *Equipoise*

*Author's first collection of stories.

AWARD WINNERS AND FINALISTS:
[1] Aurora Award, Best Short Fiction Award, finalist.
[2] ReLit Award, Best Short Fiction, winner.
[3] Bressani Literary Award, Best Novel, winner
[4] International Latino Book Award for Best Popular Fiction, winner.
[5] Danuta Gleed Award, Best First Book, finalist.
[6] ReLit Award, Best Short Fiction, finalist.

all books available at www.ExileEditions.com / free North American shipping

Exile's $15,000 Carter V. Cooper Short Fiction Competition

$10,000 for Best Story by an Emerging Writer
$5,000 for Best Story by a Writer at Any Career Point

The winners and shortlisted are published in the annual
CVC Short Fiction Anthology Series and winners in *EXILE Quarterly*

Exile's $3,000 Gwendolyn MacEwen Poetry Competition

$1,500 for Best Suite by an Emerging Writer
$1,500 for Best Suite of Poetry by Any Writer

Winners and selected shortlisted are published in *EXILE Quarterly*

These annual competitions have open calls once a year.
For Canadian Writers only.

Details at:
www.ExileQuarterly.com

STORIES OF MAGIC REALISM AND FANTASY

THIS STRANGE WAY
of DYING

SILVIA MORENO-GARCIA

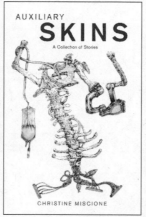

AUXILIARY
SKINS
A Collection of Stories

CHRISTINE MISCIONE

THAT
SAVAGE
WATER

STATIONS
of the HEART
STORIES

DARLENE MADOTT

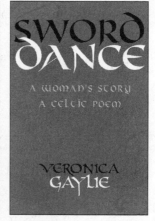

SWORD
DANCE

A WOMAN'S STORY
A CELTIC POEM

VERONICA
GAYLIE

BOZUK

LINDA ROGERS

WIDE WORLD
IN CELEBRATION
AND SORROW

LEON ROOKE

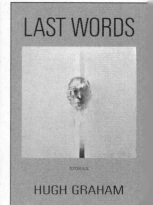

LAST WORDS

STORIES

HUGH GRAHAM